# Sefiron's Shadow

*A World Shapers Saga*

by

Mary Cilia

Copyright © 2013 by Mary E. Cilia. All rights reserved. No part of this book may be used or reproduced in whole or in part, or stored in a retrieval system, or transmitted in any form or by any means electronic, mechanical, photocopying, recording, or otherwise, without written permission of author.

For information: www. SefironsShadow.com

FIRST EDITION

Illustrations by Mary Cilia

ISBN-13: 978-1491236499

ISBN-10: 1491236493

www.SefironsShadow.com

This book is dedicated to

Dolores Cilia,
my first reader,
who taught me I could do anything I put my mind to.

I miss you.

## Chapter 1

Brandorin outpaced his escort by more than a furlong. He had not wanted to return, but the eight-man squad his father dispatched had made it very clear; whether he went voluntarily or not, son of the Protector or not, they would bring him back. His concern over Thiro's disappearance had fueled his frantic search over the last twelve days, but now the anxiety over not finding his friend and the frustration of being dragged back stoked his anger. A hawk, tied by invisible jesses, returning to its master despite its instinct to continue the hunt; he felt the strings of obligation pulling him back. He rammed his heels into his horse's flanks.

Bristo shot forward and Brandorin's arms pumped with each mile-eating stride as the war horse's muscles flexed and stretched beneath him. He didn't have to look to know the squad had spurred their mounts in an effort to keep up; thunderous pounding echoed Bristo's hoof beats, sparked by cries to rein in.

Icy wind and an hour's arduous ride had numbed Brandorin's exposed skin. His hands cramped from their unyielding grip on the reins and his face felt taut, ready to crack. Bristo's flanks were lathered, as well as his own legs, and the horse's rattled, labored breathing made him relieved to see the estate's iron gates. He felt Bristo's rear legs falter as they galloped through the turn, but the war horse dug in and hurtled down the tree-lined drive, drawing a train of dried leaves and dust in their wake.

Brandorin jumped off Bristo's back even before the chestnut steed had come to a complete stop. Throwing the reins to a groom, he raced up the wide stone stairs and across the marbled terrace; the heavy oak doors opening a second before he reached for the bronze handle. The servant on the other side stumbled back as Brandorin stormed through the foyer, taking the steps to the second level two and three at a time, nearly colliding with Ilona at the top.

"I saw you from my window," she said, reaching out to him.

"I was so worried."

He kissed her, and the familiar scent of jasmine perfume and the lingering bouquet of chamomile and honey soap took the edge off his anger. He wanted to hold her, surprised at how much he had missed her; he'd only been gone twelve days. He motioned to his dirt-smeared, sweat-soaked clothing, "I don't want to get you all . . ." that was all he had time for before she moved in close and he wrapped her in his arms, and felt her warmth take away the constant chill of the last few hours, and her soft mouth ease the sting of his own dry, cracked lips. After a time, he reluctantly placed his hands on her shoulders, and broke their embrace. "I'm sorry I worried you. You know I wouldn't be late for our wedding."

"I know that," she said. Her hand gripped his forearm. Though she lacked the strength to hold him back by force, he suddenly knew how Bristo felt when the horse wanted to bolt, but held back because of pressure on the reins. She reached up, gently touching his wind-reddened face, "Did you find any sign of him?"

"Nothing. I know something has happened to him, he wouldn't be gone this long without word," Brandorin said. This was the first time he'd voiced his greatest concern. He would only do so to Ilona.

"Go. Talk to your father." Ilona said. "If you have to be here, he can send others to keep looking."

"I'll come to see you as soon as I've talked to him." He gently removed her hand from his arm, brushed his lips across her fingers and marched down the corridor using each forceful step to stoke his anger back to its fever pitch. He wasn't running, but the forceful speed of his passing fluttered flowers in vases and wafted a hanging tapestry. Reaching the study door, he pounded once with the side of his clenched fist and entered without waiting for a response.

He stormed up the richly carpeted path down the center of the sparsely lit room. As the rug absorbed the impact of his heels, Brandorin felt his anger sapped by the authority exuded by his father's study. When Dilardin briefly glanced toward his son, before continuing his discussion with the Viceroy, Brandorin halted his forward advance, trying to fight his natural inclination to apologize for his intrusion.

He breathed deeply, concentrating on the smoky scent of the fire in the grate, his nerves crackling in counterpoint to the flames. The underlying smell of old paper and ink's tang sparked a memory of watching from the shadows as his father directed his armies. To distract himself from this reminder of his father's authority, he turned instead to the portraits of his ancestors, silently asking their help to bolster his resolve.

"Jarlin?" Dilardin's voice, though calm, jarred the Viceroy's attention back. He had been staring, rattled by Brandorin's uncharacteristic entrance.

Brandorin's heart pounded and he focused on his own quick explosive breathing to drown out Dilardin's commanding tones as the Protector continued his conversation with the Viceroy. An ache in Brandorin's jaws made him realize he was grinding his teeth, and he forced himself to relax. He watched his father, assessing him, as he had been taught; evaluating him as a stranger rather than the man and leader he knew so well.

Dilardin Adamaran, 147th Protector of Varsa, largest country on Zadania, distantly related to Hagan, last ruler of the Dravonian dynasty. In features and coloring the kinship between them was obvious. A strong brow topped deep-set blue eyes that saw everything. Dilardin's nose had been broken in battle, so the straight line that Brandorin felt was a little too long on his own face, held more character in the slightly bent bridge on his father's. Noticing the slight cleft in his father's chin, Brandorin couldn't keep from tracing the dent in his own. The artist of time had painted a stroke of gray in Dilardin's auburn hair, starting at the temples and sweeping back until it faded into the still-thick waves that mirrored Brandorin's own shoulder-length hair.

Though slightly over six feet tall, Brandorin still had to look up to his father, in height, as well as respect. Little more than an inch, but Brandorin felt miles behind when it came to wisdom and leadership skills. Fifty-four years had softened the once iron-hard muscles, but like the heated metal on a black smith's anvil, made pliable for shaping, they retained their strength and utility over the years.

Brandorin nodded to Jarlin as the Viceroy left. The older man broke protocol for the first time in Brandorin's memory, and risked a slight smile of commiseration; though he did it with his back to the Protector. Brandorin felt his father's eyes studying him, assessing him as a leader would an emissary from a foreign government. With that look, the scathing admonishments Brandorin had been rehearsing for the last three hours froze on his lips, and he knew he would bow to his father's authority, as he always did. Instead he spoke only one word, all of his anger and frustration conveyed in that one syllable. "Why?"

"You are needed here," Dilardin said.

"It's a week before the wedding. I could've kept searching." Brandorin took a deep breath and swallowed, steeling his voice to cover the pleading tone creeping through his anger. "I might have found him in the next day or two."

"You stormed out the second you heard he was missing. I understand why you did, Brandorin, but a leader cannot react so impulsively." Dilardin paused, studying his son, "Nor can he feel guilty about sending others on dangerous missions."

"I didn't send him. I was ready to go, " Brandorin said through a clenched jaw.

"No, you didn't," Dilardin interrupted. "I did. Because you were needed here. Even Thiro knew that."

Brandorin tried to hold onto his anger, but he could feel himself slipping into the role of a soldier in front of his commanding officer. "Yes, sir," the expected response, reflexive as a tick and just as annoying.

"I waited for the report from Thiro's adjutant, only to discover you'd taken off with him." Brandorin tried to speak, but his father droned on.

"We still don't know what those thieves were after. Nothing is missing, nothing damaged. Curious that they botched the burglary so badly yet managed to elude Thiro's search party so effectively."

Knowing his father's tactics, trying to defuse the volatility of the moment by leading the conversation, Brandorin blurted out, "I think they were responsible for Thiro's disappearance."

Dilardin stared at his son for a moment. Brandorin fought the urge to apologize for the interruption; the words aching for release like the rushing waters of a swollen river contained by the flanking banks. He concentrated on returning his father's gaze. Dilardin considered his response before saying, "Did you find any evidence to support that theory?"

"No, sir," Brandorin said, shaking his head reluctantly.

"The fog that separated Thiro from his men could have caused his horse to misstep and fall, leaving Thiro injured and without a mount. I sent eight squads out searching for him. They were given instructions to locate you as well. If anything, your rash action detracted from the real purpose of the search. But my men are the best. If anyone can find him, they will."

"If?" Brandorin let his anger loose for the first time since entering the room. "Have you written him off already?"

"No! You know that's not what I meant."

"They're good, but they don't know him like I do. I might see something they'd miss."

"I know that!" Dilardin shouted as he slammed his fist against the desk, for the first time speaking as a father rather than a leader. He took a deep breath, composing himself before starting again in a quieter tone. "I told them to search as if they were looking for my own son; that's why I sent so many men."

Dilardin's aggravation surprised Brandorin; he had never heard his father come so close to explaining an order.

"They'll continue the search, but you have a responsibility here."

"I wouldn't have been late. I wouldn't do that to Ilona."

"There are other things besides the ceremony: final preparations, rehearsals, receptions for foreign dignitaries. This isn't just a wedding, Brandorin; I know you're well aware of that. There are diplomatic repercussions."

Dilardin continued, but Brandorin listened only halfheartedly, his protests nothing more than a breeze against a rock wall. He was drawn back when he heard Ilona's name.

"Ilona has been frantic with worry."

"I know, sir. I should go speak with her. May I be excused?" Brandorin could read his father's expression; Dilardin had expected his son to continue the argument. Despite the fact that he seldom won, Brandorin never gave up so easily. Taking a small consolation in catching his father off guard, he left the room.

As he pulled the door closed behind him, he noticed his grandfather's portrait on the wall in front of him. He grimaced, feeling the old patriarch's disappointment, "He never ... I tried ... Never mind. I know." The hollow sound of his footfalls echoed through the empty corridors, recriminations from the generations of ancestors that hung on every wall.

*   *   *

Brandorin woke to the faint scent of baking bread, roasting meats, and the subtle sweetness of pastries and cakes riding in on the dawn breeze. A distant voice directed activities on the grounds below, while cautious whispers and the suppressed giggles of maids filtered in from the corridors.

He scrubbed his hands over the mapped lines of sleep creasing his face and shook his head, trying to shed the lingering drowsiness the way a dog shakes off water. His eyes snapped to attention as he remembered what the day held in store for him. It was his wedding day.

He swung his long legs over the edge of the bed and his feet came to rest on the flanks of his hunting dog, Rakin. The lanky, grizzled deerhound jumped up and turned to her master. Her wide eyes, topped by raised brows, her open mouth and lolling tongue conveyed her desire for a long run.

He reached out his hand and ruffled the dog's shaggy fur, "Not today, old girl."

As a puppy, Rakin's gangling form had been a constant shadow to Brandorin's own, but the stiffness of advancing years had slowed her, and she followed her master now only with her eyes.

Brandorin knew Rakin understood the subtleties of his morning routines. When he walked to the wardrobe, rather than the water basin, Rakin lifted her head and perked up her ears. But when her master looked at the clothes laid out for the wedding, the deerhound settled back down, a long exhalation of breath indicating her disappointment at the lack of a morning adventure.

Brandorin frowned at the blue velvet mantle, its collar and edges embroidered in gold. It would be worn over a black silk jacket. He reached for the gold brocade that adorned the sleeve from the cuff to the elbow, wanting to rip it off. The final fitting for these garments had been one of the reasons Dilardin had dragged him away from the search for Thiro.

Without realizing he mimicked Rakin, he let out a long, resigned sigh and turned away from the formal attire. Pulling on his robe, Brandorin walked barefoot toward the balcony door, running his hands through his thick, shoulder-length auburn hair, leaving it more ruffled than when he began. He stretched and yawned, shaking off the stiffness left from his heavy slumber. Pushing back the thick velvet draperies, he blinked at the sudden change in light, though the sun had not yet topped the trees flanking the estate.

He shivered as his feet hit the balcony's cold flagstone floor. The cool, clammy air, after the warmth of his bed, chased away the last vestiges of sleep. He gazed out over the expanse of lawn stretching from the terrace below to the edge of the forest. The morning mist shrouded the dark green pines in a gray blanket, the moisture in the air the last remnant of three days of heavy storms. A clear golden-pink sky, more typical of the crisp dry weather of Harvest month, promised warmth that would burn off the haze. The few clouds scattered overhead carried no moisture to threaten the day's events.

He looked down on the bustling servants whose muted sounds had gently roused him from sleep. The recent storms had threatened to force the wedding feast indoors, and delayed final set-up. Servants now streamed from the building, carrying tables, chairs, and benches across the terrace's herringbone brickwork to the lawn beyond.

He watched the brisk efficiency of the maids as they moved from table to table with military precision. The first maid spread linen cloths over the bare tables, a second laid out the plates and glasses, and a third positioned the cutlery. Brandorin was reminded of a supply-line as he watched the never-ending flow of pages struggling under the weight of the china, crystal, and silverware needed to accommodate the nine-course meal planned for tonight's feast. All the workers moved with an enthusiasm that could only be explained by the uniqueness of the day.

The faint aromas that had tickled Brandorin awake were stronger out on the balcony. The cooks and kitchen staff had been working through the night. Brandorin had a sudden urge to visit the kitchens, driven more by the childhood memory of long talks with Reba, a short, rotund pastry chef, than the rumblings of his stomach.

Brandorin ignored the formal clothing, and dressed so casually that Rakin sat up, alert for any sign from her master. Brandorin noticed her hopeful stare, and decided she would probably like a warm roll too. Having Rakin with him would help the day feel a little more normal.

Brandorin wanted to be married to Ilona; he just didn't like the process of getting married. He thought he would feel better about the day if he had more to do. He had only to dress for the ceremony, and his clothes were already pressed and laid out. Accustomed to preparations for a battle, inspecting swords and armor, horses and supplies, the diligence required to ensure their readiness provided a distraction from the coming attack. Without a regimen to adhere to, he needed to create his own diversion.

He patted his thigh and smiled at Rakin, signaling the dog to follow. Brandorin watched with a slight sadness as she rose with difficulty. She arched her back and walked to the door, stretching her legs out behind her, one at a time, to ease the stiffness in her joints. He crouched down, briskly ruffling the backs of both of Rakin's ears, and her eyes rolled in contentment. "We're off for a hunt, girl, this time in search of breakfast."

## Chapter 2

Ilona had finished her bath and was sitting at her dressing table. The finely crafted table was the size of her father's desk back home in Febron, its surface expansive enough for the Premier's many duties. Alabaster jars of creams, blown-glass bottles of perfumes with intricate tortoise-shell and abalone stoppers, Mother-of-Pearl combs and silver brushes had been provided by her hosts, soon to be her family by marriage, but already close to her heart.

The light scent of jasmine and honey floated through the room, mingling with the whiskery sound of brush strokes.

"It got a little wet at the base of your neck, but that'll dry in no time. We have hours before the ceremony." Her best friend, Marga, having released the golden waterfall of hair, now brushed the waist-length buttery locks. A distant cousin, Marga had come to live at the Premier's estate, orphaned at the age of twelve. Though the intention had been for her to become hand-maiden to the Premier's daughter, Ilona had seen it differently, finally having the sister she'd always wanted.

Ilona relaxed into each soothing stroke, letting the pull of the brush tilt her head back. She stared out the window, a pensive look creasing her brow.

"What's bothering you, Ilona? A girl shouldn't have any worries on her wedding day."

"I was just wondering what Brandorin's doing. He doesn't have *his* best friend to talk to." Ilona reached up and placed her hand on Marga's. "I'd be going crazy with nerves if you weren't here."

"There was no way I was going to miss your wedding, even if I did have to come to this barbaric country."

"Varsa is not barbaric," Ilona protested. They'd had this conversation dozens of times. "Everyone we've met has been courteous and kind. You're only saying that because of the swords."

"Exactly! Who ever heard of wearing uniforms and swords

at a wedding?"

"It may not be our custom, but it is theirs. They *have* been at war for a decade."

"But there hasn't been a major battle in almost a year. They just don't want to accept the fact it's over. You'd think the winners would be ready to celebrate. I can understand the Arkhanians not wanting to stop. They're blood-thirsty savages, but the N'varians..."

"Marga, I don't want to talk about war on my wedding day."

"But that's why you're here isn't it? You were promised in marriage in exchange for Febron committing her soldiers to war." Marga stopped arranging Ilona's hair to use her arms for the sweeping gestures needed to demonstrate the drama of the story. "The brave soldier wins the war; then comes home to claim his bride. It's like one of those tales the minstrels sing about."

"I hate to think my happiness depended on men dying."

"If it hadn't been your marriage, Dilardin would have found something else to use as leverage. He's the kind of man who gets what he wants. And you're marrying his son." Ilona noticed Marga's voice had slipped from the tones of melodrama to a suggestive whisper. "If Brandorin is half the man his father is, you're in for a wonderful time."

Ilona ignored the comment and handed Marga the hairpins she needed to anchor the loose curls into place. Marga's concentration on this critical part of the process stopped the conversation for a time. Ilona's thoughts drifted back to Brandorin, wondering what he was doing this morning and if he was as nervous as she was.

"There, the hard part's done," Marga said, stepping back to view the progress of her creation. In a distracted tone she continued, "I may talk about the Varsians, but there *is* one good thing about marrying a warrior."

"What's that?" Ilona asked.

"I'm sure you'll find out tonight."

Ilona blushed, and Marga said, "Oh, 'lona, you are such an innocent. If you think you won't be able to handle Brandorin, just let me know. I'd be more than happy to step in."

"If I didn't know you so well I'd be worried, but I know you're all talk."

"Not all talk all the time. But I wouldn't, not with your man. My preferences lean toward the missing friend. Ever since he came to escort us here, I've been looking forward to dancing with him at the wedding. Dancing, and hopefully something more. And now he's gone and gotten himself lost. Too bad we won't get to see the bridegroom and his attendants in their full-dress uniforms. It would have been a beautiful sight."

"You're such a hypocrite!" Ilona teased.

"You have to admit, it's pretty romantic. Brandorin agreed to ignore their customs to please you. And you were worried he wouldn't love you."

"After our first meeting, who could blame me? He hated the idea of having to marry me."

"It wasn't you, 'Iona. He didn't like the idea of being told he had to marry anyone. You didn't see it because you loved him from the second you saw him, but he resented the arrangement and didn't mind showing it. I know you don't want to hear it, but he *was* a bit of an ass."

"You didn't like him because you thought he was being mean to me." Ilona smiled, her mind elsewhere as Marga pulled the loose hair and braids up into a sweeping jumble on top of her head.

"I can't decide if I like his eyes or his smiles the best," Ilona said, ignoring the incomprehensible curses Marga was muttering. Though her hair looked like a vulture's nest now, she knew Marga would get it right. She always did.

"Did you say 'smiles', as in more than one?"

"Yes, he has a dozen different smiles that I've counted so far."

"The only one I've noticed is that one where it starts at the corners and slowly turns up. You know he's thinking something he shouldn't."

"Hopefully, it's something about me," Ilona said sheepishly, as she blushed.

"Despite my initial reservations, I do have to admit, he is rather likable."

Ilona gave her friend a satisfied look in the mirror in front of her. "What do you like best about him?" Marga's silence drew Ilona's attention, and she turned to stare at her friend, making it very clear she wanted an answer.

Marga smiled affectionately and said, "The way he treats you."

\* \* \*

Brandorin and Rakin made their way down the numerous stone corridors and stairways to the lower levels of the estate. They had to weave and dodge the many servants who passed carrying towels and bed linens, jugs of hot water and breakfasts on trays. Brandorin sensed an unusual energy to their routine tasks. For most of the staff, this would be their first state dinner, though he knew Reba had made the cakes for his parents' wedding.

With a gentle ruffle of her head, Brandorin told Rakin to wait at the door to the kitchens. He stepped inside and the heat of the ovens and the strong scents of yeast, cinnamon and nutmeg blanketed him in nostalgia. But it was the sight of an empty stool pulled up to the counter in front of a sugar bun that caused his breath to catch in his throat.

"Did you think I wouldn't be prepared for you?" Though he hadn't heard it in years, the voice was as familiar to him as his own, and turning toward it, he lowered his gaze and smiled at the small woman who beamed up at him. Her gray hair was piled on her head, resembling one of the buns she was always baking. Her rounded shape echoed two more buns, one on top of the other, hinting that not all her baked goods made it to the Protector's tables.

"You may be a great warrior now, and getting married and all, but you'll always be that little boy who looked up at me with those bright blue eyes, batting those long lashes at me," she said. Reba demonstrated the technique he had used on her so often, their positions now reversed with Brandorin towering over her.

The exaggerated blinking and coy smile made her look comical. He engulfed her in a bear hug and kissed the top of her head. "I wasn't *that* obvious was I?"

"Oh, get on with you. You don't actually think you were fooling me, do you?" Reba pulled a towel from the waistband of her apron and began to brush flour from Brandorin's tunic. Satisfied with her efforts, she shooed him over to the stool and settled him onto it before resuming her baking.

"How did you know I'd come down today, Reba? I haven't been in the kitchens for..."

"Years," she finished for him. "Thought you were too old to come sneaking treats from me once you'd been to war." Even sitting, Brandorin's head was higher than Reba's and as she looked up at him, he could see her eyes glistened with emotion.

Brandorin guessed the stool had never been put away, and reaching his hand out, he placed it on her arm. "I'm sorry, I shouldn't have stayed away so long."

"Well, at least you remembered to leave that mangy old dog in the hallway, and not bring it into my kitchen. No matter how many times I told Dilardin that, he'd try to sneak his dogs in here with him."

"Are you saying *my father* used to sneak treats too?" His voice reflected the disbelief that his father had ever been a reckless youth.

"He was worse than you. He'd try to steal my best pastries and rush out without a word. You always sat down and listened to my ramblings about the old days, or at least pretended to."

"I listened," Brandorin said with mock indignation. "I could tell you every single one of them."

She put her hand on his arm and squeezed. "I believe you could."

An apprentice had just pulled three sheets of teacakes from the ovens, and Brandorin reached for one of the honey and cinnamon scented steaming morsels. Reba rapped his knuckles with a large wooden spoon. The apprentice reeled in shock, looking for a reaction from the master's son.

"Not those. They're for the feast. Get some of the other ones." She pointed with the same spoon to a rack of cooling custard tarts behind Brandorin. "They aren't pretty enough for the guests, but they're still tasty."

"Your mother used to cook here too, didn't she, Reba?" Brandorin mumbled around a mouth full of lemony custard.

"Baked," she corrected him as she piped almond cream into bite-sized puffs, "like me. That's where I learned the trade. And she learned from her mother, and her mother before that. As far back as any of them could remember, almost back to the days of the Dravonians, we been baking for the Protector and his family. Most of these young ones," she gave the apprentice a sour look and shooed him away, "have no idea of the traditions that have gone before them."

Reba talked about past estate dinners, and about learning at her mother's side, and Brandorin listened as he ate his way through the plate of pastries. Silence and her cold blue stare brought Brandorin's attention back.

His stammered apologies met with an easy dismissal.

"Don't trouble yourself. I know your mind is elsewhere. Is it the wedding or Thiro? I would have put out two stools ... Has there been no word?"

"No. There wasn't a single sign."

The desperation in Brandorin's voice made Reba stop stirring her cream filling. "You sound like someone's taken all the breath out of your soufflé. I'm sure Thiro will be found. He's like you, very resilient."

"I should have been out looking for him this past week. I'll go back out again tomorrow."

"And leave your sweet bride so soon after the wedding?" Reba sounded as incredulous as if someone had asked her if she would serve day-old bread. "Shame on you."

"It was Ilona's idea. She said the honeymoon can wait until we find him."

"She's a rare one then. To understand. I'm glad, knowing

you'll be happy, but off you go now. There's a great deal to be done, and if you stay here much longer, you'll be eating my best pastries."

Rakin had been watching the doorway, and rose as her master appeared. Brandorin had not forgotten his unspoken promise. He reached into his pocket and pulled out an unglazed roll, which Rakin gobbled up before they were beyond the range of the kitchen's aromas.

The corridors of the estate seemed cool after the warmth of the kitchen. By the time he reached the terrace, the sun had cleared the tops of the trees, and the chill, damp shadows were beginning to warm.

Brandorin heard his father's deep, commanding voice, but before he could slip away unseen, Dilardin called out to him.

"I would ask you to join me for breakfast, but it looks like you've eaten already." Brandorin followed his father's eyes, and quickly brushed the tell-tale flour from his sleeve.

"Sorry, sir." He found it hard to picture his father sneaking into the kitchens, the image of a rebellious youth at odds with the disciplined man he knew.

"I'm just going to check on the preparations," Dilardin waved his arm across the ordered commotion around him, "then we can talk."

Brandorin nodded and watched as his father walked among the servants, talking to some, placing a hand on a shoulder, even helping to maneuver a long table around a tight corner. Brandorin checked to be sure he had removed all traces of his visit to the kitchens, wiping his mouth as well as his clothes.

Dilardin walked back to Brandorin then passed him, assuming his son would follow, their steps soon clicking off the cadence of a march. Dilardin ran down a list of the preparations taking place all around them, the many guests scheduled to attend, and specifically one that would not.

"I wish Caidos was going to be here," Dilardin said, more to himself than to Brandorin. "He's been involved in every major event in our family since he became Mirador. He was present at my wedding and at your grandfather's. I think he might have even been there for *his* father's too."

"Yes, sir," Brandorin said, acknowledging his father's statements because it was expected.

"I received a message from him last week. He was on his way here, but something came up that he had to attend to. A renegade mage they lost tabs on. They may have found him again."

"Yes, sir."

"Both Caidos and I would be more comfortable if we knew where Rhamak was. It'll be worth Caidos missing the wedding if this search will locate that mage again."

"Yes, sir."

"But I'm worried. As skilled as Caidos is, I'm not sure he's prepared to deal with Rhamak. In facing an enemy, a commander must try to think like that enemy." Brandorin cringed; thinking another lesson on command and warfare was coming, but relaxed when Dilardin continued. "As much as I care for and respect Caidos, I don't think he has it in him to think like Rhamak."

"No, sir."

Dilardin stopped so abruptly that Brandorin had gone several paces before realizing it. He turned back to find Dilardin staring at him expectantly.

"Don't you think this 'Yes, sir', 'No, sir' business is getting a little old?" Dilardin waited a moment for Brandorin to respond, but when he didn't the Protector continued, and Brandorin could hear the anger rising in his father's voice. "You're angry with me; I get it. You're worried about Thiro. Well, so am I. But as a leader you have to make decisions that are difficult and not always popular. You have to consider the greater good..."

"The greater good? Good for who? The citizens of Varsa?"

"Yes."

"Something else or someone else is always more important." Brandorin's words surged out on a wave of anger he made no effort to restraint. "I've heard about the greater good my entire life, and I've tried to understand, tried to accept my role in all of this. And I know you think that my getting married means I should take a more active role in the government of Varsa. But if being a leader means thinking velvet tunics and gold brocade are more important than finding Thiro, then I don't want to be a leader. I don't want to be the next Protector. I never have."

He stopped suddenly. He had gone further than he had intended. Seeing the stricken look on his father's face, he felt he should say something. He opened his mouth to apologize.

After a moment's stammering, a sharp voice distracted him, and he turned to see Ilona's mother bearing down on them. The tall, dark-haired woman was so unlike her daughter that Brandorin often thought of them as the human equivalents of the old fairy tale where the vulture had stolen the swan's egg and raised it as its own.

"There won't be time now," Dilardin said, taking charge of the situation. "Which one of us is in for it? You go ahead, I'll cover your retreat." Dilardin turned, striding toward the imposing woman stalking toward them. Brandorin was reluctant to leave without finishing their conversation but decided to take advantage of his reprieve.

Hoping Dilardin would handle Valira quickly, he waited on the far side of a privet hedge. He was curious to see how his father would handle his almost mother-in-law. Though Valira would be returning to Febron after the wedding, it would be useful to have a strategy for dealing with her sharp tongue. Even though Brandorin was reluctant to admit it, there was no one better to learn from than his father.

"Valira, I'm glad to see you enjoy a brisk morning walk ..."

"No you don't, Dilardin. You're not going to control this conversation." Brandorin couldn't see Valira from his refuge, but knew she would be shaking her stick-like finger in his father's face; she never tried to make a point without the use of that well-manicured pointer. "I've been trying to catch you since yesterday. I am not at all pleased with the arrangements for the cortege on the way to the cathedral."

"Is your carriage not to your liking? Too small?"

"The carriage is fine, but the route is a problem."

"The route?" Brandorin heard the surprise in his father's voice. That issue had caught him off-guard. "That route was chosen carefully, to avoid the crowds and get us to the cathedral unhindered."

"But the people are expecting us." She softened her speech, her dagger tongue sheathed in pretense. "Most citizens seldom get to see their leaders; you can't deprive them of the opportunity to do so. It could have severe ramifications."

Brandorin suspected Valira was only concerned about the citizens of Kartir getting every opportunity to see her, and her new gown. Ilona had told him her mother had five women working on it for the past year. He had missed his father's answer, but was drawn back to the conversation by the sound of his own name.

"Brandorin convinced me to lay aside our own traditions in favor of the Febronese way. He would do anything to please your daughter."

"Well, I'm glad you finally came round to seeing it my way. But where *is* Brandorin? Wasn't he with you just now? I had something to discuss with him too."

Brandorin made a hasty, but silent retreat.

## Chapter 3

As the rest of the day unfolded, Brandorin had a vague sense of being directed, like a soldier on a battlefield, moved from one campaign to the next. He had been shuttled from the tailor who fussed over his clothes to the chamberlain who reviewed protocol with him, then to the stable marshal directing the processional to the cathedral. Now the tailor was back, fussing over the wrinkles that had formed during the ride.

The old man smelled of dye and stale sweat, and his continued muttering and ministrations fueled Brandorin's growing nervousness. Though he tried to show infinite patience on the outside, Brandorin felt that if he couldn't move, even just to pace, he would bolt out the closest door. Thiro would have recognized his frustration and ripped a seam on his own clothes, just to distract the tailor.

Brandorin's aggravation was magnified by his friend's absence and his own inability to resolve the issue with his father. He had seen Dilardin twice since Valira had interrupted their talk, but they hadn't been alone. "Where are you, Thiro?" he mumbled through clenched teeth.

Mistaking what Brandorin had said, the tailor grimaced as he stood up, "Yes, I'm through," teetering slightly, his knees popped from crouching for so long. Brandorin grabbed the old man's arm until he could stand on his own, then began pacing and clenching and unclenching his fists, trying to shake off the nervous energy. He closed his eyes and took several deep, controlled breaths, and in the tailor's absence, noticed the cathedral's own smells of beeswax, incense, and wood polish.

He tried to distract himself by watching the guests through a screen in the sacristy. A river of bright colors and lace flowed into the pews, underscored by the murmured chatter and echoing footsteps reverberating from marble pillars and walls.

Slowly the chaos at the back of the church thinned, as the aisles emptied and the pews filled, and the principals were escorted in. He laughed at Valira as she strutted down the aisle, primping and preening so everyone would notice her new dress. His parents walked in with an elegant dignity, and as his mother, Corleen, took her seat she looked in Brandorin's direction and winked. Not sure she could actually see him through the screen; he hesitantly waved back at her.

Brandorin looked back and forth between the two women. Corleen radiated a quiet elegance, while Valira resounded with pretension. He knew his mother's compassion and had suffered the cut of Valira's criticism, so he understood why Ilona had grown to love his mother already.

A fanfare of trumpets announced the bride's arrival, and Brandorin inhaled deeply, squared his shoulders, and walked forward to take his place at the head of the cathedral's long center aisle. He had just enough time to be glad he didn't have to walk up that aisle, when he saw Ilona at the back, gliding forward on her father's arm.

Every face in the vast cathedral turned toward her, following her forward in unison, as if pulled by a puppet master's strings. A thin veil covered her head, but her beauty lit her face from within; he could see every detail of her lyrical face. A tentative smile showed her nervousness, but then her bright eyes turned toward him, and he felt the warmth of that smile chase away all his uneasiness, because he knew it was meant only for him.

As Ilona reached the apse and stood before him, Brandorin lifted the veil. Her skin was flawless, and he ached to touch its velvety smoothness.

As they stepped into place before the bishop, sunshine streamed through the stained glass windows of the clerestory, bathing them in a halo of light. A collective intake of breath rose throughout the vast cathedral. Brandorin had a fleeting thought that someone had planned the time for the wedding precisely, but that notion was overshadowed by the spark of golden flecks in Ilona's rich brown eyes. Many other girls had looked at him that way, but their gazes had not carried this sense of trust and devotion.

He had protested the finery he had to wear, had scoffed at the decorations adorning the estate, disapproved of the ceremonial formalities, but as he looked at Ilona now it was all forgotten. So to were the eight hundred guests in the church, honor guard and family. Whatever he must endure to have this woman by his side would be small payment.

Brandorin spoke his vows when the time came. He listened to the dulcet tones of Ilona's voice as she did the same. His father spoke and Ilona's father did as well. Yet as he walked with Ilona out of the church and into the barouche, he could remember only her face and the touch of her hand in his.

The parade route back to the estate was lined with people, packed up against the buildings and hanging from open windows. They cheered and called out, "Brandorin!" and "Ilona!" continuously. Their voices bounced off the closely packed houses and echoed down the streets.

Surrounded by thousands of excited people, Brandorin found himself getting caught up in their enthusiasm. He turned to Ilona and found her studying him with a look of skepticism furrowing her bow. He leaned over to her and spoke near her ear, so she could hear him over the storm of voices.

"Are the crowds upsetting you, 'lona?"

"Not at all. I've always thought you didn't like all this pageantry and ritual, but you seem to be handling it well."

"You don't think they can tell I'm faking it?"

"I wouldn't think you'd have to fake a smile right after marrying me," she said with mock offense.

He brought her hand to his mouth, kissing it. "That just proves I'd never make a good politician. Stuck my foot in my mouth on my very first official act. Can you imagine what I'd be like in negotiations with a foreign power?"

He made up for his misstep with a lingering kiss that elicited riotous cheers from the vigilant crowd.

"You may be right," she said, "you wouldn't be able to use that method to make up for errors with the leaders of other countries."

Brandorin had hoped that once they were out of the city, the crowds would be gone and they could pick up the pace, but the road all the way back to the estate was lined with people. By the time they passed through the gates, his face ached from smiling.

The guests for the wedding feast had followed the cortege, and they were already pouring out onto the terrace like water from a sluice. Brandorin succeeded in leading Ilona away from the crowd, and he stood with her now under the pendulous arms of a loreanna tree. Its branches hung low to the ground, and were covered with fragrant yellow blossoms, providing a cover for their first private kiss as a married couple.

"I don't know if it's you, or the heady perfume of this tree," Ilona said breathlessly as she broke their lingering kiss, "but I'm feeling a bit light-headed."

"I won't let you fall," he told her, bundling her slight frame in his arms. "Have you eaten today?"

"I don't remember."

"That means you probably haven't. Let's get you something," he said as he turned to leave, one arm still around her waist. As he reached through the hanging branches, intending to part them for her, she pulled him back in.

"They won't be serving yet," she said. She reached up, wrapping her hand behind his neck, and pulled his face down to hers.

"It's our party," Brandorin said between kisses, "I think ... we can get ... something ... if we want."

"I've waited five years for this, and Marga would be surprised to see me being so bold, but I don't want to share you with anyone just yet."

"The light in here isn't that good, but I would say you were blushing, my bride."

She buried her face in his chest and giggled. When he kissed the top of her head, she looked up at him and said, "Thirteen."

"Thirteen? I would say it was more like thirty, but I haven't been counting. Here's fourteen then." He bent to kiss her again.

"Not that," was all she had time to say for the next minute.

"There it is again. That's definitely a new one."

"What are you talking about?"

"I can't tell you, you'll think me a silly girl."

"Not married three hours and you're keeping secrets from me already. And I'll never think of you as a silly girl." He locked his arms against her meager attempts to get away. "No, not until you tell me what you're talking about."

"That's number six."

"We're getting lower. I don't know if that's good or bad."

"Your smiles," she said before burying her face in his chest again.

He placed his hand under her chin and gently turned her face up to his. "My smiles? You've been counting them?"

"Fourteen," she said before her lips were silenced once again.

\*   \*   \*

The feast lasted for hours, starting with appetizing tidbits, through savory soups, fish, fowl, and meats, ending with both ornate and simple desserts. Servants carried in loaves of warm bread and butter molded in the shapes of the Protector's and the Premier's family crests. Casks of wine had been placed at stations along the edge of the dining area and the butler and his assistants kept a continuous stream flowing from casks to ewers to goblets.

Different music preceded each course; a change in tempo or melody would silence the talk and laughter as everyone turned to see what would be carried in next. Large tureens of thick vegetable and meat soups and creamy seafood bisques were introduced by the soft tones of a dulcimer. A trio of harps accompanied platters of goose, pheasant and swan. The fish course, including oysters and lampreys, mullet and sole, salmon and trout washed in on a flourish of flutes and mandolins. A rousing chorus of drums and horns conducted in a whole cooked pig, venison and lambs. A quiet pastoral piece announced the final course: marzipan likenesses of Brandorin and Ilona were carried in before trays of sweetmeats, fruits, cheeses and nuts.

As Brandorin smiled, remembering his visit to Reba's kitchen that morning, Ilona slipped her hand into his, saying, "That's number eight." He felt content, not from the great feast they had just eaten, but in the serenity of her presence and the certainty of their love.

The uneven sound of the full complement of musical instruments being tuned seemed to jar his newfound harmony, and told him it was time for the after-dinner festivities. No one else would dance until the bride and groom had shared the traditional pavane, a slow, stately dance symbolizing their union. Brandorin took Ilona's hand and led her to the center of the dance floor. He took her in his arms in a somewhat less formal pose than the traditional stance, and began to sway with the music, clocking off the ceremonious steps that made up the dance.

The eyes of every guest were focused on the bridal couple, but Brandorin was only distantly aware of them. The music faded and even the breeze seemed to stop until he was aware only of the woman in his arms and the adoring look in her eyes as they turned upward toward his.

An unearthly howl shattered the serenity. The music stopped. No one moved, except Brandorin, who enveloped Ilona in his arms. He scanned the nearby woods, trying to determine the source of the cry. A second howl. Branches breaking. Something large crashing through the underbrush, followed by screams.

Brandorin turned toward the sound, but couldn't see the howling beast. He pushed Ilona behind him. Instinctively, he grabbed for his sword, but he wasn't wearing it. He glanced toward the tables, looking for a knife, but the dishes and cutlery had been cleared away.

He heard his father issuing orders, heard muted cries of alarm, but time seemed to stop for him. Ilona clung to him, and he felt her tremble. Whatever dread he had ever felt in battle had been for himself or his men, and it had heightened his reflexes and honed his instincts. Now he felt a fear for Ilona's safety and the weight of that responsibility chilled his blood.

"Go inside," he told her. "There's time for you to reach safety."

"No, I won't leave you," she cried through tears of terror.

Brandorin grabbed a chair; the only thing he could reach that might serve as a weapon. Even over the frenzied voices of the guests, Brandorin could hear Dilardin sending men for swords, and forming a vanguard between the guests and the beast, but they were hampered by the melee of screaming, panicking guests.

The beast barreled through the throng, swiping at anyone who stood against it. Brandorin caught flashes of white fangs, dark, matted fur, and golden eyes. It could be a bear, but the rumbling growls were not ursine.

Two guards reached the beast together. They had only chairs and ewers to use in defense. Sharp claws ripped through the flimsy shields, and raked across the men wielding them. The ewers shattered against its back like waves breaking against a rocky shore.

Brandorin knew the chair he held would not protect Ilona. He dragged her to a table, which he flipped over one-handed, then flipped a second table and sandwiched her between them. "Stay behind these," he shouted. He caught motion from the corner of his eye. He turned, and caught his first full sight of the beast.

It might have been a wolf, much larger than any he had ever seen or heard of, but its head was too big, too broad. He had seen mastiffs as fierce and large as they come, but they were like lapdogs compared to this beast. Its huge maw gaped; the jowls, pulled back in a snarl, exposed jagged fangs.

He didn't wait for it to reach him, but ran toward it, hoping to draw it away from Ilona. The beast leaped across the last ten feet, its eyes almost level with his own. Brandorin grabbed its throat, leaning forward to prevent it from knocking him over. It anchored its back legs and pushed against him with the force of a battering ram.

Its neck was too thick and muscular for him to get his hands around it, but he squeezed, pressing his thumbs into its windpipe. He could feel the guttural rumble of its snarls vibrating all the way up his arms.

He struggled to keep the fangs away from his face; gagged on the acrid smell of rotten meat engulfing him with its foul breath. Its front claws sliced down his sides, and cut into his arms and legs.

He felt no pain. Not until he heard Ilona's cries directly behind him, then his heart seemed to explode. She assailed the beast. Her small hands clenched into fists, striking, clawing at its fur, pulling. She screamed at it to stop.

"No. Go back. Get out of here!" he shouted, even as he knew he was losing the battle. The beast had pushed him back from the wooden dance floor, onto the slicker surface of the flagstone terrace. It was wet and slippery from what he could only assume was his own blood. His foot slipped and he overbalanced, bashing his head on the cobbled paving.

The beast leaped on top of him, forcing the air from his lungs. He tried to suck in air, smelled the beast's foul breath, the jagged fangs inches from his face. He saw the eyes, and the hatred they radiated stopped his breath. Then, as suddenly as it attacked, the beast left him. He struggled to rise, but the pull of unconsciousness dragged at him. His vision clouded over like warm breath on a winter-chilled window. As he blacked out, he heard Ilona scream.

\* \* \*

Brandorin fought his way back to consciousness. Even before his vision had gained full focus, he heard the sounds of a fight nearby, muffled, as if he was underwater. Shouting, snarling, and screaming blended together into a weapon of sound that sliced through his skull. He smelled the mingled scents of the evening's feast, the meaty juices and the lingering sweetness of the final course. Overlaying it all was an odd metallic smell, reminiscent of money. But he knew it was something else, something he should recognize.

He heard his father's voice in the midst of the fight. He sat up abruptly, but his vision blurred and he swayed, the pain in his head shooting through his eyes. He started to lose consciousness again, but he forced the dizziness back.

Gaining his feet, he swayed, struggling for balance. Dilardin and two guards grappled with the beast, trying to pull it off someone on the ground. Someone dressed in white. White, with splashes of red. That elusive smell, that coppery scent. It was blood.

"Ilona," he shouted. He staggered toward the beast, just as it turned and faced him again. His father bent over Ilona, as the two guards continued to fight the beast with their bare hands. But the beast offered no resistance. As Brandorin reached them, it turned, running back through the tumble of tables, chairs and guards.

A sharp bolt of pain shot through his legs as he dropped to his knees at Ilona's side, but he ignored the cuts the beast had inflicted on him. He was aware only of Ilona.

Her dress, which had been so pristine hours before, was shredded and soaked through with her blood; her frail, broken body struggling to breathe. Her once scintillating eyes, all spark now gone, stared dull and vacant.

Brandorin looked at his father for some hope, but the look of defeat he saw there told him there was none. Dilardin turned away, letting his son say farewell to his bride alone.

Brandorin knelt at her side, wanting to hold her, but afraid moving her would cause more pain. He spoke her name and her eyes focused as she turned to look at him.

Ilona tried to speak, but only a soft, gurgling sound escaped her lips. Brandorin leaned over her, speaking words of encouragement, and she answered him with a sweet desperate smile. He tried to smile back, to give her hope, even though he had none.

She spoke again, but this time he understood her. "Fifteen."

"I love you," he said, though he knew she could no longer hear him. He sat frozen, not even trying to breathe, and despite the tumultuous sound around him, he heard the delicate crack of his heart breaking. As the tears began to flow, he gulped in air, and released it in a wail flooded with sorrow and rage.

Brandorin stood; fighting back the dizziness, just as three guards came out of the estate carrying a crate full of swords. He ran up the terrace steps to meet them. The lead guard carried two swords, and Brandorin reached for the larger one. The servant, reluctant to give it up, started to protest but stopped when he saw the look of rage in Brandorin's haunted visage.

Brandorin stumbled briefly as a wave of both ice and heat surged through his blood. A spark of exhilaration revived him, and he turned to search for his prey. From his elevated position he could easily see the beast. The guards had corralled it with four long tables. It railed against them, trying to escape.

Brandorin raised the sword and shouted, "It's mine." But even as he spoke, the beast vaulted over the tables. It clawed for a purchase, mauling the backs of the men it now used as stepping-stones. It ran, weaving through the ruins of the wedding feast. It was heading back to the woods.

Brandorin sprinted down the terrace, leapt over the railing and dashed across the field at an angle, avoiding the tangle of overturned tables and chairs. The guards behind him ran to their comrades with the crate of spare swords. Now armed, a squad of ten men followed in the beast's wake, but it had outdistanced them. Brandorin was the only one with a chance to catch it.

He reached the woods in front of the beast. He turned to face it. He heard a snarling, rasping growl and saw the exposed fangs gleaming. Its eyes, catching the pure, clear light of the moon, reflected back a fierce glowing gold. Brandorin stormed forward, his sword raised.

As he charged, the beast crouched as if to pounce, a faint blue light emanated from Brandorin's sword. He could see the beast's eyes reflected in that light and he froze in his tracks, finding in those eyes the last thing he would have expected.

Brandorin collapsed to his knees and the beast brushed past him as it disappeared into the woods.

## Chapter 4

A lone traveler hurried along the southern road to Kartir, trying to reach the capital city before the gates closed at sundown. His long robes covered a thin frame of medium height. Wrinkles on his face hinted at his age. The furrows on his brow and the sword at his side reflected the seriousness of his life, but the lines around his mouth and his pale blue eyes showed those years had been sparked by laughter.

Caidos was returning to Kartir three weeks after he should have attended Brandorin's wedding. He had missed the wedding with high expectations of finding Rhamak, but his hopes had been unfounded. He had buried his disappointment by attempting to raise Vorago's spirits. It had been thirty-five years since the younger mage had lost track of Rhamak, and this had been the most promising lead in years.

Caidos' mood had not been improved by the rumors he heard on his return trip. In the last three days he had pushed his horse, Aquilo, to her limits, determined to get to the source of those rumors. He should have arrived in Kartir a day or two earlier, but had been delayed often by heavy rains; the thunder and lightning making Aquilo skittish and temperamental. Caidos yearned for the warmth of a fire and a tankard of mead, but he would forgo the comfort just to hear the rumors were unsubstantiated.

A row of hills flanked the east side of the southern road to Kartir. A thin line between the low ceiling of heavy clouds and the western horizon allowed the last rays of the setting sun to shine through. The trees on the ridge, in their full autumn colors of ambers, crimsons, and golds, caught the dying light, setting them ablaze. The trees' radiance, in stark contrast with the dark gray sky beyond, looked like tongues of flame, burning in a vast inferno along the ridge. Strong winds caused the trees to undulate, mimicking flickering flames. Normally, Caidos would have stopped to appreciate the site, but his need for information urged him on.

By the time he had reached the city gates, it was an hour past sunset and what warmth the day had held was slipping away. Kartir's walls rose above him, the pennons on the battlements fluttering and snapping in a strong wind gusting in from the Lorapan Sea. Caidos called up to the parapet. "Hail, the gatekeeper."

"The gates are closed for the night. You must wait until tomorrow to gain entrance." The voice coming from the dark at the top of the guard tower sounded harsh and intimidating, but Caidos knew it belonged to a small, quiet man with a weak chin who was one of the smallest of the Kartirian guard, though his enthusiasm more than made up for his slight stature.

"Mardeeso, your diligence is admirable," Caidos said affectionately, "but I must see the Protector. Is he in the city tonight?"

"Ah, Caidos, I didn't recognize you in the dark," Mardeeso responded, his voice changing to friendlier tones, and Caidos knew, without seeing, a broad grin now transformed the appearance of the homely little man. "Yes, the Protector is at the Residence. Give me a moment to come down and I'll let you in through the postern."

Caidos dismounted, knowing the small doorway next to the huge gate would not allow him to ride through. As he waited for Mardeeso, Caidos thought of a time when the Residence had been referred to as the Palace. But that was before Varsa had been ruled by the Protector, when Zadania's western-most country had been a monarchy.

Even though it happened hundreds of years before Caidos was born, every Westerner knew of the conflagration that had claimed the lives of the entire Dravonian dynasty. Now a fraction of the size and stripped of its full grandeur, the Residence served as a part-time home to the Protector.

Caidos' thoughts were drawn away from one of the darkest events in Varsa's history by the sound of running steps on the other side of the heavy wood door. With a rasping of metal, the bolt barring the door was drawn back. The heavy hinges creaked as the door swung outward, revealing Mardeeso, his cheerful countenance and small stature in stark contrast to the chain mail hauberk he wore.

They embraced as old friends, Caidos having known both Mardeeso and his father all their lives. They walked through the barbican as the small man, winded after running down from the tower, poured out words in short, terse phrases, punctuated by the intake of breath.

"Everyone'll be so glad to see you, Caidos," Mardeeso began. "So much has happened. I barely know where to start. The wedding, such a terrible thing. A ferocious beast. The bride killed. The son hurt. He went after the beast. Hasn't been heard from him since. And Dobbin and his ghost. Old Jorlin dying in that terrible storm, Mt. Malidar rumbling and smoking..."

"Easy, Mardeeso, catch your breath," Caidos said, trying to calm him. "Are you saying Brandorin is missing?" Mardeeso's litany of events had spluttered to a stop, but he was still panting when he came to an abrupt halt, grabbing his own head with both hands.

"Chaos take me! I've forgotten my duty. Must get back to my post." He continued to talk as he scuttled back to the gate, running half sideways, his head turned towards Caidos.

"Mardeeso, wait. What were you saying about Brandorin?" Caidos shouted after him.

"If you're going to see the Protector, he'll tell you everything. I'll be relieved at the turn of the watch. If you can make it to The Blue Gryphon..." He had reached the gate and as he mounted the stairs inside the turret, a muffled echo told Caidos he was still talking. When Mardeeso reached the top and came out into the open air again, "... I'll tell them you're back. I'm sure everything will be better now that you're here, Caidos."

He stood on the parapet, waving down to Caidos, now remounted on his courser, and hurrying down the main thoroughfare. The sound of hooves competed with Mardeeso's final farewells.

Caidos had heard rumors of the events at the wedding, but

had hoped they were exaggerated in the telling from one inn to the next. Mardeeso was a member of the Kartirian Guard, and though he wouldn't have firsthand knowledge, Caidos considered him a reliable source. The news of Brandorin's disappearance had not been part of the stories he had heard.

He was grateful for the empty streets, the hectic exchanges of the markets now quiescent. If he had arrived an hour earlier he would have had to fight against the flow of marketers hurrying home with their day's purchases. The streets would be teaming with shopkeepers hustling in and out in the flurry of end-of-day activities; bringing in their unsold wares and lowering the built-in tables and awnings that folded down to form the store's facade. Now the streets were deserted, as the shopkeepers and shoppers alike sat down to their evening meals. The palumping thud of Aquilo's hooves on the cobblestones echoed through the empty streets, as Caidos hastened her forward.

When Caidos reached the gates of the Residence, the guards on duty rushed him inside, being under strict orders from the Protector himself: Caidos was to be admitted immediately, no matter the time of day or night.

Caidos knew the layout of the Residence and on being told the Protector was in his study, he ran up the sweeping staircase. He knocked as he opened the door, and Dilardin looked up from his desk. Caidos was shocked by the drawn and haggard look of the man he knew so well.

Dilardin's hair seemed grayer, more wrinkles mapped his face, and his usually vibrant eyes were dull and red-rimmed. Worry and lack of sleep had aged him more in eight weeks than years at war had done.

"Caidos, thank the Shapers you're back. Have you heard?" He had risen from his desk and crossed the room. As Dilardin took his hand, Caidos felt the weight of the Protector's burden in the grasping strength of that grip.

"I wish I could spare you the anguish of reliving what's happened, dear friend, but I've heard only rumors. I need to know the truth."

The Protector raised his hand, stopping the mage, "No, I have to tell you. Consider it my confession. Maybe telling you will help to ease this horrible guilt."

"Guilt? How could you ...?" Caidos stopped, realizing there was much more to the story than he had heard. "Come, sit down. Tell me what happened." Caidos led him to the chairs near the fire.

Twenty minutes later, Caidos sat back, saddened by the tale and learning that there was more reality than rumor to all he had heard beforehand. So engrossed in the tale Dilardin related, the mage had not noticed the servant who had apparently come in with hot tea, a decanter of wine, as well as a light supper and a dry, clean robe. Only then did Caidos notice how damp his own robes were from his travels; steam was rising from the hem which was closest to the heat of the fire, and the smell of drying wool permeated the study. Icy fingers danced up his back; whether it was from his cold, wet clothing or the story Dilardin recounted, he couldn't tell.

"Dilardin, you have no cause to feel guilty," Caidos said as he poured a goblet of wine and handed it to the Protector, acting host in the leader's home. He changed robes while Dilardin spoke, and then poured a cup of tea for himself.

"I should have insisted the guards carry their weapons. Brandorin was influenced by his love for Ilona, but I gave in to please him, and to quiet Ilona's mother. I have never been very fond of the woman, but even Valira has not blamed me for what happened." Dilardin hadn't touched his wine, but held the goblet, staring into its garnet depths. "She must know that if we hadn't acceded to her dictates we would've been able to protect her daughter. She has that burden to carry as well as her grief. But I should have known better."

"And I should have been there. If I had been, I could have stopped it."

"Rhamak. I almost forgot why you weren't there. Did you find him?"

"No, the trail led to nothing. What looked very promising at first, just..."

"Of course, that's what it was all the time." Dilardin interrupted Caidos. "A ruse. A diversion. Rhamak allowed himself to be seen, or started the rumor himself, to draw you away from the wedding. Why didn't I see this before?"

"Because you had other concerns. But you could be right." Caidos looked into the fire, contemplating Dilardin's speculation. He continued, each word increasing the probability of the truth of it. "The trail stopped suddenly, but not before it had drawn me far enough away that I had little chance of getting to the wedding. Plus a week lost with the detour due to the collapsed bridge over Ridamon Gorge... I didn't know there was any reason to hurry until three days ago. I am so sorry, Dilardin."

"No, don't apologize. A year since our last battle with Alithia, and I've gotten complacent. I forgot we have another enemy. I've even lost track of what's happening in my own country. I hadn't heard about the bridge. When did that happen?"

"It's of no consequence. I'm sure you're people didn't want to bother you with something you could do nothing about."

Trapped moisture hissed from a log in the fire as Caidos noticed the tortured look in his friend's distant eyes. Dilardin continued, his voice barely more than a whisper.

"But the decision to put aside our swords was not my only error. When that thing attacked, I directed my men; I tried to calm the guests. They panicked, and who could blame them. That thing was horrendous. I don't know where Rhamak found it, or how he controlled it."

"You're a commander. I wouldn't have expected you to do any less."

"That's just it. I was acting like a commander, not a father."

"And what would you have done differently? Let that beast kill your guests? Women and untrained men?"

"I know I couldn't have ignored that responsibility, but I should've been there when Brandorin and Ilona needed me. You should have seen him, Caidos," Dilardin said, a sad smile of fatherly pride breaking across his face. "He ran toward that thing, didn't hesitate for a second. Tackled it with his bare hands." Dilardin mimicked Brandorin's actions, grabbing at the air in front of him, shaking from the tautness in his arms, as if he would kill the beast that had caused so much grief.

"And Ilona was right there, too. She didn't run away. She tried to help Brandorin. When the thing got him down, standing over him, she hit it with whatever she could reach. She was a tiger."

The Protector's voice dropped, carrying an uncharacteristic regret. "I tried to reach them, but there were people everywhere. A wave of them pushed me back despite all my efforts to move forward. By the time I got there, Brandorin was down and it had turned on Ilona." His voice dropped so low, Caidos had to strain to hear him. "I thought I had lost them both."

"What did the beast do after it attacked Brandorin and Ilona?"

Dilardin stared at Caidos, as if the question could not possibly matter. "It tried to get back to the woods. My men had it cornered, but it crawled right over them. Brandorin was hurt, but having Ilona die in his arms triggered a rage that fueled him for a time. Then just as he caught up to it, his energy ran out and he collapsed. I don't understand why the beast didn't kill him there and then."

"It sounds as if the beast was targeting them. Once it had attacked them, it left."

"Yet it let Brandorin live. Three times. The first time when it had him down. It might've thought he was dead then, but it faced him right after attacking Ilona, and then again near the woods." Dilardin stared out the window, but the unforgiving night reflected back his own grief. He couldn't hold the gaze for long, but turned away shaking his head.

"That would make it seem that Ilona was the target. Why would Rhamak want to kill her?"

"I can't think of any reason," Caidos said. "Vorago might have an idea. He knows Rhamak better than anyone. He headed for Tasago when we parted. It might be worth a trip out there to talk to him about this. When did Brandorin leave?"

"During the night. He had taken a blow to the head. He was unconscious when we got to him. We carried him up to his room, and Corleen sat with him all night, but she fell asleep. When she woke, Brandorin was gone. No one saw him go. He must have gone after the beast."

"You must have tried to find him?"

"We did, but there was a terrible storm during the night, and the torrential rain washed away any trace of his tracks." Dilardin's voice rose with frustration. "But even if it hadn't, I'm beginning to wonder about my men. They're getting soft. They lost the trail of the beast, which I find hard to believe. That thing was enormous. They expect me to believe it ran through those woods without breaking a branch or crushing any plants underfoot? A month and a half ago they lost the trail of some thieves trying to break into the estate."

Dilardin leaned forward, putting his face in his hands. His voice was muffled, but Caidos could understand him. "Thiro was leading that detail, and he vanished. Now both of them are missing." Dilardin shook his head and exhaled sharply.

"I don't think it's your men's fault," Caidos said, "In any of these instances. Those trails could have been cloaked, removed magically. Something is going on, Dilardin, and I don't like it. Rhamak suddenly surfacing. This strange beast. Trails that just disappear. I'll start searching for Brandorin myself, first thing tomorrow. Have there been no signs of him since?"

"No. We have no idea which way he went. The only consolation is that he has my sword."

"You gave it to him without me?" Despite all he had heard, Caidos was most surprised by this turn of events.

"He took it from one of the guards right after Ilona was killed. He had it when he faced the beast the last time. Do you think that might have saved him?"

"Fate unfolds in ways even the most imaginative playwright could not conceive. Does he understand the significance of what he carries?"

"In part. He knows about the Protector's crystal. There

was never any reason to tell him about the other."

Caidos heard the uncharacteristic despair in Dilardin's voice. He leaned forward, putting his hand on the Protector's arm, "I'll find him, old friend, and when I do, I'll bring him back here, and we'll tell him everything. I'll start at a local tavern I know, The Blue Gryphon. Simple talk over a tankard of ale often reveals things what would help a general."

*  *  *

As Caidos rode through the empty streets, he realized he had not eaten since midday. Although food had been brought for him at the Residence, he had been too concerned about Brandorin to eat. He nudged Aquilo's flanks as the staccato clicking of her hooves on the cobblestones echoed off the buildings in the deserted streets, casting the illusion of other riders.

A small stone skittered across their path, startling the tired horse. Aquilo reared slightly and Caidos cooed at her as he reined in and looked to see who had triggered the stone's ride. The alleys were cast in shadow, but he thought he heard the receding sound of hooves clacking against the pavement, no longer an echo of his own mount's. Despite a vague feeling of unease, he dismissed the phantom rider as another traveler looking for the warmth of his hearth and the food on his table.

"Just a little further, girl. Then I'll see you get plenty of sweet hay and fresh water, as well as a much deserved rest."

When they turned the final corner, Caidos heard the muffled sounds of laughter and shouting from within the tavern. As he reigned in Aquilo under the sign of the Gryphon, no longer blue due to its long years of exposure to the elements, the door of the inn opened as a patron stepped into the street. The warm glow of the fires inside enveloped Caidos and with it he felt the weariness of the road slough off.

"Caidos, is that you?" the man asked. Those just inside the door had taken up the cry of his name and it rippled through the tavern. Before he had dismounted he was surrounded by greetings and offers of ale. The flood of comments pouring over him reminded him of Mardeeso's torrent of news, but now it was multiplied tenfold. He heard only single words and short phrases, though he recognized some as the same he'd heard at the gate.

"I want to hear all you have to say," he said, his voice carrying over the clamor, "but too many voices made the dog deaf." His unusual use of an old proverb helped to stem the flow of voices, and the local magistrate, Landar, took advantage of the lull to restore some order.

"Caidos has probably been on the road for days, and I would imagine he's hungry and thirsty," he said.

"Then he's come to the right place," called Brelin, the corpulent innkeeper. "Jorba, take Caidos' horse back to the stable and see to her needs. Come everyone, back inside where it's warm."

Caidos sat at a table in the center of the great room, which was warm and dimly lit by a large stone fireplace on the back wall. The press of unwashed bodies, spilled ale in the rushes, and the heavy, smoked air from an ill-tended fireplace contrasted with the stately setting of the Protector's Residence, but the warmth of their camaraderie was as welcome and comfortable as a pair of old slippers.

There was a short scuffling as everyone adjusted chairs from other tables. By the time everyone was settled, a large bowl of beef stew, a loaf of fresh bread and some cheese had been placed in front of Caidos along with a foaming tankard of ale. He took a long draft of the brew and as he was wiping the foam from his mouth asked, "Tell me, has there been any word of the Protector's son?"

Several people started to speak at once, but the magistrate's authority had allotted him the chair closest to Caidos. Landar's voice carried over the others, who soon deferred to him.

"No, no word at all," Landar said, shaking his head dejectedly. "The wedding was three weeks ago, and he hasn't been seen or heard from since. I hate to be the one to say it, but Brandorin is likely dead."

"But he's a warrior, has survived many fierce battles," someone near Caidos' elbow said. Caidos recognized Mardeeso's voice, and turned to acknowledge the quiet man. The throng added their thoughts as Caidos dug into the steaming stew, and closed his eyes as he relished that first taste.

"There was nothing like that beast in any of those battles," Landar said with authority. "You didn't see it. Or hear it. And having his bride savaged, on his wedding day. It's enough to make a man lose his mind. Maybe he's wandering around out there with no recollection of what happened, or who he is. He did suffer a blow to the head, remember. The Protector's search parties have found nothing."

Caidos continued, "I've been to see the Protector already. I told him I would start searching for Brandorin tomorrow." Caidos was distracted by a cold wind that blew into the tavern as more people entered. He was reminded of something else Mardeeso had said, and asked, "I heard something about old Dobbin telling stories again. Could he have seen the beast?"

"No, you know Dobbin and his crazy stories. This time he claims to have seen a ghost --- and it spoke to him." Everyone laughed. As the laughter died down, several comments overlaid each other about the various wild tales Dobbin always wove.

"What did it say?" Caidos asked with amusement and affection for the old man and his imagination.

"Something like, 'The time is near'," Landar said in an ominous-sounding voice as he waggled his fingers in the air in front of his face, "and something else about a crystal. Who pays attention to what Dobbin says?"

Caidos hadn't finished his meal, but pushed it away, scraping wood against wood. He sat back, but continued to stare at the bowl as he asked, "When did he see this ghost?"

"About two weeks ago. He's talked about nothing else since. Has gone out to that same field every night, as if he wants to see it again. That's where he is now, or he'd be here telling you the story himself."

"Which field was it?"

"Out by the old abbey," Landar said. "On the hill to the west of the city. You know the place."

More stories were related, but Landar soon noticed Caidos seemed tired, almost asleep in his chair. He studied his old friend, and lines of concern wrinkled his brow, mirroring the deeper furrows on Caidos' face.

"Stop, stop!" Landar said. "There's more time for storytelling tomorrow. We're forgetting our manners. Caidos has been on the road all day, and now after his meal, in the warmth of this room he's ready to rest without having to hear all this chatter."

The mage forced himself from his reverie, and he looked at those sitting around him and sighed. "The beginning and the end reach out their hands to each other," he muttered.

"See, he's ready for the end of the day," Landar said, looking less than sure that's what Caidos had meant. "Would you like to turn in for the night, Caidos?" When the mage nodded in ascent, Landar wasn't sure the affirmation was in response to his question, but added, "I should be getting home too. Your house is close to mine, so I'll walk with you if you don't mind."

"I will be glad of your company." Caidos got to his feet and left the tavern, accompanied by the magistrate. Though everyone in the tavern wished him goodnight, Caidos left without a response. After retrieving his horse from the stable, Caidos led Aquilo through the streets, walking beside Landar. Caidos asked about his friend's family, but made no response to his answer. When they reached Landar's home, Caidos revived, perhaps by the cool night air, asked, "Mardeeso, at the gate, said something about Mt. Malidar ..."

"It's been grumbling a bit, first time in four hundred years, as far as the records show. It's making people twitchy, the noise and the smoke and all."

Staring into the dark night, Caidos' voice, barely above a whisper, "And Jorlin?"

"Oh, that was a terrible storm. I can't remember one with so much thunder. The winds were so powerful you couldn't walk against them. Lightning hit the tree outside his bedroom; split it down the middle, and it crashed through the roof; the trunk, the rafters, all of it fell on him in his sleep. Probably one of the few people sleeping that night." Landar shook his head slowly, "Jorlin's been hard of hearing for years now, but he still had a few years left."

Caidos patted the magistrate's arm in commiseration, wished him good night, and mounted his steed. Instead of riding to his own home, however, he turned Aquilo toward the west gate, more determined than ever to talk to Dobbin.

He knew the old abbey and would have no trouble finding it, even in the dark. Once through the west gate he increased to a gallop, trusting Aquilo to find the proper footing. The white stone of the old abbey reflected the feeble light of the moon as it peeked out from behind a veil of clouds.

He stumbled through the ruins, in the dark, once the clouds covered what light the moon had provided, until he stubbed his toe on a chunk of wall that had toppled into the path. He cursed the rock and himself for not thinking to create his own illumination. As he magically formed a small globe of light, he heard the startled cry of the man he was seeking.

"Lord, Caidos, ya' gave me quite a scare. I didn't expect to see anybody out here. Thought for a second, was the ghost come back," Dobbin said.

Caidos dismounted, and after anchoring Aquilo's reins under a manageable rock, he sat on the ground next to the old man. Dobbin's hair was all tazzled, his clothes rumpled, but even in the low light of a cloudy night, Caidos could see the old man's eyes glistened with anticipation, like a youngster waiting for his birthday celebration.

"Have you come to see the ghost?" Dobbin asked him.

"Not exactly, Dobbin. How many times have you seen it?"

"Just the one time."

"I would think seeing a ghost here would have scared you away from this field, at least at night."

"Oh, no, Caidos, it wasn't like that. I been calling it a ghost 'cause I don't know what else to call it, but it wasn't scary at all. It made me feel right good inside, like I haven't felt since I was a boy, cradled in my mother's arms, all peaceful like."

"Was it a woman then?"

"Yes and no, it was sorta both, at the same time. I can't explain it."

"They told me it spoke. Was it a man's or a woman's voice?"

"It was lotsa voices, as if several people, man and woman, was talking all at once, but saying the same thing. Made me think of the choir, though they was talkin' not singin'. I know it don't make any sense, Caidos. I know they all think I'm crazy, or was on the bad side of my drink, but I saw it. I know it was real. It was so beautiful I couldn't have made it up. It made its own light, from inside, flashing and glowing like a thousand jewels. And the colors, I don't think I've ever even seen some of those colors." The old man sat and looked in front of him, as if he could see it all again, and a serene look of joy seemed to light up his face.

"Do you remember what it said," Caidos whispered, not wanting to disturb the memory of the image, hoping it would help the old man remember.

"They said a lot of stuff. I don't think I understood most of it. The sight of it just knocked me over almost. It showed up right about dawn. You could wait with me and see if it comes again, then you could hear it for yourself. You'd understand it better than I did. They'd believe me if *you* saw it."

"I don't think I can wait, Dobbin. Do you think you could remember what it said? It's very important." Caidos did not want to prompt him with any of the words or phrases he had been told in the tavern. He wanted to hear it from Dobbin.

The old man closed his eyes, his features scrunching up in concentration. It was almost a minute before he spoke.

"'The time draws near', they said. 'The power of the crystal wains' or something like that. I probably have the wrong word, 'cause ev'n though I'm not sure what a crystal is, what could it have to do with a wagon?" He opened his eyes and continued,

"Something about 'The watcher must find the searcher, the defender,' some others too. I don't remember much else. Oh, I'm forgetting the most important part. It said something about the Protector. I thought I should go tell him, but I wouldn't be allowed in to see him. He'd see *you*, Caidos, maybe you could tell him." Dobbin looked to Caidos for a response, but the mage seemed lost in his own thoughts. Dobbin waited, not sure if his story had been believed.

Caidos looked at Dobbin and with a slow, sad smile, patted him on the back; "You have done well, my friend. I am sorry to tell you, it won't be coming again, not here anyway."

Caidos sat with Dobbin for a while, but his thoughts were racing, at odds with the idleness of sitting in the dark, watching the stars. "I must go, Dobbin. Are you going to go home now or wait until morning?"

"I have to wait out here, can't get back through the gate again tonight."

"I can get you back in tonight. I'm going that way myself," Caidos told him.

"I'll wait, if that's all right. Just being here where the ghost was, makes me feel good, even if it's not coming again."

Caidos said farewell and mounted Aquilo for the ride back into the city. The night sky had broken through in the west revealing a three-quarter moon riding under the stars, a ship in full sail on a sea of clouds. The familiar key-shaped feature on the moon's surface sat in blue-tinted contrast to the parchment-white glow of the lunar ship's sail. The heat of the day was long gone, but the clear night air was not responsible for the chill Caidos felt.

He reached for the amulet he wore on a chain around his neck, and wrapped his hand around it. Despite the cool of the evening, he felt the warmth it always held. Raising it to his face, he looked at the light of the moon through the crystal in its center.

## Chapter 5

Once through the city's gates, Caidos galloped toward his home, Aquilo's hooves clatteringly loud in the otherwise silent streets. On returning to Kartir he would normally walk through the rooms, opening windows to let in air, dispelling the stuffy smell that came from a house being closed and unused for months at a time. Tonight he didn't notice the staleness of the air, nor the dust accumulated on all his treasured things. He lit a candle set in a heavy pewter base and took it with him. Ignoring the front room where he met with visitors, he climbed the stairs to his private study.

The shelves and tables were crowded with books, charts and scrolls he had collected or written. They sat stacked next to objects which few if any of his visitors would understand. Devices to chart the stars, maps of lands they had never seen, a sextant, an astrolabe, jars of herbs and oils, heavy satchels laden with rare rocks; all these things were memories or interests which occupied his spare time for a week or two every few months.

Only one thing filled his thoughts now; a chart he had planned to complete but had put aside for what he had thought were more pressing matters. A strong sense of urgency gave his efforts frantic speed. Like a scared animal pursued by a predator, trying to burrow in for safety, he threw documents aside, digging for the right one. He forced himself to relax; taking deep, calming breaths, he lit more candles hoping the dim light and his haste had caused him to miss the item he needed.

At last, he found it. He cleared a space on his worktable and pulled out clean parchment, quill and ink. He scribbled calculations, wrote out long columns of numbers, put them aside and started again. Tense hours passed in silence punctuated only by scratching on parchment and frequent sighs of exasperation.

Caidos sat back, scratching his head as he shook it back and forth. "It makes no sense. It's too soon. But if it was like the other time, then why the Abbey? And what about the lost fragment.

There's no time to find it."

He picked up the amulet resting on his chest, staring at the light of the candle through its opalescent crystal. His predecessor, Mandricon, had given him the amulet, the scrolls, and the responsibility of the legend when he was thirty years old, making him the youngest Mirador in the history of the Mages of Artara. There had been some dissension among the older mages. Many thought him too young despite his considerable talent.

Mirador. The title meant Watcher. Watching was what he had done for most of the last eighty years. He had waited and listened, attuned to the stories in local taverns in case one day he would hear what he had heard tonight. Now, for the first time, he wished the dissenting mages had convinced Mandricon to pick someone else, so these tasks would have fallen on someone else's shoulders.

He shook his head again, but this time with a short expulsion of breath.

"Doesn't matter if it doesn't make sense. It *was* Sefiron's Shadow." He pushed up out of his chair and looked around his study, deciding he needed none of these things for the task that lay before him. "Even the shortest journey becomes a long one if you will not take that first step."

He grabbed a thick robe and some warm socks and added them to the clothes already in his pack. On the way out the door he picked up his wool cloak and headed to the stable. He saddled Aquilo saying, "Sorry, girl. I know it's only been a few hours, but we have to take to the road again. It is more important than ever that I find Brandorin."

He knew where Brandorin had been two weeks ago, but the question was, where was he now? The southern road out of Kartir had the most traffic, so he would start in that direction. Someone had to have seen him.

*   *   *

Caidos traveled slowly for most of the day, giving Aquilo a

chance to recover from the driven pace he had set over the past few days. He stopped often to talk to villagers and farmers working in the fields. As sunset neared, he was still within a normal half-day's ride of Kartir, but it had been almost an hour since he passed the last farmer, villager or fellow traveler.

There was not a breath of air, and a light haze covered the harvested fields on either side of the road. Caidos was suddenly aware of a total silence, undisturbed by bird or insect. An unearthly shriek made him pull up his horse and tense in his saddle. He looked up toward the source of the cry to see four creatures, swooping down on him.

They were repulsive, man-sized, bat-like creatures; their twelve-foot misshapen wings, like recently skinned hide stretched and ready for tanning. A muscular arm powered each wing tipped by razor-sharp talons. The wings ran the length of the creature's body, which ended in stunted legs and clawed feet. Each elongated head had a gnarled and twisted beak filled with needle-sharp teeth.

Caidos dodged each swooping attack, holding tight to Aquilo's reins, as the horse bucked and reared. A smell of decay emanated from the creatures, and Caidos fought a feeling of revulsion as well as Aquilo's panic.

A piercing pain shot through his shoulders as talons gripped him. Powerful leathery wings beat against his body and Aquilo's flanks as the largest raptor tried to carry him away. His feet, well planted in the stirrups, and his tight hold on the reins countered the raptor's upward pull. The creature shrieked with rage, its wing talons slashing Aquilo with each downward beat.

The horse reared in pain and the raptor lost its grip. Caidos immediately let Aquilo take the rein, and the horse bolted forward. The raptors kept pace.

Drawing on the energy in the air around him, Caidos gathered the heat into a fireball, and launched it. The helmet-sized fireball punched one creature square in the chest, but the raptor was barely affected. Caidos was dumbfounded. He had used enough power to fell a creature four times its size, yet it continued to fly unhindered, turning for another pass.

He drew more energy; creating a fireball so large it rippled the air around him. He hurled it at the closest raptor, striking it full in the face. The fire engulfed it, yet it recovered within seconds.

Drawing energy from the air gave Caidos only limited power; he needed more. Living plants would provide more energy, but the landscape was barren. He turned Aquilo toward the distant trees across the harvested fields. The transition from the well-packed surface of the road, to the uneven, furrowed soil in the field was too much for the panicked horse. She went down.

Caidos pushed off from the stirrups, and rolled away. By the time he got back on his feet, Aquilo was bolting back to the road. The raptors, sensing their advantage now that Caidos was on foot, intensified their attacks.

With his hand now free from the reins, Caidos grasped his amulet, using it to intensify the strength of his incantations. He focused the power into a narrow beam of energy, sharp as an arrow, and hurled it. Combined with the downward force of the raptor's descent, the beam should have pierced its chest. Yet it bounced off the raptor rather than impale it.

With each attack, Caidos tried stronger and more powerful bolts of energy, but nothing had any effect. The fireballs and blast arrows were getting smaller and it was taking longer to form each new one. His ragged breathing plumed as it hit the cold air. He shivered as the sweat from his exertion chilled him.

In a sudden revelation, Caidos realized the area should have been warming, as energy from each blast returned to the air after hitting its target. Instead, the air around him was noticeably colder. The creatures were absorbing the energies. Instead of tiring as Caidos was, they were getting stronger.

Instead of attacking and feeding them energy, he created a sphere of concentrated air around himself. The next raptor, diving at him, stopped in mid-flight as it hit the invisible shield. The creature lay before him, stunned, but not dead.

Caidos sprinted for the trees at the far side of the field. The raptors streaked after him. Tired from three days with little sleep, he could not run full out. His legs were sore and his chest tightened from the continued exertion. He stumbled over the furrows in the plowed field, and felt steely talons grip into his shoulders.

He grabbed at the talons, trying to prey himself loose, but his captor's grip was metal hard. The other two creatures flew across the meadow, ahead of them. The direction of the flight would take them east, over the forest. They gained height rapidly, but the extra weight his captor carried left them at the rear of the group.

Knowing fire bolts were not a solution, Caidos resorted to a non-magical one. He pulled a dagger from his boot, his sword still in its sheath on Aquilo's saddle. He swung his arm in a full arc over his head straight into the creature's belly. It shrieked as blood gushed from the wound, dark and more malodorous than the creature itself.

The creature wrapped its leathery wings around him as they both fell together from the sky. Caidos used his power to turn them as they plummeted. The creature struck the ground first, its body cushioning Caidos' impact. The combination of the knife wound and the fall succeeded where the other attacks had failed. One creature was dead.

Caidos half crawled, half stumbled toward the woods, hoping to reach its shadowy protection before the other creatures realized their companion was down. A screech from across the meadow announced the recovery of the creature felled by the air shield. It streaked at him from across the field, and he heard the echoing cries of the other two returning.

Caidos headed deeper into the woods, stumbling over tree roots and fallen branches. Crossing a stream, he tripped on the moss-draped rocks, falling face first into the water. The cold water helped to revive him and reduced the stench from the raptor's blood, but added unneeded weight to his robes. As he crawled up the far bank of the stream, his legs felt dream-dragged.

His heart pounded and each labored breath pulled a stitch in his side. He found a patch of dead scrub overgrown with vines, which formed a dense canopy over a small hollow. With the last of his strength, he crawled in to the sheltering confines.

The slashes in his head and shoulders throbbed and every muscle ached from his fall with the raptor and three days of hard riding. Magically drained and physically exhausted, he tried to calm his heart and slow his breathing. He focused on the nature of the attacks so far, weighing his options for the use of the nearly depleted state of his magical reserves.

Direct magical assaults had no effect. His knife required him to get too close to the raptors, though it would be useful if they captured him again. Defensive measures had helped, but … Caidos' speculations came to an abrupt halt as the canopy of branches and vines was ripped away.

Caidos saw two creatures perched on branches in front of him and to his right. Their comrade disposed of the debris it had removed from Caidos' refuge. Then it too settled on a low branch on his left. They had positioned themselves on separate trees, surrounding Caidos in the hollow. Their malevolent stares made him feel like a cornered mouse.

Turning slowly to keep an eye on each of the creatures in turn, his mind raced, searching for a solution to his dilemma. Two of them sat on dying trees; probably selected for the open perch the bare branches provided. All three raptors made a raspy, chittering noise and rocked back and forth on their perches.

They were prepared for an attack or for him to try to run, but his inactivity seemed to be making them nervous. He silently thanked his teachers for drilling him on the discipline it took to wait and think.

Without any time between thought and action, Caidos gathered all the power he could muster and hurled a large boulder from the edge of the clearing to the base of one of the trees. The dead tree crumpled under the force of the impact and the weight of the boulder.

The creature on it became entangled in the collapsing branches. The falling upper branches of the tree caught a second raptor as it took flight, crushing it. As the cry of their shrieks sounded through the otherwise quiet forest, Caidos had to smile as he thought of the old adage about two birds and one stone.

The remaining raptor attacked with wild savagery. It flew at him, shrieking furiously. With frenzied movements, the raptor yanked at the branches surrounding Caidos, pulling them and the clinging vines out of the way. In trying to gain better access to him, the creature had opened a path that allowed Caidos to leave the covert more easily than he had gotten in.

The creature's talons became entangled in the underbrush. It was only a few seconds, but Caidos used it to move amongst the trees, where he had more maneuverability. It followed him, but Caidos stayed under the protection of low branches or kept the trunks of the trees between himself and the creature whenever he could. He slashed at it with his knife when it moved within reach, but he inflicted little if any damage.

Though a strong breeze blowing through the woods, helped to revive him physically, casting the boulder had drained the last of his magical reserves. He had nothing left to fight with, no other defense. The last raptor hovered over him, slashing at him with the talons on both its feet and wings. Caidos' heart sank when he saw the branches of the fallen tree at the edge of the copse start to move.

As a wing and then the head of one of the fallen raptors cleared the tangle of leaves and branches, he knew any chance he might have had was gone. He had little hope of besting one creature, but if even one other joined it, he was lost.

A flash of light caught his eye, as a sword blade swung out from behind a tree, and connected with the neck of the emerging creature. There had been no sound other than a soft whistling as the blade swung through the air to its target. The creature attacking Caidos had its back to the scene, so it hadn't seen the death of its comrade.

A moment later, a man stepped out from behind the tree, and using both hands to grasp the sword by its hilt, brought it up over his head and jammed the blade down into the tangle of fallen trees. Caidos was relieved to know those two raptors would not be rejoining the attack.

The man was tall and powerfully built; the muscles in his

arms and legs obvious even through his clothes. He wore no armor or mail but he could have been a Knight Companion or a veteran warrior, for he stood with the bearing and readiness of a man who has had experience in battle. Caidos saw eyes of intense azure that shone with an inner power. The stranger locked his gaze on the remaining raptor, as he moved with a determined force toward it.

Caidos moved to turn the raptor's back to the stranger; the creature, intent on its prey, was unaware of the activity behind it. The knight studied the raptor's movements, as with a few quick strides of his long legs, he covered the distance across the clearing. He planted his feet firmly on the soft ground, and with both hands pulled the sword back over his shoulder. The power of its forward swing would cut the raptor in two.

Just as before, the sword whistled as it swept through the air in its arc toward the creature's back. The sound, much closer this time, must have alerted the raptor for it rose into the air as the sword passed through the now empty space in front of Caidos. The raptor circled around to face the warrior.

The stranger was fresh to the battle, but the creature showed no signs of fatigue as it hovered over the warrior and his sweeping sword. The warrior engaged the raptor, feinting and striking with the sword, then turning and thrusting again from the other side, each movement fluid and efficient. Both combatants were born to do battle.

The stranger soon learned how his opponent fought, and modified his tactics to misdirect and confuse the creature, but it was quick to adapt as well; and with each change in advance and parry, it reacted in kind. The raptor was able to evade each thrust of the sword, and its talons had yet to connect with the stranger.

Both combatants were evenly matched and Caidos knew only a minor mistake on the part of one of them would provide the other with the opportunity to end the fight. Caidos felt sure the stranger would not make such a mistake, but didn't want to stand by doing nothing while this man risked his own life to save his. He attempted to rise, but was not yet fully to his feet, when he was knocked back to the ground, struck from behind by a large, snarling animal.

The bear-size, wolf-like creature barreled over Caidos, and charged toward the stranger, vengeance incarnate. Caidos shouted a warning, but the warrior didn't seem to hear as he continued his fight with the raptor. The beast took flight as it vaulted off a boulder in its rush toward the stranger. Its howl sent chills down Caidos' spine.

The gaping jaws, mere inches from the warrior's head, sailed past as the stranger pivoted out of reach. The beast's momentum carried it straight into the raptor, as it clamped its powerful jaws on the creature's foot and held it, despite the blows it suffered from the talons. The knight did not waste the opportunity the beast had given him.

A flash of pale blue light blazed from the hilt of the sword as he thrust the blade up into the chest of the raptor. The creature's shriek turned into a strangled cry then was cut off abruptly as the sword point pierced its heart, and it fell to the ground at the stranger's feet.

In the silence that followed, Caidos felt a relief so profound he could barely stand. He moved to thank the warrior for his intervention, but stopped as the stranger reached out to the beast as if in friendship.

Caidos had been convinced this beast was the same monster that had killed the Protector's daughter-in-law and attacked his son, but looking at it closely now, he could see no malevolence. The beast and the warrior seemed more like a hunting dog and its master.

Before he could speak Caidos was struck by the smile of pure delight lighting the stranger's face, as he walked up to Caidos with his right arm outstretched in greeting.

"Hail Caidos, it has been many years since I've seen you." Caidos studied the stranger's face, recognizing him a second before he added, "I'm Brandorin, and this is my companion, Piritho," he said as he gestured toward the beast, "and I must thank you for the best brawl we've had in many months."

## Chapter 6

"It's been a long time, Caidos," Brandorin said. The mage's labored breathing and the rapid pulse he could feel through the tight, bolstering grip of Caidos' hand told Brandorin the mage was near exhaustion, but it was the look of open bewilderment that made him add with a suggestive tone, "I'm Dilardin's son."

Caidos' knees gave way just as Brandorin eased him down onto a fallen tree. He knew Caidos was over a hundred years old, and even though that was less than half the typical lifespan for a mage, Brandorin realized the fight against the raptors had taken its toll. Without being too obvious, he sat within an arm's reach in case the mage collapsed. The beast, Piritho, walked over and plopped down next to Brandorin. Still breathing hard, he faced away, as if standing watch.

"I recognized you, Brandorin." The words rode out on percussive bursts of shallow breathing, every few phrases delayed by a deep, controlled inhalation. "As a matter of fact, I was searching for you. It's just the surprise of you finding me instead. And you being with that ... with Piritho."

"Would you like to lie down?" Brandorin asked when the mage's wheezing breaths were punctuated with quick, shallow coughs. The mage shook his head and waved his hand in dismissal, but motioned for Brandorin to talk for awhile. "I think the last time we talked was right before I joined the cavalry, before the Battle of Dinsara. I'm not quite the same reckless youth I was then."

"And now you are quite the warrior. Your skills with a sword are very impressive – and very opportune." Caidos' breathing was starting to slow. He put his hand on Brandorin's arm, his voice conveying a profound sense of gratitude, as he said, "Thank you for saving my life."

"I'm sure it seemed more impressive because of your circumstance, but I'm happy to be of service," Brandorin said, a memory of the aftermath of his first battle tugged at him, as he recalled the sense of wonder at finding himself alive and unharmed, while so many around him were not.

"I was lucky you happened to be in the wood."

"We didn't just happen to be here. I found what I assume to be your horse, bolting down the road. I caught her and followed her trail back in time to see one of those creatures rise from the thicket and streak across the field into the forest.

"It was easy to track you from that reeking carcass in the field to the woods, but after a while all I had to do was follow the sound of the shrieking." He stopped and looked over at the last of the raptors. "What are those things?"

"I have my suspicions. It will be a long story, and I'm afraid I don't have the energy to go into it now." Caidos took a deep breath, wincing; he pressed his hand into the small of his back and stretched. "Every muscle and bone I possess is chastising me for what I've put them through. Maybe you could tell me a little about your companion and how you came to be traveling together."

Brandorin looked at Piritho, and then back at Caidos before he replied, "That's a long story too, and I have to say I don't really understand the whole thing myself, but we *are* traveling together." Acting as if he had just thought of something, he asked, "Did you have a second horse, Caidos? Or was there someone else with you?"

Caidos shook his head and gave Brandorin a you're-not-fooling-me look, very reminiscent of his father's. Knowing that it was always best to forge on through in such situations, Brandorin did just that. "I thought I saw something right after we entered the forest, just a gray, shadowy shape moving between the trees. I followed the shrieks and Piritho followed the horse but he didn't find anything." Turning to the dead raptors he asked, "What should we do with these things?"

"How do you know he didn't find anything?" Caidos asked. When Brandorin waved off the question with a hand and an oblique expression, Caidos continued, "I'm not sure where they came from, but I have no doubt they were created magically. As a result, we can't be sure they're dead." Brandorin's hand darted to the pommel of his sword and he tensed, his eyes darting from the nearby raptor to those in the tangle of the fallen trees. "I'm too exhausted to take care of it myself, but if you wouldn't mind."

"Whatever you think is necessary. Should we burn them? Cut off their heads? Both?"

Caidos chuckled at the blue twinkle of Brandorin's expression, reminiscent of the young rapscallion he used to know, now set in a more mature face. "I don't have the strength to control such a large fire in the middle of the woods, and it could too easily get out of hand. I think cutting off the heads would be a smart precaution."

"Consider it done," Brandorin said as he marched over to the closest raptor, the last to die. In one fluid motion, he withdrew his sword from its sheath and swinging it, severed the head from the body. A ringing lingered in the heavy air as he strode toward the raptors entangled in the fallen trees, where he repeated the action twice more.

"Maybe we should burn just the heads. To be sure. I imagine you'd like to rest a bit more before we start that long walk back to the horses. While they're burning, we can see to your wounds."

"That can wait. I'm too tired to even notice it right now."

The fire blazed on the dry wood as it licked at the leathery hides covering the three skulls. Although the fire's heat would have been welcome in the growing coolness of the darkening forest, the stench of the burning heads kept them at a distance. They said nothing while the fire consumed its fuel. Flames licked out through the empty eye sockets, and Caidos' skin prickled, as the charred heads mimicked the evil gaze of the live raptors.

By the time the fire had consumed its charnel fuel, Brandorin had dragged the remains of all three raptors into the shallow depression of Caidos' brief refuge. He shrouded them with the loose branches and vines.

As the burning embers reduced to a meager glow, Caidos uncurled himself from the fallen log, and Brandorin led them through the dimly lit forest, finding a smooth path in the heavy undergrowth. Though somewhat recovered, Caidos was still fatigued; he stumbled a few times, but each time Brandorin turned and caught him easily.

When they reached the meadow, Caidos rested while Brandorin dealt with the last dead raptor, cutting off the head and dragging the body into the woods. When he returned, Caidos was staring toward the now hidden raptor. "That creature didn't look as fearsome as I thought."

Brandorin added, "This one must have died first because it was the runt of the litter. Look at it; its beak is not so long and twisted; its wings are smaller, its legs a bit longer. Doesn't look quite so vicious, does it?"

As the final head burned, Caidos' stare shifted to the bare branches of a single tree, in stark contrast to the bright autumn colors of the trees around it. A thick carpet of red leaves surrounded the base of the skeletal maple.

"I'm afraid I did that," Caidos admitted with a woeful expression. "I didn't have much time to react when the raptor started flying off with me. Instead of drawing energy evenly from all of the trees, I used the nearest source."

"What would have happened if you needed more?"

"If I had continued to draw energy from that single tree, it would be gray and lifeless now. It should recover if we don't have an early or severe winter."

"I am surprised at how rested I feel," Caidos said as they trekked across the meadow. "I'm starting to believe the raptors were pulling power directly from me; with the destruction of each, I gain more and more of it back."

"Is that possible?"

"A mage *can* draw energy from a person, though the Code prohibits it. So it is possible, and based on the way I feel now, compared to the way I felt earlier, it's also probable."

When they reached the horses, Brandorin started a sizable fire. Once the blaze had caught on the tinder, he gingerly removed Aquilo's saddle. The raptor's wings had thrashed against her flanks, the talons cutting into her sides. Brandorin, seeing the wounds, said, "We can take care of these wounds as soon as we've dressed yours. You don't want those to fester. There are some plants growing on the banks of the stream I can use to prevent that."

Caidos watched as Brandorin gathered two bunches of aromatic heart-shaped leaves, which he shredded, and crushing them in the hollow of a large rock, he mixed them with some oil from his saddlebag and made up a thick salve.

"Take care of Aquilo first," Caidos told him, "I'm going to go clean up." Caidos looked longingly at the fire, but knew he wouldn't enjoy its warmth or his meal until he had washed off the stench of the raptor's blood. He took a change of clothes and a bar of soap from his pack and shuffled down to the stream.

Brandorin showed great tenderness in cleaning Aquilo's wounds; his quiet, rhythmic words calmed her as he tenderly spread the salve over the gashes in her flanks. Recognizing that she had been pushed to her limits, he spent more than the usual amount of time brushing her and rubbing liniment into her tender muscles and joints. His practiced touch massaged the overworked and bruised tendons and strained muscles; her soft whickering told him when he reached a particularly tender spot. She thanked him with a snuffling of her velvety nose against his shoulder and her clover-spiced breath brushed his face in grateful warmth.

He checked Piritho's flanks to see if he needed attention, but the beast's thick fur and quick reflexes had protected him. After grooming Bristo, he hobbled both horses and let them forage for their dinner.

By the time Caidos had washed and changed, Brandorin had finished preparing their meal. Caidos winced as he reached up to stretch his wet robe on a low branch of a nearby tree, where it would catch the rising heat from the fire.

Brandorin took the heavy wet robes and finished the job. "It's time we took care of your wounds."

Caidos sat on a large boulder as Brandorin put the last of the salve on the gashes in his shoulders and forehead. When Brandorin noticed a smile creeping across Caidos' face, he said, "Feel better? We shouldn't have waited so long."

"The farmer waits for the harvest, but still reaps the

bounty," Caidos said, the slight smile breaking into a joyous grin. Brandorin just nodded in agreement, remembering all the times in years past that he hadn't understand Caidos' remarks, thinking then it was his inexperience or lack of world knowledge, but seeing now that it was just the mage's enigmatic manner.

They huddled in the fire's pocket of warmth as the clear autumn night cloaked them in a crisp coat of stars. Caidos was munching on seconds; praising the simple fare, when Brandorin pointed out, "I think you'd say, 'Hunger makes any meal a banquet.'" Caidos smiled appreciatively around a mouthful of rabbit and bread. "Are you rested enough to tell me what you think about those creatures now?"

Caidos nodded slowly for a time, as if confirming the hypothesis that he had formed since the raptors' attack. "I think they were warded against the kind of incantations I would use against them. That's the only explanation for my power being so ineffective. The air incantations I used worked because they didn't direct energy *against* the creatures; they only served to protect me. The man who sent them hadn't accounted for that, or for someone else stepping in to help."

"But who could create such..." Brandorin trailed off; looking over at Piritho, then added with a vehement whisper, "Rhamak!"

"I'm surprised you know ...." The mage stopped, distracted by a deep, guttural growl. He turned to find the beast standing in the shadows at the edge of the fire, his hackles raised, his teeth bared, and a light in his eyes that burned with more than the reflection of the flames. Caidos tensed, glancing to his bedroll where his sword rested, but keeping a wary eye on the sharp fangs only a few feet away.

"Settle down, Piritho," Brandorin said. As the beast sat down, and the snarl reduced to a quiet but discontented woofing, he turned back to Caidos, "He's a little on edge."

Keeping a nervous eye on Piritho, Caidos asked, "What do you know of Rhamak?"

"Not much. My father has mentioned him and I know you were off looking for him recently. I take it you didn't find him."

"No we didn't," Caidos said. "If you aren't that familiar with Rhamak, why would you suspect him of creating those creatures? Have you heard news of him?"

"I know of someone who did; who actually saw him," Brandorin answered.

Caidos sat up, his eyes wide and shining in the light of the fire, "When? Where? Under what circumstances?"

"Piritho did," he said, after a moment's hesitation. "I don't know how I know that, but I do."

A cold wind blew through their secluded hollow, and Caidos pulled the front if his robes across him for additional warmth. After a moment's contemplation, Caidos asked, "Do you know what you carry with that sword?"

"I haven't carried it for long, but I know what it is."

"Where were you two weeks ago?"

Brandorin's eyes shifted up at the mage without moving his head, and he nodded knowingly as he answered, "I've been a lot of places recently, but I know what you're getting at. I was in a field outside of Kartir, near the ruins of the old abbey."

"You had the sword with you," Caidos murmured to himself, stating a fact, rather than asking a question. He continued in that same tone, "It would have been drawn to what you carry." Then suddenly aware of Brandorin again, he asked, "Then you saw the Shadow of Sefiron, heard what it said?"

"I saw it, but I didn't understand what it was at first. When I turned eighteen, my father told me what being the Protector really meant. Told me about the crystal in this sword. I know there are others, but that's about it."

Caidos' voice took on the timbre of a storyteller; practiced, with a cadence conveying the grandeur of an ancient, oft-repeated tale. "Four thousand, three hundred, and twenty years ago legend tells us the Sefiramon, the World-Shapers, came to our world and found a primeval, violent land where its few inhabitants were isolated and struggling to survive. Volcanic eruptions, ground-rending quakes, horrific storms and turbulent seas ravaged every arc of our planet.

"They imposed their power on the churning seas, calming them, sealed off the spewing volcanoes, and quelled the quaking ground.

"Each of the Sefiramon claimed a continent as their own, sculpting it into a hospitable environment. Zadan, the least of the Sefiramon, claimed an island in the middle of the vast ocean of the north. The volcanoes and quakes here were the most violent on this world, and the turbulent oceans surrounding it had claimed much of the land.

"Zadan shaped the land, sunk the highest volcano until only the caldera remained, burying it, except for the rim." As an aside, he turned to Brandorin, to clarify, "What is now the Great Central Desert. He straightened out the craggy ground, squeezed the land to sculpt rolling hills and gentle valleys, then poured down nourishing rain to wash away the dust and gather into lakes and rivers. The land had been so wasted that no life lived here, so he turned to his brethren and asked if he might make an offer to those who lived on the main continents."

Even though he had heard this story dozens of times, Brandorin was lost in the tale, hearing it for the first time from a mage of Artara, the order that had been given the task to record the history of this storm-tossed land. When Caidos paused for a sip of tea, Brandorin nodded eagerly for him to continue.

"Zadan promised special protection, special gifts to any who would come to live on this now beautiful and bountiful island. People from all over the world came to Zadania, though it wasn't called that then, and Zadan was a beneficent guardian. He gave those first settlers gifts that helped them survive. You've heard the term 'having a green thumb', well the first Zadanians had green hands; everything they planted grew, within days. If they needed anything, they would find it, or if it didn't exist, Zadan would create it for them.

"Word of their bounty spread, and more people came to Zadania. Within a few generations, the island was well populated. Have you heard of Trevarre?"

When Brandorin indicated he hadn't, Caidos continued,

"There aren't many who have. Although he might have been a well-known and revered ancestor of yours, his name was stricken from the histories."

"What did he do?"

"He grew greedy. As much as Zadan would give, Trevarre wanted more. He was intelligent and talented, in his own right, but his avarice was insatiable. Instead of directing his knowledge and ambition to helping his people thrive, he used the gifts Zadan had given him, and he created a Paragon.

"A Paragon is a talisman, a receptacle for power. That Trevarre was able to make one is a feat unto itself. Even though it allowed him to wield more power than any mortal should be able to withstand, he wanted more. He wanted what Zadan had.

"With the Paragon, he captured Zadan and held him, and turned his new found supremacy against his countryman, subjugating them to his will."

Brandorin had grabbed his sword, his fingers floating over the crystal in its hilt. "This isn't ... This isn't the Paragon?" Brandorin whispered.

"No," Caidos assured him. "Well, not exactly." When Brandorin started to protest, Caidos held up his hand and said, "Let me finish the tale."

"The Sefiramon are more spirits than flesh, but even though they are individuals, they can communicate with each other from great distances. From the moment Zadan was imprisoned within the Paragon, they lost contact with him. They came looking for Zadan, and finding him imprisoned in the Paragon, they exploded, and unleashed their wrath against the people and the land.

"The seas roiled, the earth cracked open, torrents of boulders crashed down from the mountains. In a matter of moments, the tranquil land reverted to its former state of chaos.

"But Trevarre would not be moved, and he cast a spell of protection around himself. Though it shielded him against the storms and chaotic earth, it served as a beacon to the Sefiramon, and they focused their wrath against the traitor, who was vaporized in an instant.

"Zadan was freed, but he was desolated about Trevarre's betrayal, the death of so many of his people and the destruction of the land they had made. Though he strove to repair the damage, and restore the balance, the skies churned with black clouds and ground-shaking thunder. Continual tremors threatened to dissolve all that his people had built.

"Zadan pleaded with his brethren not to punish all his people because of the betrayal of one. Reluctantly, they took the fragments of Trevarre's Paragon, for even the broken pieces still held great power. They reformed it, using their own blood, which flowed like molten metal and shined with the iridescence of gemstones.

"The calming influence of the Paragon kept the volcanic eruptions, quakes and turbulent storms at bay, and the land flourished once again. Knowing that Zadan would continue to indulge his people despite Trevarre's treachery, the Sefiramon decided to allow his indulgence, but within their own set of controls.

"They split the newly formed Paragon, which they called Sefiron, after themselves, and removed the crown piece of the great jewel, splitting the remainder into eight fragments. Each of the Sefiramon took a fragment and imbued it with some of their power to help the people. Each fragment carried a different gift, and helped its people in different ways."

Brandorin, finally getting an answer to his earlier question about the crystal fragment in his sword, "So this crystal, while not the Paragon, is a part of it?"

"Yes, one of eight fragments," Caidos confirmed. "The crown piece they gave to the race of mages. The Sefiramon called this the Dedication.

"They also gave us The Code, a set of rules that would guide us in understanding the gifts of all the fragments and to help ensure that the gifts would not be abused. As long as the Code is followed, and Sefiron is in control, the devastating force will be held back."

Caidos reached for the amulet hanging from his neck, raising it to show Brandorin the opalescent crystal at its center. "There is one in every country, one who carries a fragment, passed down to them from their forebears, in a long line since Sefiron was first formed.

"The Sefiramon set a limit on Sefiron's power. At the end of the fifth millennium there will be a great Rededication, when the Sefiramon will reassess the people of Zadania, and if judged worthy, the power of the Paragon will continue indefinitely.

"But this is too early. Sefiron's Shadow should not have appeared yet, which can only mean one thing. Someone is using a fragment in a way that violates the Sefiramon's restrictions."

"Someone?" said Brandorin, "You mean Rhamak."

"Rhamak doesn't have a fragment of Sefiron," Caidos voice trailed off, unconvinced of his own words. "Or at least he shouldn't have one. There is the Kordunan fragment which has been missing for over two hundred and fifty years. And I worry that he may have already obtained one from one of the other bearers. I am convinced today's attack was meant to get my crown piece.

"The appearance of Sefiron's Shadow, which always coincides with the New Moon, signals the time for us to come together. When we've collected all of the fragments and their bearers, we'll wait for the next New Moon. The presence of all the fragments will bring the Shadow to us. Then we will each take our fragments, and join them, and Sefiron will become whole again."

"What'll happen when the fragments are united?"

"For the true Rededication? That is something the Mages of Artara have been debating for millennia. Many believe, myself included, that if we are judged worthy, the gifts provided by the fragments will increase. The power of a united Paragon could be beyond our imagining.

"For this Rejoining, we will be told by the Spirit of the Sefiramon what we must do. About five hundred years ago, one of the fragment bearers, Gharvik of Febron, misused his power, and the Mirador of the time, Churlik, was instructed to take his fragment and give it to another. What will happen this time, I cannot say. What I do know of the history of Sefiron, I was told by my predecessor, Mandricon, as his predecessor told him. We also have scrolls, written by the first Mirador, Didonno. Although I don't know for a certainty what will happen when we rejoin the fragments, I do know what would happen if we don't succeed. Zadania would be destroyed."

"Destroyed? How?" Brandorin's sense of wonder on hearing the ancient legend vanished, replaced with the stark reality of now.

"Haven't you noticed that in the last few weeks the weather has gotten more volatile? Violent storms, earthquakes, Mt. Malidar is stirring. One of our mages, Vorago, is an expert in weather and natural phenomenon, and he says there has been nothing like the events we've been seeing since before the Dedication. It is beginning, and if we don't stop it, our island will quite literally tear itself apart."

Brandorin stared at Caidos, his mouth open in disbelief. His voice a hollow whisper, cracked with desperation, "How long do we have?"

"The scrolls say there will be seven appearances of Sefiron's Shadow, six moon cycles of forty-five days each. The World Shapers gave us the time it takes for a life to start, conception to birth. We must unite the fragments before the seventh, but I don't know if the Shadow you saw in Kartir was the first. Did it say anything that would have indicated that?"

"No, I don't remember anything like that."

Caidos' storyteller's tone was replaced by frustration and concern. "I thought it would have appeared to me first, as the Watcher. But it obviously didn't. I don't know if it's already appeared to any of the other bearers in recent months. Until we reach them, we have no way of knowing."

"The Shadow mentioned several titles: the Healer, the Defender, the Caretaker. My father is the Protector, you're the Watcher, but what about the others? Do you know who they are? Will you be able to find them?"

"That's one of the reasons I've traveled across Zadania all these years, to watch the bearers, make sure the fragments are safe, to be there when each fragment passed from generation to generation. I saw your father yesterday; he told me you had taken his sword. He's very worried about you."

"I just grabbed the first weapon I could lay my hands on," Brandorin said. "I wasn't thinking clearly at the time."

"I am sorry, Brandorin. I should have been there, maybe I could have prevented..."

"Don't blame yourself, Caidos." Brandorin wasn't ready to hear what Caidos might have been able to do. He couldn't fault the mage; he reserved that judgment for himself.

"I should bring this sword back to my father. He'll need it when he goes with you."

"No, Brandorin. You're the Protector now. Your father may hold that title publicly, but that's only a civil role. The ruler of Varsa, since the tragic death of the Dravonian family hundreds of years ago, took on the title of Protector because the man who holds that position has always come from your family, the family that holds the Varsian gem fragment.

"The bearer of the blue fragment is the Protector. You saw how the crystal blazed as you killed the raptor. It wouldn't do that for anyone but the true Protector."

"Today was the second time it gave off that blue light."

"When was the first?"

"Right after I took the sword. When I faced ... Piritho for the first time."

Caidos looked at the beast. "I think you need to tell me your long story now."

Brandorin was silent for a time. He began so quietly, Caidos might have missed it had he not been expecting it. "If you talked to my father, you know what happened at the wedding." Brandorin looked to Caidos for confirmation. When the mage nodded, he continued, "I woke in the middle of the night, thinking it had all been a nightmare. But if it hadn't, I knew where Ilona would be."

He stopped, his breathing shallow. The light of the fire glistened off his eyes. He took a long breath and continued, his voice thick with emotions he struggled to control. "I found her ... in the anteroom to the family crypt, waiting to be ..." He stopped again, taking long calming breaths. "I had to find that beast. I had to know why..."

He struggled to maintain his nebulous control. "I wasn't thinking clearly. To be honest, I wasn't even thinking. I had no idea where to look; I just had to do something. I couldn't tell you all the places I went. I was never hungry, but I ate so I could keep going. I couldn't sleep, not until I was so exhausted I just collapsed. But even after a short rest, I would wake and continue the search. It was as if the need to find him gave me all the sustenance I needed."

Brandorin stared at the fire seeing not the dancing flames before him, but the trail he followed while on the hunt for the beast.

"I don't know how long it took. I hadn't found him when I saw the Shadow; otherwise I would have gone to tell my father. But I couldn't go home, not..."

Brandorin stopped and looking at the beast, he walked over to it, crouched down by its side and placed his hand on its back. The voice that continued the story was now compassionate where it had been vengeful, sympathetic where it had been unforgiving. "I wanted to kill it. I don't think I ever wanted anything so bad. But when I came face to face with him, I couldn't do it. He was no longer the inhuman beast that had killed Ilona. I could see it in his eyes. They didn't have the fire of hatred anymore. I looked in those eyes and I knew. I couldn't kill him, so I forgave him."

The anger returned to his voice, "But I have not forgiven Rhamak. Together Piritho and I will find him and kill him."

The logs on the fire crackled in the stillness that followed. Caidos, thinking Brandorin was lost in his memories, broke the silence, "I do know how you knew." he said.

"Knew what?" Brandorin asked, startled by the question.

"How you knew Rhamak had sent the beast. You were holding the sword, and with it the Protector's crystal. The crystal fragments give the bearers special gifts, though they're different for each bearer. Have you noticed any other new abilities or knowledge since carrying that sword?"

"Not particularly, but I haven't been doing much. Davering

mostly, just wandering the back roads and villages. I can't go back home. Not yet. Not until I find Rhamak. But I don't know where to look."

A crease of concentration furrowed his brow. "I guess fighting that creature today was different. I wasn't afraid, but I should've been. Never having seen those creatures before I should've been more wary, unsure of what they could do. When I fought in battle, there was always a degree of fear that kept me sharp, kept my senses tuned, but today it was as if *I* was the weapon, as if I knew I would best it. Was that the crystal?"

"It could be. When we were walking through the woods, back to the field, you stopped me from falling at least three times. Each time when I started to stumble, your back was to me, yet you turned in time to prevent it."

"I didn't even notice that, but you're right. I just knew you were about to fall."

"We'll have time on the road. We can experiment; see what the fragment will do for you."

"I have to say, Caidos, it would make me feel a great deal better if you knew. I always thought you knew everything."

"No one is born knowing how to do more than whimper. I only seem to know so much because I've had more time to learn than most. One thing I'll never know is everything there is to know about Sefiron."

"You also seem to be assuming I'm going with you. I told you, Piritho and I are going to find Rhamak."

"But you also said you have no idea where to look. Well, it's very likely we'll run into him before this is all over. Rhamak sent that beast to kill you and it took Ilona's life instead."

"What do you mean? He could have killed me, three times, but he didn't."

"In light of the appearance of Sefiron's Shadow, I understand recent events more clearly. It was that sword Rhamak's thieves came to steal last month. And unable to get it, the beast was sent to destroy the next Protector."

"I don't think that's true, Caidos." Brandorin stared at

Piritho, shaking his head. "Why kill the *next* Protector? Wouldn't Rhamak have targeted my Father?"

"I would have thought so, but from what Dilardin told me, it seems clear you were the focus of the beast's attack. I'm sure Rhamak was responsible for those unnatural creatures that tried to kill me today. Whatever he is already up to, he wants my crystal fragment, the crown piece. With it he could control the power of a united Paragon, a power far beyond anything he has now.

"So if it's retribution you want, I think keeping him from that power would be the best revenge you can find."

Brandorin felt the familiar pull of responsibility; obligation dragging him in its predestined wake. He fought the urge to thrust the sword at Caidos; to tell him to take it back to his father. He didn't want to go back. He could admit to himself that his wandering for the last three weeks was, at least in part, because he didn't want what waited for him there: the hole where Ilona had been, and Thiro, his father's expectations, the obligations.

Now Caidos was presenting him with a new responsibility, giving him all the reasons he needed to go, but not telling him he had to. If he went with Caidos, he not only wouldn't have to go back, he might find the answer he sought, and be able to take his revenge on Rhamak.

"I understand the importance of this quest. My personal motives have to come second, but it sounds like we have a better chance of finding Rhamak if we stick with you.

"What do you think, Piritho? Shall we join Caidos?" The beast sat up and let out a bark-like growl, which even Caidos took as a voice of ascent.

"I promised Dilardin I'd bring you back when I found you, but in light of the appearance of Sefiron's Shadow, I don't think we can spare the time. We'll send a carefully worded message from the next town. I don't want to mention Sefiron's Shadow directly. Dilardin will understand. We should get an early start in the morning, and I'm drained. I'm going to turn in."

"Where do we go first?"

"N'varia," Caidos said, as he unrolled his blankets near the fire.

"To find?"

"The Searcher," he said, as he climbed under the blankets and pulled them over himself.

"All right, I can take a hint."

As Brandorin climbed into his bedroll, he felt a ripping pain in his side. He hiked up his shirt, uncovering three long scratches on his side. "I didn't think the raptor had touched me. Thought I was too fast. Looks like I could have used some of that salve myself."

"I notice there are no cuts in your shirt," Caidos said without opening his eyes.

Brandorin checked his shirt. There were no tears, nor marks on the shirt, yet the scratches on his side were deep enough that it was impossible for the talons to have left the shirt unmarked.

By the time he turned back to Caidos to ask for an explanation, the old mage had rolled over. Trying to figure out how the raptor had slashed his side, without damaging his shirt kept Brandorin awake for a long time.

## Chapter 7

Caidos slowly became aware of the quiet noises of the morning: the warbling of a wren, soon replaced by the croaking of a crow, the soft snorting of the horses, muffled clinking of pans and the fragrant aroma of bacon cooking over a campfire. Through his closed eyelids he sensed the rays of the morning sun, and bolted upright. The sun, already above the height of the trees on the eastern horizon, told him it must be hours after dawn.

"I thought the smell of breakfast might wake you."

Caidos turned to find Brandorin crouched by the fire, attending the contents of the frying pan.

"You shouldn't have let me sleep. We cannot afford the luxury of lazy mornings. We have many miles to travel and we don't know how long we have to cover them."

"You were drained, you needed the rest. We can leave within minutes, but you can't face those long miles without food."

Caidos took the steaming cup of hot tea Brandorin offered him. He stood, torn between starting their journey and knowing Brandorin was right. His stomach added its own opinion with a hunger-rumbling groan and he sat down to Brandorin's breakfast.

"I am surprised I slept so well," Caidos said, cupping his hands around the mug, relishing both the warmth of the brew and its spicy aroma. "The attack, the Shadow's appearance, finding you so fortuitously. I would have expected our journey and all we must do to be on my mind, keeping me awake."

"*You* may not have had trouble sleeping, but I was awake for a long time after you rolled over, leaving me with a mystery to solve."

"What mystery?" Caidos sipped the steaming liquid and felt its warmth course through him, staving off the slight chill of the morning. Distant thunder rumbled, and he briefly hoped they'd be travelling away from, rather than into a storm, but knew they would have many wet days on their travels.

"Those scratches on my side, and an undamaged shirt,"

Brandorin answered, as he turned, showing the mage the source of his confusion.

"Oh, that. Have you solved it then?"

"Not only haven't I solved it, it's gotten more mysterious," he added, as he raised his shirt and showed Caidos his unmarked side, no trace of the gashes remained. "And that's not all. When I went to get supplies for breakfast, I checked Aquilo, to see how her wounds were doing." He stopped, as if he expected Caidos to finish for him.

"And?" Caidos asked as he chewed on a piece of cheese and broke off some bread.

"And ... and ... they're gone." Brandorin blurted out. "Not just healed, mind you, they're gone! As if they were never there."

"You'll have to give me the name of that plant you used," Caidos mumbled around a mouth full of bread, "and how to find and prepare it." Brandorin didn't answer, but stared incredulously at Caidos. Brandorin had not responded by the time Caidos and finished his mouthful. "Unless it's a family secret."

"That was something else that kept me awake last night," Brandorin said, exasperation making his voice rise. "I don't even know how I knew that plant would help. I kept trying to remember who told me about it, and I finally decided no one had. If you hadn't seen the wounds too, both Aquilo's and mine, I'd think I was losing my mind. I'm almost afraid to ask you how your shoulders are."

"My shoulders are healed as well," Caidos said without looking. He wiped the crumbs from his hands and held one out toward Brandorin, asking, "Can I see your sword?"

"My sword? What does that have to ... The sword. Was it the crystal?"

"The sword please?" Caidos repeated, holding his hand out, flexing his fingers in a beckoning motion. Brandorin pulled the sword from its scabbard, handing it to Caidos, hilt first. Caidos took the sword with both hands; his right firmly on the hilt, his left gingerly supporting the weight by the blade.

He remembered the ease with which Brandorin had wielded

this heavy weapon; no effort wasted, every action flowing with effortless grace. He settled it onto his lap, and ran his fingers over the intricate carvings on the hilt and pommel. Curves and corners formed a complex maze, with the blue crystal at its center.

"You know what this is," he said, pointing at the blue gem set into the hilt. Without waiting for confirmation, he turned the sword over, revealing a second stone, a darker blue than the first, set in a sea of vines and leaves. "But do you know what this is?"

"Isn't it the same? I assumed it just showed from both sides."

"This is the Umari crystal," Caidos said. He glanced up at Brandorin to see if the name meant anything, but the look of confusion told Caidos it did not. "Have you heard of the Umari?"

"The legend about Sea Folk? Mermaids and sea serpents, whole cities under the sea?"

"It's not just a legend. Much of what you have heard is embellishment or outright fabrication, but the stories are based on fact. Umar was the region we call the Eastern Islands, in the sea that now bears their name. The people of that country had a strong love of the sea.

"They had a rudimentary gill system. Not enough to live underwater, but enough to be able to spend hours at a time down there. They farmed the seabed along the shores of the islands. The islands are made of volcanic rock with only a thin layer of soil, not enough to sustain a large farming operation.

"They domesticated many sea creatures: using sea turtles to tow their harvests, manta rays as message carriers. They understood the dolphins, were able to communicate with them on an elementary level. Then, almost four thousand years ago, rather suddenly, they just disappeared.

"Their crystal was lost for most of that time, but the Mages of Artara searched for it over all those millennia. That's the main reason why Artara is located where it is, in the middle of the Eastern Islands. It was essential that fragment be found; to ensure the Rejoining would succeed. They found it just over two hundred years ago.

"Where and how they found it, is a very long story, for another time, but it *was* found. On the Isle of Kenda. They debated for two decades trying to decide what to do with it. Some said the Order should keep it until it came time to rejoin Sefiron, but others, my predecessor included, felt it would be a waste of the gift it provided. Those that felt it should be kept in Artara pointed out that only an Umari would be able to use it.

"They argued for years," Caidos continued, exasperated at the foolishness his brethren had shown. "Eventually they decided they would entrust it to your line, though there are still those who voice their displeasure over that decision."

He stopped for a sip of tea, slowly shaking his head. Then suddenly, as if he had just realized he'd been telling a story, he continued.

"The Protectors would guard it; hopefully learn to use it in time, until it was needed. Each time the crystal was passed from generation to generation within your family, the Mirador would test the new bearer, to see if he could draw on the gifts it held." Caidos stared at Brandorin with a gratified smile. "You are the first to do so, and without knowing it was even a possibility."

The slow cadence with which Caidos had related the Umari story began to build. "When you started treating Aquilo's wounds, I felt a hope rise within me. I remained silent, not wanting anything I might say to affect the outcome. As you dressed my wounds, applying the salve, I could feel the wounds on my shoulder were healing. I knew that our long wait was over. You controlled the gift of the Umari fragment." He stopped, thinking for a moment and then added, almost to himself, "Maybe that's why I was able to sleep so soundly."

Caidos watched Brandorin as he contemplated this second responsibility he must accept, less than twenty-four hours after learning it would be his duty to help rejoin the crystal fragments.

"So, I'm the Protector *and* the Healer. That's convenient," he said sarcastically. "If I can't protect people, at least I can heal them afterward." Caidos did not respond to the flippant remark, knowing Brandorin was trying to deal with the reality he was being asked to accept.

"I can't believe my father never told me. I've known about the other fragment for eight years. I think he told me to let me know he considered me to be a man," Brandorin said. "Why wouldn't he have told me about both?"

"I know he planned to tell you about the Umari crystal when he gave you the sword. He thought telling you about both fragments at once would be too overwhelming."

"I remember being stunned when he told me what being the Protector really meant. I guess finding out about the Healer at the same time *would* have been too much." Brandorin stopped, realizing what he had said earlier. "Oh, Caidos, I'm sorry about that 'if I can't protect them, I'll heal them' comment."

Caidos shook his head and waved his hand in dismissal, "Already forgotten."

Neither of them said anything for a few minutes, and then Brandorin asked with a wry grin. "I'm not going to grow gills, am I?"

"No, I don't think you'll have to worry about that," Caidos said, chuckling. "That was a physical trait of the Umari."

"This explains something the Shadow's voices said, 'The Protector and the Healer are one.' It didn't make any sense at the time, but it sure does now."

"The Shadow knew you'd become the Healer?" It was Caidos' turn to look confused. "But you hadn't shown that you could heal until last night. Or did you? Was there anything you might have done before the Shadow appeared?"

"I can't think of anything. I was alone most of the time, no one to heal."

"What else did the Shadow say?"

Brandorin stared into the distance, concentrating, trying to remember the Shadow's words. "It mentioned all the titles. That the Watcher had to bring everyone together. What I said just now about Protector and Healer. Then it said something about a scroll." He shook his head. "Look for the scroll ... find the scroll ... I'm sorry, Caidos. I should have paid closer attention."

"Don't worry, Brandorin. I've read Didonno's scrolls many times. It would be nice to have them here to consult, but I feel confident I remember everything they have to say about Sefiron."

"My having the Umari crystal explains why all our wounds disappeared, but it still doesn't solve the mystery of my undamaged shirt."

"Brandorin, when were you first aware of the wounds on your side?"

"Last night when I lay down; I stretched that side."

"Not earlier when you were disposing of the remains of each raptor, or when you were collecting wood for the fire?"

"No, I didn't," Brandorin said, giving the idea some thought, he moved his arms, mimicking his actions of the night before. "But I should have. Reaching over, I would have felt it then. I can understand not feeling the wounds when it happened. I've seen men take worse wounds in battle, and not notice them until after the fight was over. You're concentrating so hard on your opponent's moves, on how you're going to defeat him. You don't notice minor wounds; sometimes, not even serious ones. But none of this explains why my shirt wasn't damaged. The talons had to have gone through the cloth to gouge my side."

"Your shirt wasn't damaged, Brandorin, because the raptor's talons never touched you." Caidos paused, giving Brandorin a moment to think, then continued. "Your wounds were on your sides. Aquilo's were on her sides."

"Are you saying my wounds came from Aquilo?"

"It's how the healing process works," Caidos said, nodding his head vigorously, his voice almost squeaking with excitement. "The Healer takes the pain into himself, and then completes the healing. Your shirt wasn't damaged because your wounds weren't inflicted from outside. They came from within, so to speak."

Brandorin looked over at the horse then put his hand to his side. "How did I do all of that without even knowing I could? Did that salve do anything? Why didn't I feel a pain in my shoulders if I cured your wounds?"

"I can't give you complete answers, remember it's been

thousands of years since anyone has been able to control the Umari crystal, but I can tell you what I think. Either my wounds transferred to you after you were asleep or the salve, and the fact that you applied it, did all the work. Aquilo's wounds may have taken longer because she is a horse. I am very encouraged by the fact you accomplished all of this without even knowing it was a possibility. It may indicate the strength of your gifts as the Healer."

"So, do you think I did something like this before the Shadow appeared, and didn't realize I was doing it then either."

"Undoubtedly, otherwise the voices would not have called you the Healer. Think about it, there must have been something." Caidos got up and started packing up his bedroll. Brandorin, taking his lead, began to clear up the rest of the campsite.

"I was in a daze during most of that time, Caidos. I'm sorry. The only thing I can think of is how a short rest would revive me, so I could continue searching."

"It's all right, Brandorin. *What* you did is not as important as the fact that you *did* it. We'll just have to learn how it works as you use these gifts. It should be quite fascinating to see."

"Why was I able to use the crystal when no one else could?" Brandorin asked.

"That's the big question," Caidos said, dropping the blankets he'd just rolled, throwing his arms open wide, to demonstrate the magnitude of the mystery. An edge of the blanket fell precariously close to the fire, but Caidos didn't notice; Brandorin pushed it aside with the toe of his boot, as Caidos started pacing around the campfire, too excited to sit still. "It could be the appearance of Sefiron's Shadow. The fragments draw it, and you hold two."

He seemed to be talking more to himself than to Brandorin, trying to reconcile the legends he had been told, and the reality of recent events. Brandorin continued to pack, dodging around Caidos as he continued his animated pacing. "I don't believe it was a coincidence you were on the road yesterday. You were drawn to the fragment I carry."

He reached for his amulet, and looking at it he continued in a distant voice. "The times, the Shadow, the nearness of two other fragments, any or all of that could have awakened the latent gifts of the Umari stone. Or it could be you, Brandorin. If I had to pick, that would be my choice. It could be a reflection of your strengths as both the Protector and the Healer, at a time when we will need them the most."

He picked up the tumbled blanket, and rerolled it, now relating the legends to the man who had inherited them. "Mandricon decided to give the Healer's stone to the Protector because the gift of your fragment enhances innate abilities already present in the holder. Your courage yesterday, in fighting the raptors, was enhanced by the gift of the crystal. If you didn't already possess the courage it took to face such a dreadful adversary, the stone would have done nothing to help you."

When Caidos saw Brandorin still had many questions about the stones and their gifts, he suggested, "There's a great deal more I could say about Sefiron, but we must get started. We've tarried too long as it is. We can continue to talk on the road."

He surveyed the area for the third member of their party, "Where is Piritho? Won't he be traveling with us?"

"Oh, he's going with us all right. He wouldn't miss this for the world. He's off hunting his own breakfast, but he'll be back before we leave."

They smothered the fire and finished breaking camp. While Brandorin saddled the horses, Caidos went to the stream to clean the pans and fill their water skins.

By the time he returned, Brandorin had the horses packed and Piritho was back, looking less like the ferocious beast Caidos had first perceived him to be, and more like an extremely large lap dog, ready to play or fetch a stick. Caidos stopped in front of him, and looking into his eyes, saw a gentleness in stark contrast to the large mouth and threatening fangs. He shivered, thinking how dreadful an attack by this creature could be, and he struggled to understand the change in the beast's demeanor.

\* \* \*

They headed south. Piritho loped along beside them for a time, running ahead whenever the road led them within a hundred feet of the woods. His forays into a stand of trees or around a thicket would occasionally scare out a bevy of quail or a covey of grouse. After an extended absence into the woods, he came out barking and whining in a way that made even Caidos feel he was talking to them.

"He says there're pheasant just into the woods," Brandorin interpreted. "This would be a good place to rest the horses." As he dismounted, he removed his sword from its sheath. He tossed Caidos the reins before running into the woods behind Piritho. "There's water just over there," he called back over his shoulder, pointing to the left, as he disappeared under the cover of the trees.

"Don't take a sword to kill a mouse," Caidos said to the empty space where Brandorin had been, "but it's probably the sport you're after anyway." He walked the horses to the small stream and hobbled them so they could obtain water and grass, then he found a quiet spot against a large boulder where he could rest in the sun.

The sun beamed though a break in the heavy storm clouds that seemed the only constant on their journey. The usual crisp air of autumn smelled dank and fetid from the excess rain. The scant sunlight warmed his aching, horse-ridden muscles and reflected off the leaves the light breeze had coaxed from their berths as they floated earthward to join hundreds of others that covered the ground with a patchwork quilt. The trees applauded the scene as their dying leaf coats chaffed in the soughing wind.

Caidos was jarred from a gentle slumber as a rustling of the underbrush signaled the hunters' return. He turned in time to see Piritho come gamboling out of the woods, his mouth open and tongue lolling out in a fashion that betokened success. Brandorin followed, carrying two large pheasants by the neck. On seeing Caidos watching he brandished them in the air, shouting, "We'll have a fine dinner tonight."

"I would think one would have been enough."

"One is for you and me, the other is for Piritho. He found them; he should get one for himself."

"It doesn't look like you used your sword after all. I pictured you coming back with a headless bird that would have dripped blood all along our trail. How did you catch them?" Caidos asked as Brandorin tied the fowl to his saddle.

"I'd like to say I didn't use the sword at all, but it played its part. I caught those birds, with my bare hands, as Piritho flushed them from the thicket. Not both at once, mind you, but I caught each one as it took flight out of the undergrowth." Piritho barked once, as if to confirm the unbelievable story.

"It had to have been the sword. My reflexes are good, but not that good. This has to be how a hawk feels catching her prey. I could learn to like this."

They climbed back onto their horses and resumed their journey. Caidos said, "We'll test your theory tonight, while those birds roast."

"Test it how?"

"I'm sure I can come up with something," Caidos said, a mischievous glint lighting his pale blue eyes. "Something ... challenging." A peal of thunder added an ominous note to his insinuation, and they pulled up their hoods as the dark clouds released a heavy downpour.

\*   \*   \*

They made camp for the night in the shelter of a rocky outcropping, the air spiked with the resinous smell of the surrounding pines. Brandorin dressed the pheasants and spitted the pieces on a steel rod he carried for such purposes. Caidos cast an incantation on the rod, so that it would turn slowly on its own, as he tested Brandorin's gifts with the Protector's crystal.

"What did you have in mind?" Brandorin asked.

"Since you were so impressed with the crystal's apparent effect on your reflexes, why not start with that. I'll hurl small rocks in your direction; you see how well you can stop them with your sword."

"That's not so difficult. I could do that before I had this sword. We used to play like that when I was small. One kid threw the stones; the others had to bash them back with sticks."

"I would imagine you did that during the day. There's not much light tonight and I won't be throwing them." Caidos flicked his first two fingers, and a small rock flew from Brandorin's left, passing close to his face.

Brandorin leaned back as the rock flew by, narrowly missing his nose, "A bit more challenging. Can we use something other than rocks though? I don't want to dull the blade."

Caidos surveyed the area, and a pinecone suddenly flew up from the ground under the nearby tree and shot toward Brandorin, who cut it in two with his sword as it passed. "Is that better?"

"Much better. For my head too, if I miss."

Caidos started a barrage of pinecones flying at Brandorin. They came from every direction, at a variety of speeds. Some caught the light of the nearby campfire, while others flew from out of the shadows, giving little warning before they sailed within range of the sword's arc.

Yet Brandorin's effortless swing sliced each pinecone with minimal movement. When the projectiles shot at him from behind, he didn't even turn, catching them in a single fluid motion as the sword swung around and back. After over thirty cones had been split in two, Brandorin shouted, "Faster."

The cones shot up from the ground, and came at him more frequently. Caidos started sending them from two directions at once, but Brandorin's sword raced to meet them. The glade was filled with a soft whistling and snicking as the blade blurred through the air, slicing each projectile. When a pinecone hit Brandorin in the back of the head, as he was slicing two others in front of him, Brandorin lowered his sword saying, "That's not good."

"That was *very* good, Brandorin," Caidos said. I've never seen anyone move so fast. You missed one, out of what," he scanned the pile of pinecone halves at Brandorin's feet, "sixty or seventy at least. The crystal's not going to make you infallible. Plus there's no danger. You feel no threat from these pinecones. The more you need it, the more it will help you. Let's try something else. Use my sword."

Brandorin placed his sword in the sheath hanging from his belt and picked up Caidos' sword. The pinecones sailed at him again, at first one at a time, then in increasing number and speed. Two out of twenty cones got past him.

"Now put your sword down, somewhere away from you," Caidos said. Brandorin removed his sword belt and took it over to the fire, laying it down next to Piritho. Without the crystal, Brandorin hit six out of the next ten Caidos sailed at him.

"That's to be expected," Caidos said. "Having the fragment nearby helps, but not as much as direct contact. How did it feel? Did you hit more with your sword because you could see them better, or hear them coming?"

"I'm not sure I can explain it. In some ways it felt like I had more time to react, even though they were moving pretty fast. When you sent them from behind me, I didn't hear them or see them; it was more a feeling they were there.

"I would have thought using the crystal's gift would have been more – intentional, instead it's almost like a reflex. It's a little unsettling."

"The crystal is not doing these things without you, Brandorin, or controlling your muscles without your volition. It is simply enhancing your own abilities."

They returned to the fire, checking that the pheasants were finished cooking, and they sat down to eat. Brandorin tossed a few pieces to Piritho, who quickly devoured them, prompting Brandorin to ask, "Did you even have time to enjoy that?" A bark and a whining growl were Piritho's response.

"No, you can't have ours too."

"Are you joking when you talk to him in that way, or do you really understand him?"

"I understand him. At least I think I do." He turned to Piritho and asked, "Is that what you said? That you wanted some of ours, too?" A decisive bark and a quick movement of his head indicated Piritho's confirmation. "You must have understood that," he said to Caidos.

"I would accept that as a 'yes'. Did you understand him before you carried the sword?"

Brandorin looked at Piritho for a long time before answering. "I've only carried the sword since the wedding."

Caidos winced. "I'm sorry, Brandorin. I forgot. It just seems as if you and Piritho have been together for years. But as for the rest, it must be the crystal. Have you found you understand other animals as well? That's how it works with the Larians."

"No, just Piritho."

"Interesting. It may be because you had just taken the sword. Your first act as the Protector was to track him down. It may also be the reason he understands you so well."

"Who's Didonno?" Brandorin asked after a long silence. "You mentioned him this morning and yesterday."

"He was the first Mirador. He wrote twenty-one scrolls detailing the Sefiramon's instructions to the first bearers. The scrolls are passed from Mirador to Mirador, along with this amulet, which holds the crown piece, and the responsibility of watching the bearers."

"What's in the scrolls? What kinds of instructions?"

"That's a mountain of knowledge, Brandorin, and I know myself well enough to admit that once I got started telling that story, I could talk for hours. Let's save that for another time. I'm ready to turn in."

## Chapter 8

Rhamak's fortress sat on the rim of the Chiron Ridge, overlooking the Great Central Desert. Built on a steep, weathered butte, its walls rose seamlessly from the craggy slopes to twin towers one hundred fifty feet above the surface of the plateau. Rhamak called his fortress Kalarak, behemoth in the ancient tongue, for he had designed it to resemble the head of a monster rising up over the escarpment. The towers formed threatening horns, while the central tunnel opening, which allowed access to the fortress, mimicked the gaping mouth of the beast.

The fortress had been built with the sweat, blood, and energies of thousands of forced laborers, toiling in the heat of the region. The task of bringing the endless tons of rock up the steep slopes had almost proven insurmountable, but Rhamak had not chosen the location lightly. The height of the towers, added to the one hundred-fifty feet of the escarpment, provided an unobstructed view for miles to the east.

Two men stood at the top of the northern parapet. Rhamak waited, leaning against the battlement, his eyes and his thoughts focused on the western horizon. Chaubrel watched him from the shadows.

They had climbed the turret stairs, coming out onto the parapet when the sun was directly overhead. As the sun worked its way toward the western horizon, Chaubrel had shifted his position, moving with the elusive shade. The light of the setting sun now cast Rhamak into silhouette.

The heat of the day had almost proven too much for Chaubrel, who normally relished any opportunity to escape the chill stone interior of the fortress. His heavy robes and the lack of food or water since breakfast had threatened to put him to sleep, or worse. Although his mind had drifted often throughout the day, Chaubrel now watched Rhamak's every move. A single finger tapping on the stone surface of the embrasure, his straight back tilted forward, the tempo of his breathing, even his silence.

Chaubrel had learned to recognize the subtle signs of Rhamak's moods, adjusting his behaviour accordingly. As chamberlain, Chaubrel was the only servant who spoke directly to Rhamak. But not because Rhamak demanded it.

Chaubrel had instituted that rule in order to shield the other servants from Rhamak's punishment for their missteps. He was haunted by his failures. Many years ago, one had occurred on this very parapet. Rhamak had ordered wine and a servant had ascended the stairs to deliver it. He had come up the stairs, but he had not gone down that way. It had been the wrong wine.

Chaubrel shielded them because he knew he would not suffer the same fate, but he had no desire to expose himself to Rhamak's castigation if he could avoid it. He moved out of the shadows, to be closer to Rhamak, edging toward the battlement. Heights bothered Chaubrel. He turned, avoiding the view to the plateau below, and checked the south tower. The extra guard was in place, watching, as they were, for any sign of Rhamak's messengers.

Rhamak's first words in over an hour startled Chaubrel.

"I want to be here when they bring that meddling Mage to me. He will see me, will finally see Kalarak the way he should, as my prisoner." Rhamak had stepped away from the battlement, his arms outstretched to encompass the vastness of his fortress. "He has no clue of its existence."

Rhamak squinted toward the horizon. "Is that them? No, just an eagle. Useless birds! They call them predators!"

"They haven't seen your Talondrin, sire," Chaubrel said as he stepped away from the edge.

"But by now, Caidos has. He is getting a very close look at them." Rhamak's laughter made Chaubrel nervous, but then again, so did his silence.

Rhamak paced the thirty feet across the parapet, his voice now reflecting the frustration his actions demonstrated. "That old fool has gotten fat in his dotage, making them fly slower. I should have just told them to kill him. They could bring me the amulet, but I want to see his face when he knows I have it.

"Perhaps they had trouble locating Caidos, sire."

"He was returning to Kartir. I expected him to leave right away. He has two excellent reasons for doing so."

"Two are much better than one."

Rhamak began to speak, then stopped, scrutinizing Chaubrel. A sardonic grin cracked across his face. "You've gotten very good at this, Chaubrel. Did you ever suspect we would come to this?"

"No, sire."

"As I said, very good. It took a long time didn't it? Before you knew just what to say, or what to do."

Chaubrel could feel Rhamak's eyes on him. He felt an urge to return that look. No, not an urge, a compulsion; to be drawn to, yet repelled by the same magnetic gaze. Those tawny, cat-like eyes, so unnatural, yet so compelling. But it wouldn't do to defy Rhamak. Chaubrel also knew what not to do.

Rhamak broke the silence and his stare at the same time. "Since you *asked* so carefully ... Caidos will have heard of the Shadow's appearance, and of the events at the recent wedding. He must stick his nose into everyone's affairs, so he would not have stayed in Kartir for long. When he left, the Talondrin were waiting."

"Thank you, sire."

"I'll want to use them again. I'll create an army of Talondrin. My enforcers. These first four will be the leaders, the generals of an army of predators, whose only desire is to carry out my will."

Rhamak paraded across the parapet, sweeping his arms across the plateau to demonstrate the vastness of the force he would create. "They'll fear nothing. Other than me, of course.

"Where are they?" The tone of Rhamak's voice had changed from exhilaration to anger between strides. "They couldn't have failed. It was impossible for Caidos to defeat them, impossible even to escape them."

Rhamak stopped; the look of discovery on his face. "That's it, Chaubrel. They lost him somehow and they're trying to find him again, afraid to return without the prize. They are tenacious; they won't leave the trail, not until they've acquired their target. I'll give them another day."

He turned and entered the turret, descending the long staircase to his private chamber. Chaubrel followed close behind him, sighing with relief at the coolness within the stone walls and at the ease with which Rhamak accepted this delay. He descended the steps with deliberate care, his hunger making him light-headed. Rhamak's footsteps echoed in the winding staircase, his voice sepulchral as it resounded within the circular stone walls.

"I must be told as soon as they are spotted."

"I have already sent word to the command post to put out an extra man on all shifts until they return. Their sole duty will be to watch for the Talondrin," he answered.

They emerged into Rhamak's private chamber at the foot of the turret.

"Do you wish to be awakened if they come back during the night?" He was startled by the anger in Rhamak's answering words.

"Did I not just say that?"

"Yes, you did, my Lord," he responded, stepping back reflexively. "The second they are spotted."

"Dinner," Rhamak said, leaving the room. "It will be a distraction while I wait for Caidos' arrival," he said.

They walked through the sporadically lit corridors, the flickering of each wall-mounted torch alternately lighting their faces and leaving them in shadow. The rhythmic striking of Rhamak's boots on the hard stone floors echoed through the room-wide hallways, blending with the susurrus of his long robe stroking the pathway behind him. Chaubrel walked three paces behind Rhamak, making no sound with his soft-soled shoes.

As Chaubrel scurried to keep pace with Rhamak's long legs, he marveled at Rhamak's energy and appearance. How could a man who performed no labors more intensive than lifting a full goblet of wine, be so slender and appear so muscular? Chaubrel never had an excess of food growing up, but as Rhamak's chamberlain he had his choice of whatever food Rhamak did not select. The rich food and minimal exercise had made him pudgy.

Chaubrel found comfort in the contrasts between himself and Rhamak. The chamberlain's dark tea-colored eyes, olive skin, and chestnut hair seemed almost the opposite of the mage's whiskey eyes, fair complexion, and sandy hair. Rhamak wore only simple, fitted robes, of single, dark colors; Chaubrel wore bright, multi-colored robes of damask, with velvet and gold braid trim.

Rhamak's only adornment was a simple gold headband with a solitary stone of pure white, which rested on his brow. Chaubrel had a chest filled with treasures no longer needed by their former owners.

Chaubrel was allowed to choose what he wanted; what he did not select was buried with its owner. Each morning he would sift through the many necklaces, rings, bracelets, and other baubles, deciding what would best match the robes he had selected for the day. He had grown up in a society that valued the simple life and had had few luxuries. His role as Rhamak's chamberlain provided him with excesses he had never experienced and he found them hard to resist. As long as his destiny was interwoven with Rhamak's he might as well enjoy the few benefits, though they could never replace what he had lost.

As they approached the immense dining hall, Chaubrel could smell the mélange of aromas, the succulent roasts and spiced stews, the freshly baked breads, roasted potatoes and sautéed mushrooms, already laid out for Rhamak's review. He licked his lips in anticipation of the feast ahead, and his stomach grumbled.

Rhamak dined alone; Chaubrel selected what he wanted from the food remaining, always enough for a banquet. The kitchens prepared everything Rhamak liked, not knowing what his tastes would be on any particular day.

Rhamak paced along the length of the thirty-foot ebony dining table, reviewing the evening's fare. Chaubrel went to stand with the steward by the sideboard, when the sound of metal hitting stone drew his attention back to the table. A dish and its contents now lay strewn across the stone floor.

"They serve me fowl when I'm waiting for my Talondrin to return." Rhamak's voice was low and controlled, yet carried a venom that oozed from his lips just as the grease from the pheasant now spread out from under the bird on the floor. "Are they mocking me, Chaubrel?"

The chamberlain was already advancing. He was as wary of his words and actions as he was of the slippery grease on the floor, knowing a misstep in either case would be disastrous. "It is my fault, my Lord. I should have told them to hold the fowl courses."

"Don't take the blame for others, Chaubrel; it's beneath your station. Just have it removed. I'll have the venison tonight," he said as he moved to the only chair at the table.

Chaubrel directed the servants, who moved silently to clear away the spilled pheasant, while the steward served the steaks Rhamak had selected. He filled Rhamak's goblet with wine and placed bread, cheeses and fruits close at hand.

Rhamak sat, with the food before him, holding the wine goblet, and stared out at the western sky as the red sunset deepened to a dull purple glow. He picked at the meal. Chaubrel stood to the right and slightly behind Rhamak's high backed chair, ready to respond to even the slightest indication of his desires.

Tentatively, he asked, "Is the food not to your liking, sire? I can have the kitchens bring out anything you would like." He knew Rhamak would expect no less, but had often found the sound of his voice helped to soothe Rhamak's errant moods. There was no response, however, so Chaubrel waited; knowing that to probe further would be foolhardy.

It had taken years for Chaubrel to learn the limits of his nebulous freedom with Rhamak, each punishment overly sufficient to ensure the singularity of the action. Afraid the grumbling from his empty stomach would draw a reaction from Rhamak, Chaubrel retreated to the sideboard to await the end of the meal.

A distant and muffled sound made him think he was not the only one in the room that had missed a meal. He froze, waiting to see if Rhamak had heard it too. Rhamak made no sign he was aware of anything in the room; instead his eyes were focused on the night outside the dining hall's twelve-foot windows.

A recurrence of the distant sound came from the open window, much closer and clearer now, and this time Chaubrel recognized a raven's caw. The bird flew in through the west window, its five-foot wingspan dwarfed by the vastness of the room. It circled once, repeating its call, then settled on a perch at the far side of the room.

Rhamak had risen at the entrance of the bird, dropping his goblet and its contents on the floor, the ringing of the metal joining the call of the bird in the emptiness of the twenty-foot vaulted ceiling. His long-legged strides spanned the distance, as a servant retrieved the forgotten cup, removed the spilled wine and placed a new goblet on the table.

"You have news for me, Juar." He spoke to the bird, gently, expectantly, and reached up to stroke its glossy black feathers. The air around the perch rippled, distorting the image of the raven. When the air stilled, a man stood in front of the perch, and the bird was gone. Juar, returned to his natural state, crumbled to the floor, groveling before his master. Rhamak's expression changed from anticipation to anger.

"There is no need to be afraid of me, Juar," he said, his voice as smooth as melted chocolate, seemingly warm and comforting as it poured over the frightened man. Rhamak reached down and brought Juar to his feet, lifting him until their faces were inches apart, Juar's feet dangling six inches off the floor. Chaubrel shivered as he saw Rhamak lock his eyes on the helpless man in his grip. Though he had not dared to look directly into Rhamak's eyes for years, he could still picture the copper flecks within their tawny depths; could almost feel his muscles liquefying under that penetrating gaze.

Juar could not turn away once pinioned by Rhamak's gaze. Sweat beaded on his brow. Though he had no control of his limbs, they shuddered with tremors of fear. Chaubrel stood behind Rhamak, ready to respond, but not wanting to watch.

"You should not be afraid of me, Juar," Rhamak repeated as he released his hold on the man's arms and stepped back. Juar's body remained floating in the air in front of Rhamak, his eyes hypnotically holding the man in place. "It's not as if I am a venomous snake or spider. I won't bite you. Would you even be afraid of such things?" he asked.

There was no verbal response from Juar, but Rhamak continued as if he had heard one, his voice soothing, without menace, almost sympathetic. "No, of course not. You'd just catch them, and destroy them, thus ending the threat."

A ripple of fear ran through the man's entire form as Rhamak spoke the word *destroy*, and it intensified as Rhamak's voice slithered on. "What *are* you afraid of, Juar? We all have something we fear, something that forms icicles in our veins and haunts our nightmares. What is your deepest ... ah, fire!" he said, though Juar had yet to utter a word.

"But I don't have to use fire against you, do I? You *want* to tell me your news, let me see what you saw." Rhamak's words had slowed, and the pitch of his voice was barely more than a whisper.

Only Chaubrel was close enough to hear. Close enough to hear the whimpers and moans growing deep in Juar's throat. Chaubrel knew from first-hand experience that Juar's gaze no longer saw Rhamak's face in front of him, but saw a personal hell Rhamak had created for him.

"Wouldn't you rather be somewhere else?" Rhamak continued. "Perhaps back on the road near Kartir, watching for Caidos. Yes, that's it, show me what you saw." Rhamak paused, as he took in the scene Juar's memories revealed to him.

"Oh, that was beautiful! He never saw them coming. Look at the symmetry of their attacks, almost poetic in form and grace." Rhamak reveled in Juar's memory as it replayed the attack for his viewing. His voice modulated in pitch as the excitement of seeing Caidos' frustration took all menace from his words.

"Yes, they are my greatest endeavor. His bolts of fire are useless." His voice spiced with a sardonic laughter, "Look at his face! Oh, it's priceless, to be able to witness Caidos' first taste of failure.

"What? What stopped it? How clever of you, Caidos, but air

shields won't work for long. They won't be fooled. I taught them to reason," he said triumphantly, pride in his creations reflected in his voice.

"Go ahead, run. It will do you no good. You will tire, but they will not. They'll drain the very energy from your body and use it to defeat you.

"Ah, wonderful, he has you! You must be on the way to me now. No!" his voice rose in a shout of disbelief. "But you must have been hurt in the fall. Your cleverness won't get you out of this, Caidos.

"Well, follow him you fools!" Rhamak, his gaze still locked with Juar's, watched for a time without further comment.

Chaubrel, knowing what the silence meant, watched as Rhamak's fists clenched in frustration. He knew Rhamak would like to pace, but could not release his gaze from Juar, because he would lose the image of the memory playing out in his mind.

"Find him. Don't lose him, don't give him time to regain his strength." Rhamak viewed Juar's memories in silence for a time, his body weaving back and forth as Juar, the raven, flew after the raptors.

"They have you now." His voice rose to a cheer. "You know you are beaten, you have nothing left." He was silent for a moment, then a single word, spoken in an angry whisper. "No. They just sat there, waiting?

"Only one," he said dejectedly. "But he's the best. Look at his fierceness. You're drained, Caidos, you can't have anything left," he said, but Chaubrel could tell by the tone of his voice, he was not convinced.

Rhamak had finally remembered that Juar's return so obviously bespoke the failure of his raptors. Even Chaubrel was surprised Caidos had somehow managed to defeat four of Rhamak's supposedly unbeatable predators.

"Move in. Take him. How could he beat you? He couldn't." Rhamak's voice dropped to a shocked whisper for the final word, "You!" Chaubrel understood Rhamak did not refer to Caidos or the remaining raptor, and he stepped back, knowing what was to come.

"What are you ...? Why would .... Where did ...?" Rhamak's anger and his voice had soared to the point he could no longer complete a thought, but the target he longed for was not there. Juar was, however.

The heat of his anger seemed to subside, but it was not gone. It was now focused and controlled. Juar's moans increased. His mouth worked as if he was trying to speak but could not. He tried to lift his hands to cover his eyes, not wanting to see the image before him, but Rhamak had him locked in position. He hung there, twisting and writhing against invisible bonds, struggling to escape the tortuous images that were all too real.

Chaubrel smelled the burning flesh before he saw the smoke rising from Juar. He stared, frozen in shock at a man, burning to death in front of his eyes without a single flame in sight. Not in his sight. He knew Juar saw nothing else.

Chaubrel watched as the flesh of Juar's arms and legs started to shrivel up and blacken. Watched his mouth, wide open in a silent scream of pain so intense it stopped the sound deep in his throat. He wanted to run from the sight, but was unable to move, frozen not by Rhamak but by the terror of what he saw, combined with a morbid curiosity preventing him from turning away.

For what seemed an eternity Juar hung before them, slowly being consumed by an invisible conflagration. There was an unnatural silence in the room, as if the sounds themselves had escaped the horrific scene. Juar unable to scream was held in Rhamak's spell; no crackling or hissing as the invisible flames painstakingly consumed their fuel. The room too, was silent; all of the servants had fled soon after Rhamak began his interrogation. The lack of sound made the vision all the more intense.

The absolute silence was broken. Screams gushed from Juar's mouth as his body disintegrated into ash. The cries rang through the vast emptiness of the room, growing in intensity, rather than fading as they echoed throughout the chamber. The screams did not fade away, but came to a strangled stop as Rhamak turned from the residue that was all that was left of Juar.

He walked slowly, each step in synch with each purposeful breath. He passed Chaubrel and without breaking his stride, struck out with his left arm, hitting him in the face with enough force to knock him to the ground, unconscious.

## Chapter 9

M'drani gazed out over the Rensiri River, toward Varsa on the northwestern bank. The docks of B'zuri teamed with the activity of river-born commerce, but she was barely aware of the shouts of stevedores, the thuds of crates being dumped on the piers, or the creaking of ships straining against their dock-bound ropes. She focused her attention on the approaching ferry, as it bobbed its way across the surging river. Too distant to visually recognize the individuals on board, she sensed the presence of the person she had come to meet.

The many recent thunderstorms had raised the level of the river to near flood stage. Its normally gentle flow now teamed with the flotsam of broken branches, loose timber and an occasional dead animal. Strong cross winds buffeted the heavy transport boat, and the deckhands scurried to keep her on course. A water-heavy log thudded into the prow of the ferry, turning the nose down-river; the sound of the impact taking a few seconds to reach M'drani's ears. By that time the crew had already started to steer the craft back on course.

She was distracted by the cry of seagulls fighting over scraps of food, and she smiled at their playful banter. A boat, pulling into the slip in front of her, blocked M'drani's view of the inbound vessel. By the time she had walked to the ferry's usual berth at the end of the pier, she could distinguish the two men standing on the deck at the prow.

She shielded her eyes from the brightness of the late afternoon sun and the force of a brief gust of wind, and recognized the older man as Caidos, but the younger, taller man was a stranger. At first she thought they had three horses: a large, chestnut war-horse, Caidos' courser, and a smaller, dark horse. As they drew closer, she realized the smaller horse was in fact a large dog or wolf, the largest she had ever seen.

When the ferry pulled up to the pier, M'drani waved to Caidos, and was able to see the other man clearly for the first time.

She brought her arm down and touched the amethyst stone in the torque around her neck, as a strong blend of feelings rushed through her.

Caidos' mind was very open and receptive to her gift, and she sensed an uncharacteristic concern. She could not concentrate on Caidos, however, because the feelings coming from the stranger were overpowering her.

She sorted through the jumble of emotions, as if they were the separate colors in a great work of art, now recognizing individual hues within the composition. She sensed the grays and browns of grief and anger, the reds and yellows of excitement and anticipation, and the blues and greens of compassion, loyalty and integrity. She had never sensed anyone so immediately and so intensely before, and the stranger's feelings now mingled with her own, as she felt her heart quicken. She withdrew her hand from the crystal at her neck, but her awareness did not lessen.

His dark auburn hair framed a strong, handsome face, dominated by intense blue eyes that sparked a warm sense of trust. As he met her gaze, a slight, sweet smile broke across his face, and she sensed the grief and anger recede. Despite the cold wind, she felt warmth in her cheeks, and knew she was blushing, but hoped he would think her face reddened by the wind.

\* \* \*

Caidos had told Brandorin the woman on the pier was M'drani, of the family E'varania, current N'varian fragment holder, in an unbroken line since the Sefiramon had originally bestowed the crystals upon the leaders of Zadania. Brandorin watched her as the ferry approached the pier. Putting aside the formality of M'drani's role, he saw a small woman, her long feathery hair fanned out behind her by the blustering wind as the sun highlighted its sand-colored strands with threads of gold.

As the ferry docked, Brandorin caught her gaze, and was startled by vibrant, violet eyes. He marveled at the delicate beauty that robed a woman who conveyed both a compassionate nature and a quiet strength. He smiled as a feeling of recognition swept through him, though he knew he had never seen her before.

His right hand was on the sword at his side, and he wondered if the crystal in its hilt was heightening his senses. Even at this distance he was sure he could smell the fragrance of her perfume and feel the softness of her flawless skin. He was reminded of the day Ilona arrived in Kartir, and a feeling of guilt welled within him, though he wasn't sure why it should.

"Brandorin, are you coming with us?" Caidos' voice cut into his thoughts, and he looked to find the mage already on the dock. By the time he joined them; M'drani had walked up to Caidos and embraced him in greeting. Caidos introduced them. Brandorin, suddenly sure she could read his thoughts, stammered a greeting as he shook her hand.

"Brandorin?" M'drani said. "Of Kartir?"

Brandorin noticed her furtive glances at Piritho. As she looked back to him, a small crease appeared between her brows and he could see a question hovering on her lips. He guessed she had heard of the events at the wedding, and he prepared himself for her question.

"I sensed you would be here today, Caidos," she said, though she still looked at Brandorin, her head tilted up, to compensate for the disparity in their heights. She looked at Piritho, her eyes only inches above his.

When she looked back to Brandorin, he blurted out, "This is Piritho. He's with me."

Although it was apparent from M'drani's reaction that she expected a further explanation, she didn't ask for one, but instead said, "Are you all right, Caidos? Has something happened? You seem ..." she struggled for the right word, "burdened."

"I'm fine. We'll talk, but not here.

We can talk when we get to my home." She looked at Piritho again, then after a hesitation, "Will he be coming with us?"

"He won't hurt anyone," Brandorin said, "but if you think people will be afraid, he could stay here at the docks."

"I don't think that's necessary," Caidos said. "He's very

gentle, despite his appearance. He can walk between the horses. That will block him from most people's view."

As they rode through the streets of B'zuri, Brandorin noticed the stark differences between this city and his own. The buildings and homes of Kartir were packed tightly together, in some cases two buildings sharing one common wall. In B'zuri the houses and other buildings were separated by lawns or gardens dotted with trees. Brandorin couldn't remember a single tree anywhere within the city walls of Kartir, other than those at the Protector's Residence.

The buildings in B'zuri had porches, balconies, and open pavilions on the roofs. Kartirian streets were narrow, opening onto an occasional square with buildings crowding around on every side. B'zurian streets were wide, and every few blocks there was a park, bordered by arcades or colonnades.

Scattered across the lawns was evidence of a recent storm, undoubtedly the same one that had soaked the three of them the night before. Broken branches and crushed flowers added to the piles of raked leaves, some already being burned.

When they passed through the markets, Brandorin missed the familiar calls of street vendors hawking their wares; instead he heard the soft lilting voices of a bevy of merchants and bargaining shoppers, waging the age-old battle of striking a balance between seller and buyer.

M'drani's home was large and set on a quiet side street, adjacent to a park. The upper story had a covered balcony that mirrored the one on ground level. A small woman sat in a cushioned chair on the open porch that ran across the front and down the park side of the house.

The woman stood with her arms open wide; a bird in flight, as she fluttered down to Caidos.

"M'dori, how good it is to see you again," Caidos said as he handed his reins to M'drani, and walked to greet her mother. Brandorin was treated as if he was a long lost cousin, and he soon felt as welcome as Caidos, who had been there scores of times. Piritho accepted the need to stay in the barn, and once he was given an ample supply of meat, he seemed anxious for Brandorin and the others to leave, so he could enjoy it in peace.

"M'drani knew you would be here today, Caidos, so we have made a special effort with the evening meal," M'dori said as they walked back to the house. "I know you'll say you aren't hungry, but Brandorin looks like he wouldn't mind an early supper."

"Don't make a special effort for me, ma'am," Brandorin started to say, but was stopped by M'dori's fussing.

"Nothing special. It will be ready in a little while," M'dori said. She ushered them into the kitchen, and Brandorin was immediately reminded of home, but where Reba was a mother hen, clucking commands and pecking at slackers; M'dori was a partridge, scurrying through her domain, a line of children following in her wake.

All four kitchen walls were covered with shelves, packed with glass jars of spices, bottles of oils, stacks of stoneware bowls and crocks, wooden spoons and every kitchen implement Brandorin had ever seen, as well as some he hadn't. Steaming pots simmered on the stove, filling the air with fragrant bouquets of dill, thyme, basil and sage. Brandorin's mouth watered and his stomach grumbled; before he knew it M'dori had plopped a hot roll slathered in butter and dripping with golden honey into his open hand.

"If we can drag Brandorin away, M'drani," Caidos said, "could we have a talk out in the garden?"

The glory of summer was long gone, but sedum and mums leant dots of color to the browns of stark empty bushes. The fading fragrance of spearmint and lemon balm sparked the air. They sat on a set of curved stone benches at the center of the garden; the separate pieces of a broken circle, they reminded Brandorin of the crystal's fragment.

Caidos sat next to M'drani, and taking her small hand in his, he told her, "Sefiron's Shadow has appeared. Almost five weeks ago outside Kartir."

M'drani's surprise was evident, as her mouth dropped open and she looked at Brandorin, suddenly realizing the significance of his presence. She turned back to Caidos and said, "This is the burden you carry.

"It's a responsibility I have been trained for, but truly never expected. Have you experienced more than the usual number of storms this season? Stronger downpours, more lightning and thunder."

"Yes, we had a terrible hail storm just last night, and the river has been running very high for this time of year; it's usually at its lowest at the end of summer. There are rumors of quakes coming up from the south. But all this can't be connected to the Shadow's appearance. That was planned —"

"But not for six hundred and eighty years. The volatile weather and the Shadow's appearance are an indication that someone is misusing a crystal. It will only get worse until we can rejoin the fragments." Brandorin wondered why Caidos had not mentioned his concerns about Rhamak, but decided it wasn't his place to do so.

"Then we should leave immediately," M'drani said. Brandorin watched her face, reading in her expression the determination to do her duty, as well as reluctance, even fear of leaving her home and family. Or was it a fear for her family's safety? Probably both.

"In the morning," Caidos said. "We go to Medora next."

Brandorin, expecting Caidos to say more, turned to him, surprised by his silence, but it was M'drani who spoke next.

"It'll be fine, Caidos. There'll be enough time. My mother may already know the reason for your visit. She carried the fragment before I did. Why else would you have brought Brandorin with you?"

"Maybe I should have let you come into the city without me," Brandorin said.

"And let my mother miss the opportunity to feed you? She lives for moments such as this." Brandorin wondered if Caidos had told her about his healthy appetite. "My mother is a wonderful cook, and there's nothing she loves more than to see people enjoy her cooking, especially new people."

"I'll do my best to make her happy," Brandorin said.

By the time they reached the dining area in the central courtyard, other members of the family were already present, bringing dishes to the large circular table, or returning to the kitchen for more.

Each person stopped on their way back to the kitchen to greet Caidos and meet Brandorin. There seemed to be so many and they looked so akin to one another, Brandorin was convinced he had met some of them twice.

N'varian homes were expansive and several generations of a family resided together. M'drani's parents, M'dori and J'roba, her sister and brother-in-law, as well as aunts, uncles and cousins, all lived together. The house was built around a central courtyard, structured so each smaller family within the larger one could find privacy.

Brandorin had thought Caidos led a very lonely life, always on the road, never at home anywhere, but it was apparent he was considered to be a member of this family. Knowing how his own family viewed Caidos, Brandorin started to suspect it was like this everywhere he went.

The flow of people coming from the kitchen trickled to a stop and everyone sat to eat. The table was covered with dishes that were unfamiliar to Brandorin, but the aromas wafting up from the plates stoked his appetite, and his first taste of each was a wonderful surprise.

As they ate, Brandorin noticed M'drani's family shared many of her physical traits. They were small of stature. Brandorin towered over all of them, except M'drani's brother-in-law. J'shurla was tall and muscular, had an aquiline nose, and clear, sharp, oval eyes. The others had delicate features and large, round eyes. They spoke with a slight trill, their voices melodic like a flock of larks chittering to each other.

He was moved by the closeness of this family and he began to think of their large home as a great nest. M'dori cooed as she fussed over her family, including Caidos and Brandorin, as she assured herself they had had enough to eat.

He was reminded of a nest once again when he lay down to sleep and was engulfed in a large, deep comfortable mattress. He was almost asleep when he realized that despite the size and satisfaction of the evening meal, there had been no meat served. If it wasn't for the fact that Piritho undoubtedly finished his meal soon after he left them, Brandorin might have gone to join him in the barn.

* * *

In the morning, Brandorin and Caidos found M'drani in the kitchen helping her mother pack food for the trip. M'drani still wore the dress she had on the day before, making Brandorin suspect the two women had talked through the night.

They stayed to keep M'dori company while M'drani went to change. When she returned, M'drani wore a tunic of thick fabric, belted over a pair of loose trousers, and a pair of soft leather boots laced around the calves. She still wore the torque that held her crystal fragment, and her feathery hair was pulled back into a braid. She carried a rolled blanket, wrapped around her changes of clothing, and a cinched bag holding other items she could not leave behind. A knife in its scabbard hung from her belt.

"I've said my farewells. To everyone but you, Mother."

"Honey," M'dori said gazing at her daughter with mixed emotions of concern and regret. "You should take some honey. It will sweeten the plain food you'll find on the road." M'dori continued to busy herself with the preparations, and Brandorin suspected she was avoiding having to say farewell to her daughter. He caught Caidos' attention and together they left the room.

When the women met them on the porch a few minutes later, M'dori was sniffling and wiping her eyes.

"I know how important this is, Caidos. If anyone can see that this quest succeeds, it's you," she said. Turning to Brandorin, she added, "Protect her, and bring her back to us."

He bent down and embraced M'dori, whispering to her, "I will." Although he had only known M'drani for a little over twelve hours, he added, "... with my life."

A cyclone of dry leaves swirled through the street, a trio of little girls chasing after it. The towering pin oak that shadowed over them played host to a thousand birds, if their chattering talk was any indication of their numbers. The rest of the family had joined M'dori on the porch, and they waved in farewell as the three horses and Piritho turned to walk down the street, heading east.

An overcast sky seemed low enough to touch; the dreary day mirroring M'drani's mood. Brandorin tried to engage her in conversation, but every time he asked a question Caidos would answer, and despite several tries, he could not come up with a topic the mage was unfamiliar with. They were ten miles out before M'drani broke her silence by asking, "What kind of an animal is Piritho?"

"One of a kind," Caidos answered, when Brandorin did not. "I have never seen anything else like him."

"I must admit, he startled me at first," M'drani said, "but once I looked in his eyes, I could sense his gentleness."

"He would never hurt you," Brandorin said.

"I know that now. Why did you give him the name Piritho?"

"Why do you assume I named him?" Brandorin asked.

"It's a natural assumption. He couldn't tell you his name after all."

"I wouldn't be so sure of that," Caidos said. "Brandorin can understand him quite well."

"I can understand birds," M'drani said, "but I've never had one tell me his name."

*　*　*

That evening, when they made camp, Brandorin could tell by the stiffness in M'drani's walk and the slow deliberate way she sat or bent down that the day's ride had taken its toll. He picked up his sword and walked over to join her.

"You look like you're in pain. Can I try to help?"

"Are you going to cut off my legs?" she asked, looking at the sword.

"No, nothing like that," he said, hurrying to dispel her concern.

"I was just teasing, Brandorin," she said. "But you're right, I have aches in places I don't care to mention, though I can't imagine how your sword could help."

"I carry two fragments of the crystal," Brandorin said, flipping the sword back and forth so she could see both crystals imbedded in its hilt. "The Protector's stone and the Umari stone."

"The Umari fragment? I thought that had been lost long ago."

Brandorin explained the finding of the Umari crystal, and the reason the Protector carried it. "I haven't done much with its healing powers, but I would think I could take care of some soreness. It works better if I'm holding the sword, touching the crystal."

"The same way I touch my crystal when I Search." She reached for the stone in the torque around her neck.

"The only other time I did this, I didn't even realize I was doing it, so I'm not sure what to do next."

"Start by holding the sword," Caidos said walking over to them. "I'm curious to see how this will work now that you're doing so consciously. Sit next to M'drani and relax."

"Nothing's happening," Brandorin said after a minute.

"Try touching her hand or her shoulder."

Brandorin placed his left hand on the crystal and reached his right hand out toward M'drani, who put her hand in his. She jumped and tried to pull her hand back, but Brandorin held it tightly. She relaxed, closing her eyes. A troubled look crossed her face, then her eyes darted open in surprise. M'drani jumped up with no apparent discomfort, strode across the campsite and back and sat down again.

"No pain at all. I felt it disappear as quickly as the light from a snuffed candle."

"I felt the pain in my legs for a few seconds," Brandorin said, "then it was gone." He stood and walked a few paces away and back. "I was a little sore before we started. Just what's normal after a day's ride, but that's gone too. How about you, Caidos? Are you sore?"

"Very," he said as he stretched his back and grimaced at the aches and stiffness. "I was asleep before the wounds in my shoulder healed. It will be interesting to see how this works."

Brandorin repeated the process with Caidos, who seemed to be concentrating as hard as Brandorin, then he burst out with a sudden, "Ah. Incredible! All my aches are gone, from my legs, and back, and shoulders. Brandorin, that is a wonderful gift. Thank you."

"Yes, thank you, Brandorin," M'drani added. "I was so surprised by how it worked, I forgot to say so."

"That was so easy, and it worked so much faster this time. Maybe because I'm doing it intentionally. We'll have to make it a part of every evening. No sense sitting around aching when it's not necessary. Since I was able to heal Aquilo's wounds, we know I can heal the horses too. If I can heal their tired muscles each night, we'll be able to push them harder and cover greater distances than we would otherwise."

"That alone would help me sleep better," Caidos said. "Excellent idea."

Brandorin stood and walked across to the fire, "Piritho, how are you feeling? Any aches?"

Caidos shook his head. "Leave it to Brandorin to treat the crystal's gift like a new toy."

*   *   *

The sun would not rise for thirty minutes, but M'drani was already awake. She normally woke with the dawn, but whether it was the unaccustomed setting, the excitement of their journey or an echo of the spark that had coursed through her with Brandorin's healing; she had not slept well.

She sat near the fire, long since burned out, listening to the wakening sounds of the surrounding forest. She heard the clear, mellow whistle of the meadowlark, the soft warbling notes of the bluebird, and the subtle rustling of leaves as field mice skittered through the underbrush.

A long exhalation of breath drew her attention back to her traveling companions. In the soft light of the breaking dawn, she studied Brandorin's features. Awake, his lucent blue eyes dominated his features, and commanded her attention.

In repose, however, she noticed the slope of his nose, the strong, high cheek bones and the barest hint of a cleft in his chin. The crease of concern between his eyes was gone, though a hint of it remained.

Her fingers ached to trace his features, even though she felt silly for wanting to do so. She would be able to feel the stubble of his beard and the hard line of his muscular jaw. But she couldn't, knowing that even a gentle touch would disturb his sleep, a warrior's reflexes readying for battle the instant he woke.

A warrior and fragment bearer, but he was also heir to the leadership of the largest country in Zadania. He bore his responsibilities with a reluctant nobility, like a tailor's custom-made clothing on a soldier, it fit well, but it still seemed to chafe.

His mouth slowly curved into an achingly sweet smile, M'drani unaware that her own mirrored his in response. She shifted her eyes to find him looking back at her, and she was glad the low light prevented him from seeing her blush. She struggled for a reason for watching him sleep, but he didn't seem to need one. She had no sense of what he was thinking, but felt he was somehow aware of her thoughts, and her blush deepened. Still he said nothing.

Just when she'd convinced herself he was still asleep, he whispered, though it seemed louder in the stillness. "Did the birds wake you? They sound like they're having quite a conversation." He stood, stretching muscles stiffened by a night on the cold ground. He looked briefly at Caidos, still in a heavy slumber. "He'll be awake soon," Brandorin whispered, "and wanting us to leave, so

I better get started on breakfast." He grabbed a pot and a couple of water skins, and headed for the stream. M'drani watched him walk away.

\* \* \*

After breakfast, while Brandorin saddled the horses, M'drani and Caidos went to the stream to clean-up and fill their water skins.

"We heard rumors in N'varia about what happened at Brandorin's wedding, but the stories I heard make no sense considering Brandorin's attitude toward Piritho. Yet the sorrow I sensed when Brandorin healed my aches seemed to match the rumors. I don't want to pry, but can you tell me what really happened?"

"I can tell you what happened, but I can't shed any light on their mismatched companionship."

Caidos told M'drani the story of Brandorin's wedding and how he and Piritho had met. M'drani wiped her hand across her face, brushing a tear away. "He's a good man, Caidos. Brave, intelligent, compassionate. He'll make a good healer. He's grieving, but he's also very angry about Ilona's death. He may *say* he's forgiven Piritho, and his actions show that, but I sense a bitter resentment. It's very deep; I doubt he's even aware of it. After he has some experience healing others, maybe he can turn it inward and help himself."

"Perhaps we can help," Caidos said. "It will be good for him to have you on this trip." He reached over and hugged her. "I know it's good for me."

\* \* \*

The sky churned with thick, charcoal clouds, sparked by sporadic lightning. The wind kept the clouds moving before them. Though it kept them dry, they were forced to pull out their warmer cloaks and put up the collars against the cold wind at their backs. The howling winds competed with any attempts to talk, so they road in silence seeking warmth in their separate cocoons.

When they passed through a small, but dense wood, the moist, chill air dropped on them like velvet curtains, cutting off the wind, the dim light causing them to rein in their horses. Even at the slower pace, distracted by their first conversation in hours, they nearly collided with a gray, speckled horse standing in the middle of the road on the blind side of a curve. There was no rider in sight.

Brandorin dismounted, took the horse and led it to the side of the road, tying its reins to one of three dead trees. He scanned the area, looking for the owner. A low, deep growl from Piritho pulled Brandorin's attention. Piritho's hackles bristled, as Brandorin slowly drew his sword, the almost imperceptible scraping of metal against metal dull in the heavy air. The noise of breaking twigs and rustling leaves signaled someone's approach moments before a black-haired man in brown robes emerged from the darkness of the woods.

"You there, what are you doing with my horse?" he called. The stranger marched forward to take charge of his horse, and Piritho repositioned himself between Brandorin and the stranger; an air-rippling snarl stopped the man in mid-step. The man's complexion faded to a mushroom pallor and the still air began to ripple in front of him, as a fireball formed above his outstretched hand.

"Vorago, stop!" yelled Caidos. The stranger had already launched the fireball at Piritho, but it crashed against an invisible wall of air Caidos had just cast, dissipating harmlessly into the dim light of the woods. "He won't hurt you, Vorago. He is one of our companions, as odd as that may seem. Brandorin and M'drani, this is Vorago, one of the mages of Artara. Brandorin, I was with Vorago, searching for Rhamak at the time of ..." Caidos trailed off, not wanting to make a specific reference to the tragedy at the wedding.

Vorago stammered a bit, stepping around and away from Piritho before extending his hand to Brandorin, all the while keeping an eye on the snarling animal staring him down. "I thought -- I heard stories -- I'm sorry."

"He won't hurt you as long as your intentions are fair," Brandorin told him. "We weren't trying to steal your horse. He wandered into the road and we almost ran into him."

Vorago accepted Brandorin's explanation, but his wariness was still dagger-sharp, and he sidled toward his horse, giving Piritho a wide berth.

"Vorago, what are you doing in N'varia?" Caidos asked. "You were going to Tasago. Have you had any further news of Rhamak?" Vorago didn't seem to hear, distracted by Piritho's low, guttural growl.

"It's all right, Piritho," Brandorin whispered out the side of his mouth, "he's a friend." To Vorago, he added, with a slight bow of the head, "Sorry for the scare."

"No harm done. I think we just surprised each other," Vorago said in commiseration, though he kept a watchful eye on Piritho nonetheless. "As a matter of fact, I'm on my way to track down another lead," he said, finally answering Caidos' question. "Rhamak may have been seen in Dachara."

"Is it a reliable lead? As strong as the one we followed last month?"

"No, I don't have as much faith in this as I did the other." Vorago's voice dropped, and he looked away from Caidos before continuing. "And we know how that turned out."

"But we must track down all possibilities. I admire you for being so diligent over all these years. But be wary; it may be a trap."

"Rhamak has been missing for thirty-five years, with virtually no sign of his whereabouts for most of that time," Vorago said. "Now, here's the second lead, only a few weeks after the first. What do you make of it?"

"Some odd things have happened, and I think he may be involved. We're heading to Medora now, and then we'll be going to Setabri. If you hear anything in the next week or so, even if it's only an unsubstantiated rumor, leave word for me at the docks."

"Something serious must be happening if you're going to Medora again," Vorago said expectantly, but when Caidos gave no sign of enlightening him, Vorago asked no further. He walked to his horse and remounted. "You may want to go through B'rona, even though it'd take a bit more time. The Miara River is running extremely high, and you won't be able to cross at the ford along this road. Mount C'Zada is smoking and causing the ground to rumble, so you may want to check that out. I've heard rumors of Mt. Malidor doing the same. I'll send word if I find anything." He rode off westward.

"Rhamak is definitely active again," Caidos said after Vorago had ridden off, "and I can't believe it's a coincidence that this comes at a time when Sefiron's Shadow has appeared.

"I don't think it's a coincidence either," Brandorin said, "but I have no idea what it might mean. Is Vorago the mage that was monitoring Rhamak when he disappeared?"

"Yes, over thirty-five years ago. I've tried to get him to come back to Artara, but he feels responsible for losing Rhamak and is determined to find him. He's very skilled in alchemy, weather, and plant and herb lore. That knowledge should be passed on to others. He would make a great teacher, but the black ox has trod upon his foot."

Brandorin and M'drani looked at each other as they mumbled a courteous, though perplexed acknowledgement. "And you think it's odd I understand Piritho," Brandorin whispered.

As they started out again, Brandorin asked, "Are we going to head toward B'rona?"

"As much as it might be helpful to get a firsthand view of what's happening, there is really nothing I could do about it. We can't afford a delay, and I can get us across the Miara no matter how high its waters might be. An air bridge is easy to cast, even if it might be a little unsettling for the horses to cross."

"That's probably better," Brandorin said. "I know Vorago is one of your Order, but Piritho really doesn't like him."

Caidos chuckled, "He's probably just put out from being caught off guard ..." Caidos stopped and shook his head as if shaking off rainwater. "Now you've got me doing it. Attributing human behavior to him. He is just an animal after all."

Piritho responded to that last remark with a derisive snort. "Don't be so sure of that, Caidos. There's nothing 'just' about him," Brandorin said.

They resumed their faster pace and had covered a sizeable distance, when M'drani suddenly reined in and sat in the middle of the road, as if listening. Caidos and Brandorin stopped and returned to her once they realized she was no longer riding with them.

"What is it? Caidos asked.

"We're being watched," she whispered.

"This looks like a good place to stop for a while," Caidos said in a normal voice, then quieter again, he added, "Can you tell the direction?"

"No, but if we stop here, I can Search and find out."

"No, Piritho and I will do the searching," Brandorin said. "You and Caidos can stay with the horses. If there's any sign of trouble, you ride out of here."

"I think she'll do a better job of it," Caidos said. "Just watch."

They moved off the road and dismounted. M'drani handed her reins to Caidos, and sat on the ground, her legs folded in front of her. She closed her eyes and rested one hand on her knee while the other touched lightly on the crystal fragment in her necklace. She took a deep breath, letting it out slowly, her entire body relaxing with the exhalation. A transparent image of a white dove rose above her head and hovered there.

"What is that?" Brandorin asked, startled by the ghost-like bird.

"She's Searching," Caidos whispered. "This is the N'Varian gift."

M'drani raised her head and the dove soared, sweeping out over the road and flying in ever-increasing circles centered on their position.

"M'drani can see what the spirit dove shows her. If someone is watching us, she'll find him."

As the dove flew over the wood for the third time, a large

hawk broke out of the trees and streaked toward it.

"It's going to get her," Brandorin shouted, as the hawk streaked through the dove and flew off. M'drani's body shivered; then settled back into a restful pose. The dove returned to her, hovering over her body, then merged into her until it disappeared completely. M'drani opened her eyes.

"First time that's happened," she said; she shivered as if showered with ice water. "That was not like any hawk I ever encountered. As it flew through me it was as if we were one, and I could read its thoughts. I sensed fear and pain, and a feeling of utter helplessness. There was an image of a man, a man it was very afraid of."

Both Caidos and Brandorin spoke at once. "Rhamak!"

"How would Rhamak be connected to a hawk?"

Caidos said, "He sent five creatures, which were like nothing I've ever seen before, to attack me, and he is responsible for – a recent attack in Kartir."

"Piritho," Brandorin added. "He sent Piritho to kill me."

"We'd heard rumors here in N'varia," M'drani said as she placed her hand on his arm. "I'm very sorry, Brandorin."

He patted her hand and acknowledged her concern, but changed the subject. "And now he's watching us. I don't like it."

"There's not much we can do about it," Caidos said, the frustration in his voice betraying the nonchalant comment. "At least M'drani will be able to sense when it's happening."

"As long as it's a bird," she said.

"If he can't use birds anymore, then he won't be able to get his messages as fast. That will be good," Brandorin said.

## Chapter 10

Chaubrel always rose before dawn. He had done so since childhood, but it was also best to be ready before Rhamak rose. He had been to the kitchens already, had gone down while still in his nightrobe. He used the excuse of checking on supplies, but he enjoyed the warmth of the kitchens. The heat from the ovens and cooking fires helped to chase away the chill he always felt within the walls of Kalarak. He had gotten himself a warm cup of tea and a freshly baked roll, and returned to his chambers to prepare for the day.

He was fully dressed and now looking through his chest of jewels. He held out his arm, so the red stone in his cuff bracelet caught the light of the candles, turning his wrist to watch it shimmer. He remembered a ring he thought would match, and even though he already wore two rings, he searched through half the contents of the chest until he found it. He added a long gold chain with a heavy pendant, and stepped to the polished brass he used as a mirror to check his appearance.

He was pleased with the overall effect, but grimaced when he saw the cut above and the bruises around his left eye. The bleeding had stopped before he had awakened on the floor in the dining hall. He had been there all that night, but he was neither surprised nor angry that none of the servants had come to aid him. Rhamak's blow had put him there, and they would not risk the Master's anger by interfering.

The blow had not been severe enough to knock him out for so long. Most of the jewels he had worn that night had turned dark and cloudy, and he felt a weariness not attributable to the blow to his head. Rhamak had needed energy for his attack on Juar. The many jewels Chaubrel wore provided a powerful source of energy, but they had not been enough. Rhamak had pulled energy directly from his chamberlain, a sure sign of the magnitude of his anger at the failure of his plans.

He leaned in toward the mirror and touched the bruise

gingerly, wincing at the puffiness around the cut, still tender after four days.

"Admiring your battle wounds, Chaubrel?" Rhamak said as he strode into the room. "It gives you a sinister look, with those tilted eyes and your swarthy skin. It's a big improvement."

"Yes, sire, I was just thinking that," Chaubrel said, "makes me look a little like my father." Why had he said that?

"I don't recall you ever mentioning anyone in your family before." Rhamak's gaze had an almost tangible effect; the crawling, spine-cringing feel of a spider slithering up his back. Chaubrel stepped away from the mirror, not wanting to catch even the reflection of those quicksand eyes.

"You're much like me in that regard; I never think about my family. They demanded so much, yet provided so little." Rhamak's denigrating tone slipped into perplexity as he added, "But I did have a nostalgic lapse just last night. This will undoubtedly surprise you as much as it did me, but I suddenly realized how similar my early years were to Brandorin's."

Rhamak caught Chaubrel's gaze as the chamberlain stared back at him, drop-mouthed and wide-eyed.

"I know; who would expect that? I was the only son of a powerful man, as is Brandorin. We were both raised in privilege, tested in war, and destined to inherit our role in life. But, of course, I wasn't constrained by the limits of my ancestor's lack of foresight and adherence to their archaic views. Laws are meant for the commoner, not the rulers, but Brandorin follows the family line. That's what makes him so predictable."

Rhamak continued talking as he walked from Chaubrel's room and down the long corridor. "But he *is* managing to become a thorn in my side. I was awake most of the night, thinking about it, rereading all the relevant scrolls. They were of little help. I learned more four months ago, from our special visitor. Brandorin and his amazing sword." Rhamak's words dripped with sarcasm.

"What will you do now, sire?" Chaubrel asked.

"I'll get ahead of them. They're in N'varia and my spies don't work well there, but I will prepare a surprise for them in

Medora. I'll eliminate the Builder and retrieve his stone. The stonemason will see to that."

"Jarvin, sire?"

"Is that his name?" He waved a hand at Chaubrel, as if to say it did not matter.

They had arrived in the solar, where large open windows let in the warmth of the outside. Chaubrel spent much of his limited free time in this room, but not only because of the warmth it provided. The solar was filled with a wide variety of plants and trees, giving it an exotic atmosphere, totally at odds with Kalarak's setting. The occasional moments he spent here made him feel he was free, yet, because it was so different from his native land, he never felt homesick.

Rhamak walked through the winding path set amongst the densely placed plants to a set of perches where many birds of different varieties were tethered. Some stood erect and preened their feathers as if seeking his praise, but most cowered, fearing his touch.

"Which is the stonemason's brother?" he asked.

"The peregrine falcon, sire."

He strode past the other birds, and stopped before the slate-gray falcon, as it puffed out its pale-feathered chest. "You are ready to fly for me," Rhamak said, as he passed his hand over the bird. The air shimmered, and a short man with a grizzled beard stood before him, blinking his eyes and shaking his head to clear the cloudiness from his brain.

"Your instructions, sire," he whispered. Rhamak looked back at Chaubrel with a question wrinkling his brow.

"Willem, sire," Chaubrel told him.

"Willem, I have a task for your brother to perform." Rhamak locked his gaze on the man standing before him. "He must lead the Builder to a place where he can be dispatched without too much fuss. Stone will do the trick for us this time. Hard, cold stone, impervious and heavy. There will be no saving him."

Rhamak's words were spoken simply for their hypnotic effect. He sent his message directly into Willem's mind, casting a message to be received by Jarvin. He took no risks with the possibility of misinterpreted instructions. The images of the Builder's destruction were being burned into Willem's memory. The man flinched and squirmed. Chaubrel was glad he didn't know what lay in store for the Builder.

"Handle this well, Willem, and bring me back the crystal when it is finished, and I will release you and your brother. You will have served me well."

"Thank you, sire. We won't fail you." He bowed over and over, until Rhamak raised his hand again, passing it over the man. The air around Willem wavered. When it cleared, the falcon was once again on its perch, bobbing its head.

Rhamak released its leather jesses, and it launched itself from the perch with such force the stand rocked back. Willem was through the window and soaring across the plateau, heading southwest, even before the perch had stopped teetering.

Chaubrel noted the shriveled plants that surrounded the perch on which Willem had roosted. They had provided Rhamak with the energy he needed to transform and instruct his messenger.

Rhamak watched the falcon fly, until it was far out over the plateau. When he turned and walked back through the solar toward Chaubrel, he had a look of dissatisfaction on his face.

"Something troubles you, my Lord?" Chaubrel was concerned only because he was clueless about the source of Rhamak's frustration.

"It's too easy," Rhamak said, then on seeing Chaubrel was still unclear, "This controlling of men's minds. They are so open, so easy to read. It was challenging in the beginning, but not any longer. It gives me no pleasure. Sometimes I feel I should go myself."

"Sire, that would be too dangerous a risk."

"Don't you think I would be victorious? That foolish old man? He couldn't stand against my power. And that inexperienced oaf, Brandorin? I am not afraid of him, though our visitors said I should be. You haven't seen me in action. If you had, you wouldn't doubt my success. But I'll get my chance before this is over. There is still much to do here."

Rhamak sat on a bench in the solar, looking at the birds on their perches. Chaubrel waited for him to speak again.

"I can admit to you, Chaubrel, I'm somewhat jealous of these men." Chaubrel said nothing.

"The ability to fly, to soar above the trees, across the rivers, to know how they feel when they are up there. When they return, I see what they saw, but I don't get a sense of the exhilaration they must feel. If I could just transform myself." He jumped up from the bench in frustration. "If I had the Arkhanian stone, I wouldn't have these limitations."

## Chapter 11

They crested the hill, the city of Medora nestled in the valley on the other side, along the banks of the Nebar River. The closely packed houses and buildings leaned up against the inside of the city walls, the only thing that kept them from overflowing into the river and surrounding countryside.

A large section on the north side of the city had been cleared, and from that incongruous open area sprouted the skeleton of a new cathedral, its tall spires and buttresses rising sixty feet above the roofs of the closest buildings. The late afternoon sun, reflected from the surface of the river behind the city, silhouetted the workmen climbing the columns like a swarm of insects stripping the needles from a stand of pine trees.

A quick yap from Piritho stopped Brandorin and M'drani as they rode down the far side of the hill. He stood above them, looking back up at the crest where Caidos, seated on Aquilo, seemed to be lost in his reverie of the city below. When repeated calls failed to get his attention, M'drani turned her mount and rode back up the hill.

"Are you all right, Caidos?" she asked. He didn't answer; showed no sign he had even heard her. Anyone could see the distant, unfocused look, the pain-weary crease of his brow and the weight-worn slump of his shoulders, but M'drani could also sense an inner turmoil. Her deep affection for Caidos tempted her to go beyond the point of courtesy and search further into his mind.

She scanned the vista, but saw nothing that could have triggered her inborn instincts for danger. Laying her hand gently on the Mage's arm, she whispered, "Caidos, what is it? What's wrong?"

His whispered response carried the haunting echo of old and troubled memories. "I was born here," Caidos said. "I had just turned nine when we left." His words came haltingly, reluctantly, as if he was trying to tear down a brick wall that guarded him from memories cordoned off behind mortared protection.

As he continued, Brandorin joined them, flanking Caidos on the side opposite M'drani. Piritho sat back on his haunches in front of the three of them, as if listening intently.

"My parents sent me away. For my own safety. But it wasn't soon enough. Not for them. The council knew. They killed them anyway."

"I don't understand, Caidos," Brandorin said. A concerned look from M'drani stopped any further questions. Caidos' emotions were too strong for her to ignore. He had removed enough of the barrier to let her glimpse what lay beyond; she knew what had happened.

"Did you ever come back, Caidos?" she asked.

He shook his head wearily; a vulnerable smile banished the haunted look, though it barely touched his eyes. "You can tell Brandorin," he told her.

"Are you sure?"

"There are no secrets among companions who have traveled many leagues together."

"Correct me if I tell it wrong," she said to Caidos. Then she began to tell Brandorin the story Caidos' memory had revealed. "The people of Febron discourage the use of magic. Anyone who uses it is considered an outcast; but in Medora it is forbidden, in any form."

When Caidos responded to her statement with a derisive splutter, she added, "They forbid it on religious grounds. They feel it's demonic, believing only someone possessed by evil forces could perform such feats. People who show signs of using or even understanding magic are put on trial. But they are always found guilty, and the punishment is always death. Enchantments, incantations, transfiguration, mind reading, your healing; any of these 'unnatural abilities' as they call them, are forbidden. Caidos showed signs of his abilities even in the cradle."

She smiled as she shared Caidos' memory of his early achievements. "He was able to retrieve his rattle when it rolled beyond his reach, floating it back through the air. Slowing himself when falling so he wouldn't get hurt. Creating light when he was scared of the dark. His parents were both proud and afraid. They themselves had limited power, but never used it. Not living here.

"They thought of moving to another town, one that would not view their son as a demon, but times were tough in those years. His father was afraid he might not find work elsewhere, and he didn't want his family to starve. They discouraged Caidos from using his ability, making it clear he should never let anyone outside the family know what he could do." She stopped, puzzled and turned to Caidos to ask, "How did they find out?"

"I never knew," he said with a profound regret. "Someone must have seen. We felt lucky to have gotten word of their suspicions." Caidos continued his own story now, past the resurgence of emotion caused by seeing Medora again. "My parents had always felt we might have to leave, probably in a hurry. They were prepared. They'd lived here all their lives, as had their parents, all their ancestors. Strong ties to family and tradition kept them here long after they knew we should have left.

"We left the city the next day, telling the neighbors we planned to take advantage of the fine spring day and have a picnic in the countryside. Maybe we would've been better off to leave without any excuses. I always suspected one of those neighbors had been set the task of watching us, maybe had even been the one to turn in the report against me.

"The Council recognized citizens who gave witness, rewarding them with medals and certificates, and even Council jobs if they were especially good at it," he said, with disdain. "I always suspected many were sent to their deaths having never performed the slightest magic, but simply as the terrible result of a bad incentive system.

"The plan had been for us to picnic on a quiet, tree-shaded knoll near an old, abandoned barn." He stopped for a moment, and pointed to the right, "That one down there."

They saw a picturesque spot down the hill, about fifty feet from the road, under a stand of oak trees. The barn had collapsed, its roof covering the remains like a blanket trying to hide the shame of failure.

He continued, "I was to start ahead, leaving under cover of the wood, while they stayed and ate lunch. They would pretend to call me occasionally; giving the impression I was just off climbing trees. We had picked a meeting point, another abandoned barn. That would have been back down the way we came today, but it wasn't there. There were many such buildings then; left behind when their owners went to find something better." He paused in his story, lost in his regrets.

"How long did you wait for them?" Brandorin asked.

"All that day, through the first night and into the next. I had hoped they were just delayed, would catch up with me. I was afraid to leave and miss them, or to leave and be caught. Hunger finally got me moving. They had given me some money, but a young boy didn't travel alone, and I didn't have the courage to go into an inn too close to Medora.

"We had a second meeting place; a small ruin on the far side of Talrom. It took me a week to travel the fifty miles on foot. They had warned me against travel on the road, so I went across the fields and through the woods, going out of my way to avoid meeting anyone.

"Just before I reached Talrom, I overheard some travelers coming from Medora, talking about a recent demon trial." Caidos stopped, and when he didn't continue after a few minutes, M'drani continued for him.

"His parents had been found guilty of harboring a demon." She looked at Caidos. How could anyone consider this sweet man, or the innocent child he must have been, a demon? "They could've been accused of being demons themselves, but it really didn't matter, since the punishment was the same in either case. They'd been dead for five days by the time Caidos heard about it."

Brandorin grasped the hilt of his sword, and M'drani could feel the red flames of his anger flare. The silence that followed was broken not by any of the three companions, but by a low and mournful moan from Piritho. Caidos looked at Piritho for a long time.

"It's an old fool that frets over the misgivings of his youth.

We have to find the Builder, and he's down there in Medora." Without another word, Caidos nudged Aquilo's flanks and started the descent down the hill. Brandorin, M'drani, and Piritho followed and in the silent understanding of friends who have shared a profound moment, they made their way toward the city.

As they got closer to the city, and encountered more and more travelers, many who cast suspicious glances at their group, Brandorin called to Piritho, who had been running ahead of the horses. Caidos turned to Brandorin and Piritho and added, "Piritho, the sight of you in this city's streets would cause a panic. I'm sorry, but they're sure to think you're a demon.

Brandorin nodded, understanding what Caidos had in mind, and he finished for him, "I think it'd be best for you to wait out here. Looks like a small stream runs through those woods," he said as he indicated the trees set back from the road. "It'd be a good place for you to wait."

Turning to Caidos, he said, "I imagine we'll spend the night at an inn in the city, won't we?"

"In all likelihood" Caidos answered. "Even if we find the Builder today, it'll be too late to set out on the road again. There is no sense spending a night on the road when we can spend it in the warmth of a local inn." Piritho snorted.

"Well, you heard him, Piritho. Make camp and stay out of sight. We'll see you in the morning."

The beast looked at the woods Brandorin had indicated, then to the walls of the city. After a low reverberant growl and a lip-curling snarl, he loped across the grass between the road and the trees, where he disappeared into the shadows. Brandorin turned to his traveling companions and said, "He didn't really mean that. He'll get over it."

Caidos and M'drani exchanged a doubtful look. M'drani seemed about to question Brandorin's comments, but Caidos waved dismissively and said, "Don't even bother."

As they entered the gates of the city a short time later, M'drani sensed a surge of emotions from Caidos. Wanting to distract him she asked, "How will we find this Builder? Are you sure he is here?"

"Salis Braena, the man we are looking for, is an old friend of mine. He used to live in Setabri, the southern port, but he travels quite a bit. As to how we'll find him? He has a passion for contraptions and building things. He's the Builder, and what else would he be building, if not that?"

He pointed to the columns towering over the city, the tips of the spires clearly visible from the barbican just inside the city gates. "We'll have no trouble finding him there."

Their progress through the narrow streets of the city was hampered by the activity of commerce. They were forced to dodge wagons laden with bolts of cloth, crates of chickens, or mounds of cabbages, turnips or potatoes. For a time, they followed a squealing cart of pigs, until the smell encouraged a detour. They had to pull over and wait while a lorry bearing a large block of granite maneuvered through a narrow lane; Brandorin was very tempted to tap one of several kegs of ale that sat, unwatched, in a stack outside a local inn.

Though the close proximity of the lower shops and homes blocked their view of the towers at times, and the bustling, crowded streets forced them to change direction often, they never lost their way. Whenever the streets opened onto a small square, they would get another glimpse of the spires, closer and larger each time.

Before they turned the final corner, they could hear the unmistakable rhythmic ring of hammers and chisels striking stone, the rasping of saws on wood, and the voices of hundreds of workmen. At the end of the street, the small buildings ended and they got their first direct look at the building site.

Hundreds of men toiled: cutting templates for arches, chipping away at large blocks of granite, moving stone, wood and other supplies, all in a struggle to raise the columns and walls of the cathedral. The air was thick with the woodsy smell of sawdust and shavings, the tangy scent of freshly mixed mortar, and the sharp odor of resin. The hectic traffic of craftsman and laborers amid the warren of scaffolds, work tables and stacks of building supplies prevented them from riding any further.

    Brandorin caught the arm of a local lad as he scurried through, to ask where they could stable their horses and find a comfortable night's lodgings. The inn he directed them to, The Steeple's Cellar, was only two blocks from the southern end of the building site. After determining there were accommodations available, they left their horses with the stable boy, along with instructions for him to take their belongings to their rooms. They walked back to the cathedral through the crowded streets. Brandorin held M'drani's hand, recognizing her unfamiliarity with the anthill flurry of activity that was so alien to B'zuri, but so reminiscent of Kartir.

    By the time they arrived back at the site, the bustling had escalated to a frenzy, as each man hurried to finish his task and put away his tools before going home for the night. They caught sight of a well-muscled man who, with a continuous flow of words, barked orders to several small groups of men all at one time. Deciding he must be a foreman, they wove their way over to him, sidestepping or ducking constantly to avoid men carrying long boards or wheeling barrows loaded down with stone, tools or dirt.

    Caidos reached the man first. "If I could have a moment of your time, sir. I am looking for someone who is most likely working on this beautiful cathedral"

    "I got no time to be giving out directions right now. Can't you see I'm busy here?" he barked back at Caidos. Then, without a pause, the gruff foreman marched over to a man nearby who was trying to unload an armful of tools onto a worktable. "You can't leave those there, Caleb. Put 'em away in the tool shed. If Salis saw you trying that again, he'd be telling me to send you packing."

    "Now that's precisely who I'm looking for. Can you tell me where I could find Salis?" Caidos shouted as he hurried to catch up with the man.

    "The Master Builder? That's who you're looking for?" he said with great surprise. Without waiting for a reply, the waterfall of words continued. "He's not here today. He went out to the quarry. They cut the altar stone today. He didn't trust that to anyone else. Garvon, run over to the apse, and tell Dorsic I have to see him - here - now!" The sluice of words slowed just enough to give each of the final words an emphasis that got poor Garvon running across the site and into the shelter of the partially finished west end of the cathedral.

"He's coming back tonight. Late though. You could see him in the morning, but not too early. He'll be busy. Come back about three hours after dawn. All right, Treniff, I'll have to show you myself, but this is going to be the last time." He marched across the square toward a young apprentice who was having difficulty with an adze and a large wooden board.

He was already gone by the time Brandorin and M'drani had caught up to Caidos, who stood looking after the man. The mage's face reflected wonder and admiration at the tempo of the foreman's speech and his apparent grasp of everything going on around him.

"Do you think we should split up to look for Salis? Brandorin asked as they walked up to Caidos.

"No need. I already found out he is not here right now. We can go back to the inn, have dinner, a good night's rest, and even a relaxing breakfast in the morning." Caidos stopped; the foreman's racing speech had proven contagious. He started again, at a normal pace. "We won't be able to talk to Salis until mid-morning tomorrow."

"That was quick! Use a little you-know-what on him?" Brandorin waggled his fingers in imitation of casting a spell.

"Don't forget where you are!" Caidos replied brusquely, pushing Brandorin's hand down. "Even joking about 'you-know-what' is discouraged here. And, no, I didn't need to. I just happened to pick the right man to ask, and was apparently lucky to get a word in. Now, I don't know about you two, but I could use a warm cup of mead."

"Ale for me. And lots of it," Brandorin said with relish. "And something substantial to eat. I've had nothing but 'on the road' food for so long, I can't remember when I had a real hearty, fill-up-the-corners kind of meal."

"Didn't you care for N'varian food?" M'drani asked, with more than a little disappointment in her voice.

"Oh, that was very tasty," Brandorin stammered, trying to cover for his lapse, "but, don't mind the expression, your people eat like birds. The flavor of the food was wonderful, like nothing I've ever had before, but it just doesn't stay with you very long."

"I understand." she said sarcastically. "You need a man's meal, something that's going to sit in your stomach for a few hours. Carry you through the next couple of days."

"Yes, that's it." He had started to agree before she had finished her thought, but once she had, he added, "No, I'm not that bad. It's just that ..." he cut off as a whimsical smile broke across her face. "All right, I guess I had that coming."

"You do realize the expression 'eat like a bird' is totally inaccurate. A bird, for its weight, eats a great deal. I doubt you could keep up."

"Right now, I'd be more than willing to give it a try." He laughed with her as they headed back to the inn.

They checked at the stables to ensure their horses were well tended. Aquilo was lazily munching some hay, and whinnied as Caidos stroked her forelock. M'drani cooed to her white palfrey as she borrowed the stable's brush and gave N'jari some extra attention. Brandorin, after seeing Bristo had been groomed and fed, was more than anxious to get into the inn and have that substantial meal and ale. The closeness of both seemed to have a strong pull on him.

"Come on you two. They're well taken care of, and probably wish you'd leave them alone so they can finish eating and get to sleep."

"I think we better see to Brandorin's needs now, Caidos, or he's going to be stealing hay from Bristo," M'drani said as she put down the brush and left the stall. Brandorin was already at the door of the stable, but Caidos and M'drani caught up to him before he reached the door of the inn.

"You can always tell from the smells coming from an inn ..." Brandorin's words froze on his lips when he looked into the common room of The Steeple's Cellar. When Caidos and M'drani joined them, they too stood speechless.

The inn opened onto a small entranceway, which had doorways on either end, one leading to the stairs up to the rooms, and the other leading presumably to the kitchen. Straight across from the outside door was a wide stairway of five steps that led down to the common room. The stairway was not unheard of, but the ceiling to the common room was what drew their attention, for it was little more than five feet above the floor.

Once sitting at a table, a patron would be more than comfortable, but walking to that table would require a person to bend over and walk slowly and uncomfortably to a chair. As they stood at the top of the stairs, they saw the waitresses, all at least an inch or two shorter than the low ceiling, delivering tankards of ale and bowls of stew.

"Looks a little odd to you, doesn't it?" a gentile female voice from behind them asked. They turned to the speaker, expecting to see another of the diminutive waitresses, but instead found a tall, handsome woman, with long flowing curls of near-black hair. "I am Mirséd, and this is my place. I had three other taverns before this, but was never able to turn a profit, what with all the fights and broken chairs and bottles. Then I found this place. It used to belong to a wine-maker, and he used this area to store his kegs of wine and spirits. But he wasn't making any money either. So I got the idea to turn it into a tavern.

"We have very few fights in here, and the ones we do have are pretty minor. No one can lift a chair over his head to hit anyone. If they jump up out of their chair to join in, they usually forget about the ceiling. By the time they come to their senses again the fight is over. I make sure my food, ale, and wine are the best, so no one is bothered by the tight quarters. They even seem to like it."

"An excellent solution to a long-standing and troublesome problem. I am Caidos, and this is M'drani and Brandorin. We reserved rooms for the night."

"My stable boy told me you were back. Come on in and I'll

have your dinners brought to you. Let me find you a table near the fire. Looks like you've been on the road for awhile and could use the warmth."

She talked as she led them into the common room. She walked into the low-ceilinged room with the grace of a dancer. M'drani didn't have to stoop at all, and Caidos only a little, but Brandorin, well over six feet tall, after bumping his head on the ceiling a few times, walked almost doubled over to avoid doing so again.

Within minutes, a sweet girl with a pug nose and long brown braids brought their dinners and drinks to the table. She looked warily at M'drani before turning her charm on for Brandorin, who only had eyes for the refreshments she carried. With a pouting look she retreated, perhaps to launch another assault after his stomach was full.

*   *   *

In the morning, Brandorin was half way through his eggs, bread and cheese when he stopped to comment, "This is as good as what we had last night, and the beds were up to the same standards. I don't mind having to duck walk in here to get it."

"It's good you're enjoying it, because there probably won't be a chance for such luxurious accommodations for quite some time after today," Caidos said. "We have three more bearers to reach after Salis and there are many leagues to travel before we're done."

"That may be why I'm enjoying this place so much, but you never know what we'll find on the road. We didn't expect to find this place. We may have other surprises."

"Surprises? I have no doubt of that, but they're more likely to be bad ones than good."

"Why are you so cheery this morning?" Brandorin asked sarcastically. "Wasn't your bed comfortable?"

"I'm sorry. I just feel uneasy, as if something is wrong. Maybe we should have gone out to the quarry last night. Do you sense anything, M'drani?"

"Yes, I do. There *is* something, but I don't know where, or who, it's coming from."

"That does it. If you're feeling it too, it's not just my imagination. Let's get to the cathedral and find Salis. I don't care if he's busy." Caidos jumped to his feet, forgetting the low ceiling, and was rewarded with a bump on the head. His mood was not improved by Brandorin's snickering.

Caidos set a fast pace through the empty streets to the cathedral. His mood focused him on his objective, so it was Brandorin who noticed and said, "Where are all the people? We haven't passed a single person since leaving the inn. At this time of day, there should be shopkeepers, tradesman, carters, all sorts of activity."

"Something is wrong. We must hurry," Caidos shouted back, as he ran ahead of them to the building site. Brandorin and M'drani caught up with him by the time he reached the cathedral square, jammed with people looking up at the eastern wall, unfinished, but already over sixty feet high. Caidos asked an almost toothless man at the back of the crowd, "What has happened here?"

"Scaffold gave way whilst workmen were a' top." The air whistled in the open spaces between the few rotting teeth in the old man's mouth, giving his speech a wet muffled sound. "Last one's still up there. See'm?" he said, pointing midway between two support columns, at the crown of the wall. "He's been holding on for some time now. I missed the first, but he'll prob'ly fall soon," he said with a relish.

Caidos, afraid of hearing Salis had been one of those who had fallen, said, "We're here to meet with the Master Builder, but I suppose he's busy with all this commotion." He tensed, preparing for bad news. He had not, however, been prepared for the man's macabre chortle.

"Busy? I'd say he's busy, sir, he's the one what's hanging from the wall up there." He continued his cackling, and turned to the man standing next to him; apparently deciding the joke was too good not to share.

Caidos forced his way through the crowd. "Hurry, we must save him!"

The mass of unwashed bodies added an acrid scent to the normal smells of the construction site. All of the citizens of Medora appeared to be present, packed in shoulder to shoulder, pressing forward to gain a better view. Many bowed over books, held hands and chanted prayers. The rest craned their necks aloft, watching the man hanging from the top of the unfinished wall.

They struggled to make progress, until Brandorin, a head taller than most, plowed a path through the crowd, Caidos and M'drani following closely in his wake.

They could now clearly see a tangled mound of wood planking stretched out in front of the crowd. A single stone eye stared out of the rubble, fixing Caidos with its granite gaze. That, as much as the three bodies covered by blankets, sent an icicle of apprehension down Caidos' spine.

The mage went immediately to the man directing the cleanup and asked, "Is that really the Master Builder up there?" then held his breath, waiting for the answer.

"Aye, it is. He was up there directing the work. They were preparing to add the drain spouts." He paused before adding with an obvious sense of guilt, "The scaffolding gave way. I don't know how that could have happened. With all the tremors lately we've built them extra strong."

"Are you the Master Carpenter?" Caidos guessed.

"Yes," he admitted reluctantly.

"What can be done to get him down?" Brandorin asked.

"I don't know what we can do. There's a staircase in the turret there." He pointed to the right about thirty feet away, where a doorway opened into a tower that rose above the height of the wall. The workers had concentrated on clearing a path to the doorway in the turret and the base of the spiral staircase inside was now visible through the opening. "It used to meet up with the scaffold at the top, but without that I don't know how we'll reach him."

"Could a rope be thrown or shot to him from the top of the stairs?" Brandorin asked.

"If we could get it to him, there's nothing where he's hanging for it to be tied to. The only thing up there is the next column, just as far away on the other side. Without something to anchor the rope to, he would swing down in an arc of almost fifty feet and smash into the side of the tower."

Caidos motioned for Brandorin and M'drani to follow him off to the side, where they could talk without being overheard. "We'll have to intervene. They don't know how to save him. I could easily help him, but that would mean openly using magic, which these people would not accept. We can work from the top of the tower, where the people on the ground won't be able to see us clearly. M'drani, you can help provide our actions a non-magical appearance. The dove that appears when you search will carry the rope to Salis."

"The dove is only a spirit, Caidos," M'drani whispered. "It can't carry anything."

"I will levitate the rope to him. From the ground, the dove will appear to carry it."

"But Salis will know we're using magic," Brandorin said.

"He won't give us away, especially after we save his life."

"The rope will have to appear to be anchored," M'drani noted.

"It can be looped around the wall, going through the window opening just past him," Caidos said, as he reached into his robes and pulled out a small cage holding a white dove, startling both Brandorin and M'drani. "It's just an illusion, but it should convince everyone we have a trained bird that can carry the rope."

After telling the Master Carpenter they were members of a traveling carnival, they explained the non-magical version of their plan. Brandorin picked up a coil of rope, brought from the tool shed, hefting it onto his shoulder and they started toward the tower stairwell. The Master Carpenter joined them as they started up the stairs. They stopped; he couldn't be with them at the top of the tower.

Brandorin, thinking quickly, said, "The bird can be skittish around strangers. It would be better if you stayed here."

"The scaffolding was made by my workmen. It's my responsibility. I've already cost three men their lives, I need to help save one," he said in desperation.

"I understand your concern, but if the bird is nervous and can't be directed, the Master Builder won't be saved," Caidos told him. The bird in the cage fluttered its wings, as if startled. "See, she's getting riled."

The Master Carpenter wavered, wanting to help save Salis, but not wanting his participation to prevent the rescue from succeeding. Reluctantly, he said, "I'll wait down here. But, please, call me if I can help."

He left the tower in order to watch their rescue from the ground below Salis. When he had left, they started up the stairs, and Caidos released the illusion of the bird in the cage.

Brandorin said. "This rope is far too heavy for a dove to be able to carry. Even though it's only carrying the end, the weight pulling on that end will be heavier than the bird long before it reaches Salis. I know there isn't really a bird, and it won't really be carrying the rope," he added when Caidos started to protest, "but will the people below believe the dove can carry it?"

"That's a valid point," Caidos conceded, "but I can't think of anything else we can use to cover our actions. I could create an illusion of a larger bird, but I couldn't be hiding an eagle under my robes. We'll have to rely on the excitement of the rescue to distract the people from realizing the flaw in our plan.

"We have another, more serious problem, however," Caidos continued. "There are no good sources of energy here. No plants, no trees. I hesitate to use the stone or the ground in this area; it could weaken the structure. If not right away, it could cause a collapse as more weight is built on top."

"You could use me, Caidos," Brandorin said. "There isn't anything else I can do to help anyway."

"That's very generous of you, Brandorin, but you don't know what you're volunteering for. If I concentrated on you, even for this minor use of magic, you'd be off your feet for at least a day or two. And we can't afford that."

"What about the crowd out there? Could you pull a little from each of them? Evenly, so as not to hurt anyone."

"I think I'll have to, though I detest the idea. But it may actually help us with the other problem. The energy I pull from them will make them a bit muzzy, less likely to realize the bird couldn't be carrying the rope. They may think about it later, but by then we'll be gone."

"It's up to the two of you then," Brandorin said. "I'll stay down here, and keep anyone else from coming up and seeing what you're really doing."

Caidos took the rope from Brandorin as he and M'drani continued up the stairs by themselves. Brandorin waited in the turret, out of sight from anyone in the square, but still in a position to watch the doorway. Once at the top they could see Salis clearly.

"Looks like you could use a hand," Caidos called to him.

"Caidos! What are you doing here in Medora?" Salis responded casually, as if he wasn't hanging precariously sixty feet above the ground. "Aren't you going to introduce me to your friend?" he added, noticing M'drani, and releasing his right hand from the wall in order to tip an imaginary hat.

"This is M'drani, and she's going to create a cover for my levitating you over here," Caidos said. Even as he spoke, M'drani sat cross-legged on the floor of the tower and began to send her mind out to Salis. The ghost dove, the image of her spirit, rose from her and hovered in the opening next to Caidos, who held the end of the rope out. Using an air incantation he fed the rope out of the tower slowly, giving M'drani time to adjust the dove's movements to that of the rope.

As the rope and dove moved together toward Salis, a cry of surprise rose from the crowd below. From the top of the tower, the dove was obviously insubstantial; anyone seeing it would know it was not a real bird, but from the ground, the illusion was effective. The crowd shouted words of encouragement as the dove and rope reached the place where Salis was hanging.

"Do you want me to grab it?" Salis asked.

"No, we have a plan to tie it off," Caidos answered, as the bird and rope snaked through the unglazed window beyond Salis and came up again from inside, looping the rope around the empty window frame. Caidos had attached the other end to a support within the tower.

Once it was secured, Caidos released his air incantation on the rope and transferred it to Salis, who felt the support, relieving the drag on his arms. "Now make it look real. Hang from the rope. I won't let you fall."

Salis grabbed the rope with both hands, and as he allowed his body to swing away from the wall, a small piece of wood that had provided him with some support, clattered earthward. The crowd let out a collective cry of alarm, but when they realized the rope now held the Master Builder, they cheered him on.

Salis worked his way, hand over hand, thirty feet to the tower, supported by Caidos' incantation. Once he was safely inside, the crowd roared, and Salis leaned out of the opening and waved to them, as if he was an acrobat who had just successfully walked the tightrope.

"You better bring the rope back. Someone is bound to test it, to see if it would really hold a man," Salis said.

"Oh, it would, I just thought your arms would be a bit tired by now. Thought I would give you a hand, so to speak. Still, you're probably right. Are you ready, M'drani?"

While in this state, M'drani could not respond verbally, but the dove flapped its wings and flew to the end of the rope, where, with Caidos' assistance, it unwound the rope from the window and brought it back. The dove returned to the tower and floated above M'drani's head before fading away.

As she stood, Salis took her hand to help her up, then gallantly kissed it as he said, "I owe you my life, dear lady. I am eternally in your debt." M'drani smiled at the strange little man in front of her. He had large, slightly bulging eyes, a large mouth full of uneven teeth, and scraggly hair of indeterminate color, yet seemed to possess the confidence and charm of a handsome man of stature. She liked him immediately.

"I had a little to do with this myself, you know, Salis," Caidos said, sounding a little wounded.

Salis turned to Caidos, and casting aside all hint of sarcasm, said, "I know you did, Caidos. Thank you." He gave Caidos a quick hug, then with a dramatic change of tone, he added with a wink, "But, I'm already in your debt, dozens of times over. I have no hope of ever breaking even. So why try?"

The cries of cheering from below grew louder. The crowd was trying to enter the tower in their excitement to congratulate the rescuers.

"We better get downstairs and let you take your bows," Salis said. "You should conjure up a bird for them to lavish their praises on, or your elaborately detailed ruse will fall apart."

As they started down the spiral staircase, they heard Brandorin calling to them from his station at the bottom of the stairs. Caidos, grabbing Salis by the arm, held him back for a moment.

"The Master Carpenter said the scaffolding gave way. It seemed difficult for him to accept that, and frankly, I'm not sure I believe it either. What really happened?"

"Oh, the scaffolding gave way all right, but even I find it hard to believe what caused it." Salis paused, and Caidos was suddenly struck by the stone-cold chill within the turret's thick walls. "One of the gargoyles - it came to life! A heavy, stone gargoyle took flight and started to attack us. It flew into the scaffold, and collapsed it out from under us."

## Chapter 12

When they emerged from the turret, the crowd surrounded them; clapping Caidos on the back, and trying to get a good look at the remarkable, trick bird. Caidos made the illusion flap its wings in simulated aggravation, then pulled a cloth from inside his robes, to cover the cage, saying the bird needed to rest after its strenuous activity.

The companions tried to make excuses about being tired, or having to get on the road, but the crowd would not listen. Although they had suffered a great loss in the deaths of the three workmen who fell from the scaffolding, they needed to rejoice in the salvation of one. Many men in the crowd insisted on escorting the companions back to The Steeple's Cellar, where they bought round after round of drinks, and the sound of their cheers and laughter was soon bouncing off the low ceiling of the common room.

Caidos realized once the celebration was well underway, the participants would not even notice if the guests of honor had gone. He instructed each of the others to slip away, one at a time, and to go upstairs to their rooms.

M'drani's departure caught the attention of a pair of inebriated patrons. Caidos, pretending to be responding to a question that no one had actually asked, shouted over the crowd, inviting everyone to a special show that very evening; one that would feature the heroic dove. He distracted them by asking where the event should take place, and in the ensuing debate as one after the other vied for the privilege, she slipped out unnoticed.

"They will celebrate for hours yet. We can join them again in a little while," Caidos added when he noticed the disappointed look on Brandorin's face because he thought he was going to miss so many free drinks. "I want to talk about what happened today. Did you tell them what you told me, Salis?"

"No, not yet. I don't like thinking about it. The sight of that creature, flying at us, it makes my skin crawl."

"Was it another one of those raptors, Caidos?" Brandorin

asked.

"You've seen these things before?" Salis asked, his voice rising in surprise.

"No, to both of you. What attacked me four weeks ago was very different, though they had one thing in common. Tell us everything that happened today, Salis. I think you'll find talking about it will make it seem less bizarre."

"We had hoisted one of the gargoyles up, to see how it would look on the drain spout." Though he started slowly, his pace quickened as he revealed more and more of the story. "We weren't ready to be attaching them permanently, but Jarvin, the Master Stonemason wanted to see one in place, before they continued making the others. I didn't want to go up there today; the winds were very strong this morning, but Jarvin insisted. At least he was pleased with what they had done." He smiled a sad, regretful smile that gave a certain beauty to his plain features.

"We were talking about the way the statue would attach to the water feeds from the roof. So the water would pour out through the mouth of the gargoyle. We weren't even looking at the statue. The sound got our attention."

His pace slowed again, as he reached the part of his story that was so difficult to accept. "The winds had died by that time. Everything was so still it felt as if we were waiting for the world to exhale. Then that horrible sound, like a blade scraping against stone. That, more than the sight of that stone monster taking flight, that's what sends chills up my spine. It shrieked. A horrible cry. A grating, raspy, shriek. Even though the wings flapped and the neck moved, it still looked like stone. Except for the eyes, they glowed like the heart of a fire. Daken was ready to jump, just to get away from the thing, but Jarvin grabbed his arm to stop him.

"That's when it started to attack the scaffolding. It was made of stone. It shouldn't have been able to move, let alone reason, yet it realized that destroying the scaffold would kill us too. How could it know that?"

"It didn't know that, Salis. The man who sent it did" Caidos answered.

"I don't know how I managed to grab on. I tried to save the others; it just happened so fast. Then while I was hanging there a falcon started to fly at me, as if it thought I was something to eat. At least there was no one below to see the gargoyle's attack, or that crowd would be denouncing me, saying I am in league with the devil. How else would I have survived?"

"How long before we got there did this occur?" Caidos asked.

"I wasn't in a good position to be watching the clock, but I'd say it was fifteen, twenty minutes at least. Wilton, the Master Carpenter, had come up the turret to see what he could do, and he assured me he would find a way to get me down. He blamed himself, but I couldn't tell him what really broke the scaffold."

"You were using a little magic of your own, weren't you, Salis? That's how you managed to hang on for so long," Caidos said. "I sensed something, even at the inn. It was the magic that empowered that gargoyle, and then your own I felt. M'drani, you felt the strong emotions, the fear."

"That and their deaths. When someone dies like that, in such fear, and so violently, it's more powerful," she said, shivering at the memory.

"I couldn't hold myself up. I can control other things, move them, levitate them, but I can't use it on myself. I held a piece of scaffolding against the wall, and used it as a step."

"That's what fell to the ground when you shifted your weight to the rope and the air cushion," Caidos said.

"I could have created a set of steps for myself, levitated pieces of wood up from the ground, to walk on over to the tower. But using magic to save myself would have been a temporary solution. The crowd would have seen, would have known it wasn't natural. I would have saved myself from falling, only to be executed by their barbaric superstitions," Salis finished with anger.

"Are there some who'll be suspicious of the methods we used?" Brandorin asked.

"There's a good chance a member of the Council may be here to visit us before the end of the day," Salis answered.

"If anyone thinks to question a dove being able to support a long rope, it will be a member of the Council," Caidos added. "They're probably questioning witnesses now. It would be best if we weren't here. How soon can you be ready to join us, Salis?"

"Join you? I'm not leaving! I have a cathedral to build."

"Do you feel safe here, by yourself? This attempt failed, but there are likely to be others. Don't you realize what's happening? The time has come."

"But the cathedral? I'll never get this chance again. This is my design, my work. It will be here for years after I'm gone. My testament. I can't just walk away," Salis pleaded.

"It's taken fifteen years to get this far. How long will it take to finish? Thirty years? Forty? More? We'll only be gone a few months. And success at the goal we face will be a far greater testament for you to give the world, not just this city. You know what's at stake. You know I'm right." Caidos stopped, waiting for Salis to make the decision he knew he must.

After a few moments, Salis responded, "Yeah, I know you're right, but the timing stinks. I won't be able to come back and finish. They won't take me back after I run out of here with no explanation - especially after today's misadventure. They'll be convinced magic was involved, in the rescue at least, if not in the failure of the scaffold. I'm sure I'll have a price on my head within hours of them discovering we're gone."

He paused, accepting his fate, then added, "I just hope it's a big one. I'm worth five hundred tansur at least, don't you think? I have nothing at home that can't be left behind," he said as he touched the yellow stone in the buckle of his belt. "We can leave as soon as you're ready."

"We'll need a distraction if we're to slip away unnoticed," Caidos said. "I'll go back to the common room, and recreate the illusion of the dove. I'll hold their attention away from the doorway, while you leave. Get the horses and meet me at the Farmer's Market near the city gates ... let's say thirty minutes."

"I have a better idea, Caidos," Brandorin said. "We shouldn't use any magic if we don't have to. Since I didn't do much at the cathedral, let me go back to the common room and do the distracting. It'll be easier for me to get away if there are problems, and I can catch up to you at the market in fifteen minutes. The sooner we're out of this city, the better I'll feel."

"How will you keep their attention without magic?" Caidos asked.

"I have dozens of interesting stories to draw on," Brandorin said with bravado. "Ones that aren't at all related to anything magical," he added when he felt that Caidos was about to protest. "Give me three minutes to get things started. By the time you get your things together and come down the stairs, you should hear the laughter from the common room to tell you they're engrossed in my story."

"What story is that?" Salis asked.

"I don't know yet, but I'm sure I will by the time I get down there."

"He's going to wing it! Do you think that's safe, Caidos?" Salis was openly nervous.

"He'll do just fine."

Salis turned to Brandorin, "I don't suppose the fact you'll get a couple tankards of ale in the process has anything to do with your volunteering for this potentially dangerous mission," he said sarcastically.

"No one ever said danger couldn't be fun," Brandorin said as he headed down to the common room.

It took only minutes for Caidos and M'drani to pack up their things, and grab Brandorin's. When they reached the bottom of the stairs, raucous laughter and suggestive sneers erupted from the common room. Brandorin could be heard over the sound of the patrons, telling a story of a brawl and missing clothing. They made their way to the stables unobserved.

"You can take Brandorin's horse for now, Salis. Do you have one of your own we should pick up on the way out of town?" Caidos said as they slipped into the stables.

"Actually, that one back there, in the far stall, *is* mine," he said, as he made his way back to saddle up the tan cob. They were finished and mounted within minutes and left the inn behind, with Caidos leading Brandorin's horse.

They reached the market without drawing anyone's attention, and Brandorin joined them twelve minutes later. He was clearly agitated and he quickened their pace as they pushed their way through the crowds toward the city's gates.

"Did you have any trouble breaking away? Caidos asked.

"A great deal," Brandorin told him, breathing hard and glancing back suspiciously the way he had come. "Four members of the Council arrived, asking questions about the rescue. They wanted to see the bird, and the rest of you. They became suspicious when they learned you weren't in the common room. I volunteered to go get you, but they didn't want me to leave. One of them went to go find you while the others stayed with me. I'm sure they thought they were being subtle, but they were quite obviously guarding me, to prevent me from leaving. I knew I only had a little time; as soon as your departure was discovered, I'd have no chance of getting away."

"How *did* you get away?" M'drani asked, her eyes wide with curiosity.

"I told them I had to visit the outbuilding," Brandorin answered sheepishly. "No man would question another about that, especially after he's had as much ale as they saw me drink. One of the Council members went with me, so I had to hit him over the head. I hid him in the shack, hoping they wouldn't think to look in there, and we would have a few extra minutes."

"There's an ironic justice to your solution," Salis said with admiration. "For years I've thought that's exactly where the Council belonged."

Brandorin was ready to ride into the bailey just inside the main gate, when Salis warned him. Two men, wearing the insignia of the Council, stood with three guards each, on either side of the open portcullis. "They beat us here."

The companions rode past the gate and into the shadows of an abutment on the far side. "They'll be looking for three men and a woman," Salis said. "I'm the only one they'll know by sight, and since I'm not often seen in the company of women, M'drani and I can ride out together. The two of you can follow soon after."

"That's too risky by itself," Brandorin said. "Can you create an illusion to make us look different? Or at least Salis?"

"That's a great deal of magic. The Council may not use magic, but they can sense it, if it's strong."

"I have an idea," Salis said. Caidos recognized the conspiratorial tone of his friend's voice, but before he could counsel against it, a rumbling clatter, followed by shouts, came from the bailey. A wagon carrying a large load of ale kegs had broken a wheel and the loose barrels were rolling in every direction. One had smashed into the gate and a spray of ale now spewed through the resultant crack, showering one of the Councilmen and his waiting guards.

In the chaos, the companions ambled through the gate in single file. A few hundred feet down the road, they abandoned any pretense of subtlety, and galloped away from the city.

As they approached the small woods where they had left Piritho, Brandorin spurred ahead and pulled off the road toward the trees, calling back to them to continue.

A few minutes later, Salis, who had been checking over his shoulder, saw Brandorin gaining on them, followed closely by a large beast. "What is that?" Salis said, as he started to draw his dagger.

M'drani tried to calm him. "Don't worry. He's one of our traveling companions."

Brandorin reached them and slowed from the full gallop it had taken to catch up; to the light gallop they had adopted to avoid too much attention.

He rode next to Salis to make the introductions. "Salis, this is Piritho. Piritho, Salis."

Turning to Caidos and M'drani, he continued, "I gave him a quick rendition of what happened. He can wait for the full details until we stop. I think he'd like to hear it from you, Salis."

As Piritho, running in the center of the pack, let out a low howl in response, Salis turned to the others, "I think our big friend here had more than just a couple of ales after we left the tavern."

"Don't worry, Salis, he always does that," M'drani laughed.

"Nice traveling companions you've hooked me up with, Caidos. I notice you didn't tell me about *this* when you were talking me into coming with you," Salis said. He turned to Brandorin and asked, "You call that a dog?"

"No, I call him Piritho," Brandorin responded, then to Caidos, "Didn't I just tell him that?"

\* \* \*

They kept up a fast pace for the rest of the day, stopping only when it was fully dark, making camp for the night under cover of a small copse of trees, fifty feet from the road.

"Caidos, do you think it's safe for me to heal the horses? Brandorin asked. "We pushed them pretty hard today, and being in Medora, I didn't do it last night."

"I think it'll be fine. There's no outward sign of what you're doing and we're well off the road. Just make it look like you're grooming them."

While Brandorin curried the horses, removing mud from their hooves, rubbing their coats and massaging their overworked muscles and tendons, Salis volunteered to collect wood for the fire. Caidos, who knew his friend well, thought it best to follow him at a short distance.

As piece after piece of wood floated up from the ground and formed a bundle in the air in front of Salis, Caidos, laughing to himself said, "I might have known there would be an ulterior motive for you volunteering for work." The mage's voice coming unexpectedly from the otherwise silent woods, startled Salis, and the bundle of wood dropped to the ground, one piece landing firmly on his right foot.

"Ow, what're you doing sneaking up on me like that?" he said, hopping on his left foot as he massaged the sore spot where the log had hit.

"We aren't that far out of Medora. It's not safe to use magic yet."

"You let Brandorin ..." Salis said, though the tone of his voice told Caidos he knew it was a lame excuse.

"Brandorin's healing is not at all evident, but logs floating in the air simply screams magic."

"I thought here in the woods I'd be safe from prying eyes, but I forgot about yours. You know how muscles ache when they aren't used enough. You just want to stretch them. If they aren't used enough they get rusty, don't work as well when you try them again. I wouldn't want to be out on the road, and have to use my talents in defense against another attack, and have them wilt out on me."

"Your motives are admirable, but discretion, please. Even I wouldn't expect to find a member of the Council in these woods, but we have a time limit to our task, and it's all the more urgent because I don't know what that limit is. We can't afford to get caught up in a Medoran Demon Trial."

"Don't worry about me, Caidos," Salis said as the pieces of wood began to float up and reform the bundle. "I'm the very soul of discretion." He stretched out his arms under the suspended bundle of wood, which still floated a fraction of an inch above his sleeves. "I've lived in Febron all my life, a great deal of it in Medora, using magic when I could." Another log rose from the underbrush and was added to the top of the stack.

"You like the challenge a little too much for my tastes, Salis. Do me a favor and wait another couple of days before you do too much more stretching."

They walked back to the campsite, where Salis faked a grimace as he struggled under the supposed strain of carrying so much wood.

"Salis, let me help you with that," Brandorin said, as he hurried over to them, and took the logs away from the smaller man. "That's a large load for one night. We'll want to keep the fire low. Don't need to draw attention to ourselves." Brandorin grunted as he lowered the wood to the ground near the shallow pit he had dug for the fire.

"See, Caidos, had the big guy fooled."

"The clever rooster crows from the egg," Caidos said to Salis, "but he still ends up as Sunday dinner."

"Yeah, well, he who lies on the ground, has no place to fall," Salis responded and walked away.

When Brandorin looked after Salis and then at Caidos with a puzzled look on his face, Caidos told him, "He's been saving that one up for awhile." Then he too walked away; leaving Brandorin more confused than ever.

They started a fire and began to prepare their evening meal. A heavy rain started soon after, extinguishing the fire and soaking them quite thoroughly before they could put up a canvas awning. The weather made them miserable, but also made it more difficult to spot them from the road. Once they finally settled for the night, wanting to test a suspicion, Caidos asked, "That's a fine horse you have there, Salis. What's his name?"

"Name? Oh, it's ... I call him ..." After floundering for a few seconds Salis confessed, "All right, you got me. It wasn't my horse. It was just so convenient, and I didn't want to unduly delay our departure."

"You stole that horse!" M'drani said.

"I noticed that none of you stopped to pay your bill at the inn before we sneaked out of there," he responded defensively.

"Oh, my! I hadn't thought about that. Mirséd was so nice to us. Is there some way we can send the money to her?"

"Don't worry, M'drani. I left more than enough to cover the bill on the nightstand in my room. But I didn't leave enough to cover the cost of that horse," Caidos said.

"If it helps, the city owes me this month's wages. When our furtive departure is uncovered, the owner of the horse will go to the Council to complain. They'll volunteer to cover the man's losses with my unclaimed wages, and they'll still be ahead, and look magnanimous in the process. So, despite the fact that I hate making the Council look good, taking that horse was really a good deed all around."

Caidos looked at him disapprovingly; then a slow smile broke the tense moment. "You haven't changed at all," he said laughing.

"Would you really want me to?"

"No, the joy of a friend adds laughter as well as years to one's life."

"I know you think all those sage proverbs make you seem wise beyond your years," Salis said, "but come on Caidos, remember how old you are. You've got a lot of catching up to do!"

Continued conversation was stopped by a prolonged volley of thunder and lightning and a squall of almost horizontal rain gusted in under their awning. Caidos felt the use of air shields to block the wind was justified in this dark corner of the woods. When they settled down again Brandorin asked, "Where do we go now, Caidos?"

"There are three more companions. The next one geographically is in Laria. Matu Lairom, the Counselor. After that, Ilyan and Arkhan. The Caretaker and the Defender. We'll make a circuitous trip of most of Zadania.

"It's a great deal of ground to cover, and after what happened to Salis, I'm very worried about the three remaining fragment holders. Well, mainly two of them. TA-KA, the Arkhanian bearer can easily take care of himself. The Larians have weapons but they can be too trusting, and the Ilyani are totally defenseless. They're innocents, no weapons, no defenses. They can barely conceive of violence; it's so alien to their culture."

"Larians? Ilyani? You talk about them as if there are a lot of them. There're no cities in either of those two countries. Who could we be looking for there?" Salis asked.

"There are no traditional cities, but I've visited there often. The Axana Mountains are a natural barrier on the west. Few people have ever made the trip by sea, under the false assumption the country is wild and untamed. If you went there on your own, you'd probably have difficulty finding a Larian city; would probably pass within sight of one without realizing it. You would most likely just get lost in Ilyan.

"That's the way both the Larians and the Ilyani want it. You were surprised at Piritho, Salis. Don't understand how Brandorin communicates with him, and frankly, I have to confess a certain bewilderment at that myself." He looked at the two friends sitting together on the far side of the campfire.

"But there are many different types of people in this world, and some of them, because they are different from the rest of us, have chosen to remain isolated. You'll be meeting all of them before our travels are finished, and I know I can trust you to approach each of them with an open mind. Not to judge them because they're different than yourselves."

"I've heard of the Larians and the Arkhanians, but what are the Ilyani like?" M'drani asked.

"I think they're the most interesting people in Zadania, though I think I'm the only outsider who knows of their existence. Their appearance, their very nature is unique. It's very hard to describe them to someone who hasn't met them, not without making them sound unreal. Maybe I should leave most of it for you to discover for yourselves.

"Ilyan is a natural paradise. No trees have ever been cut down there, no ground tilled. The Ilyani understand plant life, the way you understand birds, M'drani, or the way Salis understands buildings, or Brandorin battle or even Piritho."

"What about the Larians?" Salis asked.

"They are most like the N'varians, wouldn't you say M'drani?" He continued, while she nodded in ascent. "At least in custom and abilities, if not in appearance. They have what you'll probably consider to be a very primitive culture, Salis, because they don't build the way you do. They don't charter cities, or know anything about mechanisms, nor do they want to. They don't even use wheels nor have money."

"No money!" Salis shouted. Caidos smiled, having saved that announcement for the last, knowing Salis's likely reaction. "How can you call that a culture, Caidos? No cities, no commerce? What are there, four of them sitting in a tent somewhere in the woods just talking to the animals?"

"You're more correct than you realize, Salis. They do have cities, just not the type you'd expect. They have no money because they have no needs that aren't fulfilled by the community in which they live. And there are far more Larians than there are Febronese. But the number four is very important to them. And, in a way, they do talk to the animals, but more correctly, they understand all animals. I'm most anxious to see what they make of Piritho."

Brandorin looked a little uneasy, but Caidos continued. "You may feel they're primitives, and know nothing compared to your modern civilization, Salis, but what they do know is life, all forms of it. And if you go there with an open mind, I think you'll find they have a great deal to teach you."

Caidos looked back at the horses, then turned to Brandorin to ask, "How did your 'work' on the horses go? Do you think it helped?"

"Oh, yes. I'd say they're fresh for another day like today, without a problem. Their muscles were tender and their tendons a bit swollen after today's push, but once I used the crystal, the swelling was down and there's no sign of tenderness."

"Good. Then I think we should all turn in for the night. I want to be up well before Day-Spring. Then soon after dawn, we'll head out. We'll continue south to Setabri where we'll take ship around the Axanas to reach the Larian shore. I want to cover as many miles each day as we can get out of the horses. They can rest once we are on the ship."

"Why get up before dawn, if we aren't leaving until after?" Salis asked.

"It may be for no reason at all, but I suspect we'll be visited in the morning," Caidos said.

"Do you think the Council will catch up to us?

"No, not the Council. If I thought that, we would have traveled farther before stopping, despite the darkness. No, this will be a friendly visit." But he would say no more.

"With that definite explanation of what awaits us in the morning, I know I'll be able to sleep soundly tonight," Salis said sarcastically, as he climbed under his blanket.

*   *   *

Despite his protests, Salis slept well. Enough that Brandorin had to shake him roughly to wake him. "It's still dark," he protested, trying to roll over and go back to sleep.

"I think you're going to want to see this," Brandorin said, seriously nudging him with the toe of his boot.

"If this is how this trip is going to be I may head back to Medora and take my chances with the Council," Salis said, as he grudgingly got to his feet.

The others were already up and they stood silently looking toward the road. The faint sound of many voices chanting and a low glimmer of light in the meadow between them and the road stopped any further complaints Salis may have been planning to voice. "What *is* that?" he whispered instead.

"Today will be the dawn of the new moon," Caidos said reverently. "It's the Shadow of Sefiron. I had hoped the combined presence of five fragments would draw it to us." He spoke in a whisper, not wanting to miss the song, or any message it would impart to them.

The light grew stronger, forming into an ephemeral image of a being or beings. As Dobbin had described so well, it was impossible to tell if it was male or female, yet it seemed to be both at once. The voices, too, were a harmonious mix of alto and soprano, bass and tenor, and they built to an exquisite crescendo that seemed to illuminate their very souls with its purity. They all felt renewed, as if they had reached the end of their journey and were reaping the reward, rather than having most of their struggle still ahead of them.

As the dawn began to lighten the sky over the eastern horizon, the song softened to a murmur, and the lights within began to swirl and pulse with colors none of them had ever seen before, nor had words to describe. The voices, though continuing their song, also spoke to them.

"Caidos, the Watcher, you are doing well, but there is much yet to do, and the time draws near. Only two cycles left. Beware the Life Stealer."

"Brandorin, Protector and Healer, you doubt yourself. Will you rise to the challenges ahead? Only you can say."

"M'drani, the Searcher. You fear that for which you search. Have faith and it will find you."

"Salis, the Builder. A testament for countless generations awaits you."

"Piritho, your sacrifice will be rewarded. Your time will come."

The sun crested the horizon and the Shadow and its song faded, until it was only an echo in their minds. None of them could speak or move, the experience of what they had seen and heard had left them numb.

## Chapter 13

The morning sky, marbled with feathery clouds, caught the light of the rising sun, replacing the fading lights of Sefiron's Shadow. The companions drifted back to the campsite in silence, trying to cling to the memory of the song and the feeling of joy and serenity it instilled in them. Brandorin's sense of wonder was no less for having seen the Shadow before.

Caidos was the first to recover from the effect of the Shadow's presence. "We must hurry; we have far less time than I had hoped for."

Salis, who didn't seem to have heard what Caidos said, asked, "Why do you think the voices singled me out like that? Do you think they meant the cathedral?"

"Singled you out? The Cathedral?" Brandorin said, shaking his head in confusion. He turned to Caidos, "What's happened that makes you think we have less time?"

"'Only two cycles left' they said. If this was only the second appearance, we should have five left."

"I didn't hear that," Salis said. "They talked about 'a testament'. I thought they meant me. It seemed like they were talking to me, but I guess it could have been all of us."

"I didn't hear anything about a testament," Brandorin said. "It was about a challenge. Then they said M'drani's name, then yours, then Piritho's, and then they faded away."

"You didn't hear that?" Salis said, his eyes bulging in disbelief. "It was so clear. Caidos, you must have heard it."

Caidos shook his head. "There wasn't anything about a testament or a challenge. Just that we have much to do, 'only two cycles left,' and to be careful of Rhamak."

"Rhamak?" Salis and Brandorin said simultaneously. Brandorin added, "They didn't say anything about Rhamak."

"Not directly. But who did you think the Life Stealer was?" Caidos asked.

"I didn't hear what any of you are talking about," M'drani

said. "I only heard what they said to me, just as each of you heard only what they said to you."

The looks of confusion on their faces slowly changed to wonder. "Of course," Caidos said. "The messages were very personal, and they were delivered in a personal manner. But 'two cycles left', which is one of the things they told me, can only mean one thing. We have less than half the time that I had hoped for. If we don't reunite the crystal within two full cycles of the moon, ninety days, we will fail and all of Zadania will pay the price."

\* \* \*

When they stopped to rest the horses, M'drani felt an urgent need to immediately take to the road again. She sensed they were being followed, at a distance, but the strong emotions of suspicion and vengeance carried across the miles that separated them from their pursuers. Caidos allowed only a brief stop for a midday meal, and pushed them hard for the rest of the day.

It was still two hours before sunset when M'drani reined in her horse as she shouted to the others, "We have to get off the road now." When the others had stopped too, she added, "I can feel them, feel their desperation as well as their vengeance. They're close, too close to outrun."

Brandorin surveyed the road ahead; it ran straight to the horizon, unhidden by trees or hills. "Those trees," he said, pointing across a wide meadow to a dense wood beyond, "would make an excellent cover and there are enough tracks on the road from other horses passing that ours won't be missed, but we'll leave a trail as we cross the meadow."

"I can take care of that," Caidos said. "You go ahead." As they sprinted across the meadow, Caidos walked Aquilo, his body turned in the saddle, aiming backward. The depressions made by their horses mysteriously rose back up behind them as Caidos created concentrated flows of air that lifted the bent grasses.

Once they were well hidden in the woods, Caidos asked, "M'drani, could you Search, to see how many are following us, and where they are now?"

"I was thinking I should, but wasn't sure it was a good idea."

"Stay high above the road. They will be looking ahead, not above."

The dove had been gone for only ten minutes when it returned and M'drani told them what she saw. "It's a good thing we stopped when we did, they were only a mile behind us. They rode right past where we exited the road. There are eight of them, and they were traveling very fast. "

Salis asked, "What were they wearing?"

"Dark gray robes, the hoods up. I don't know why but the sight of them made me uneasy. Their horses, their clothes, everything about them seemed colorless, as if the joy of life had been drained from them."

"That's a very good description. They are the Council's enforcers, the Watch. They track down those accused of using magic, what they call 'devilry', and bring them back to be tried and executed. They enjoy their work." He spat out the last statement, making it very clear what he thought of members of the Watch.

"What are the limits of their jurisdiction, Salis," Caidos asked.

"They've never gone any further south than Embara, which is a half day's ride from here. Most likely they'll turn around before reaching the outskirts of the city. The Embarans have made it very clear they don't approve of the Watch. They incarcerated the last patrol that entered their city, and threatened to put *them* on trial. I've always liked the Embarans."

"Then I say we camp here for the night," Brandorin said.

"There is still some light left," Caidos protested.

"Caidos, we can't push the horses any more today. Look how lathered they are; their breathing is beyond labored. We all know how urgent this is, but those short rests we took today were not enough. Much more and one of these horses will fall and break a leg. I don't know if I could heal that. Besides, if we continue, we could encounter the Watch on their way back if they turn around when they reach Embara."

Caidos reluctantly agreed, but added, "We are going to have to continue at this pace in the coming days. After what happened with Salis at the cathedral I am worried about the other fragment bearers, and our time is so short. Could you add a healing at midday, too?"

"I suppose so, but it may not be enough if we have to keep up this pace for too many days in a row."

"They will get a much deserved rest once we reach Setabri, where we will book passage on a ship, to go around the Axana Mountains."

"How many days will that be?"

"Six, or seven at most."

"That's longer than I'd like, but I'll see if I can make the evening sessions more intense."

M'drani, still sitting from her Search, struggled to stand, and Salis put out a hand to help her. She limped slightly as she walked over to the horses, to see to her palfrey.

"I can see how sore you are, M'drani," Brandorin said. "I'll take care of that shortly. If you don't mind, I'll help the horses first. I was very tired last night after healing them, but healing other people seems to refresh me too."

"Whatever you think is best. The horses did all of the work today, it's only right that they get taken care of first."

Brandorin began the process of grooming the horses and healing their overstrained muscles. He inspected their hooves for stones, and massaged their tender tendons, as he felt the surge of power from the crystal in the sword on his belt. When their small fire had had time to warm some water, he washed the lather from their sides, all the time talking softly to them, and easing their spirits as well as their muscles. M'drani watched him surreptitiously as she laid out the bedrolls.

Salis had collected the firewood, but now sat enjoying its meager warmth. Caidos stooped beside him, "What do you say we put you in charge of supplies and meal planning?"

"Sure, I can do that," Salis said. "I better go find something for our dinner then."

"Be careful, Salis," Caidos warned him. "Don't let anyone see you, and absolutely no ..."

"I know. I live here, remember. I know what's at stake."

Salis headed into the woods, returning a half an hour later brandishing a young wild turkey.

"Caidos thought he was sticking me with a thankless job, but you'll see I don't take my responsibilities lightly. We'll eat well tonight. Once I have cleaned and dressed this bird, and it starts to roast, I am going back for some more delicacies to add to our grand fare."

"You don't expect *me* to eat that bird, do you?" M'drani said.

Salis stammered in response, "Don't you ... I mean ... I didn't think ... You don't eat fowl?"

"Eat a bird! I couldn't. They're such beautiful, noble creatures. Soaring on high, moving with the winds, floating and climbing so gracefully. It's like a prayer. They must certainly have a soul. "

"But this is a wild turkey. I don't think it *can* fly, let alone soar," Salis said, getting his stride back. "It's really quite an ugly bird, actually."

M'drani gave him a look which told him his argument was feeble at best. "I couldn't," she insisted.

"All right. But you wouldn't mind if we did, would you?" Salis looked to Caidos and Brandorin for help. Caidos looked amused at his predicament, and Brandorin rather obviously looked away so he wouldn't have to answer.

"I can't expect others to change their habits for me," M'drani conceded.

"That's quite fair of you, my dear lady. I'll be sure to find some fresh root, vegetables or berries for your meal. But for future reference," he continued, as he looked at Caidos with a look of a man who knows he has been had, "do you eat meat at all: rabbit, deer, chicken... Oh, sorry, you know what I mean. How about fish?"

"Fish, yes, and some meat, but not a great deal. I don't eat much meat because I don't like the taste, feel it's heavy. Some N'varians, the Falconry for example, eat a great deal of meat. But my family, we eat mostly fruit, vegetables, grains, nuts, and beans."

Brandorin whispered to Caidos, "I should have eaten with the Falconry when we were there."

"I heard that, Brandorin," M'drani said without looking back at him.

Feeling it was better to be elsewhere, Brandorin said, "I better get some more wood for the fire, Salis. That bird will need a bit of roasting." Then very quietly to Salis, as he passed him on his way to the woods he added, "But it'll be worth the wait."

"I heard that, too," M'drani said, and Brandorin, being as smart as he was brave, chose not to respond.

Salis, considerate of M'drani's sensibilities, took the bird downstream, out of sight, to prepare it for cooking. By the time he returned, Brandorin had stoked up a sizable fire. Roasting the bird whole would have taken hours, so Salis had cut the bird into pieces, wrapped them in grass and packed them in mud. He placed them in the hot coals where they could roast. Brandorin promised to keep an eye on the cooking while Salis went back into the woods to find something for M'drani, who decided to accompany him.

"I don't think she likes me too much, Caidos," Brandorin said after they had gone.

"Why do you say that?"

"She makes me nervous. I never seem to say the right thing."

"I've noticed that. Why do you think that is? You don't seem to be tongue-tied with me, or Salis."

"I guess it's because she can read my mind. I always feel I have to be so careful around her, yet I keep making a mess of it."

"She doesn't go around reading people's thoughts all day, Brandorin. She can do it if she concentrates, but it's like reading. Unless you look directly at the words on the page, you don't know what it says. Reading a person's thoughts without their consent would be, well, rude. She wouldn't do it."

"Oh, that's good to know," Brandorin said, feeling relieved. "It doesn't seem to bother Salis. He's always sweet-talking her. He makes a big mistake with the turkey for dinner, and the next thing you know she's going off into the woods with him."

"Strong emotions will come through to her unbidden. You've seen that happen. Like the emotions coming from the Watch. Fear, anger, or hatred, for example, she can feel, even from a distance. Love, or care or concern, she'll get a sense of, but only when close."

"What do you mean?" Brandorin asked.

"Well, for example, what happened with that bird. M'drani could tell Salis was trying to please her, not offend her. Not only by his actions, but also by her internal senses. She would've been able to feel his concern. I would imagine that's why she went with him; to let him know she wasn't offended by what happened.

"You or I would get a similar sense of someone's intentions by looking in their eyes. By their stance, their mannerisms, though to a lesser degree..." Caidos glanced sideways at Brandorin before continuing, "and perhaps not as accurately. M'drani and most of her family have more of an inner sense for such things. They feel it rather than see it. Understand?"

"I guess so," Brandorin said turning the turkey in the coals.

They heard the sound of M'drani's laughter coming from the woods. She and Salis soon followed, both with an armload of apples. They set the apples down only seconds before they would have fallen from their arms.

"Oh, Caidos, you should have seen him. He was magnificent," M'drani said, as she sat down on the ground next to the Mage.

"It wasn't that special, M'drani," Salis said, "Maybe you shouldn't bother Caidos with it."

"What were you doing, Salis?" Caidos asked suspiciously.

"We were very careful, Caidos," M'drani explained. "I Searched the area; we're the only people for miles. There was this tree, and it was covered with these big beautiful apples. Look at them," she declared, as she picked one up for their inspection. Brandorin noticed how enthusiasm lit her face and sparked her violet eyes.

"But there was this rather large bull in the field with the tree, and every time we tried to climb the fence to get some of the apples, he would come running up and chase us away."

"A fence?" Brandorin asked. "That means the tree was on someone's farm. You stole their apples."

M'drani stared at him, then she turned to Salis and said, "Kind of reminds you of that bull, doesn't he?"

Brandorin held his hands up in surrender, and turned back to the fire as M'drani continued. "It was obvious the bull wasn't going to let us get in there to get any apples. I was ready to walk away and see what else we could find, when Salis here," she said, placing her hand on his arm, "said he could take care of things." Brandorin noticed the gesture and let out a little snort.

"I wasn't going to let him get gored, but he didn't have to go inside the fence. Suddenly the apples started rising up from the ground under the tree, and floating over to us, all by themselves. We were alone," she added when she saw the concern on Caidos' face.

"But most of the apples from the ground were wormy or rotten," Salis said, "so I started picking them off the tree."

"That bull looked as surprised as a human would have been," M'drani said laughing again. "He started pawing the ground, and snorting, and I thought he was going to storm the fence. But by that time, Salis had gotten more apples than we could carry anyway. We grabbed up as many as we could, and we ran almost all the way back. I haven't done anything like that since I was a child."

She sat back, with a smile of contentment on her face, and picking up one of the apples, she wiped it off on her pants leg, and took a big bite. She kept smiling as she chewed her apple and wiped the juice from her chin. "They're so good," she said as soon as she could, "So sweet and juicy."

Caidos was visibly upset over Salis' use of magic. "I'm glad you checked the area, M'drani." He turned and glared at Salis before continuing, "because Salis doesn't seem to have enough sense to know when he's doing something dangerous. The Watch is on our trail and we're still within a hundred miles of Medora and ..., and ... it's just foolhardy taking such chances."

His voice had slowly started to rise as he talked, until at the end he squeaked out, "For apples."

"I'm sorry, Caidos," M'drani said.

"M'drani, it's not you I'm worried about. I warned you yesterday, Salis, when you were levitating that stack of wood. And now we are being chased ..."

"You weren't carrying that wood?" Brandorin jumped in. "I took that from you because I thought you were straining under the load."

"Don't pick on him," M'drani said, coming to Salis' defense.

"I wasn't picking on him." Brandorin said defensively, then to Salis in a conspiratorial whisper, "That was actually pretty good. You had me fooled. No one else would have known, Caidos."

"You're teasing the tiger," he said, as he jumped up, ruffling his hair into a tangle of frustration. "We can't afford to get cooked in that pot right now." Caidos stalked off muttering to himself.

"What does that mean?" Brandorin asked.

"It means he's very upset with me," Salis said. "He's misquoting his own proverbs, mixing them up, which means he's very angry. He asked me yesterday to wait a couple of days. It's just been so long, and I was trying to ..." He stopped. "He's right. I shouldn't have done it, even if there's no one else around. I know he's worried about the other bearers and our deadline. What I did didn't help any. I'll go apologize and promise not to do it again until he says we're clear." Salis got up and followed after Caidos.

"I guess I made it worse, by making him seem like a hero," M'drani said to Brandorin, after Salis was gone. "Maybe I should go apologize too."

"No!" Brandorin blurted out. "I don't think that's necessary. Salis will smooth it over."

Brandorin struggled for something to talk about, choosing

something that seemed safe. "Can I try one of those apples?"

He bit into the apple, the crunch loud in the quiet woods. He added in a muffled voice, "They *are* good,"

They sat without talking, as they both ate their apples. "I think Salis was trying to impress you," he finally said to break the uncomfortable silence.

"Why would he want to do that?" she said.

"He likes you."

"I like him too, but why …? Oh, what a sweet little man. I guess I'll have to be careful with him. I don't want to give him the wrong idea."

"Couldn't you tell how he felt? I thought you could…"

"Read people's minds," she finished for him. "It's not like that, Brandorin. I can read feelings, somewhat, but not more than a person wants me to know."

"I'm beginning to realize that," he said, starting to feel at ease. "Will it bother you to watch us eat this bird?"

"I guess I feel the way you would if someone were eating a horse, or a dog."

"Understood. No more bird for dinner. There's enough other things to eat."

A silence followed, no longer uncomfortable, punctuated by an occasional crunching sound as they each finished their apples.

Caidos and Salis returned to the campfire, and as they sat back down, Salis told them, "I've promised Caidos I'll wait until he says it's safe. But when he does, watch out, because I'm going to need to stretch."

"Where is Piritho, Brandorin?" Caidos asked.

"He's off hunting his dinner. Why?"

"We've been careless with him so far, letting him run along the road with us. Very few people travel between Medora and Embara, but if the Watch saw him, they'd declare him to be a demon and would hunt him down and kill him, and us along with him. If the Watch has any doubts about us, Piritho's traveling with us would just seal our fate. Can you call him? Would he come if he heard you?"

"If he hears me, he'll come back. It's going to depend on how far away he is," Brandorin said as he got up, calling and whistling. After a few minutes, Piritho trotted into the clearing, preceded by a small flock of birds.

"I told him about your worries. He appreciates your concern. What do you think we should do?" Brandorin said.

"The farther south we go, the safer we'll be," Caidos said. "Tomorrow we'll be passing through Embara. It's not as large a town as either Medora or Setabri, nor are they as superstitious about magic as the Medorans, but I don't think they'll accept Piritho as a large dog. The road swings around to the west about four miles before Embara.

"When we start heading west on the road, Piritho, I think it would be best for you to continue straight south, through the woods the road sweeps around. If you head straight south, you'll come out of the woods well past Embara, and we can rejoin you there."

"There's a small village down there," Salis added. "He'll have to swing around it to the east, but just beyond it there's a rather dense stand of pine and beech trees. It's not a good place for hunting, so it should be a good meeting place. That is if Piritho can be made to understand all that."

Piritho barked and sort of nodded his head, making it apparent he did in fact understand.

"Maybe Salis should go with him, Caidos," Brandorin suggested. "They're most likely to recognize Salis, and it will change our numbers."

"That might be the best plan. M'drani and I can handle the provisions, but there's something else..."

"What other things?" Brandorin asked when he realized Caidos was hesitant to discuss whatever was on his mind.

"South of there, all the way to Setabri, the roads are more traveled," Caidos said. "From a distance people are likely to think Piritho's a small horse, but on closer inspection it's impossible to accept either. I no longer see him as dangerous, but a passing stranger is more likely to run in fear."

When Piritho protested with a low growl, Caidos added, "I'm sorry, Piritho, that's how it's likely to be." Caidos stopped, throwing his hands up in exasperation. "There I go again."

"It's hard not to when you get to know him," Brandorin said.

"Getting him into Setabri and onto a boat is going to be impossible, unless ..."

"Go ahead, Caidos. You won't hurt his feelings."

"I fear we're going to have to buy a wagon and a cage." Piritho snarled, dissatisfied with the way the conversation was going. "It's either that or you won't be able to come with us the rest of the way. I can think of no other way to get you through Setabri and onto a ship. And that's the only way to get to Laria."

"You can ride in the wagon, Piritho, next to the cage, until we meet people on the road," Brandorin said, trying to make the best of the situation. "At night you'll be fine with us by the campfire, like this. You'll only have to stay in the cage once we reach the outskirts of Setabri and until we land in Laria. Right, Caidos?"

"Yes, they like all animals there."

Piritho made no sound to indicate he accepted or rejected the idea, but he rose up on his front legs, and swiveling around, turned his back on them, his nose in the air, indignation evident in every muscle. "It's better than being left behind. Why don't you sleep on it? See how you feel in the morning."

\* \* \*

Rhamak reached for another slice of apple, eating it as distractedly as he had the rest of the meal. Chaubrel stood at the sideboard waiting for the right moment to tell him of the falcon's return. Although he knew it was risky to delay, he also knew that the news from the falcon could be good or bad, and whenever he told Rhamak, he would have to accompany him to the solar.

Chaubrel was interested in a savory rabbit stew Rhamak had ignored. Though he knew the servants feared Rhamak, they disliked Chaubrel's favored status, and he was sure the stew would be gone before he returned. But if Rhamak left the table before he was finished, no one would dare clear the foods away.

Seeing that Rhamak was not enjoying his meal anyway, Chaubrel passed on the news.

"Does he have the stone?" Rhamak asked, jumping up from his seat and striding out of the room.

"They didn't say, sire," Chaubrel answered, following closely behind him. "They knew you were anxious to hear of the falcon's return."

The solar was directly above the dining hall. Rhamak hurried to the stairs, and taking the steps two at a time, he soon reached the solar. He brushed past the other birds, and went immediately to the peregrine falcon's perch. He waved his hand across the bird, and the air shimmered and once again, Willem stood cowering in front of Rhamak.

"I fear your news is not good," Rhamak said, his voice low and controlled. Chaubrel was not fooled by the soothing tones. Like a peacefully flowing river, the underlying stone of his heart was moss covered from lack of use and treacherous to tread upon.

Willem was quick to defend himself. "I have other news for you, my Lord, aside from the attack at the Cathedral. About what happened after."

"Fine, let me see," Rhamak said. Willem reluctantly raised his head, hesitating for only a second before meeting Rhamak's tawny gaze.

Rhamak stared into Willem's eyes, and was soon viewing his memories. Rhamak was not happy with the results of Willem's and Jarvin's efforts. He was even less happy with Caidos' appearance and interference.

"What's your other news, Willem? It will have to be very special to save you from joining your brother.

"The beast rides with them? That's an interesting twist, but good news. Is that all you have?

"Yes, the Shadow, I've seen it. Months ago. That's nothing new." Rhamak released Willem from his gaze, having seen all that interested him, but the man was still frozen where he stood.

"You did what I asked of you, Willem. You won't return to the form of the falcon." Willem heaved a sigh of relief.

"It was your brother that failed me," Rhamak continued, "but he is beyond my punishments. He deprived me of that pleasure as well. But without your brother, you are no good to me as a messenger anymore." Something in his voice caused Willem to shiver. Chaubrel held his breath, waiting for the sentence.

"But you will be good for a meal or two." The look of confusion on Willem's face didn't last long. Rhamak waved his hand and instead of a man standing before him there was a rabbit. Rhamak turned and walked from the solar, petting a large hawk as he passed it on its perch. "Enjoy."

Rhamak was already out of the room when the hawk leapt from its perch at the rabbit, still immobile. Chaubrel watched as the hawk reached its prey and began to use its sharp beak and talons, and a scream, both animal and human, broke the silence in the solar.

"Come, Chaubrel, time to finish our dinner."

Chaubrel turned to follow Rhamak and decided he was glad he had not already eaten. He wasn't sure he would be able to eat this evening, but if he did, he knew it would not be the rabbit stew.

## Chapter 14

They continued their journey south under an overcast sky and a curtain of drizzle; clouds as gray as the Watch's robes sailed like a flotilla of ships across a sea of trees. When the road turned to the west as Caidos had predicted, Piritho headed off into the woods, without a backward glance.

"I'm not sure what's worse," Salis said as he turned to follow, "running into the Watch on the road, or traipsing around in the woods with - our furry friend." Salis gave them a mock salute as he entered the wood, and they turned to follow the road as it curved to the west.

They stopped in Embara, picking up provisions and buying a wagon. They selected an old one, since it would only be needed for four days, and would be left behind in Setabri, but it proved difficult to find a cage large enough to accommodate Piritho. They ended up taking the tops off of two large cages and having a blacksmith connect them together sideways.

The blacksmith was concerned that the makeshift cage would not be strong enough to hold an animal large enough to fill it, but the companions knew it was only for appearance sake. After buying more supplies, they left Embara behind, and soon reached the designated meeting place where Salis waited under the sheltering arms of a hemlock tree.

Caidos, who was driving the wagon, pulled by Salis' horse with Aquilo in tow, veered off the road toward Salis' refuge.

"Piritho waiting in the woods?" Brandorin asked, as he surveyed the trees in search of the beast.

Salis hesitated before answering, looking everywhere except at Brandorin. "I don't know where he is."

"What do you mean? What happened?"

"We got separated."

"Separated? How?" Brandorin said, the first sign of worry now creeping into his voice.

"He ran off to the east, when we should have been heading

south. I tried to tell him ... Maybe he just doesn't understand me as well as he does you."

"Maybe he changed his mind about going with," Caidos suggested. "He didn't seem to like the idea of riding in the cage."

"No, he wants to go with us," Brandorin said. He started to pace along the edge of the wood, peering through the thick trees. "Something has happened to him. I don't like this. If he's not here soon, I'm going looking for him."

"Look where? Through the entire forest between here and where he left us," Caidos pointed out. "He'll show up after you've gone, then we'll have to go looking for you."

"I could Search for him," M'drani volunteered.

"That's probably the best idea, but you should go into the woods before you ...," Caidos began to say, but he was interrupted by rustling deep in the woods, that got increasingly louder. Then a single muffled bark.

A moment later, Piritho sprinted out of the woods. Caidos was about to say something, but stopped when he realized the urgency of the beast's flight. Piritho sprinted for the wagon and jumped in; trying to hide under the cloth they had gotten to cover the cage, just as a group of five men ran out of the woods where Piritho had emerged moments before. M'drani already standing by the wagon, covered him with the cloth.

They were carrying pikes and clubs. They looked in every direction, searching for something. They all shouted at once.

"Did you see it?"

"Did it come through here?"

"It's as big as a horse, you couldn'a missed it."

"Maybe we lost it in the woods."

Salis was the first to respond, speaking in an excited manner, matching the tone of the farmers or hunters. "What was that thing? I never saw anything like it. It came crashing out of the woods, and almost ran me over." They responded to his cries, and looked to him for direction.

"It took off for the woods on the other side of the road," he continued. As he pointed across the road, "There, toward that stand of trees. You can see its tracks going in," he added as he pointed to the flattened footprints in the moisture-laden grass on the far side of the road. The prints trailed from the road, across the grass and into the trees.

The men ran in the indicated direction, and were soon out of sight.

Brandorin stared at the prints that ran across the field, knowing Piritho had not gone that far.

"Come on. We have to go now," Salis said in an urgent whisper. "Do you want to wait until they come back?"

Salis detached Aquilo's reins from the wagon and jumped in. He drove off, expecting to be followed. He was several hundred feet down the road by the time the rest remounted and started after him. They galloped for over two miles. The road had curved twice; the place where they had waited no longer visible. Slowing to a walk, Brandorin, Caidos and M'drani pulled up and rode alongside the wagon as they continued south.

"I'm sorry, Caidos, I had to do it. There was no time to ask permission," Salis said.

"I thought so. You were right, Salis. There was no other way," Caidos responded.

"What are you two talking about?" Brandorin asked, as Piritho sat up in the back of the wagon, and the cloth slipped off. He was still panting, despite the ten minutes of rest he'd had in the back of the wagon. He was wet, and his fur was matted and full of burrs.

"I created the trail for those men to follow," Salis admitted. "Piritho's prints were obvious in the grass between the woods and the back of the wagon. I used my power to push the grass down in spots, to try to make it look like he had run straight across the road into the other woods.

"They weren't good trackers, I could tell by the way they were looking around when they came out of the woods. They weren't looking down at the marks in the grass; they were looking for Piritho himself."

"Quick thinking, Salis," Brandorin said, the admiration clear in his voice. Piritho added his thanks with a big sloppy lick on the side of Salis' face.

"You're welcome, Piritho," Salis said, as he wiped the beast's gratitude off his face.

"I would guess they were farmers; they saw Piritho and thought he was after their sheep or cattle." Caidos' speculation was confirmed by a quick decisive bark from the back of the wagon. "He must have had to run them in circles, to delay until we got there." Another bark.

"If he had come out of those woods before we arrived, he would have had to do exactly what Salis said he did. I take it you aren't questioning my reasons for the wagon anymore, are you, Piritho?" The last statement received a reluctant snort, the closest to agreement that Caidos was likely to receive.

"We saw some men in Embara who looked like members of the Watch," Brandorin said, "and even though Salis is sure they'll head back north now, I think we should put some distance between ourselves and both the Watch and those farmers."

They'd had a brief lunch while in Embara, and Salis had eaten while waiting for Piritho, so they rode straight through to nightfall, putting over twenty miles behind them by the time they stopped. They chose a secluded section of wood, well off the road, even though it was not close to a source of water. They had full water bags and were a quarter mile from a small stream, if they needed more.

Piritho did not go hunting that night; Caidos suspected he had given the farmers good reason for chasing him. After Brandorin healed the beast's aching muscles and the few cuts he had suffered from his chase in the woods, Piritho stayed close to the fire and the companions.

*   *   *

"Salis, you showed good judgment the other day, saving Piritho," Caidos said. "You used your power, but it was an emergency, and you were discreet. We're three days from Embara and there has been no further sign of the Watch. If you can maintain that level of discretion, I think it's safe for you to start stretching those muscles now."

"I notice you're telling me this after we collected firewood, and after we carried everything from the wagon, but I appreciate the trust," Salis responded.

The next morning Salis used his liberty to move supplies to the wagon and to take care of cleaning up. Unused firewood was scattered back into the woods, and dirt was moved to cover the remains of the campfire, all without any visible help. By the time they left, there was no sign they had been there. Caidos voiced no complaint, knowing they would not be observed this far into the woods.

They had left the wagon just inside the forest; the trees were too close for it to be driven any further, but it was so old, it looked like it had been abandoned there. The ride in the wagon across the meadow had been very bumpy. Piritho had jumped out after a minute of bouncing and ran the rest of the way. When Caidos noticed the return trip back to the road was so smooth they seemed to be riding on a well-packed road, he glared at Salis, who shrugged and gave Caidos a can't-blame-a-man-for-trying look and the wagon resumed its bouncy jaunt across the field.

Out of the shelter of the trees, the sky churned with roiling, dark clouds, sparked by sporadic lightning. The wind kept the clouds moving before them. Though it kept them dry, they were forced to pull out their warmer cloaks and put up the collars against the cold wind at their backs. The howling winds competed with any attempts to talk, so they road in silence seeking warmth in their separate cocoons.

Brandorin caught movement out of the corner of his eye. A dark bluish-green creature swooped down from the sky, directly at Caidos, sweeping in close enough to lift the hood off his head. Brandorin drew his sword and pulled Bristo around to face Caidos. He was standing in his stirrups, ready to strike as the creature came back for another pass.

Brandorin brought the sword up and began the swing

toward the creature in a blurred motion. Caidos shouted, "No" as he saw Brandorin strike. The movement of the sword and arm slowed and Brandorin's face strained to fight against an unseen barrier. He stopped as he saw the creature come to rest on Aquilo's back, and nestle down in front of Caidos.

What appeared to be a cat-size dragon flicked its tail and flexed leathery wings before furling them. Odd crackling and gurgles emanated from the creature; they seemed to indicate its contentment as Caidos stroked it and talked to it.

"I'm sorry she scared you, Brandorin," Caidos said. "This is a friend of mine, Zephyr. She's a firedrake. She's just a young one, only five years old. She'll reach a size of about three feet in length when she's fully-grown; by then she'll be able to live up to her name. Firedrakes are called that because the adults can breathe fire, just like the legendary dragons of old. She's just learning how to do that."

"Was that one of your air cushions that stopped my arm?" Brandorin asked.

"Yes. I was as surprised as you were by her arrival," Caidos said, as he looked around and both up and down the road.

"Is there another one?"

"No, but Zephyr didn't arrive here by herself. I left her in Artara with my apprentice, who I suspect will be joining us shortly." Two minutes later a horse could be heard approaching from the south; a girl on a tan stallion rode up to join them. She appeared to be in her late teens, and she wore the brown robes of a mage.

"Zephyr, you found him, good girl. Caidos, I brought you important news," the girl said as she reined her horse in next to the Mage.

"Icara Mar, my apprentice. This is Brandorin Adamaran, from Kartir, and M'drani E'varania from B'zuri. Salis you already know." A loud bark from the back of the wagon caused him to add, "and that's Piritho, origin unknown. What is this news?"

Icara looked at Caidos' traveling companions, hesitant about making an announcement in front of them. "Maybe we should talk privately," she said.

"If it's about Sefiron, they have the right to hear it. They are the Protector and the Healer," he said pointing to Brandorin, "the Searcher and the Builder," he finished, indicating M'drani and Salis in turn.

Icara's look of surprise was almost comical as she stared at Salis and then back at Caidos. "I didn't know ... you never said ..."

"Icara," Caidos said with a slight tone of command. "You have some important news?"

She reached into her saddlebag and pulled out a roll of parchment with a dramatic flourish. "This scroll appeared in the midst of Didonno's scrolls. I know I haven't studied them as much as you have, but I know this one was never there before."

"Let me see that," Caidos said, reaching for the scroll Icara held, his lips pursed in a skeptical frown. After taking a cursory look at the scroll, Caidos' eyes widened and the frown was replaced with a wide grin.

"It's definitely Didonno's writing, but I've never seen it before. This must be the scroll the Shadow mentioned in Kartir, Brandorin." Caidos looked around him, debating the best course of action. "I have to read this immediately, but I don't want to delay our journey."

"You can ride in the wagon with me, Caidos," Salis said. "You can read while I drive."

\* \* \*

After reading through the scroll three times, Caidos returned to his horse, riding alongside Brandorin.

"Part of what's in this scroll concerns you," Caidos told him. "It indirectly answers the question we had on that first morning of our journey."

"What question?"

"About when you became the Healer. It happened the moment you picked up the sword."

"What? What are you saying?" The disbelief in Brandorin's voice surprised Caidos.

"This new scroll indicates an enhanced role for the Protector. It says the Protector will be able to draw on the powers of any of the fragments 'at need'." Caidos' voice crackled with excitement. "I think that means you could use any of the fragments if the bearer of that fragment could not do so. You were able to heal from the moment you took the sword."

Caidos waited for Brandorin to comment, but he did not. When Caidos turned in his saddle, he was surprised by a single tear trailing down Brandorin's face. "What is it, Brandorin? I consider this to be good news."

"It was only a couple of minutes. If I had known ... I might have been able to save her."

"Ilona," Caidos whispered, as he remembered that Brandorin had taken his father's sword only minutes after Ilona had been killed by the beast that now rode in the wagon behind them. Brandorin prodded Bristo's flanks and spurred out ahead of the rest of the party.

\* \* \*

Icara joined them on their journey south, riding along with Caidos, while he told her of recent events: from hearing about the Shadow's appearance near Kartir to saving Salis at the cathedral and their journey from Medora.

"Caidos, considering what country we're in, I was surprised to feel you using your power before. Zephyr felt it too, that's why she took off and got so far ahead of me."

"That was Salis going a little crazy with his new-found freedom. He's promised to be discreet. Then I had to stop Brandorin from splitting Zephyr in two. I'm sure he thought it was another raptor attack. How long have you been looking for me?"

"Almost five weeks. The scroll must have appeared after the first cycle, six months ago, but I didn't see it right away. After I found it, everyone debated what to do for a couple of weeks. But when the next supply ship came through, I decided it couldn't wait any longer, so I grabbed the scroll and Zephyr and came looking for you."

"Good for you," Caidos said with pride. "Those old fools will still be debating when we're finished."

"I got to Kartir about a week after you'd been there. I've been following your trail ever since. I must have passed you while you were in the woods, but I felt the use of power, so I turned around and came back and that's when we found you."

"You made the right decision, Icara. I needed to see this scroll. You read it, I assume." When she nodded, he continued, "The Kordunan fragment is no longer an issue. I've debated sending you back, to tell the rest of the Order what is happening, but I think having you here will be helpful in making another. It may be dangerous, and I am worried for your safety, but we must succeed."

"You'll be glad I'm with you before this is all over," she said with bravado.

"I'm glad now," Caidos added.

## Chapter 15

When they made camp for the night, as Brandorin went through his nightly ritual of grooming and healing the horses, Caidos walked over to talk to him. He accepted Caidos' apology for not connecting the timing between acquiring the sword and Ilona's death, but silently focused on his task, until the mage quietly walked away.

Caidos sat apart from the rest of the companions, talking with Icara, referring often to the scroll the young mage had brought with her. Brandorin watched him, thinking he had been abrupt with the older mage. It was not his fault after all, and even knowing he could heal at that time could not have brought Ilona back from the dead. He finished grooming and healing the horses and strolled over to the mages, not wanting to interrupt, but wanting to make up for his curtness earlier.

"But where will we get that?" Icara was asking.

"It's possible the Larians could have one, but even more likely that the Arkhanians will," Caidos said.

"Anything I can help with?" Brandorin asked, and the two mages looked up as he approached.

"You wouldn't happen to have a Kordunan artifact on you, would you?" Icara joked.

"No, I'm afraid not," Brandorin said with a bit of confusion, not able to see the relevancy in the question.

"My young apprentice is making light of a very serious situation," said Caidos, who despite his serious tone, had a twinkle of pleasure in his eyes for the first time since before they first entered Febron.

"My concern of getting to the other three fragment bearers in time has not been the only worry weighing on me. You may recall that on that first night of our journey together, Brandorin, I mentioned the Kordunan fragment that has been missing for over 250 years. I have been concerned that we may not be able to complete the rejoining if we don't have that fragment."

"Just vaguely. There were a lot of new ideas I had to get a grasp of that night," said Brandorin.

"Didonno's scrolls have intimated that if a fragment was lost or broken that there would be 'other options'. There has been great debate among the Mages of Artara over this point in the scrolls. What it means or doesn't mean."

Seeing the look of concern and confusion on Brandorin's face, Caidos hastened to add, "That is why I haven't mentioned it before this." He pointed at Brandorin's face. "I didn't want to worry you, because I have been confident that something could be done about it."

"Why would you jump to that conclusion?" Brandorin asked.

"It's not really a jump. In the 3900's a Dark Age began, especially in Febron, and the bearer of the Febronese fragment, a man by the name of Gharvik, started using the fragment's gift to wield power over his people. Sefiron's Shadow appeared to direct the Mirador to gather the other bearers and stop Gharvik. Ultimately it was those times and Gharvik's actions that lead to the Medoran distaste for magic.

"At that time, a new scroll appeared among Didonno's original twenty-one scrolls. It had never been there before, but then one day, there it was. It gave very specific instructions on how to select a new bearer of the Febronese fragment. That is when it was given to Salis' ancestors.

"The World Shapers, who gave us the fragments to begin with, have provided the necessary information we need to use them properly, and to deal with problems. Problems that may seem unexpected to us, but were anticipated by the Sefiramon."

"And the new scroll tells us how to make a new fragment to replace the Kordunan's lost fragment," Icara said quickly.

"I was getting to that," said Caidos, giving her the look of a teacher who has had his moment of revelation stolen from him by his star pupil.

"Sorry," muttered Icara.

"So you need a Kordunan artifact to make this new fragment?" Brandorin asked, agreeing with Icara that this was not a time for a history lesson.

"That would be necessary for someone other than the Mirador," Caidos answered. "But the Crown piece has the essence of all other fragments. Once we have all the fragments, except the Kordunan, the Crown piece will sense which fragment is not present and we'll be able to make the missing one."

"Then why were you asking about an artifact?" Brandorin asked Icara.

"Because I thought that if we had one, we could try to make one now, before we had the rest of the pieces collected."

"Not waiting until the last minute isn't a bad idea," Brandorin said.

"We won't be waiting until the last minute, "Caidos pointed out. "We can start collecting the other things we'll need once we're in Laria. We will need a piece of Zadanite to make the new fragment. We can find it in either Laria or Arkhan. Even if we had the Zadanite, we couldn't make it in Febron. It is very strong and visible magic. We would not be able to hide what we were doing.

"At least I can rest easy about the missing fragment. It's the other bearers and the road we have yet to travel that concerns me."

"It may not seem like much time, Caidos, but we can do it," said Icara. "We have almost two months to get through Laria, Ilyan and north to Arkhan. You've come this far in a little over a month."

Caidos smiled, though it didn't last long; the weight he carried was evident in his tired eyes and bowed back. "There won't be roads like this in Laria and Ilyan. We won't be able to travel as fast. If there has been as much rain in the east as we've had in the west, the going will be rough. We can do it, if we're not delayed. Rhamak has tried at least three times to interfere. He'll try again, we can be sure of that.

"That worries me, but I also have a nagging feeling that there is something I am forgetting. Something about the first three appearances of the Shadow. Rhamak is a problem we know of. Whatever I am forgetting makes me think there is a problem we don't know about."

\*   \*   \*

The remainder of the journey to Setabri passed without event, and M'drani had no further sense of being pursued. The volatile nature of the weather continued, overcast and drizzly one day, torrential rain and powerful winds the next. Brandorin cursed the need for the wagon often, as it got mired in the mud and the slippery ruts in the road at least three or four times a day. The only good thing about the terrible weather was that most travelers stayed in, so that when they were alone on the road, Salis could help get the wheels out of the ruts.

The one good thing about the wagon, and Icara's presence, was that they no longer looked like the group the Watch was after. On the clearer days, the traffic on the road surpassed Caidos' predictions and slowed them down, but they took advantage of the congestion whenever possible, riding along behind other groups to appear to be a part of them.

When a particularly large group of an extended family, their children and goats took up the road, heading north, the companions pulled their horses to the side of the road to let them pass rather than buffet their way through. Brandorin listened to their gentle banter about purchases at the market, smiling as he felt some of the tension of their frenzied pace leave him. He noticed Caidos' impatience, and though he understood the mage's concern, he couldn't help but wonder how the mage could seem to be pacing while sitting on a stationary horse.

Piritho remained in the cage while they were on the road, and limited his roaming to within a few hundred feet of the campsite at night. The last day of travel before reaching the outskirts of the city had them passing or being passed by another group of travelers at least three times an hour.

Setabri was situated due west of the Axana Mountains, which formed a natural barrier between Febron and Laria. The terrain surrounding Setabri was hilly, and all along the road north of the city, the Mountains could be seen on the eastern horizon, stark and foreboding, their tops snow-covered and their passes narrow and treacherous. Clouds heavy with rain seemed stuck to their peaks, threatening to release a torrent with little or no warning.

Though the land was fertile, it undulated with low hills and narrow valleys. Farmers had created stepped terraces to plant their crops, which they carted into Setabri at harvest time. From there it was shipped to ports of call throughout the west.

When they reached the crest of the last hill before the city, they pulled the wagon off the road at a secluded spot and made their plans.

"Salis, you and I know the city best," said Caidos, "so why don't we split up. You take Brandorin and M'drani and get some more provisions, while Icara and I go down to the docks and book us passage around the mountains to Laria. Take the wagon and Piritho with you. I think it would be best for one of you to stay with him at all times. We don't want a curious official looking under that cloth while you are all inside a shop.

"Meet us at the docks when you've finished," Caidos continued, "we'll wait for you at The Laden Vessel Inn. Don't take too long. If I am not mistaken, there'll be an outbound tide this evening, so we may be able to leave right away. It shouldn't take more than an hour or two for each of us to do what's needed."

*   *   *

Setabri sat at the edge of a natural harbor, protected on the east by an offshoot of the Axana Mountains, which jutted out into the Mardanic Sea for over a mile. The city had sprawled out to the foot of the mountains on the east and stretched for three miles along the shore to the west.

When looking at the city from the hills to the north, Caidos could see where Salis had learned such a love of buildings. There were buildings of every style and size; some of them seeming to mirror the high peaks of the mountains, with tall spires and towers sprouting from every corner. Others seemed to mimic the farms in the surrounding countryside, sporting stepped terraces and balconies providing more rooftops and windows.

It was a city controlled by its surroundings, but driven by trade. Though a third the size of Kartir, it boasted of commerce surpassing that of the larger city. Most people would agree Setabri was the busier port. The docks were always filled with ships waiting to unload their cargo and take on more, with additional ships waiting at anchor out in the harbor for the next available pier. It was because of this continual flow of ships, that Caidos felt confident in finding one to take them to Laria.

The companions separated soon after entering the city. Caidos and Icara headed for the docks, with Zephyr hiding in the folds of Caidos' robes. On reaching the docks, they were swallowed by the currents of men flowing around the many ships anchored there.

Most ships were in some stage of loading or unloading cargo. Crewmen worked barefooted and without shirts; their tan, muscular backs straining with the weight of the crates and barrels they wrestled in or out of the holds. They glistened with the sweat of their labors despite the coolness of the autumn breezes blowing in from the sea. The energy of the bustling workers and the sharp tang of the sea air revived Caidos who was tired from the sustained pace he had been setting. Brandorin's healings revived him physically each evening but the responsibility of their goal carried a weight that Brandorin could not relieve.

As they walked along the piers, Caidos saw a ship he had sailed on many times: the Noki, named after a legendary water sprite. As they walked out onto the dock that berthed the Noki, a booming voice, rising above the noises of the many other ships at the pier, drew their attention to a muscular man standing in the middle of the deck. His leathery skin was tanned to a golden bronze. His shaved head and bare torso displayed tattoos of every legendary creature of the sea. From the sprite for which his ship was named, to the giant dragon-like serpents said to roam the depths of the oceans before the World Shapers calmed the chaos. He didn't bark the orders at the crew, but seemed to croon at them, his commands sounding more like an old sea shanty.

In the midst of his chant, he noticed them approaching, and he raised his hand in a salute. He shouted, "Caidos, you old Mage! May the Gods Shape you! I suppose you'll be wanting to go to Laria again. I don't know why you keep going there," he bellowed as he loped down the gangplank toward them to meet Caidos on the dock. "But don't ask a Mage his business; you're just wasting your breath." He reached Caidos, and wrapped him in a bear hug, lifting him from his feet in the process.

"We're forgetting our manners, Caidos. Who is your fair companion?" he asked, as he took Icara's hand and bowed over it, so she could clearly see the mermaid on the top of his head, and the fearsome octopus on the back.

After he had kissed her hand she exclaimed, "That's not a mustache!"

"You're a smart one, you are. Fools most people." Largo stroked the twin sea serpents facing each other across his upper lip.

Caidos made the introductions and asked, "Largo, do you have room for five, plus our horses and a large crate?"

"Now you're moving in. Starting a city? You'd let me know, wouldn't you? Give me exclusive rights? Have you found gold there, perhaps?"

"Always looking for the angle to fortune, Largo. But I'm sorry to disappoint you. No fortune, just five weary travelers. Can you take us? The sooner the better."

"You have your luck with you today, you do. We're waiting on a shipment that's been delayed due to storms. Happening more and more often these days. The hold is not even half full and his lordship doesn't want to make the trip all the way to Kartir with half a load."

He looked around to see if anyone was near, but dropped his voice even though no one could have heard him more than three feet away among the bustle of the docks. "I don't normally agree with him, but a bit more ballast is just smart sailing with the seas rolling the way they've been."

He put his arm on Caidos' shoulder, steering him up the ramp onto the ship, "Come, I'll take you to our beloved captain.

We'll have you to the shores of Laria and be back in time to load up that cargo when it gets here." Leaning over, he whispered to Caidos, "Do you have the little darlin' with you this trip?" Caidos nodded his head in answer, and a wide grin spread across the First Mate's face, stretching the twin sea serpents across his upper lip.

Captain Teves was a small, inconsequential man who tried to compensate for his small stature by wearing formal, military-like attire. He sat behind a small desk on a chair with longer than normal legs. Caidos thought he should have shielded the front of the desk if he hoped the furniture would make him appear taller. The captain's legs could be seen below, dangling an inch above the floor. He looked like a young boy dressed up in his father's uniform.

When Largo had explained the request to Captain Teves, his expressionless face lit up. "Can you get enough of the crew back? It doesn't have to be a full compliment. We'll only be gone for a day, there and back."

"I'll take care of it, sir," Largo responded. "Most of the men will be at the inns in the quarter here. We'll leave a man at the dock, so no one will panic if they see we've gone. Don't want to lose our crew for the trip to Kartir."

"Good thinking. Take care of it, Largo. We'll leave on the evening tide. Dismissed."

"Aye, sir." Largo saluted and led Caidos and Icara from the cabin and back on deck.

"We didn't even discuss the fare," Icara whispered to Caidos on the way up.

"There are standard fees for passage and cargo, Miss," Largo explained. "Fee for this trip of yours is pure profit. He has to pay the crew anyway, to keep them from taking on with another ship leaving today or tomorrow. Plus you've saved him a day's docking fees. We've just made my captain a happy man, which will make our trip to Kartir all the more pleasant."

"But will the crew want to go? If they are being paid anyway, why wouldn't they want to stay, and take advantage of the taverns?" Caidos asked.

"Some will, but others, who don't have the extra money it

takes to use those taverns, would rather get the free food and daily ration of grog. And some of them just hate being on the land. We'll find our numbers, don't you worry. You just get the rest of your party here within the next two hours, so we can get them on board and be prepared to sail with the tide." Largo gave his crew on board some quick instructions to get the ship ready to depart, and then headed for the taverns to collect the crew he would need.

Caidos and Icara followed behind him, as far as The Laden Vessel Inn to wait for the others, who arrived half an hour later. Brandorin was disappointed to hear he would not have the chance to sample the local brew, but was glad Piritho wouldn't have to spend an extra day in the cage.

The horses and Piritho in his cage were loaded and the crew began to ready the ship for departure. The travelers were fascinated by the efficiency of the crew as they scaled the ladders and walked the yardarms dozens of feet above the deck.

"Hold on your departure." A nasally voice called from the dock, and they looked down to find eight members of the Watch standing at the foot of the boarding ramp.

Brandorin scanned the deck, relieved to see Salis was still below. Realizing M'drani could not be seen from the dock, he asked her, "Can you make sure Salis remains below? He's the only one of us they'd know by sight. Then stay down there with him."

"Who are you to be telling us we can't take sail?" Largo had stepped forward, standing firmly at the head of the gangplank, daring them with his stare to even try to board his ship. Brandorin walked up next to the First Mate, his hand on the hilt of his sword, his azure blue eyes fixed on the man who'd spoken. The man had thrown back the hood of the dark gray robes, revealing greased-back hair with a receding hairline. His thin lips were set in a disdainful sneer, and his dark eyes seemed colorless and resentful.

"I am Deneva, Commander of the Watch, here on the authority of the Council of Medora to take those men and that woman into custody. Where is the Master Builder?"

"Who?" Caidos asked. He and Icara were standing behind Brandorin. "Builder of what?"

"This isn't Medora, Commander. This is Setabri," Largo said, "and we don't know you or recognize your authority here."

"I have a Writ of Seizure, signed by the Counselor himself." Deneva brandished a scroll, unrolling it to show the seal at the bottom.

"Oh now you've done it," Largo declared. "If you're talking writs, I have to get our legal counsel involved. He'll have to be fetched to read it and make sure it's valid. But if it is, he'll insist we comply."

Largo turned to Caidos to apologize. "If what he's saying is valid, and he has a legal right to take you and we hinder him, they can seize this vessel and its contents. There's nothing I can do, Caidos."

Largo swung about and climbed the ladder to the foredeck. Deneva swaggered up the ramp, his seven guards in tow. He stood, staring at Caidos and Brandorin, with a smug look of victory etched across his weasely face.

Brandorin stepped forward, pulling his sword six inches from its scabbard, but Caidos laid a hand on his arm, restraining him. Brandorin locked eyes with the Watch commander, who could only maintain his gaze for a moment before turning away from Brandorin's steel-hard stare.

Largo returned, a rolled parchment in hand, as he called his boson. "Bim, take this note to Lathan at his law offices. You know where they are. Hurry man, we want to sail on the tide. We've got less than an hour."

Deneva directed his men onto the deck, "Take charge of the prisoners."

"They aren't prisoners yet," Largo said. "Not until we determine if that writ is valid."

The Watch ignored Largo's comments, following the orders of their commander. They faced Brandorin first, demanding his sword. Brandorin, never taking his eyes off the commander, grabbed the hilt of his sword and drew it with lightening speed, making a statement with the slicing ring of steel on scabbard.

"I am not surrendering my sword."

Four swords arced through the air and would have come to rest on Brandorin's chest, if the Protector's blade had not stopped them. A fifth and sixth sword pointed at Caidos and Icara. Though the two mages jumped slightly, Brandorin had not budged, not even to blink.

"I know we are in the right," Deneva declared, though Brandorin's steely demeanor seemed to be flustering him. "I will agree to wait until your counsel arrives, but I cannot risk these prisoners getting away. They fled Medora, and given the chance they will run again."

"I am not giving that man my sword," Brandorin said, his teeth clenched and every muscle in his body tensed for a fight.

"If you will not release your weapons, I will not wait for the lawyer."

"What if I hold the sword?" Largo asked, stepping in front of Brandorin, between him and the sword points, his back to the Watch. Brandorin met the First Mate's imploring green eyes, which darted to Caidos, seeking his help.

"It is an agreeable solution, don't you think, Brandorin?" Caidos said. "I'm confident in our legal position. The Watch carries no authority in Setabri." Brandorin was reluctant to agree, but seeing assurance in the First Mate's eyes, he acceded to Caidos' request and handed Largo his sword.

"Bind him!" Without his sword, Brandorin's reactions and strength were insufficient to stop the three men who grabbed him. He struggled, throwing one man to the deck and had almost knocked the two remaining men off their feet, when a fourth stepped up and pressed the tip of his sword against the base of Brandorin's throat. They tied his hands behind him; then secured him to the rail. The guard who had been thrown to the deck, punched Brandorin in the stomach. When he bent over in pain, as far as the bonds would allow, the guard fisted Brandorin across the mouth.

Deneva, ignoring the guard's bullying, turned to Largo, "Thank you for your co-operation in disarming him. You saved a great deal of bloodshed."

Brandorin strained against his bonds, trying to reach the First Mate. "I trusted you." The blood in his mouth tasted bitter, and he spit it out in Largo's direction. Largo avoided returning Brandorin's hateful stare; he stepped away from the Watch, holding Brandorin's sword, the hilt tight in a two-handed white-knuckled grip.

"Bind them all," Deneva ordered, but before his men could react a loud explosion at the head of the quay stopped them. Sparks of fire and bright flashes lit the docks in the diminishing light of twilight, and the distant sound of shouting and cries of agony reached them on the wind.

"Guard them," Deneva shouted, as he marched to the dockside rail. At the head of the pier, the shouting continued as men poured from the buildings, shouting and running in panic. Brandorin whispered to Caidos, "Cut these ropes; give me your sword." But the mage hadn't heard him, his attention locked on the commander at the rail.

One man broke away from the crowd, stumbling toward the ship, a bloody rag held to his head, shouting, "It's a Mage. He's killing them all. My eye!" The sailor collapsed at the base of the gangplank as Largo sent two crewmen to his aid.

Deneva gaped at Caidos, then Brandorin and Icara, then back to the commotion on the quay, before he stammered, "I was sure ... you fit the description ..." He turned and charged down the boarding ramp, "Hurry men! This way!"

Largo started shouting orders to his crew, and the two men on the dock, along with the sailor with the bloody rag, ran up the ramp and pulled it in behind them. The injured sailor removed the bloody cloth to reveal two healthy, bright, mischievous eyes, and Brandorin's jaw dropped as he recognized the man as Bim, the boson who had taken the message to the lawyer.

Crewman scaled up the rope ladders, and released the gaskets and halyards that harnessed the bilious sails. As they struck the sails, the wind caught the volumes of canvas and they blossomed open, pulling the ship out to sea. The Noki answered the sea's call like a horse released from the stables into an open meadow. The sails snapped open, the creaking strain of the halyards reining the canvas to the mast. The winds gripped her as she skimmed over the waves and sailed out of the harbor.

Icara cut the ropes that held Brandorin to the rail, as Largo walked up to them. Brandorin's temporary suspicion of the First Mate had changed to admiration. "What was really in that note you sent?"

"I sent Bim to get our shore crew to create a diversion. If Deneva thought there was a Mage on the docks, they'd be convinced you weren't the ones they wanted."

Brandorin shook Largo's hand as Caidos added his thanks, "Brandorin, I was worried you were going to start a fight and ruin what Largo was setting up."

"You knew..."

"I suspected. The ship's counsel story just sounded made up to me. I know this man; knew we could trust him."

Salis and M'drani joined them on deck and M'drani asked Largo, "Will you get into trouble with the Watch?"

"I didn't hear them ask us to wait, did you?" A wide grin caused the tattoos on his face to spread, seeming to move on their own. "My men on shore will convince them the Mage and the others they are looking for are headed out of Setabri. Before they know any better, we'll have slipped back into port, loaded up and be well on our way to Kartir."

\* \* \*

The companions stood at the ship's port railing and gaped at the majesty of the jagged cliffs that stopped abruptly at the sea's edge. The waves fought a continual struggle against the rocks, crashing against the granite walls before returning to sea. The Noki sailed a mile from the cliffs, but the travelers still had to lift their heads and crane back to see the peaks towering thousands of feet above them. An arm of the Axanas occasionally tried to reach out beyond the rest of the cliffs, but the sea protected its boundaries, beating at the walls, trying to break them down with their persistence.

As the sun set and the sky darkened, the companions remained at the rails and watched the battle between sea and mountain until the lack of light and the cold sea air drove them below. Largo walked up to them as they swayed across the deck. "You feel it don't you? The slow, pulsing creak of the ship as it rides the waves, as if we're resting on the back of a great beast, rising and falling with each intake and release of his breath."

Caidos pulled Largo aside. "Perhaps you'd like to meet our cargo. A little thanks for your help today." Largo's eyes widened in anticipation and a devilish grin broke across his face. He followed Caidos into the hold and Brandorin uncovered the cage.

The lantern light gave Piritho a fierce countenance, and his eyes glowed back golden. Caidos was startled by the effect, but Largo was enthralled. He walked around the cage, trying to see Piritho from every angle. Caidos suggested they let Piritho out.

Without a moment's hesitation, Largo responded with enthusiastic approval. "You can see in his eyes he isn't mean. I know you, Caidos, you wouldn't have offered if you thought he was dangerous."

Once released from the cage, Piritho stretched and yawned, revealing large fangs.

"Oh, he's a beauty. You wouldn't think of selling him, would you?" Largo asked. Piritho responded with a guttural growl that set Largo back for a moment. "I didn't mean to offend you, you handsome thing, you. You look hungry. I bet you'd like something to eat." He backed up to the ladder, never taking his eyes from Piritho. He shouted an order up for a couple of steaks to be sent down.

"We don't normally have fresh meat on board, but since this was such a quick trip, out and back, the captain brought a few with. Spending a little of your money. He can have mine." Piritho enjoyed the attention and the steaks.

"Does he get along with the little darlin'?" Largo asked. Caidos nodded again, and took Zephyr out. "There she is. Oh, she's growing up, isn't she? Can she hiss the fire yet?"

"Not yet, but she's been trying. She's managed a spark or two."

Largo sat with Zephyr in his lap, next to Piritho. "If I had known you would have two such beauties with you, I would have paid your passage myself."

The ship continued its journey throughout the night, and Piritho was given free use of the hold area. Largo spent as much time as he could spare, splitting his time between just sitting and looking at him, and playing with Zephyr.

When the companions woke in the morning and came on deck, they found Piritho already there, Zephyr sitting on his back. By this time the mountains had receded back from the shore, revealing isolated beaches and dense jungles. A tapestry of lush vegetation covered the cliffs. Buttery yellow clouds caught the light of the morning sun, like a flock of sheep huddling together against the cold, bitter wind driving them forward.

About three hours after dawn, Largo directed the crew to furl the sails, and the ship slowed as it turned toward the shore. A small but deep inlet with a dock allowed the travelers to disembark and get their horses ashore. Caidos led them away from the dock, into the dense wall of trees that surrounded the peaceful inlet. Largo watched as Piritho traipsed off after them; Zephyr still perched upon his back.

At home even isolated paths were beaten down by those who had gone before them, but aside from the dock in the inlet, Laria looked as if no man had ever set foot here.

Deer munching on grass near a stand of trees looked at them with curiosity, but not fear. A beautiful teal-feathered bird, the size of a falcon, flew over them, then swung back and came to rest on M'drani's outstretched arm. She cooed at it and it sang back to her, a sweet, lilting call.

"I've never seen a bird like that before," she said, as it took flight and returned to the trees. "From the songs I hear from the trees, I would say there are dozens of other varieties I've never seen either."

"We've seen nothing man-made since the dock at the

beach, Caidos," Salis said. "Where did that come from? It seems out of place here."

"The Larians built that for me, over fifty years ago. I used to need a rowboat, which meant I couldn't bring my horse with me. They built up the shore at the edge of the inlet and installed the dock. They maintain it, too."

"You said they didn't build. But that was a solid, well constructed dock."

"I said they didn't build traditional cities, didn't use the kind of mechanisms you're used to. But they're good engineers. You should be able to learn a few things while you are here, Salis."

"Caidos, would it be all right if I Searched the area?" M'drani asked. "I've felt a sense of exhilaration ever since we approached the dock. I feel I have to soar, or I'll burst."

"It's perfectly safe here, M'drani. I just wish I could go with you," Caidos said.

"It might be possible, Caidos," she told him. "Your mind is very open. It might be possible for us to link, before I begin my Search. And if we can, then you should be able to see what I see."

"It's worth a try," Caidos said enthusiastically. "What do I do?"

"Sit here, in front of me." She sat down, cross-legged on the ground. Caidos joined her, and she took each of his hands in hers. "Relax. Try to think of nothing at all."

They sat in silence for awhile, and then M'drani whispered, "Good, that's it." The spirit of the dove rose from her and hovered for a moment above them; it was larger but still as insubstantial.

Caidos was dizzy at first. He could still feel his body sitting firmly on the ground, but his vision showed everyone, himself included, from a great height. When the dove turned away from them and showed him the vast field they sat in, he forgot everything except what he could see.

He saw the landscape gradually change from the palm trees, thick vegetation and hilly terrain near the shore, to vast fields of tall grass, flanked by trees and lakes. Though Caidos had traveled this land numerous times, he didn't recognize the terrain; this new viewpoint was so different that he felt he was seeing it for the first time.

They dove down the far side of a hill, and turned along the bed of a rushing river. Swaying with the bends of the river, they traced its course for more than a mile, before soaring up and over a tree covered knoll. They banked to the right and stopped, hovering over a field of wild flowers.

Scents of a dozen different blossoms filled Caidos' head, and he suddenly realized he could separate the scents into their individual sources. The sound of a bird's trilling call started their flight again as they turned into a forest, dodging between the branches, yet disturbing none of them. A viridian and golden bird sailed along with them for a time, serenading them with its plaintive song.

They chased a small herd of goats and outpaced a blue heron. They floated with a swarm of blue and green butterflies and seemed to take a ride on the back of a wild stallion. When they arched upward and looped around, Caidos could sense their ride coming to an end even before he saw the companions and horses far down below them.

Brandorin had groomed and hobbled the horses, and Salis had dinner well underway when the dove returned and settled over M'drani, and then merged back into her. Both she and Caidos opened their eyes at once, and Caidos let out a long breath and looked in awe at the small woman in front of him.

"That is the most marvelous gift. I must admit to being envious of your ability. I didn't realize you could smell and hear when you Searched. All of the senses are involved." He stood, a little unsteady on his feet. Brandorin put a hand out to keep him from toppling over, and helped ease him back down. "I feel as if I have been drinking ale; I am light-headed and wonder-struck. Thank you. I've always known this was a beautiful country, but to see it from up there. Incredible!"

"I never tried that before," M'drani said, her voice hoarse whisper. "I feel drained, both by what I saw and sharing it with you. Could I have some water?" Both Brandorin and Salis handed her a water skin.

* * *

"We will reach Numina shortly," Caidos said as their horses slowed to climb a small hill, "but I feel more and more anxious the closer we get. What if Rhamak has gotten here before us?"

"I've been wondering about that, Caidos," Brandorin said. He and Caidos rode together in the lead, but he turned to see how close the others were. He lowered his voice as he continued. "Why has Rhamak suddenly gotten so active? How would he know Sefiron's Shadow had been seen? If he sent those thieves to the estate, wouldn't that indicate he knew what would happen before the Shadow appeared to me outside of Kartir?"

"I have been wondering that myself. When I heard the Shadow had been seen in Kartir, I was astounded. I was afraid I had somehow missed some sign that the time had come. I went to my home and consulted my charts and did some calculations. I calculated the number of New Moons since the Dedication, trying to see if the number revealed something. But the numbers were not significant.

"The new scroll Icara brought didn't explain the reason for the Shadow's appearance. The rest of Didonno's scrolls are in Artara, but I have read them so many times, I could practically quote them to you verbatim. There was nothing in those scrolls to indicate the Shadow would return now. It must be similar to the time when Gharvik abused his gifts, yet I know the three remaining bearers, and can't believe that of them. I can't believe that of any of you."

"I don't believe the attempted burglary at the estate and the attack at the wedding were a coincidence. Was there anything else in that new scroll said that I should know about?" They had not discussed the scroll since the day Icara brought it.

"The Shadow's appearance has strengthened your powers as the Protector. It helped you use the Umari crystal when no one else had been able to do so."

"I've realized when I performed my first healing," Brandorin said quietly. "When I first took the sword, I felt an odd sensation of both cold and heat race through my blood. I thought it was from the blow to my head, but thinking about it now, since I've been using the Umari stone, I realize it was the healing. When the beast attacked me at the wedding, it raked my sides and arms with its claws, yet there was no sign of the wounds the next day."

"You had other things on your mind." Caidos didn't want Brandorin to dwell on what might have been, so he continued talking about the new scroll. "It said 'at need'. That means that if there was any reason why one of the bearers could not complete the journey, you could carry their fragment for them, rejoin it with the others when the time comes."

"Hopefully it won't come to that."

As they topped the hill, they saw a vast forest. It spanned the horizon, made up of trees with massive trunks, both in width and in height. The trunks grew straight for forty feet before opening into a wide canopy of leaves that covered the forest like an umbrella.

"What kind of trees are those?" Salis asked when he caught up to them, "They're incredible. The buildings I could make with beams that long."

"I hate to tell you this Salis, but you couldn't use those trees to build," Caidos told him.

"Why not? Not hardwood?"

"No, they aren't really trees."

"What? They're beautiful trees."

"It's not a forest. It's a Larian city. That's where we're going. That's Numina."

## Chapter 16

What had appeared to be trees from a distance were in reality the walls of a great city. Crafted to blend with the neighboring forest and hills, the fortifications grew from the sloping lawns to a height of forty feet. A canopy of thatch at the top branched out to form crenellations and battlements, though no sentries stood their post as the companions drew near.

When they reached the entrance into Numina, Brandorin exclaimed, "There are no gates!"

"Everyone is welcome to enter," Caidos told him. "The walls were built in a time when defense was necessary, but the Larians have had no enemy for thousands of years. The Larians didn't want to mar the harmony of the landscape, so they tore down most of the walls, but left these, covering them with a more natural face. They serve as a reminder of those troubled times, in hopes that they would not be repeated."

Brandorin found it hard to think of a city without defenses. He soon saw that the buildings within the city walls were as natural in their surroundings as the walls themselves. Some buildings were molded by the hills that served as a natural wall to the west, while others were built around or between real trees. Instead of cutting them down to make room for the homes, and using their wood for building materials, the Larians had created a harmony between nature and their constructions.

Brandorin noticed Salis shaking his head and staring open-mouthed at the buildings. "What's wrong, Salis? You're not saying very much."

"I've always been so proud of the work I've done. I designed buildings in Setabri that mirrored the mountains and steppes of the surrounding countryside."

"I liked those buildings."

"But they were separate from their background. The Larians have melded their buildings *with* the background, as if they have been here all along. I couldn't go back to the cathedral now, even if they wanted me."

"Forget about the buildings for now, Salis," whispered Icara. "Look at the people."

The buildings of Numina blended with their surroundings, but the people seemed to share a kinship with the animals that inhabited the land. Their facial features were reminiscent of wolves or dogs, cats or foxes, with broad noses and muzzle-like mouths and chins. Honey or wheat colored eyes, topped by prominent brows, were most common, but many were sage, willow, or moss, with pointed-oval irises instead of round. Their hairlines started low on the forehead, forming a peak between the eyes, and came out farther into their face on the sides, covering half of the cheek. Their hands had dark nails and only three fingers and a thumb each.

Despite the differences in their appearance, and the obvious fact the travelers did not belong there, the Larians didn't stare at them. Brandorin knew that if a similar group of Larians had walked through the city gates of Kartir, they would have been ridiculed or driven from the city, and he didn't want to think what would have happened if Larians walked into Medora. Several people greeted Caidos as they passed, but showed no surprise at his companions, even greeted them as well, and welcomed them to their city.

In the streets of Kartir, merchants and shoppers alike hurried from task to task, brushing against their fellow citizens without acknowledging them. The Larians moved slowly through the wide avenues of their city, greeting their fellows and stopping often to talk.

Brandorin noticed a young girl whose long red hair matched her vixen features. She stopped as she walked into the brighter sun of an open square. She turned her head up to the warmth of golden light, and breathing deeply, relishing the beauty of the clear day.

The Larians approached routine daily tasks with a dignity and grace reserved for formal ceremonies in the west. Selecting ears of corn or squashes from market stalls was more than just a monotonous task, but recognition of the bounty the land had provided. The women at the wells moved with reverent grace as they bent to raise and withdraw the full bucket of water. Each time, they stopped, and using a ladle, they would draw water from the bucket and holding it for a moment, would then return it to the well.

"Caidos, what is the significance of the ceremony the Larians follow when drawing water from the well?" M'drani asked.

"Remember I told you they have no money? They don't pay for the goods they select from the market, not directly, as we would in the west. They pay for what they take from the community by the work they do in other areas. They believe that for everything they take from the land, they must give something back. So they return a ladle of water back to the well. When they eat, they leave a small portion, to be returned to the land."

"It's like a form of prayer."

Salis said, "They build their homes in groups of four, the decorations on the buildings are four-pointed stars or scrollwork with four sections. Is it because they have only four fingers on each hand?"

"Partially. Just as we have five fingers on each hand, the numbers five and ten are significant for us. We reflect that in our money: coins are made in five and ten tansur denominations. We count in tens, hundreds, and thousands. But for the Larians it goes deeper than that. They see the four phases of the moon: new, quarter, half and full; the four seasons of the year, the four directions; the four powers of the world: air, earth, fire and water; the four phases of life: childhood, adolescence, adulthood, and wisdom. They have a reverence for life and the wonders of the world in which they live. I always feel renewed every time I come here."

\* \* \*

They had been in the city for twenty minutes when a very regal man, with russet hair rode up to them on a flaxen colored horse. The wolf-like features of his face conveyed a serious demeanor, but his honey-colored eyes reflected warmth and a whimsical nature.

He wore a tightly woven jerkin with a crest quilted on the chest. The crest had four points and in its center rested an amber stone. He raised his hand in greeting, palm open with the three fingers together and the thumb to the side, "Hail, Caidos Batana. We have watched for your return."

"Hail, Matu Lairom," Caidos responded in kind, his hand raised in greeting. "I am glad to return to Numina again." Caidos and Matu rode toward each other, each taking the others forearm in his hand. The formal greeting over, Matu laughed and his smile transformed his stern lupine visage and his golden eyes sparkled. He warmly clasped Caidos' back with his free hand.

He drew back from Caidos, and resumed the formal pose of greeting, and raising his hand again as he rode toward the others, he called, "Hail, Brandorin Adamaran, Protector and Healer, Numina welcomes you." He grasped Brandorin's arm as he had done with Caidos.

Brandorin, temporarily surprised by the greeting, responded as he had seen Caidos do. "Hail, Matu Lairom, Counselor. I am honored to be here." Matu laughed again, and clasped Brandorin as he had Caidos.

He greeted the others in turn, calling each by their full name as well as their title. He was confused by Icara, not being able to link her to a crystal fragment. When Caidos told him who she was, he smiled in recognition and said, "Caidos has spoken very highly of you and your talents. Numina welcomes you."

When Matu looked at Piritho, he stopped abruptly, and whispered, "A lapithi?"

He swung his leg over his horse's neck, slipping to the ground, and went to him. Holding Piritho's massive head between his hands, Matu looked into his eyes. He stared into their dark depths for a long time before standing and saying, "Piritho, I welcome you." Then to the others, "We will care for him. Come." He jumped effortlessly onto his horse's bare back.

"Finally someone who knows what he is," Salis said to Brandorin. "Maybe he comes from Laria."

Brandorin made no response, but watched Matu suspiciously.

As they rode through the city Caidos talked with Matu.

"Can I assume from your companions, Caidos, that the time has come for the Rejoining?"

"Yes, it has. But surely our arrival is not the first indication you've had of this? Has Sefiron's Shadow not visited you?"

"No, but clearly you expected it to have appeared here."

"There were supposed to be seven sightings in all, yet I can account for only two, and the Shadow has told us there will only be two more."

"Only two?" Matu sounded worried as well as surprised. "That doesn't leave us much time."

"I would have been much more comfortable if we'd been given the full seven cycles." Caidos surveyed the area. "This isn't the way to your home, Matu. Are we going to the Chamber of the Elders?"

"The Elders read the shifting of the winds and knew of your coming. They sent me to greet you, with strict instructions to bring you to them as soon as you arrived. They'll want to hear the news of Sefiron immediately. They'll also want to meet your friend, Piritho. It's many years since we've seen a lapithi, but the Elders will know what to do."

"What do you mean 'do'?" Brandorin asked. "What do you think you are going to do to him?" Matu would say no more.

They rode without further comment for fifteen minutes, arriving in front of a large pavilion at the center of the great city. Grooms stepped up to greet them and take the horses, as Matu led them inside.

The vast interior of the pavilion had been divided into individual rooms; hanging panels of woven fabric separated one section from the next. They walked through a central corridor flanked by small rooms or other corridors. They passed through a wide archway and the corridor opened out into a spacious chamber. A fire burned in the center of the chamber, the smoke rising through a funnel-like structure vented to the sky above.

The chamber made Brandorin think of the cathedral back home, though its interior was not so vast nor its ceiling as lofty. In fact, it wasn't the visual aspects of the place, but a feeling of spirituality that filled the room. The other companions seemed to sense it as well, for their casual conversation had dropped to respectful whispers.

Around the fire sat eight men and women, their lupine, feline and vixen features animated in conversation. There was a natural grace to their movements, a reverence in their voices. They stopped when they saw Matu, Caidos and his companions. A few nodded silently as if the arrival of the travelers confirmed their expectations.

The companions were welcomed and asked to sit with the Elders. When they had been made comfortable and food and drink had been brought to them, all talk ceased and the Larians turned to look at the man sitting in the center at the far side of the chamber.

He appeared to be the eldest of the Larians, his hair a pure white and his face a tan and leathery map of the years he had seen. His features, similar to Matu's, carried the keen-eyed understanding of age. He sat in silence and looked at the companions, each in turn, evaluating them with intense, mahogany eyes. When he spoke, he did so with quiet reverence, hallowed whispers in a holy place. His voice resonated as if it crossed the vast gulf of time.

"Caidos, old friend, it is good to see you again. We welcome you and all of your companions to Laria. But first you must rest from your journey. And I see one among you is lapithi. We will see to his needs while you eat. Lata, Gaila, take him. We will wait for your return."

Two of the Elders rose from the circle and walked to where Piritho sat. They spoke no words, but he rose and followed them toward a curtain behind Korlu, the Elder who had spoken.

Brandorin started to rise, but Matu put a hand on his arm and said, "He doesn't need you in this. They won't harm him. They'll bring him back to you as before." Brandorin continued to rise. He looked to Caidos, who nodded in agreement with Matu.

"He'll be fine, Brandorin. Wait with us." Brandorin watched

the back of the chamber, where Piritho had been taken to the antechamber beyond. Matu reached for him, gently pulling him back down. Though food and drink were placed before him, he didn't touch them.

"Korlu, we are thankful for your hospitality," Caidos said, directing his words to the Elder, out of respect for his position. "May I introduce my companions?" Korlu nodded in ascent, and Caidos introduced each of the companions, in turn, giving full name, country, and title. The Elders understood what the presence of the companions meant, but they made no comment other than silent nodding and knowing looks toward one another.

"And what of your winged companion?" Korlu asked, indicating Zephyr. She had been sitting quietly next to Caidos, partially hiding in the folds of his robes. Caidos reached down and picked up the firedrake, setting her on his lap.

"This is Zephyr. I found her in Arkhan, five years ago. A tiger had killed her mother, and she was barely old enough to survive. She is very rare; few of her kind survive."

"Will you come to me, Zephyr," Korlu asked, "that I may understand your spirit?" Zephyr, who was normally quite shy, flew to the old man without hesitation. She sat on his lap, as she had done for Caidos, facing him, as he gently touched her, looking into her eyes. After only a moment, she began to purr in contentment. "You are of an ancient race, a noble one, and brave." Zephyr fluttered her wings in response, and settled down to rest.

"We are not often visited by the people of the west," Korlu said. "How do you find your first sight of Laria?" M'drani, Icara, and Salis all began to answer together. Brandorin, still watching the curtain where Piritho had gone, came out of his reverie to add his praise of the beauty of their land.

Salis, after a moment's hesitation said, "I'm overwhelmed by the nature of your buildings. If there's time, could I talk to some of your engineers? I know it would take years of study to fully understand what you've done here, but if they could answer a few questions ... " A strong wind blew through the chamber; the gust swirled around the fire, raising a cloud of smoke.

Salis coughed on the smoke and was just about to speak again when a mournful howl from the antechamber sent a shiver up his spine. Brandorin jumped to his feet and was half way to the curtain before Matu stopped him. They struggled as Matu fought to hold him back.

"He's not hurt, Brandorin," Matu told him. "He'll be back with you shortly." Brandorin reluctantly agreed to wait but did not return to his seat by the fire, his eyes fixed to the curtain as he paced.

"Yes, Builder, our people would be pleased to share their knowledge with you," Korlu continued. "I am sure they would be anxious to hear of your methods of building as well, though they have never seen your structures. We would be happy for you to spend those years with us, but I fear you will have only days, if that."

Before Salis could respond, Lata and Gaila emerged from behind the curtain, accompanied by a tall bearded man, with unkempt, long brown hair and an unhealthy pallor. He wore a loose-fitting robe, but had neither shoes nor sandals. It took a moment for the companions to realize this third man was not Larian, but a Westerner.

The lost and hunted look on his face made him seem old and tired. He walked forward, staggering a little. He glanced around the fire as if searching for someone. A smile broke across the stranger's face as he noticed Brandorin standing in the shadows, and with its appearance the aged look of his countenance vanished. He strode toward Brandorin.

When the stranger was two paces away, Brandorin put an arm out to stop him, and whispered, "No!" Brandorin shook his head, a pained look on his face. He said it again, louder, his voice laden with a mixture of anger and grief. He turned abruptly and ran from the chamber.

\* \* \*

The joy on the stranger's face vanished, and he stared after

Brandorin, crestfallen. Matu rose, and walking to the stranger, took him by the arm and led him to the fire.

Matu said, "You remembered Brandorin. Do you know the others?" The man looked at them in confusion. Slowly recognition lit his face, and turning first to M'drani, he extended his hand in greeting. He opened his mouth as if to speak, but no sound came out.

M'drani cautiously took his hand, and looking into his eyes, she inhaled audibly, and whispered, "Piritho?"

The man, still unable to speak, nodded gratefully. Caidos, understanding what had happened, said, "Of course. It makes sense now." He stood and walked over to him, taking his hand, "Piritho, it's good to have you back with us."

"Caidos," Piritho whispered hoarsely. He looked down the corridor where Brandorin had gone. "I thought he'd forgiven me," his voice barely audible, was scratchy and choked with emotion.

"I'm glad you understand what's going on," Salis complained, "but could someone please explain it to me?"

"He was a lapithi," Matu answered, "a human spirit in animal form. We have not seen such a thing in many years, but any Larian would recognize one. Lata and Gaila are two who still possess the skill to bring him back. Your memory will be cloudy," he said to Piritho, "but more will return with each passing hour."

"How does someone become a lapithi?" Salis asked.

"Rhamak!" Piritho's answer was heavy with anger. Breathing in short quick gasps, he stared into the fire, trying to cope with the flood of memories pouring over him.

M'drani and Matu tried to console him, telling him his attack on Brandorin and Ilona at the wedding feast was not his fault. Korlu stood, and nodding to the other Elders, they left the chamber to the companions. Zephyr fluttered over to Piritho, and settled down next to him.

"A lapithi has a human spirit," Matu explained, "but it is controlled by the animal's instincts and senses. Once you had been given the form of the beast, you were no longer truly a man. Most of your understanding of what is right and what is wrong would have been overshadowed by the beast's primitive senses. Survival alone would have become your primary goal."

"What do you remember, Piritho?" M'drani asked him.

"Only brief flashes from the wedding," he said, his voice coming back to him as he used it more. "I didn't see it as a wedding at the time. I wasn't thinking in words, just feelings, emotions, raw, primitive emotions. I don't know where I was before that; I was just there. I was consumed with fear and hatred."

He stopped, closing his eyes, and he trembled, shaking his head. He opened his eyes again, staring into the fire and continued, "I could smell the remnants of the feast; I could pick out each course that had been served. The smells of the people too. Their perfumes and their sweat, but most specifically their fear. It was intoxicating, driving me forward.

"I knew someone there was going to kill me. The only way to save myself was to kill him first. There were hundreds of people, but the threat came from one person, and I was being drawn to him.

"I ignored anyone else that got in my way. I had to find him. I knew the face I was looking for. It was as if I was hunting him." His fists clenched. His breathing came in ragged gasps.

"Then he was there. Waiting for me. Then running toward me. I leaped at him. Was soon standing over him. He lay on the ground beneath me. Kill him. Kill him. That's all I could hear. All I could feel.

"Then I saw who it was. Some part of me recognized him. I couldn't do it. But the urge to kill was still so strong. I couldn't fight it. But I couldn't kill him. She was there, striking me. There was some emotion I didn't understand. Something drew me to her. No thought, I just attacked," he stopped, breathing deeply, images of what he had done and seen flashing through his mind, as a tear coursed down his cheek.

He looked up, and seeing the others were waiting, he continued, "The murder lust was gone. The raw emotions, the savage instinct for survival, gone. I turned and he was there. I had thought I'd killed him too. I was so relieved, but I was also ashamed. I ran. I just wanted to get away."

"He caught up with me as I reached the woods. He hated me. I could see it in his eyes. Then there was a light, and it was different. He wouldn't strike. I wanted him to. I didn't want to live knowing what I had done. Living as a beast. But he knew who I was, even the way I was."

"You said you recognized Brandorin? That he knew you?" Piritho nodded his head, but would say nothing else. "Piritho, look at me." Caidos looked at Piritho closely, trying to picture the man behind the beard. Recognition lit up the mage's face.

"You wouldn't kill him. He wouldn't strike you. I told Brandorin it seemed like you'd known each other for years. You're Thiro aren't you? Brandorin's friend." Piritho nodded once. "I haven't seen you for a very long time. Why has Brandorin been calling you Piritho?"

"It's my actual name. He's called me Thiro since we were very young. He couldn't say Piritho very well, and it came out Thiro." Piritho looked in the direction Brandorin had gone. "The way he's acted all these months ... I thought he'd forgiven me."

"He probably just needs time," Caidos told him. "Let me talk to him."

"No, Caidos, let me," Matu said. "I can explain the nature of the lapithi, help him to understand his friend was not in control. I'll go now to find him."

"We'll be at my house," Caidos told Matu, "you can bring Brandorin there when he's ready."

*   *   *

Matu found Brandorin on the parapet, near the entrance to the city. Brandorin stood looking out over the plain at the half moon as it cleared the horizon. Despite a thin veil of clouds, it stood out starkly, a porcelain cup against the gray-blue velvet sky of early evening. Brandorin was reminded of the way Ilona's face seemed to glow from beneath her bridal veil in that moment before they took their vows.

"Did they send you to talk to me?" Brandorin asked without turning around. "Are you supposed to explain how he wasn't responsible for his actions?"

"I don't have to explain to you what you already know."

"Knowing it doesn't seem to help." The frustration he felt was obvious in his voice. "Yesterday I knew the beast was Piritho. I've known it since I caught up to him, and looked in his eyes. I thought I'd forgiven him. But seeing him again, as my old friend, back to the way he was. I don't know, I can't explain it."

"When you thought he was always going to be the beast maybe you felt he was being punished enough. It was easier to forgive him."

"He could have killed me. I have to believe Rhamak ordered that. Why did he leave me alive, and kill Ilona?"

"You'll have to ask *him* that. You can do that now."

"But that's part of the problem. I'm not sure I'm ready for that answer." Brandorin turned and looked at Matu for the first time since their conversation began. He saw a man, whose features should have made him seem foreign and unfamiliar, but he felt comfortable, sensed he could trust this man to understand. "I don't even know why I'm telling you all these things. I don't know you."

"Some things are easier to discuss with a stranger. A friend would understand too easily. Maybe there's something you'd rather not talk about with Piritho; something he will too readily understand."

"If understanding too easily is a problem, then Piritho may not be the only one I have to worry about," Brandorin said, laughing a little as he said it. "I may not know you, but you seem to be reading me pretty well."

"Part of being the Counselor, I guess." Matu followed Brandorin's lead and tried to joke with him. Brandorin looked at Matu for a moment, then turned back to the parapet.

After a minute he said, "I think I'm angry with him for leaving me alive. Does that make any sense?"

"I can understand that," Matu said as he stepped up to the battlement, staring out over the surrounding fields. After a moment he added, "My wife died three years ago. We both fell ill. Strong fever, a terrible weakness. None of the medicines helped. Hundreds of people were sick, it wasn't just us. Most people were able to fight it; about one in twenty could not. She was one of those that could not." He stopped, and Brandorin suspected he was feeling the pain of her loss even after all the intervening time. "In my grief, I kept asking why I didn't die too. I wished for a long time I had. There was no one to blame."

Neither of them said anything for some time, each remembering the woman taken from their lives. Matu broke the silence. "I'll show you where you can spend the night. We can talk more in the morning."

As they walked through the city, Matu acted as a guide, talking about the buildings and the city. Brandorin knew Matu was trying to distract him, but after awhile he stopped listening.

"This is Caidos' home," Matu said as they walked up to a large house built amidst four tall fir trees. "Your companions are within." As Matu walked toward the house, Brandorin stood still, looking at the house. Matu added, "Or if you would prefer, I have an extra room in my home."

"This will be fine," Brandorin said, catching up with Matu."

As Matu stepped aside, he saw Piritho standing there, looking at him, waiting for him to speak. Brandorin tried to think of him as Thiro, tried to say he needed time, but all that came out was, "I can't."

"I can't expect you to forgive me, when I haven't forgiven myself. Even though I couldn't speak, we made a vow to seek our revenge on Rhamak. I will fulfill that vow, and I promise you, here in front of all of these people; if I don't die in the effort, you can take my life. And if you won't, then I will."

Piritho didn't wait for Brandorin's reaction, but left the house. The companions looked to Brandorin. When he didn't go after his friend, Matu said, "I'll bring him to my home, then I'll be back."

After Piritho and Matu had left, the companions waited for Brandorin to speak. He felt their disapproval, and part of him agreed, but he couldn't stop the images of that day from coming back. He knew the man responsible was the one they expected him to forgive. He couldn't look at M'drani, knowing she could sense his frustration, guilt and anger.

When he didn't speak, Caidos showed him to a room where he could rest.

* * *

It was three hours before Matu returned. Only Caidos and M'drani were still waiting for him.

"We had a good, long talk," Matu said. "He knows Rhamak transformed him into the beast, but he has little recollection of how and where it happened. Most of his memory is back, but the events between his capture and the wedding are still cloudy. I think I have a fairly good idea of what happened."

"Maybe I shouldn't hear this," M'drani said, starting to rise as if to leave the room.

"No, I think you should stay, M'drani," Caidos told her. "Your abilities as well as your caring nature, and your feelings for both these men, will be of help as they try to deal with this. Go ahead, Matu."

"Rhamak apparently sent some of his men to break into Brandorin's home. He had hoped to secure the Protector's sword and the crystals it holds, but it was also a trap. Whether they obtained the sword or not, he expected Brandorin would come after them. But *he* didn't. Piritho did.

"It was shortly before the wedding. Piritho told Brandorin he couldn't let him get all cut up and bruised, that he would make a scary looking groom. So it was Piritho that went after Rhamak's men, and was caught in the trap instead."

"Then Brandorin is also feeling guilty for what happened to his friend, feels it should have been him," M'drani said.

"Yes, I'm sure that's part of it," Caidos agreed.

"Rhamak was undoubtedly disappointed he didn't get his intended quarry," Matu continued, "but he learned from questioning Piritho, that he had another way to get to Brandorin. Piritho's memory of that time is murky, but it seems Rhamak has abilities similar to yours, M'drani. He can read another's thoughts. But he uses his ability to torture and control his victims." Matu's voice reflected the anger he felt, and he stopped, taking a deep breath to gain control of himself again.

"Once Rhamak had transformed Piritho into the beast, the emotions had more control over his actions. He was still a man, spiritually, as well as intellectually, but instincts and emotions overrode reason, and Rhamak used that too. But in the end the man won out over the primitive beast, and Piritho was able to stop himself from killing Brandorin.

"The drive to kill, the hatred Rhamak had fueled in him was still there, however. I would guess Piritho didn't know Ilona well, and she was there, and perhaps, in the blind rage Rhamak had created, he saw her as a threat."

"Has Piritho given up his desire to die?" Caidos asked.

"No, he won't give that up so easily. But as long as Rhamak is alive, he is dedicated to seeking revenge. He won't do anything until that happens. What about Brandorin?"

"He would say nothing. He turned in right after you left, though I doubt he's sleeping," Caidos said. "We can only hope time and our mission will help them both get through this."

"Do you think it would help Brandorin understand, if I told him these things?" Matu asked.

"I don't know. It could even make it worse," Caidos said. "Because Piritho took his place in the chase for the intruders, he was captured by Rhamak, tortured, changed into a beast, and sent to kill his best friend. Then, Brandorin is spared, but not Ilona. I have to admit, I don't know how I'd react in such a situation."

"We must give them both time," M'drani said, "time to heal."

## Chapter 17

The next morning the companions were called to the Chamber, where they met with the Elders again. When Caidos, Brandorin and the others walked into the Chamber, the Elders, Matu and Piritho were already there. Brandorin looked at Piritho only briefly, then averted his eyes and sat in a position that would prevent him from having to look in his friend's direction.

"I have called this council, Caidos," Korlu said, "for we would have you tell us the full significance of the Shadow's appearance. I know the legend of the crystal, having carried the Larian fragment for many moons before passing it to my son, Matu. The other Elders, as well as some of your companions, I suspect, do not know the full history of the crystal. Can you speak of these things to all of us?

"Yes, I can tell you. But it is important the full story, and many of the things we'll talk about, stay with those in this chamber." Caidos related the story of the crystal's formation and the powers the World Shapers endowed into the eight fragments and the crown piece. Because many in the chamber were unfamiliar with the history of the fragment holders, he explained some of that as well.

Korlu was the first to break the silence. "The signs we have observed are explained by your tale, Caidos, but why did the Shadow appear at this time? Since the gods gave our ancestors Sefiron's powers to help us survive, why would the Shadow come to us before we are able to live without Sefiron's protection?"

"I don't know, Korlu. I'm afraid the scrolls do not address the reasons for the Shadow's appearance at this time."

"Perhaps it is a trial," Korlu said, "like the Rites of Manhood." Many of the Elders nodded their heads in agreement. "We must prove that we deserve the right to continue to hold the powers Sefiron gives us."

"Perhaps," Caidos said. "But with all the other information in the scrolls, I would think the reasons for the Shadow's appearance would be explained."

"Life cannot be explained ahead of time, Caidos. We must learn its ways as we walk its path."

Salis asked, "Caidos, you said there were nine fragments created by the World Shapers: yours, mine, Brandorin has two, that's four. M'drani's and Matu's make six. Then there are the Ilyani and Arkhanian fragments we must get yet. But that's only eight."

"The Korduna had one too. They lived in The Void."

"How could anyone survive up there? It's barren and rocky. Little or nothing grows there," Salis said. "I never thought I was so ill informed about Zadania, but I was unaware of the Larians. Sorry about that," he said to the Elders, "or the Ilyani. Now you're saying there are people called the Korduna that live in The Void."

"Lived," Caidos corrected him. "They're gone. They were wanderers; that's what Korduna means. They had no cities. During Mandricon's tenure as Mirador, they died. There have been no Korduna for two hundred and fifty years. Mandricon was convinced Rhamak was involved."

"That's why the new scroll explained how to make a replacement fragment," Brandorin said.

"The Sefiramon anticipated every contingency," said Caidos. "Korlu, would your people have a piece of Zadanite? It is essential to making the replacement."

"I will ensure you have one. If we don't have one in Numina, I will send runners to find one for you."

"Could Rhamak have been responsible for the loss of the Umari?" Piritho asked.

"No, we can't blame him for that," Caidos said. "They disappeared four thousand years ago. Rhamak is close to six hundred years old, but he's not old enough to have known the Umari. I'm sure he was looking for their fragment as well, but luckily the Mages of Artara found it."

"How can a man live so long?" Gaila asked.

Caidos explained. "Rhamak was one of my order, but he experimented with incantations that were against our code. We haven't had direct word of his actions for thirty-five years. But he is obviously still alive," he said looking at Piritho. "The incantation that transformed Piritho was one he was expelled for. He also has learned how to take the life of another, adding their unused years to his own. I had heard rumors of this, but had no confirmation until we saw Sefiron's Shadow; they called him the Life Stealer."

\* \* \*

Rhamak was not eating his breakfast. Kalga and the other servants waiting by the sideboard were openly nervous. It was normally Chaubrel's task to talk to Rhamak, find out what he wanted, but he was not here. That alone could be cause for Rhamak's moodiness. Chaubrel was always wherever Rhamak wanted him to be, even if Rhamak had not spoken his desires.

Kalga was not as afraid of Rhamak as the others. He even tried to spend more time around him, where others preferred to work in the kitchens, the armory, or other places where Rhamak never went. He had heard stories of what Rhamak had done to servants, but he believed most of these stories to be exaggerations. He had never found anyone, other than Chaubrel, who had been present when these atrocities supposedly took place.

But he had seen the special treatment Chaubrel received. The clothes, the jewels, and the food were evident. He had watched Chaubrel dine on the sumptuous dishes Rhamak had left behind. Chaubrel had his own chambers, with a big comfortable bed, and chests filled with gold and jewels. There was enough for two special servants, and if Kalga had his own way, he would supplant Chaubrel and be Rhamak's new chamberlain.

This would be the perfect time. Rhamak was not eating and Chaubrel was not here. Kalga approached him now, hoping he could resolve his dissatisfaction with breakfast. Such service would bring him the recognition he felt he deserved.

"Sire, is there something else you would prefer to eat?" Kalga asked, trying very hard to prevent the trembling he felt in his knees from coming through in his voice. Rhamak didn't react at first, and Kalga began to think he hadn't been heard. He was about to try again, when Rhamak turned his gaze on Kalga, and the words stopped in the servant's throat. Kalga felt like an insect locked in the mage's amber gaze.

"What is your name?" Rhamak asked him. "Kalga," he heard Rhamak say, though the servant had not spoken. The inside of his eyes began to itch, but he could not blink. He began to feel approaching Rhamak had been a mistake. "Of course it was a mistake," Rhamak said as he rose, keeping his eyes locked on Kalga, who could no longer control the trembling in his knees; it had now spread to his entire body. He thought he would fall, but he did not; Rhamak's will held him up.

Chaubrel walked into the dining hall. Recognizing Rhamak's impatience, he started to speak from the middle of the room, "We have confirmation, my Lord, you were, of course, correct in your suspicions."

Rhamak turned toward Chaubrel, and Kalga, now forgotten by his master, slumped to the floor, as he sat in a puddle of his own urine. "How was it done?" Rhamak asked.

"The Larians, sire. They sensed the human spirit within the beast. They were able to change him back."

"How dare they? I control my creations, where they go, when they come back, when they are transformed. I was not done with that one. He failed to fulfill his assignment."

Rhamak paused, distracted by the beast's failure. "That was such a marvelous plan. I don't know what went wrong there. It was perfect. Brandorin's best friend, under my control. Kill Brandorin before he becomes the threat the Shadow foretold, and use his best friend to do it." Rhamak shivered with delight at the beauty of his plan. Chaubrel noticed that the success or failure of a plan never seemed to effect Rhamak's enjoyment at his own cleverness.

"That was the crowning glory. He had no idea how envious he was of Brandorin. It was almost too easy to use that to turn him to my will. It's always too easy, Chaubrel, not even an effort anymore." Rhamak's sighed. When he spoke again his voice was on the edge of whining; something Chaubrel had never heard him do. "Well, Brandorin is probably gloating now. My plan failed and he has his friend back."

"That's not how it appears, sire." Chaubrel said gently.

"What?" Rhamak said, turning toward Chaubrel so quickly, the chamberlain became flustered.

"When the Larians changed Piritho back into a man, Brandorin refused to talk to him. Stormed out of the room."

"Hasn't forgiven him after all. Interesting. That could prove very helpful. The Larians may have transformed him back, but once a man is under my control, only I can truly release him. And there is only one release."

Rhamak thought for a moment before asking, "Is everything in place for the next attack?"

"Yes, sire, they are in position."

"They have their instructions. They won't fail me. It will be like a dance, well orchestrated, perfectly timed. An attack within an attack. They'll see the first one. Counter it, or not, it doesn't matter, but they won't see the second attack. But that's only the third act of my little play. We must prepare for the next acts as well, and for the finale."

"The subjects are waiting below, sire."

"Tomorrow, I think." He turned toward his chamber, then stopped and turned back to Chaubrel. "You distracted me from that fool in the dining hall."

"I am so sorry, sire. I didn't realize you found him entertaining. I was so anxious to bring you the news. Should I bring him to you now?"

"Perhaps another time.

## Chapter 18

They assembled outside the pavilion, checking their horses, saddles and packs. The Larians promised to provide a horse for Piritho, though they had no saddles. Larians never used leather, and though they could have made a workable saddle out of other materials, they felt a horse allowed a man to ride him. There was better communication between horse and rider if there was no saddle to interfere. Matu arrived with a black stallion and a large roan horse with a black mane.

"This is Kahdu, Piritho," Matu told him, indicating the roan; "he's one of our larger horses, but he's very good with new riders. I've talked with him about your unfamiliarity with riding bareback. He says he will help you, and promises you'll never want to use a saddle again. He's agreed to use a bridle until you are comfortable in signaling with your knees and are confident he won't let you fall. He is friends with the horse I will be riding, so we'll ride together."

Piritho walked over to Kahdu. "I won't be able to understand you as Matu does, but I'll try. Thank you for agreeing to carry me."

Turning to Salis, who gave him a strange look, he said, "It may seem strange, and he may not even understand me, but I appreciate animals' feelings much more than I used to."

"That makes sense," Salis conceded. "As long as we're on that subject, did you really understand everything we were saying, before, when you were ..."

"When I was 'the beast'? For the most part, I guess I did, but it was different than hearing the words and knowing what they meant. It was as if I understood the meaning even though the words didn't always make sense to me."

Piritho was relieved someone was finally talking about the way things had been. Looking around, and realizing no one else was close enough to hear, he added, "It's all right to talk about this. Everyone seems to be taking a great deal of care not to offend me, mostly by ignoring the fact there's been any change at all. Only

Brandorin knew who I was, and he had no reason to believe my form could be changed."

"I see you've shaved your beard off," Salis said.

"Over two months without shaving or visiting a barber," Piritho said, rubbing his chin. "I was looking rather scruffy. Feels better without all that fur. Any other questions?" he ended with a smile.

"Just one. I got stuck with the job of procuring food for this trip. You aren't going to want live meat for dinner, are you?" Piritho, surprised by the question, saw the glint in Salis' eyes, and they both started to laugh.

"Just what everyone else is having will be fine with me," Piritho said.

"Good man," Salis said.

"You don't know how good it feels to hear someone call me that."

\* \* \*

The travelers left Numina by the north gate, heading toward Ilyan. Since there were no roads in Laria, they relied on Caidos and Matu to lead them, traveling from one landmark to the next. The first was a bare rocky butte, which could be seen on the horizon, rising abruptly from the flatness of the plain, and signaling the change from grassland to forest. Despite the lack of a well-worn road, they were able to ride at a light gallop, the ground level enough for the horses to easily find their footing.

They reached the butte by late morning, and took a short break, allowing the horses to water at a nearby stream. Piritho, whose face had been protected by heavy fur for months, now suffered in the bright sun and strong winds. The skin on his face was red and dry, but Matu found an aloe plant, and breaking off a stem, directed Piritho to rub the sap on his aching skin.

The path for the rest of the day would take them through a dense forest, which would eventually open again at the edge of a large lake. To save time, they planned to angle slightly to the east as they rode through the forest, coming out at the eastern shore of the lake. Matu took over the lead, knowing the signs in the forest better than Caidos.

The companions were grateful for the protection of the trees, which blocked the cold wind that had been biting at them all morning. Piritho, who had suffered the most, sighed with relief. The closeness of the trees required their path to continually weave back and forth. Only Matu was able to maintain a sense of direction and ensure they didn't lose their way.

The trees and undergrowth were so dense it was necessary to travel single file through most of the forest. Conversation had stopped and after a time even the wind had died. The heavy carpet of dead leaves beneath the horses' hooves muffled the sound of their passage. The silence was oppressive, and the enthusiasm that had started out the day, faded with the sound.

When the trees thinned and they entered a small clearing, Piritho took advantage of the extra room, and rode up alongside Caidos.

"Caidos," he said. His voice sounded loud and harsh in the quiet of the woods; he dropped it to little more than a whisper. "I wanted to thank you for allowing me to go along."

"You've been a member of this quest since the beginning. And as long as we are expressing gratitude, I should thank you for the part you played in saving my life." When he saw confusion in Piritho's eyes, he added, "With the raptors, back in Varsa. I have to admit when you came crashing through the woods, I thought the battle was over, though I thought you were on the wrong side at first. But a wolf at the door doesn't always mean a fight for the chickens."

"No, I guess it doesn't," Piritho said, with a slight confusion in his voice.

"See, it wasn't just because you were a beast, Piritho," Salis said from behind them, "he doesn't make any sense to me half the time, and sometimes less than that."

"Salis," Caidos told him without looking back, "You always forget, it's the quiet waters that ..."

Caidos never finished his proverb, for the silence of the forest was rent by a high pitched squeal and the sound of breaking branches being trampled by heavy feet.

A huge boar came crashing into the clearing, swinging its massive head from side to side, in an attempt to gore them with its saber-like tusks. The boar was as large as Piritho had been as the beast, but broader in girth. The usual, incongruously small cloven hooves of a boar were replaced by heavily clawed feet; the claws digging into the ground and kicking up clods of earth as it thundered past.

It swung its massive head at the horse's legs, barreling through them like a plow. Foot long tusks, added to the two-foot wide mouth, gave it a wide cutting swath. As it swung its head from side to side, it raised and lowered its jaws, trying to rip its prey with the jagged fangs pointing outward along the edge.

For something so large and heavy, its movements were swift. It had easily avoided the hooves of the frightened horses as they reared up and pawed at it. It had passed the travelers, and was turning for another charge as each of them tried to calm their mounts.

Brandorin was the first to react. He had jumped from Bristo's back and drawn his sword in one fluid motion. He swatted the horse's hindquarters to send him off and out of harm's way.

Kahdu had reared, but true to Matu's promise, Piritho had not fallen from his back. He was second to reach the ground, his sword out of its sheath before he landed.

Caidos and Icara stayed on their mounts, ready to use their incantations in defense of their companions. Matu was helping to calm M'drani's horse, so she could dismount safely.

The first boar had just begun another charge, as a second boar broke through the undergrowth. Brandorin and Piritho turned in opposite directions, each facing their own adversary. Even as the two boars were storming toward the swordsmen, the trampling and snarling of a third could be heard coming toward them through the woods.

Brandorin, closer to his target, held his sword steady, ready to strike the boar heading straight for him. The boar had just come within range, his sword slicing down its back when Matu shouted, "Stop, they are lapithi! Don't kill them."

Brandorin pulled the sword back and jumped. Reaching a low-hanging branch, he swung his legs clear of the passing tusks. Piritho dodged the boar attacking him, rather than striking it.

"What do you suggest we do?" Piritho called to Matu. "Can you reason with them?"

Brandorin dropped back to the ground, immediately ready to fight again. "I can appreciate trying to save them," Brandorin shouted, as he dodged the third boar as it plowed through the clearing, "but it doesn't look like they're planning to be reasonable."

"Let us try," Caidos said, as he and Icara prepared to use magic. As the first boar came back, Caidos cast an air incantation, trying to divert it away from them yet not hurt the man within. Though an air incantation had diverted the raptors; this time his magic had no effect, and the boar continued its charge directly at the mage. Zephyr, who had flown to a tree with the first attack, swept down toward the beast, hissing and sparking, distracting it. At the last second she flew up again, out of its reach.

Icara, seeing the ineffectiveness of Caidos' incantation, decided on fire as the other boar charged at her. She hit the boar with a barrage of fireballs. It yelped in pain as the fire ignited along its back, but it didn't divert from its charge. She ducked and rolled at the last second, the boar's tusk catching and ripping her robe.

The third boar ran toward the horses, where M'drani and Matu stood. M'drani had only a dagger to defend herself. Matu was prepared to defend her with his sword, if his attempts to reach the man within the boar failed.

Knowing they could not survive by continually dodging the boar's attacks, Brandorin and Piritho took action. The boars' grunts and growls changed to squeals of pain, as Brandorin's sword sliced the side of one boar and Piritho's sword came down on the back of the other. The boar's leathery hide and bristly mane deflected Piritho's sword, causing only minor damage.

The third boar bore down on M'drani and Matu. "Get into the tree, M'drani," Matu told her, "I'll deal with him." The branches in the closest tree were too high for M'drani to reach, so she stood her ground, ready to strike. The boar headed straight for her. Matu stepped to the side, trying to draw the boar toward him and away from M'drani. It ignored him, and continued its charge at M'drani. He dove toward it and reaching with his sword cut a glancing blow in its side as it passed.

It continued its charge, undaunted. When within five feet of M'drani, it wailed in pain, and swerved aside, missing her by inches. Brandorin ran up behind it, and as it turned, thrust his sword into its side, piercing its heart. It fell dead at his feet.

The other two boars had run out of the clearing after their last charges, but Brandorin could feel their pounding hooves in the hard-packed ground upon which he stood. The strong, pungent animal smell lingered in the clearing even though they had passed out of sight, into the wood.

The pounding increased in intensity, and the harsh breathing could be heard once again, as one of the boars returned, heading toward Piritho, who stood directly in front of it waiting. At the last second, he stepped to the side, and swung his sword, slicing into its rear flank. But it continued its run, heading now for Brandorin, who stood with his sword in front of him, holding it with both hands. He didn't jump to the side as the boar reached him, but used the forward movement of the charge to drive the sword into its throat, the impact knocking him off his feet.

A deathly silence filled the clearing, broken only by the heavy breathing of the companions, who turned looking for the remaining boar. Minutes passed, but the final boar did not return.

"Looks like we got that one too," Brandorin said as he turned to Piritho, clapping him on the back. "Either that or we scared him so bad, he ran off to nurse his wounds rather than face us again." Piritho, surprised by his friend's casual manner, hesitated before responding.

"We've always fought well together," Piritho said.

The excitement of the fight receding, Brandorin realized he

had spoken to Piritho for the first time since his retransformation. Feeling suddenly uncomfortable, and not knowing what else to say, he turned to Matu.

"It took a little while for your blow to stop it," he said.

"I didn't think I'd caused that much damage."

Brandorin, who had reached the carcass, crouched to get a closer look.

"There's an arrow in its side," he said with surprise. "Who had a bow?" Brandorin stood and looked at the other companions. "Salis? Where's Salis?" he asked, turning slowly around to search the entire area, not seeing the little man.

"His horse reared, then bolted away," M'drani said, "but he managed to stay on."

"Which way?" Piritho called, as he ran to Kahdu and jumped on his back. M'drani pointed in the direction she had last seen Salis and his horse, and Kahdu took off with a start.

"Then who shot this arrow?" Brandorin asked.

"I did." A female voice spoke from the far side of the clearing, and a tall, dark-haired woman, with cool penetrating eyes, walked into the dim light. She wore a deerskin tunic and pants, and carried a long bow. A shorter bow and a quiver full of arrows were slung over her shoulder. A large hunting knife was strapped to her thigh. Brandorin stepped between the woman and the rest of the companions. He had not yet sheathed his sword; though its point was lowered, he was ready in case of trouble.

"Who are you?" he asked.

"My name is Lanata. It looked like you could use a little help." Turning to M'drani she asked, "Are you all right? That thing got awfully close to you."

"I'm fine. Thank you for your intervention. I am M'drani," she said, stepping toward Lanata, her hand extended in friendship. Brandorin, clearly nervous about the presence of this unknown, well-armed woman, stepped up as well, introducing himself and the rest of the companions still in the clearing.

"And who was the one that went riding out of here?" Lanata asked, an intense interest in her voice.

"That was Piritho," Caidos said, "he went to find the last member of our party, Salis. And if I'm not mistaken, they're coming back now." The pounding of hooves approaching at a full gallop was clear. Piritho skidded to a halt, a bleeding man draped over the back of the horse in front of him.

"Salis!" Icara cried, before she saw a second horse, a short distance behind Kahdu.

"Salis found this man on his way back," Piritho said as he slid from the horse, the injured man in his arms. "He couldn't lift him to bring him back here. He's been gored by at least one of those boars. Has lost a great deal of blood."

He laid the man down and everyone could see he was a Larian. He had dark hair and a feline appearance, but his face was deathly pale. They could see the front of his shirt was soaked in blood, a gash torn in his side. M'drani grabbed a cloth from her saddlebag and pressed it to the man's side, trying to staunch the flow of blood.

"He has a second injury on his back," Piritho said.

"Let me see him," Brandorin said, kneeling next to the dying man, who looked up at him and then at the others.

"Matu, help me," the injured man whispered and tried to raise his hand to reach for his fellow Larian. Brandorin grasped his sword, placing his hand over the crystal in the hilt, and reached for the dying man with his other arm.

"Help me lift him," he said. Piritho bent to raise the man up so Brandorin could wrap his arms around the injured man.

The dying gasps of the wounded man and Brandorin's ragged breathing were the only sounds in the clearing. A pale, blue light slowly emanated from under Brandorin's hand on the sword's hilt. The gasps of the dying man seemed to even out and fall into synch with Brandorin's, the two men now breathing as one.

The glow intensified, illuminating the clearing in a blue nimbus of light. An agonized cry burst from Brandorin, as his arms and body convulsed. The stranger slumped to the ground and lay still, now breathing peacefully.

Brandorin wrapped his arms around his own stomach, as he

teetered on his knees. The companions gasped as they saw blood seep from his shirt, on both his side and on his back. Sweat broke out on his brow, and his face contorted around clenched teeth, as he held in another cry. He gasped as if each breath caused him excruciating pain. He could no longer remain kneeling, and fell over, his arms at his side as his body bucked and his back arched in the throes of agony. Despite the wrenching contortions, he held the sword in a white-knuckled grip. M'drani moved to go to him, but Caidos reached out his hand and stopped her, shaking his head.

Slowly the blue light faded and Brandorin's breathing eased. He laid still, his face relaxing as he controlled the wounds he had taken from the dying man. He opened his eyes and tried to sit up, but the ordeal had left him exhausted. Caidos and M'drani knelt on either side of him, supporting his back. His breathing had not returned to normal, but it was nothing more than the sound of a man who had been running fast and hard. M'drani saw, after wiping the sweat from his brow, that no more returned.

The man, whose wounds had been healed, sat up, touching his side and his back, and said, "My wounds, they're gone. I felt them leave me," his face a mix of joy and incredulity. He saw the blood on Brandorin's shirt matching the stains on his own. A look of awe and disbelief replaced the surprise and confusion on his face. "How did you ...? Why would you?"

"You're fine then?" Brandorin said, the words riding out on each exhalation of breath.

"It's as if it never happened. But what about you?" He moved, taking Caidos' place in supporting the man who had saved his life. "How could I ever thank you?"

"You could get me some water," Brandorin said weakly. The man jumped up, and Matu went with him to the horses where they got a water skin. After a long drink, Brandorin asked the man, "What's your name?"

The man, still in shock over what this stranger had done for him, had to stare at Brandorin for a second before answering, "Sadro."

"I'm Brandorin," he said as he feebly put his hand out.

Sadro clasped the offered hand and shook it fiercely. "Easy," Brandorin said, "you'll knock me over."

"I think we should camp here for tonight," Caidos said, "I don't imagine Brandorin will feel like riding before morning."

"That's the best idea I've heard all month," Brandorin said, as he collapsed back against Sadro and M'drani.

* * *

The travelers, well accustomed to the process of setting up camp, worked efficiently to unload the horses, lay out the bedrolls and find the closest source of water. The strangers had joined in, but though Sadro's wounds had been healed, the process had drained him. M'drani noticed him stumbling as he unsaddled Brandorin's horse.

"Why don't you sit with Brandorin, Sadro? See how he's..." She stopped, looking around the clearing, not seeing Brandorin. "Where is he?" she asked. The concern in her voice caught Piritho's attention as he passed.

"Where's who?"

"Brandorin."

"He's right over .... Well, he was there a minute ago. Maybe he went for some water," Piritho suggested, though the sound of his voice indicated he didn't place much confidence in his own suggestion.

"That healing exhausted him so badly, I think he would have asked if he needed anything," M'drani said. "Something's wrong, I can feel it," she said as she ran to the spot where Brandorin had last been seen. Piritho, who had followed close behind her, crouched to check the ground where Brandorin had been sitting.

"I don't like the looks of this," Piritho said as he jumped up and sprinted across the clearing to his bedroll, and pulled out his sword. "I think you're right, M'drani. Something is wrong."

Piritho's and M'drani's actions and the distress in their voices had drawn everyone's attention. Caidos stopped Piritho as he started to follow the trail into the woods. "What is it?" he asked.

"Brandorin's gone," Piritho said, "and from these marks on the ground, I would say he *crawled* away, but that doesn't make any sense. We've got to find him."

Caidos couldn't stop Piritho, but he took command of the rest of the companions. "If Brandorin is indeed missing, it will be best to search for him in pairs. Get your weapons." When everyone had left, he quietly asked, "M'drani, do you sense anything?"

"I can't say for sure. It's very confusing. I think it's Brandorin, at least part of it. It's all scrambled. Some of the feelings have to be from someone else. Those can't be Brandorin ..."

She was stopped by Piritho's return and the shocked look on his face.

"You found him?" she asked quietly.

He nodded hesitantly.

"He's not ...?" Caidos could not finish the question. The others had returned with their weapons.

"Caidos, M'drani, you better come with me. The rest of you, please wait here." The tone of Piritho's voice stilled any protest. He turned silently and walked back into the woods. M'drani and Caidos walked behind him but they had gone only a short distance when he stopped. Piritho said nothing, but the pain and confusion in his eyes and the direction of his glance told them all they needed to know. Even in the low light of the woods, they could see Brandorin plainly; curled up at the base of a large oak tree, cowering in fear.

## Chapter 19

Though she had not known Brandorin as long as either Piritho or Caidos, M'drani was shocked by Brandorin's condition. Bravery was as much a part of Brandorin as his auburn hair or his long legs; he wore his courage as naturally as his skin. Piritho, no longer able to watch his friend in so uncharacteristic a state, had turned to Caidos and M'drani, hoping they would have an answer.

"Brandorin, it's me, M'drani. We're here to help you."

The words, though spoken softly, had a major impact. Brandorin recoiled from her. He tried to back away, but the trunk of the oak held him in place. He began to mutter incoherently. Most of the words were incomprehensible but M'drani was able to discern one phrase. "Don't hurt me." She stepped back a few feet to lessen his distress.

"He had the same reaction when I first found him," Piritho said. "He was fine after healing Sadro. Exhausted, but otherwise fine."

"His shirt is all bloody from the wounds he took from Sadro," M'drani said. "Maybe there are new wounds. Could something have happened in the clearing? Something the rest of us didn't see?"

"I checked when I first found him. He's not wounded. Nothing natural would make him react this way. Rhamak did something. A spell. A poison." Piritho's voice intensified with each phrase, and Brandorin recoiled from the anger they reflected.

"Yes, undoubtedly Rhamak," Caidos said, keeping his voice low. "But I don't understand how. Brandorin wasn't injured by the boars; he only healed someone who was. The incantation would have had to transfer from the boars, to Sadro, and then to Brandorin."

"That can't be done?"

"*I* don't know how to do it. Rhamak may have found a way."

"How do we counter it?"

Caidos shook his head slowly, his voice dejected. "I don't

know."

"How can you not know, Caidos," Piritho burst out. He dropped his voice when he saw Brandorin's fear intensify, but his frustration and anger were still evident. "You're the Mirador. You're supposed to know all the tricks."

"I'm sorry, Piritho, I wish I could ..." Caidos began.

M'drani put her hand on Caidos' arm to stop him and quietly said, "Piritho, he doesn't know the incantation. How can he know how to counter it?"

Piritho, calmed by M'drani's words, stammered an apology to Caidos. M'drani decided Piritho and Caidos were too close to Brandorin. She took control of the situation.

"Why don't you two go back to camp," M'drani said. "Let the others know what's happening. Talk to Sadro. See what he knows. Maybe he felt this way too for a time. If he did, that would mean it wears off. In the meantime, let me try to help Brandorin."

"I don't think we should say anything just yet," Caidos said. "I'd like to know a little more about Sadro and Lanata and why they were in these woods, at this particular time. For all we know they had a hand in all of this."

Once Caidos and Piritho had gone, M'drani watched Brandorin from a short distance. From the clearing she had sensed his distress, felt a deep and utter sense of loss. Now that she was close to him, the fear overshadowed any other feelings. The intensity increased the closer she got to him, until she could smell the rank fear pouring off him.

M'drani spoke soothingly, trying to calm him, as she reached for him with her thoughts. She tried to wrap her thoughts around the fear, envelop it, and control it, but it was different than any fear she had ever felt, either her own or anyone else's.

This fear was vile, infused with the brownish green of rot and decay. M'drani felt its long, clinging tentacles trying to reach her. If she didn't do something soon Brandorin would be permanently locked in its grip.

She ran forward and dropped to her knees in front of Brandorin. She took his arms, and unwrapping them from around his torso, put them around her own. Cradling his head between her hands, she looked deeply into his panicked gaze and with her thoughts, reached into his.

Brandorin fought her, trying to hide in the recesses of his mind. M'drani ignored his plaintive cries and reached for the fear. It waited for her, turning on her the second she touched it. It washed over her, threatening to drown her.

She choked on its sour stench, was swamped under by the raw power of it. M'drani called to Brandorin, asking for his help, but all she heard were his denials. She felt his arms grip her more tightly, and the urgency of that embrace gave her the strength to push the fear back.

It began to recede, but would not surrender. The fear still held him like a vise and M'drani could feel Brandorin's despair of ever breaking free.

The fear surged over her in waves, each one stronger than the last. She was losing the fight. M'drani's instincts told her to get out. She couldn't save him. Brandorin didn't want to be saved. She tried to pull away, separate her thoughts from his, but the draw of the fear gripped her.

M'drani reached up, trying to pull herself out, but there was nothing to grab onto. The wave receded, and she reached again. Then she felt it, a tentative touch.

Brandorin was trying to help. She called to him again, and this time felt his thoughts join hers, and together they surrounded the fear, pushing it back.

As it receded, a black iciness seized her, like the powerful undertow of a wave breaking on the shore. It pulled at M'drani until it had engulfed her in a cold desolation that wormed through her veins, threatening to freeze her heart. She felt bereft, completely alone in a great void. There was no way to fight it, no one to help her. She was being dragged down.

M'drani heard Brandorin's thoughts call out to her. They anchored her. He was losing the battle with the fear. It was returning, overpowering his tenuous control. M'drani turned from the pull of the void, focused on the fear and with Brandorin's strength, felt it slowly retreat.

*   *   *

Brandorin and M'drani walked back into the clearing, leaning on each other, like two fallen trees supporting each other, though it seemed that the willow held up the oak. Caidos and Piritho had been watching the woods and joined them as they collapsed near Brandorin's bedroll.

"We told them you were having a reaction to healing Sadro, but didn't provide any details," Caidos told them.

"Mostly because we didn't have any," Piritho added.

Brandorin smiled weakly and looked at his friend for a long time, until Caidos said, "Are you going to tell us what happened?"

M'drani started to speak, but Brandorin stopped her. "I will." The exhaustion he felt was evident in his voice, little more than a whisper, the phrases gasped out more than spoken. "But what I want - more than anything - is to get out - of this bloody shirt. And have something to eat. Is there any dinner left?"

"Dinner? It will be another couple of hours before we eat."

"It feels like days since I ate last."

"I'll get you a spare shirt and some food," Piritho said.

"Stalling, Brandorin?" Caidos asked.

He turned his eyes up to Caidos, his head felt too heavy to move. "A little. Mostly just exhausted. I don't remember ever being this tired."

"That was quite a dramatic healing, very different than anything you'd done before. But I have a feeling that was nothing compared to what you went through in the last half hour."

"Half an hour?" M'drani said, surprise making her voice squeak. "Is that all it's been? Brandorin's right, it seems more like days. I hope Piritho brings enough food for two."

"I did," Piritho said, opening the bundle he carried. Brandorin's change of shirt was wrapped around a full loaf of bread, a wheel of cheese, a water skin, and a clean rag.

Brandorin needed help to change shirts and clean the

remainder of the blood off with a damp rag. Once he had consumed a fair quantity of bread and cheese, Caidos gave him a look that clearly said he should begin his story.

He took a long drink of water and said quietly, "I wasn't prepared for the pain. I hadn't felt anything that first time, when I cured Aquilo's side and your shoulder, Caidos. When I've healed our aches each night, I could feel some discomfort, but nothing like this. I know these wounds were worse, but it was more than that."

"More pain?"

"More pain, yes, a lot more. More than those wounds should have caused. It seemed to hurt everywhere, not just my side and back. It felt as if my entire body was being stretched and contorted.

"But I also felt fear. I've been scared before. But nothing like this. I'd never felt so afraid. And alone. I knew you were all there, but I felt - abandoned. It almost overwhelmed me it was so strong. But when the pain left, so did the fear. At least I thought it did.

"Everyone was setting up camp. Sadro had brought my saddle, bedroll and other things over after unsaddling Bristo. I figured I should be doing something, so I started to set up my bed. Then it suddenly came rushing back, stronger than before. I was suddenly terrified." He stopped. Just talking about it built up a pressure in the pit of his stomach, as if the fear would break through the fragile barrier that held it in. He took a deep breath and continued, but his voice was controlled, the words measured.

"I was terrified of all of you. It wasn't any one person or thing; I just knew I had to get away. I was even afraid to stand up; afraid you'd see me, so I ..." He turned his face away, unable to look at them as he finished. "I crawled out of here on my belly.

"But that didn't help. I was just as afraid when I was out of your sight. Then Piritho found me. I didn't even recognize him. All I knew was the fear."

"What happened after we left you?" Caidos asked.

"M'drani helped me to control it. But it's not gone, not totally. I can feel it, hiding; like an echo, it keeps threatening to come back."

"Brandorin, you said you were setting up your bed," Caidos said. "What exactly did you do?"

"Nothing to be afraid of. I unrolled my blanket. Threw my cloak over the saddle, and picked up my ..." He stared at Caidos, his mouth hanging open, "Oh, no! My sword. I had just picked up my sword."

Caidos reached for Brandorin's sword, handing it to him he said, "Here, take it. Put your hand on the crystals."

Brandorin stared at the sword for a moment, took a couple of deep breaths, and grasped the hilt. He felt his mouth go dry. He gulped air, struggling for each breath. His hand started to shake and he dropped the sword.

"Was it the same?" Caidos asked.

"Not as intense, but it was growing. Quickly."

"Hold the sword, but don't touch the crystals."

Brandorin tried to swallow but couldn't; it was as if he had forgotten how. He took the sword reluctantly, avoiding the stones in its hilt. His hand gripped the sword so tightly his arm shook. Piritho reached out, wanting to help his friend, but Caidos put up a hand and shook his head.

"It's there, but more distant, less severe."

"Now see if you can hold it and touch only the Protector's crystal." Brandorin shifted his hand on the hilt so his palm was on the light blue crystal, but his fingers were not wrapped around far enough to touch the Umari stone. He had barely touched the stone when a jolt of ice-cold fear shot through him, burning from the inside out. He threw the sword to the ground.

"You don't have to tell me that was worse," Caidos said. "Now turn it, and touch only the Umari crystal." Brandorin clenched his fist, holding his arm against his stomach. "You must, Brandorin."

His fingers trembled as he reached out to touch the indigo crystal lightly with his fingers, ready to pull them back if he felt even a spark of the fear. When he didn't feel anything, he grasped the hilt, being very careful to touch only the Umari stone. He held it for a long time.

"Nothing. Not even the distant echo. But that's not going to work if we have to fight again. I can't handle the sword properly if I have to hold like that. And I can't be afraid to grab my sword. Those few seconds could mean someone's life. Could we temporarily remove the Protector's stone?"

"No, it will only be released at the Rejoining. We have to hope the feeling will fade. Perhaps holding the Umari stone will help heal that as well."

"Rhamak planned this." Brandorin felt a heat rise in his throat, but it was anger and frustration, rather than fear. "He knows I have the Umari stone, doesn't he?"

"I would think so," Caidos said, nodding in confirmation.

"So he knew I would try to heal anyone who got hurt."

"I still don't understand how he did it, though." Caidos shook his head slowly, his lips pressed tightly together. When he spoke again, he seemed to be talking more to himself than the others. "It didn't happen with the raptors. But he could have added this twist after their failure."

He turned to Brandorin, with a crinkle at the corners of his eyes. "I'm sure he was quite angry with you for foiling that attack. Let me at least see if I can tell what we're dealing with."

Brandorin still held the sword, while Caidos puzzled over what to do. "Keep your hand on the Umari crystal while I try this. It seems to help you, so it probably can't hurt."

"Probably? Doesn't sound encouraging," Brandorin said.

Caidos ignored him, and slowly reached his hands out, one near Brandorin's hand, the other near the former location of the wound that had started the problem. A pulse of light jumped from Brandorin to Caidos' hands, and the mage flew backward falling flat on his back. Piritho reached down to help him up. Caidos had a look of annoyance on his face.

"It was Rhamak all right. Chaos take him!" Caidos shouted, then stopped and regained his composure. "He expected me to try that. In addition to a shock of power there was a lingering sound of laughter. He was laughing at me! He knew I'd try, and he knew I'd fail." He looked at Brandorin, and saw the utter disappointment he tried to hide. "I'm sorry, Brandorin. There's nothing I can do. Just keep your hand on the Umari crystal as much as you can. And don't try to test the other stone until at least tomorrow."

The sound of voices drifted over from the others sitting on the opposite side of the clearing. "What are we going to tell them?" M'drani asked.

"I'm not sure we have to tell them anything just yet. Let's see how Brandorin feels in the morning. With your help, and the Umari stone, he may be able to conquer Rhamak's little surprise.

"M'drani, Caidos, would you mind letting me talk to Brandorin alone?" Piritho looked at his friend to see if he was agreeable.

When Brandorin nodded hesitantly, Caidos smiled and said, "It would be my pleasure. Come, M'drani, we'll get you something to eat. Brandorin didn't give you much of a chance with that bread and cheese."

After they had left to join the rest on the other side of the clearing, Piritho looked at his friend. "This must be very hard for you."

"It can't be any harder than what you went through."

"I don't know. I don't remember much before ... Caidos said the crystal in the sword helped you recognize me." When Brandorin didn't say anything else, Piritho continued, "I can't imagine what this must be like for you. I've seen you in battle, I know you don't feel fear ..."

"Everyone feels fear."

"Well, I've never seen you let it get the better of you. It's something you've never had to deal with, so ... if you want to talk about it ... I understand what it's like being forced to act in a way that's so out of character."

The two friends sat without talking for a time. Piritho started to get up when Brandorin asked, "What do you remember of the last few weeks?"

"As much as you do, I guess, though not necessarily in the same fashion. I know it must have looked odd, the two of us traveling together, but it seemed pretty natural to me."

"You're right, it did. But it was different. Different enough to let us forget what had happened. But now that you're back ... I can't. I should have gone after Rhamak that day," Brandorin said. "It should have been me."

"If you had gone, you'd be dead now. I may not remember much about what Rhamak did to me, but I know that." An awkward silence fell between them. Piritho finally broke it.

"I know you can't forgive me for what I did. I don't ..."

"It's not that," Brandorin interrupted. "I know it wasn't your fault. I know that better now than I did a couple of hours ago. It's just that I need to know why. Why Ilona and not me?"

Piritho closed his eyes and turned away. Brandorin watched as he struggled for an explanation. He continued to look away as he answered Brandorin's question. "I recognized you. I knew I was supposed to kill you, but I couldn't. Ilona was there. I didn't recognize her, but I think I saw her as a threat. I can't explain it."

"I think I understand; when you found me before, I didn't see you as a friend. I was terrified of you." Another silence fell between them, but it was no longer awkward. Brandorin knew Piritho's true feelings had nothing to do with what he had done at the wedding. He continued, "It's going to take a little longer for me to deal with all of this. But I will."

"I've found I'm more patient than I used to be," Piritho said. "I don't know if that bread was enough to satisfy your hunger, but I think we should find Salis and see when we're going to eat."

Brandorin wrapped a blanket around his shoulders, to hide the sword while he held the Umari crystal. He needed help getting up and walking across the clearing, but as they approached the others, they could tell that the discussion about their evening meal had already started.

"Now let me get this straight. You, M'drani, won't eat fowl, but you'll eat fish, and some meat. But Matu, and undoubtedly Sadro, won't eat any kind of meat," Salis said.

"We don't eat the flesh of creatures we communicate with."

"What about fish then," Salis asked.

"Fish is fine."

"Caidos did this to me on purpose," Salis muttered, "he knew this was going to happen. Meat, no meat. Fowl, no fowl. I can't wait until we get to Ilyan and Arkhan."

Matu agreed to go with him in search of food that would be agreeable to everyone. Brandorin pulled him aside for a quick question before he left, then turning he saw M'drani watching him. Not wanting to talk further about the fear, he turned to the others and said, "Lanata, I didn't thank you for your help," Brandorin said. "Convenient, you being nearby."

"Oh, she explained that before, Brandorin," Piritho said. "She's quite a hunter, and came to Laria to see what the land is like. You probably don't realize what a shot that was. She showed us where she was standing. Shooting from between the trees, the distance, the low light. It was an incredible shot!" Brandorin looked at Piritho and smiled inwardly at his friend's reaction to Lanata's skill.

"Have you already explored the entire west?" Brandorin asked, trying to find out about Lanata through more objective eyes.

"A great deal of it, yes. I was born in Bortira in Varsa. It's a very little town, in the northeast, up near the Arkidan Mountains. You've probably never heard of it. My mother died when I was young, so my father taught me to track and hunt along with my brothers. I feel uncomfortable in a city, and even worse in a dress. I wanted to see someplace new, different. So I rode across the Central Desert, traveling at night, when it was cool, under the Harvest Moon, so I could see. Thought I'd work my way through Laria and up to Ilyan."

"We're heading that way ourselves," Piritho volunteered. Caidos and Brandorin both gave him a look, trying to stop him, but he didn't see them, or chose to ignore them. "You can ride along with us."

Before she could accept an offer Brandorin would have preferred had not been made, he asked, "Have you seen anyone else? Especially in the last day or so?"

"You're the first people, Larian or Westerners that I've seen since leaving the Chiron Ridge. But I did see some wagon tracks to the north of these woods. I thought the Larians didn't use wheels, so I found that curious. I followed them. That's what brought me into this area. When I heard those snorts and squeals, I left the trail and followed the sounds."

"Did you have a wagon, Sadro?"

"No, I was on horseback."

"Maybe we should follow those tracks tomorrow," Brandorin said. "Caidos, should we take care of the dead boars? The way we did with the raptors."

"No, just leave them for now. I don't know about everyone else, but I'm hungry. Where is Salis? He's supposed to be working on dinner."

The companions continued setting up camp, getting ready to cook whatever the others brought back. Brandorin and Caidos conferred over the sudden appearance of two strangers and the possible impact on their quest. They approached Sadro, who was seeing to the horses.

What happened to your horse, Sadro?" Caidos asked.

"She reared up when the boars came at us. I was thrown and she took off; I had to run for it. My sword and all my supplies were with her. I could try looking for her tomorrow, but it's likely she just headed home."

"Where is home?" Caidos asked, watching the stranger's cat-like eyes carefully for any sign of deceit.

"Adina, it's north and east of here.

"That's quite a way. What were you doing this far from home?"

"Heading to Numina."

"We just left there this morning, but it will take a couple of days for you to walk it. I'm sure we can spare some supplies."

"There is nothing special awaiting me in Numina. I feel I owe you a Debt of Life," he said to Brandorin. "I will travel with you, until I can repay that debt." He looked to Brandorin, touching his hand to his brow, then added; "I need to get fodder for the horses."

"Debt of Life? Is that a Larian term?" Brandorin asked Caidos, after Sadro had left.

"Yes, and they're very serious about fulfilling such debts. You saved his life. He must do a great favor for you. If he can save yours, he'll consider the debt repaid in kind. Despite what he said, he may have been driving the wagon. It would have been the best way to get those boars here."

"It shouldn't be too far. If it was used to bring the boars into the area, their tracks should lead away from it."

"He may be telling the truth, Brandorin. He's obviously a Larian, and the Debt of Life is valid. And he knows Matu."

"I asked Matu about that. He doesn't know Sadro. Though he admitted Sadro could know him due to his father's position of Elder."

"Lanata's presence has me more concerned," Caidos said. "There's no logical reason for her to be here. And the fact Piritho has now invited her to go along with us, doesn't help."

"I think the two of you are being overly cautious," M'drani interjected. "Sadro could have died, and he probably would have if Brandorin didn't intervene. Lanata saved my life. If she hadn't shot that boar, it would have gored me, so I guess I owe her a Debt of Life. I don't sense any danger from either of them."

"Maybe I'm overreacting," Brandorin muttered. He reached for the sword at his side, and put his hand on the Umari crystal again.

"I don't think we can be too careful," Caidos added, "there's too much at stake. But there may be other factors at work here. Maybe these people were meant to find us. Still, it's foolish to put money into a sack, without first checking if it has a hole."

"Do you want me to try to get a better feeling from them?" M'drani asked.

"You understood that?" Brandorin whispered to her.

"I heard that, Brandorin," Caidos said, then to M'drani, "If you can. And don't be worrying about being rude. See what you can get from each of them tonight, so we can make a decision before we leave in the morning."

The sound of voices coming through the woods ended the conversation. "Another fabulous dinner coming up," Salis called. "But I must give credit to Matu here. He's deadly accurate with a spear. We have enough fish here to make everyone happy." He looked at Brandorin suspiciously, "Unless you're going to tell me now you don't like fish."

"I wouldn't do that," he said. "Even if it were true."

\* \* \*

After the fish had been cooked and everyone had their fill, the companions sat around the campfire and relaxed. Caidos had watched Lanata and Sadro throughout the evening. M'drani had managed to engage them both in conversation and he felt she was ready to tell him what she had learned. He was just trying to get her attention when Salis, who had gone off to bury the remains of their dinner, called out in alarm.

"Caidos, Brandorin, come quickly. Hurry." Everyone jumped up from the fire and ran over to him. As M'drani, Icara and Lanata approached, he motioned for them to stop. "You ladies better wait there."

When they reached Salis they looked over his shoulder and saw a naked man, covered with blood.

"I expected this," Caidos said. Salis looked at him, startled at his reaction. When he started to say something, Caidos added, "You should find another over there." He pointed to the opposite side of the clearing. Salis, confused by his friend's reaction, walked in the direction he had pointed. As he walked, Caidos directed him more specifically to the spot he meant.

"You're right, there's another man here. He's dead too," Salis added after checking.

"The lapithi," Matu said quietly.

"Lapithi?" Salis asked, "Like Piritho?"

Matu nodded. "Your horse had bolted and you were gone before I realized the boars attacking us had human spirits."

"What do you mean, 'like Piritho'?" Lanata asked.

"Thank goodness we decided to have fish," Salis said, "For a while there I thought having pork might be nice."

"Salis!" Matu, M'drani and Brandorin all said at once.

"All right everyone," Caidos said, taking charge of the situation, "let's settle down. I'll explain everything, after we bury these men; they deserve that. But first, I need to check something." He raised his hand, forming a ball of cool flame and went back to the body of the first man. Rolling him over, he checked his face and the wounds that had killed him. He did the same for the second. After they had buried both men, they returned to the fire and Caidos provided the explanation he promised.

"As Matu said, the boars that attacked us were lapithi," he began. He turned to Lanata, who had not been with them in Numina, "That means they were human spirits in an animal's body." She turned to look at Piritho, remembering Salis' comment.

"Yes, Piritho was a lapithi, up until two days ago. Though he wasn't a boar like the creatures that attacked us. He was a much more lovable beast," he said, smiling at Piritho, "a very large dog, for lack of a better description.

"There is a third man out there in the woods. He may still be a lapithi. We don't know if the wounds he incurred were enough to kill him. All four of these men were transformed and sent after us by a man named Rhamak." Caidos gave a brief rendition of the raptor attack for Lanata's and Sadro's benefit.

"But you'll remember, Brandorin, as we came out of the woods and saw the raptor in the field; it didn't look as fierce as the others. You called it a runt. I think they too were lapithi, and after death, they were returning to their natural form.

"There was still a slightly non-human look to the men we just buried. They were not quite back to their original form. From their features, I would say they were Varsians. I regret having to kill them, but we had no other choice. If Rhamak had sent three men that had attacked us with such ferocity, we would have done the same."

"They had no choice in their actions," Matu said, "I understand why we had to kill them. I just wish there had been another way."

"As do I, Matu," Caidos continued. "Lanata, Sadro, you have talked about joining us on our journey, but you may want to rethink that decision. This was the third time Rhamak has sent lapithi after one or all of us. I have no doubt he will try again."

He had talked briefly to M'drani before they had all returned to the campfire. Based on what she had told him, he continued. "The quest we are on is of vital importance. The survival of Zadania depends on our success. Your lives will be in danger if you continue to travel with us, but we could use your help, if you're willing to give it."

When Lanata made a move to speak, he stopped her. "No, don't answer yet. It's late, and we should all get some sleep. We'll start early in the morning. From here we go to Ilyan, and then to Arkhan. We hope that will be the end of our journey, but it may not be. We may have to find Rhamak to complete our quest. Fighting those boars, or those raptors, will be nothing compared to facing Rhamak directly.

"Think about your choice. If you wish to go your own way in the morning, no one here will blame you. We must go, you do not."

## Chapter 20

Rhamak and Chaubrel left the solar. Rhamak had viewed the boar attack and the events following from the memory of a man that had witnessed it as a raven. The man had flown through the night, under strict instructions from Rhamak, to return to Kalarak as soon as possible. After viewing everything the man had seen; Rhamak had sent him back to catch up with the companions. The presence of six crystal fragments would help him find them even in the wilderness of Laria or Ilyan.

"They think they have won another victory because they stopped my Suidar, Chaubrel, but they didn't see the second attack within. That seed is planted now. Brandorin and his precious gift of Healing. He won't be so anxious to try *that* the next time. Caidos and his young apprentice are easy to handle. But what was that little dragonfly?"

"I'm sorry, sire, I don't understand," Chaubrel said.

"Oh, of course, you didn't see it. Caidos' pet. It's of no consequence. Brandorin won't be wielding that troublesome sword with quite the same vigor, but they all have swords. I'll make the next attackers more impervious to cuts, and their target will be Brandorin. He's vulnerable now. The subjects are ready?"

"Yes, sire."

"You go ahead, I will be down in a while."

Chaubrel was unsure of Rhamak's mood. The news from the raven had been mixed. The boars had failed to hurt, let alone kill any of the companions, but whatever Rhamak had seen had made up for their failure. He hadn't told Chaubrel what the second attack was, but it had been successful. Yet despite its success, Rhamak was distracted. He wasn't angry, as he had been when Juar brought back the news of the Talondrin's failure. Chaubrel was wary of Rhamak when he was in a pensive mood. He was glad he had been dismissed.

\* \* \*

"See these marks," Matu said as they inspected the bed of the wagon Lanata had found, "clawed feet, and big ones. The boars arrived here in this wagon. And there was one man, the driver of the wagon. Nothing distinctive about his footprints. He released the boars, unharnessed the horse that pulled the wagon, and rode away. Looks like he followed the boars."

They followed the horse's trail. It led back toward the clearing, stopped for a time in one spot, though the boars had continued on. When the rider did move on, he went in a different direction.

"He headed northwest after that. We'd have to go out of our way to keep tracking him."

"We don't have the time for that," Caidos said. "He has up to a half day's lead on us, depending on how long he stopped for the night."

As they walked back to camp, Caidos pulled Brandorin aside. "Could those prints have been a woman's, instead of a man's?"

"Do you want to know if they could have been Lanata's? No they aren't. I compared the footprints to hers; they aren't even close. Her feet are not only smaller, but also narrower. And before you ask, they aren't Sadro's either."

"Just a dead end for now. How are you feeling this morning?"

"Refreshed. I'll have no trouble riding today," he said. Caidos raised an eyebrow and stood waiting for the real answer to his question. Brandorin added, "About the other, I don't know. You said not to touch the Protector's crystal again."

"A blacksmith's children are not afraid of sparks. Go ahead, try it now." He suspected Brandorin had tried it on his own, but had not been happy with the results. Brandorin hesitated, then steeled himself against the fear.

He held it far longer than the previous evening. Caidos could see the distended muscles and veins in his arm, saw a slight tremor. Brandorin said, "Much better," through clenched teeth. Caidos could see by subtle changes in his expression and his breathing, the feeling of fear was creeping up on him. Brandorin held on for much longer than Caidos had expected, but the strain was apparent, as was the relief on his face when he finally released the sword.

"Time and the Umari stone seemed to have helped. Keep your hand on the stone as you ride today, and we'll test it again tonight."

"But what if we run into trouble again today? I won't be at my best. It could cost us a life."

"That's why I must ask your permission to talk to Matu about this. I think it prudent to keep it from Sadro and Lanata, however, until we are sure about them, but at least Piritho and Matu will be prepared to cover for you."

Brandorin flared with anger, but it was not directed at Caidos. "I've never hesitated when action was required, not in training, not in battle."

"There is no reason to be embarrassed, Brandorin. It isn't your fault." Caidos wanted Brandorin to feel more at ease, "I know this is as unnatural to you as ... as doing hard work is to Salis." Caidos was glad to see a smile break across Brandorin's face.

"You and Salis are very good friends, aren't you?"

"I've known him since he was a boy. I know a great many people, in cities and towns all across Zadania. But there are very few I consider good friends. Someone I can tell *my* troubles to. Salis has always looked at me as just another man, not letting the title and my abilities keep him at a distance, as so many others do.

"Don't get me wrong, they are all wonderful people, and I care for them deeply, but Salis feels like family. And if I can tell you a little secret, I think by the time this journey is finished, I'll have a few more names to add to that short list." He put his hand on Brandorin's arm, and winked. "I don't have to tell Matu the real reason, if you would rather I not. I can tell him you are still tired from yesterday's healing. It's mostly the truth."

"You can tell him the truth. This is only temporary, but we need to be alert. What do you think about Lanata now that we've confirmed her story about the wagon?"

"I tend to believe her. If she had anything to do with that wagon bringing the boars here, she wouldn't have mentioned it to begin with. Remember the raptor attack? You thought you saw someone else in the woods that day. You said Piritho went to investigate."

"But he didn't find anyone."

"Still, there could have been someone controlling the raptors, just as someone brought the boars here, and was probably controlling them."

"Do you think it wise to allow Lanata and Sadro to come with us?"

"Maybe it isn't wise, but I think we should. It's just a feeling, but I think it will be worse if they aren't with us.

\*   \*   \*

Rhamak crossed to the stairs, which he descended to the dungeon. Chaubrel waited at the bottom of the stair, wishing he could be anywhere else, but Rhamak expected him to attend the transformations.

At the bottom of the stairs the hallway opened out onto a large circular room. A large stone table, made from a single block of basalt, dominated the center of the room, its ebon surface smooth and unmarked.

The mélange of human sweat and waste, spiced with the acrid scent of fear permeated the room. The flames of six torches did little to illuminate the horrific scene. At the far end of the room, a cage held thirty men, packed in so tightly they were forced to stand. Twelve men stood along the walls of the room. Their arms and legs chained, forcing them to face the table, to watch what took place there.

Rhamak's marshals had brought all forty-two men to Kalarak, but Rhamak had selected these twelve himself. They were candidates for his elite cadre of assassins. Their strength and their intelligence would be supplemented by powers Rhamak would give them. The commonality and vulnerability of their human form would be replaced with something more threatening and durable.

Rhamak walked around the room, inspecting the twelve men, judging them, rating them. Chaubrel stood at the foot of the block of stone, two guards at his sides, waiting for Rhamak to indicate his selection.

"I haven't prepared such a group since I created the Talondrin," he said, the excitement of the adventure ahead of him making the timbre and pitch of his voice rise. "I made them invulnerable to Caidos' magic, but that wasn't enough. I intend on instilling in these creations the same skills and defenses the Talondrin were privy to, but I will improve them. I will provide them with an armor their swords won't be able to pierce. I will make them indestructible."

He stopped before one man, a malevolent smile hinted at his plans. "Yes, I remember this one. He will be the best." The man stood tall, showing pride in being singled out. "He will be the leader. This one last, Chaubrel."

"Yes, sire," Chaubrel said, as he made a mental note of Rhamak's choice.

Rhamak continued his circuit of the room, and indicating the smallest of the twelve, he said, "I'll start with this one." He stepped to the table in the center of the room, and ran his hand over its glossy black surface.

The guards released the man from his chains, and brought him to the table. They laid him on the surface, stripped him of the few clothes he was wearing, and held him. Rhamak swept his arm over the man, and he remained motionless, unable to move. The guards withdrew, standing in the entrance to the chamber.

The man gulped air in deep, grasping breaths, and his mouth and eyes widened with fear. Chaubrel tried to see the man the way Rhamak did, but he had never been able to do so. Rhamak looked at the man on the table before him, but saw only clay, a medium with which to sculpt his new creation. Chaubrel could smell the man's fear, and felt his own cold sweat break out along his spine.

Rhamak held his arms out over the table, passing them slowly above the reclining figure, feeling the bones, muscle and sinew within without touching him. His lips moved slightly, as if he was speaking, but even the man closest to him heard no words.

The man began to moan and writhe, as the muscles in his legs began to pulse and expand. His thighs and calves distorted until they were twice their size in girth, and each muscle was clearly defined, distended and knotted. As Rhamak swept his arms up the man's torso, the muscles in his abdomen, chest, and arms grew and bulged, just as the moaning grew from sobs to screams. Rhamak's eyes glistened with excitement and a grin of utter satisfaction looked foreign on his usually stern face.

Those watching from the walls began to sweat and struggle against their chains. Moans and cries came too from the cage at the far side of the room, as the men in it were slowly consumed by Rhamak's incantations; their energies sacrificed to power the transformation.

Rhamak walked to the head of the table, a bounce in his step that betokened his enjoyment of the process. He stretched his hands out, a few inches above the man's face. The man's nose slowly disappeared as his face widened and then elongated and stretched forward. His mouth gaped from ear to ear, wide open in a silent scream. Double rows of sharp, dagger-pointed, jagged-edged teeth sprouted along the full length of both upper and lower jaw. The lids of the subject's eyes disappeared as they grew in size and stared back, black and lifeless.

The rise and fall of his chest had stopped, and Chaubrel thought he had died from the ordeal. Then he noticed gills in the neck, which pulsed as air was passed through.

Rhamak now worked on the creature's hands. The tendons stood out in stark relief as the muscles expanded. Webbing appeared between the elongated fingers. Next, Rhamak broadened the feet, the arch flattened and the toes merged together. The shape looked odd to Chaubrel, until he realized that the fin shape would help the creature swim, but the flat structure would also allow it to walk on dry land.

Rhamak held his arms out, encompassing his creation, looking at the overall affect of his effort. He looked up at Chaubrel and slowly nodded his head in affirmation of the changes.

"Now, to provide my Maken with a natural armor."

Rhamak raised his arms again, spreading them wide over the creature; he closed his eyes and began to utter an incantation. Chaubrel recognized the words as those of the ancient tongue, though he didn't understand them. It was a harsh and guttural language that echoed dully throughout the room. The skin covering the creature's body began to ripple and darken. It thickened and separated into scales that grew smaller and tighter, until it became a tough hide of dark gray. It resembled chain mail, but with links so tight and small they could barely be differentiated.

"Shall we test it?" Rhamak asked. Chaubrel stared at the creature on the table. Only five minutes before this had been a man, now even Chaubrel didn't think of him as one. "A sword, Chaubrel."

The tone of Rhamak's voice brought Chaubrel out of his stupor, and he looked up at Rhamak, trying to hide his disdain. He decided he must have been successful for Rhamak looked back at him with a sense of pride, as if Chaubrel had been admiring his handiwork. Chaubrel motioned to the guards standing against the wall. One of them walked to the table, his sword drawn. He stood rigid, awaiting further instructions.

"Strike him ... it," Chaubrel told them, but the guard hesitated, looking to Rhamak for confirmation before destroying what had been so painstakingly created.

"Try to kill it," Rhamak said calmly, and he stepped back to allow the man room to swing.

The guard swept his sword down onto the creature's midsection. He had not applied a great deal of force, the sharpness of his blade and the downward movement being sufficient to cut. The blade bounced back, ringing with a dull metallic sound; a slight expulsion of air the creature's only reaction.

"Good," Rhamak said, "but more force."

The guard swung again, as the creature's stomach muscles tensed in preparation for the blow. He hit it with enough force to split a six-inch log. The blade bounced back again, a slight cut in the hide, not even deep enough to draw blood.

"Very good," Rhamak said. "Now stand," he told the creature. It struggled to sit up, unaccustomed to the new muscles Rhamak had given it. Chaubrel moved forward to aid it, but Rhamak motioned him back. The creature sat and then swinging its legs off of the table slipped to the floor, almost overbalancing, not familiar with the heavier upper body and head.

"Again."

The guard brought his sword back, holding it with both hands and swung it across the creature's abdomen, putting his entire weight behind the blow. A small slice cut through the tough hide, and a slight trickle of blood seeped out.

"Yes, yes. Now a thrust."

The guard repositioned himself and stepped forward as he struck a blow, point-first into the creature. He rebounded back as the hide held firm.

"More force. Use all your strength."

The guard stepped back, and grabbing the sword in both hands, rushed forward, leaning into the thrust. The blade pierced the creature's stomach, impaling it on the sword. The creature wrapped webbed hands around the blade protruding from its stomach, as a faint gurgling sound escaped its mouth. It crumbled to the floor; the guard extracting the sword as it fell.

"That was too easy. The skin must be tougher," Rhamak said. Ignoring the body lying on the floor before him, he walked back to the wall to select the next subject.

He selected the next smallest. The man, having seen the transformation and murder of the first victim, struggled violently against the guards dragging him to the table. His fear provided his frenzied struggles the strength to hinder the guards; one lost his footing and the man nearly broke free of the remaining guard.

"Enough," Rhamak said impatiently, and he turned toward the men behind him. He stepped toward the three men, the prisoner still struggling against the guards restraining him. He would not voluntarily look into Rhamak's eyes, but was unable to fight against the hands that tilted his head back. Once he had seen the eyes, his struggles ceased.

Rhamak looked into his soul for a time, then motioning to the guards, he said, "Take him back to the wall. He has a strong will. I won't waste him in experimentation."

Rhamak selected another man. Despite the new man's desperate attempts to fight back, he was easily brought to the middle of the room and placed on the table, where the process of transformation was repeated. Rhamak worked faster than before, enhancing the shape, making the creature sleeker, but still strongly muscled. He added razor-sharp claws at the end of each finger. The sword tests provided the same results; though the guard needed to apply much more force to get the sword to pierce the hide.

"Arkhanians. I need Arkhanians. They are tougher, though they are bad subjects for transformation. The new form is not retained."

"Could you reinforce them with magic, sire?" Chaubrel asked.

"Yes, I can, but it will be vulnerable to Caidos reversing the incantation." He paused frustrated at the failure of the tough hide to stop a sword thrust. He thought for a few seconds, then added, "I will empower the Maken to deflect all energies directed at them. They won't get stronger as my Talondrin did, but Caidos won't be able to reverse the incantations I use to shield them. The Maken will be victorious."

## Chapter 21

When Brandorin and Caidos returned to the camp, the mage walked over to where M'drani was talking with Icara. "Icara, may I interrupt you. I need to talk to M'drani," he said. When Icara got up to leave them alone, he added, "No, you can stay. You may have discussed this already, and you can voice your opinion as well. M'drani, last night you said you had read Lanata and Sadro, and you sensed no danger from them. I was wondering; would you be able to sense if they were hiding something, holding something back?"

"If I'm trying to read someone, as I was with Lanata and Sadro last night, I can usually tell if they're covering up feelings or fears. It's never anything definite, just a faint feeling, like hearing voices in another room. You can't tell what's being said, but you know there's something there. I didn't have that feeling at all. There *was* a fear in Sadro, a deep fear he has buried. It could have been from the boar attack, or more likely a childhood fear he never got over completely. Many people have that. I don't think it's anything to be concerned about."

"And Lanata."

"Oh, she's wonderful," Icara said eagerly, "she's not afraid of anything."

"But should we be afraid, or rather, wary of her?"

"I don't think so, Caidos," M'drani said. "She's very open, very easy to read. And remember, she saved my life. If she was sent to hurt us, why would she have done that? And she is very interested in Piritho."

"Piritho? Do you think they met before? Maybe she was with Rhamak when he transformed Piritho."

"No, Caidos, not like that. Interested, romantically."

"Oh, that. Maybe Piritho is interested in her as well. He keeps telling her things I wish he would keep quiet about. He's another one I want to talk to this morning.

"Of course he's interested in her," Icara said. "Can't you tell by the way he looks at her?"

"I don't have an eye for such things. Well, M'drani, if you

give them your approval, I'll go see if they've decided to join us."

"Lanata will," Icara said. Caidos gave her a look as he walked over to Lanata and Piritho. He would have to teach her to be objective when making decisions of this kind.

"Piritho, can I ask you to go find Matu. There is something I need to talk to both of you about." When Lanata started to follow him, Caidos motioned for her to stay and said, "Did you think about our talk last night?"

"Yes, I'll go with you."

"This is not going to be an adventure, Lanata. It will be quite perilous."

"I know, Caidos. Piritho was telling me more about your quest."

Caidos sighed quietly, wishing he had talked with Piritho last night.

Lanata continued, "I don't think he told me everything he could have, Caidos, so don't blame him for giving away your secrets. You don't have to worry about me. I can take care of myself, and others, too." She saw Piritho returning with Matu, and she added, "So if there's something about our defenses you're going to be telling them, maybe I should hear it too."

"I am sure you'll be very helpful in a fight, and I'll be glad to have you with us," Caidos said.

"But?" Lanata asked.

"But, I need to talk to Piritho and Matu, alone. Please don't be offended."

"I won't be," she said, as she went to saddle her horse.

Caidos watched to be sure that she was not within hearing, then checked to see where Sadro was before continuing. "Matu, I want to let you know; we have a little problem. Just a temporary one, I hope. Brandorin has not completely recovered from healing Sadro yesterday. There was more than just the pain caused by taking on the wounds the boars inflicted."

Caidos glanced at Piritho, silently asking him to go along with the white lie he was about to tell. "Both Brandorin and I feel he'll be back to normal in another day or two, but we're concerned what might happen if there's another attack before he recovers completely. He won't be fighting at his best, and I want you both to be prepared to help cover for him."

"What do you mean about there being more than pain?"

Brandorin told him he could tell them the truth, but Caidos decided it was better not to discuss Brandorin's fear. "It's left him with an unexplained tiredness. I think it will pass. I think it best to keep this quiet."

"You mean don't tell Sadro and Lanata?" Matu asked.

"Yes. At least for now. Matu, I need to have a word with Piritho. After that I must talk to Sadro and Salis, and then we can leave. Can you make sure we'll be ready? I'll send Piritho to help you in a minute."

Matu went to see the horses were saddled and the packs loaded, while Piritho stayed to talk to Caidos.

"Piritho, what do you think of Lanata?"

"She's amazing, ..." he began, but Caidos stopped him.

"I meant, do you think we can trust her? We know nothing about her other than what she has told us herself, and I think it would be best if we didn't share everything we know with her."

"And I went and invited her to go with us. I guess I should have checked with you first, Caidos. I'm sorry. It's just that it felt so good to be talking to someone who didn't look at me as that guy who used to be a beast. I just found myself talking to her as if we had known each other for years." Excitement was evident in his voice, but then he slowed down, and spoke quietly. "I even told her about what I did to Ilona and Brandorin."

"You have to stop blaming yourself for that, but it's good to talk to someone about it. What was her reaction?"

"She said what you've said; that it wasn't my fault." He spoke the words, but the emotion in his voice indicated he did not believe them.

"An objective opinion. How did your talk with Brandorin go yesterday?"

"It was a start. We're not back to the way things were before, but it felt good to be talking to him again."

"As to the other," Caidos said, "about how we've been acting toward you, you have a point, Piritho. We have probably been overly careful about how we're treating you. I'm sorry. Do you want me to talk to the others?"

He shook his head, "It's getting better. I'm comfortable with Salis; he just says what he's thinking. *I* look at it as if we've been traveling together for weeks, but to you it just seems like a couple of days. It'll work out on its own. And I promise I won't tell Lanata so much about our quest and Rhamak."

"Or Sadro either for that matter. Good. If you want to go help Matu get ready, I'll go have my last two talks." He signaled to Salis, and stepped aside to talk to him.

"Salis, where did you find Sadro? What was his condition when you found him?"

"What are you onto, Caidos?"

"Just trying to tie up loose ends."

"My horse had bolted when the boar came crashing into the clearing, and you know me, I'm not much of a horseman. I'm frankly surprised I managed to stay on. By the time he settled down and I had him under control again, we were quite a ways away. I was riding back when Sadro came staggering across my path. By the time I dismounted, Sadro had collapsed and was barely conscious. I couldn't get him up on the horse by myself, and I was just about to remount, and come to get one of you, when Piritho came riding up. He grabbed Sadro and got him onto his horse and headed back here."

"Did you see any sign of the third boar?"

"Third boar? I hadn't even seen a second one. I thought there was only one until I got back to the clearing. How's Brandorin doing this morning? That healing must have really taken it out of him."

"Not quite recovered yet. But I'd like to get back to Sadro. Did you see any sign of a wagon or his horse, the one that bolted and left him?"

"No wagon, no horse either. Why all the questions?"

"I just want to be sure. There he is now. Sadro," Caidos

called, and when Sadro joined them, he asked, "Have you decided if you're going on to Numina or are you going with us?"

"If it was not for the Debt of Life I must honor, I would probably go on to Numina. I can see no other way to repay the debt, unless I stay with you. From what you told us last night, I could easily have the opportunity to do so. My sword and my honor are yours," he said, touching his fist to his heart, in the Larian manner of sealing a vow.

"Then we are nine," Caidos said.

\* \* \*

A short time later, they had finished the preparations for their departure. Sadro rode double with Piritho until they found a herd of horses. Matu and Sadro communicated with the herd and soon returned with a young dappled stallion that was willing to join them.

"They've seen no sign of Sadro's horse," Matu told them, "but they'll watch for him, and if they see him, they'll let him know Sadro is well. This is Tasina and he has agreed to carry Sadro and go with us on our journey. The young stallions often tire of following the herd, and he is excited about the change, and the new places we'll see." The stallion whinnied in ascent.

With everyone on their own mount, and the weather favorable, they were able to make good time. Their route passed through lush pastures of wild grasses, browned by the autumn sun. The rolling hills gave way to meadows of fragrant grasses and wildflowers. Yarrow, wolf-bane, fox-brush and larkspur dotted the landscape with color. The trip from the dock to Numina had overwhelmed the Westerners with both the beauty of the landscape and the lack of any sign of man's existence. They had long since grown accustomed to the absence of man, but not to the vastness and beauty of this untouched land.

When they stopped for the evening and dismounted, the companions stretched to ease the aches of the road out of their muscles.

"I like to have a good run at the end of the day," Lanata told the others, "anyone up for a little race? It really shakes out those stiff muscles."

"I'm ready," Piritho said.

"Count me out," Salis said.

"A run is just what I need," Matu said.

"Me too," Sadro added.

"What about you, Brandorin?" Lanata asked.

"Sure, why not?" Caidos looked at him, questioning his choice. "I'm well rested. I doubt I'll win, but someone has to bring up the rear."

They had stopped by a small lake, and Lanata suggested they run around it.

"That has to be at least a mile and a half," Salis said, making it clear he thought the entire idea was absurd.

"Then maybe twice around," Lanata suggested.

"Once should do it," Brandorin said.

"Once, then," Lanata conceded. "Ready?" When all four men had confirmed, she turned to Caidos, and asked. "Will you serve as judge?"

"Judge of what?"

"Of who wins."

"So when you said 'race' you meant it." He smiled, realizing Lanata had thrown down a challenge. After looking at the men, he realized Matu and Piritho had accepted that challenge, while Sadro and Brandorin still considered it to be a friendly run. He laughed to himself when he remembered what Icara had told him about her observations concerning Lanata and Piritho. He felt she should have added Matu as well.

"I'll be the judge then. If you're ready," they all said they were, "then ... go."

The five runners took off; Matu and Sadro in the lead, with Piritho close behind. Larians were natural runners, often preferring to go by foot rather than ride for shorter distances. Lanata seemed at ease, as her long legs clocked off the path beaten down by the three men in front of her. Brandorin, still not recognizing the challenge that had been laid down, was running along easily next to Lanata.

"I thought she would have been in the lead," Icara said, disappointed in Lanata's performance.

"I think she's toying with them," M'drani said. "She challenged them because she's confident she's going to win."

After they had rounded the first curve of the lake and were racing across the opposite side, Lanata increased her pace, effortlessly leaving Brandorin behind, and passing first Piritho, and then the Larians. All four men, temporarily startled by the new leader, stepped up their pace as well, and there was a jostling for position; the lead being held by Matu, then Piritho, then Lanata again.

"Get ready, Caidos," Icara shouted, "here they come. Watch Lanata's mark."

The observers stepped back from the mark Lanata had made in the dirt at their starting point; as the three leaders came around the last curve of the pond and sprinted for the end.

Piritho crossed the mark first, but only by a small lead ahead of Lanata, who was only a short distance in front of Matu. Sadro and then Brandorin followed, all five runners panting from the exertion.

"Well, who won, Caidos?" Brandorin asked.

"Piritho."

Caidos was surprised by everyone's reaction. He thought he understood men and women and the roles they played, but none of the participants in the race seemed to be following the rules he thought he understood.

He had expected Lanata to be disappointed she had lost the challenge she had cast; instead she seemed very pleased Piritho had won. He would have thought the men Lanata had beaten would have been upset, but instead they were congratulating her on her success. He would not have been surprised had Piritho gloated over his victory, but instead he looked at Lanata with pride. Caidos left them to their celebrations, shaking his head in confusion.

\* \* \*

They had their camp set up and were preparing dinner and settling in when the sound of someone or something approaching put everyone on edge. Caidos glanced at Brandorin who held his sword, but not as he would if he were prepared to use it. Piritho had taken up position close to Brandorin, slightly in front of him, between Brandorin and the oncoming intruder.

All of the built up tension was unwarranted, for the visitor turned out to be Larian, sent by Korlu with the much needed Zadanite. Caidos and Icara took the rare metal and found a quiet place away from the others to begin the process of making the Kordunan replacement fragment.

The mages had set up outside the light of the campfire, but before long a pulsing nimbus of blue, green and yellow light emanated around them. Beams of pure white light sparked from the center, shooting into the black velvet sky above. A low hum vibrated, in ever increasing pitch, until an ear-piercing shriek blasted through the quiet night. The noise and lights ceased abruptly and Caidos' heavy expulsion of air signaling completion of a difficult task seemed to echo through the resultant silence.

Caidos walked back toward the companions, Icara close behind him. He held out his hand, palm up, carrying a dark, dull oval that appeared to be more rock than gem, saying, "It is not complete yet. We don't have a Kordunan artifact." Turning to Brandorin, he added, "But it's possible that the Protector can complete the process. Would you like to give it a try?"

Brandorin looked less than confident, but didn't want to refuse the attempt with everyone watching. "What would I need to do? Was there anything in the instructions in that scroll?"

"No, nothing specific," Caidos said. "It would likely be automatic, much the same as you're taking on the healing powers of the Umarian fragment." Caidos tried to speak with the confidence he would have felt before the boar attack and the triggering of the fear spell.

Brandorin reached out his hand. An almost imperceptible

tremor caused him to fist up his hand, as if flexing it, then open it again as he took the stone from Caidos. The mage noticed relief flood Brandorin as he closed his hand around the replacement fragment. Apparently it didn't trigger the fear, but Brandorin's slow shaking of his head also told him that there was no other reaction either.

"We will need a Kordunan artifact then, or else the presence of all the other fragments. We'll have both when we reach Arkhan." Caidos took the stone back from Brandorin, after deciding he would not ask Brandorin to try it with the Protector's crystal, at least not in front of the others.

*   *   *

The boar attack in the vastness of the Larian wilderness, made Caidos afraid for the Ilyani. The rough terrain and Brandorin's inability to heal the horses over the next two nights slowed their journey, but escalated Caidos' concern. All of the companions felt his concern, and they agreed to start earlier and ride longer through the cold wind that whipped across the open plains each day.

Each morning and evening Brandorin held his sword, touching both the Protector and Umari stones. He claimed the fear was lessening every time, but Caidos suspected there had been little change, except Brandorin's ability to hide the fear he still felt. His apprehension for the Ilyani's safety was heightened by Brandorin's inability to help should the need arise. At night when they camped, his anxiety increased, until his nerves crackled like the logs on the fire.

They reached Ilyan on their ninth day out from Numina. Their progress slowed even further as the separate stands of trees grew together into one vast forest. In many areas they had to dismount and walk their horses, for there were no roads, and the route Caidos took passed through forests thick with vines and undergrowth. But despite the dense growth, there was generally a path of sorts, and they were able to continue moving forward, never having to backtrack or turn aside due to thickets or hedges too dense to pass through.

The Larian landscape had been open, consisting of prairies and meadows, interspersed with an occasional wood or lake. Ilyan was a primeval forest, however, which in some places cut off the light of the sun so dramatically it was difficult to tell the time of day.

The light through the canopy of leaves created a dappled effect on the forest floor where it mingled with the fallen leaves of seasons past. The animals that lived among the trees seldom made it to the ground, scurrying from branch to branch in search of food. The larger, older trees, covered in moss and lichen, towered over the young saplings, which struggled to reach the light, striving to survive in the shadows of those that had come before them. The roots of the great trees spread across the forest floor, tunneling into the ground, and creating a web of obstacles to their passage.

On the eighth day after crossing into Ilyan, they had traveled for hours through the densest undergrowth they had yet encountered. Though they knew it was mid-afternoon, the light filtering through the canopy was barely enough to see by. A sudden clap of thunder startled them only moments before the sound of a great downpour hitting the roof of leaves told them a storm was breaking.

The thick canopy prevented most of the water from reaching them, but they were soon drenched by the soft shower that dripped from the leaves above. They could tell the thick trees and vegetation were sheltering them from the worst of the storm, though they could see high winds were buffeting the upper branches. Peals of thunder were joined on occasion by the ripping sound of branches being torn from the sturdy trunks.

The storm lasted less than an hour, stopping as suddenly as it had begun. They knew the high winds had blown the heavy cloud cover away as the dimness of the forest brightened into a myriad of light, shining and reflecting from the droplets of rain that continued to drip from the canopy above.

Long after the storm had ended, they were still plagued by the cold drops of rain dribbling down the backs of their necks and keeping their clothes damp.  Salis tried to convince them that there was some physical law that attracted cold rain drops to unprotected warm necks.  Though no one accepted his theory, the jest helped lift their spirits.

They trudged across the muddy floor of the forest, but they forgot about being wet and miserable when they suddenly broke through into the clear, warm sun, and looked out over a scene that stopped all conversation.

They stood on a high ridge, looking out over a beautiful, verdant valley, cut by a river that had just dropped two hundred feet from the forest floor.  The waterfall had been split just prior to its crest, by an island in the middle of the river.  The water careened off the outer banks on either side of the island, creating a double waterfall that flowed back onto itself and merged into a single fan-like fall before reaching the valley floor.  The bright noon sun, caught on the mist rising from the rushing water, formed a double rainbow.  The arched light formed the colorful wings of a giant bird rising from the white water, the single fall below forming a spectacular tail of white plumes.

"Well, Salis, you were impressed with Larian architecture," Caidos said.  "What do you think of that?"

"It's beautiful.  The difficulty is trying to duplicate nature, or simulate it, as the Larians do," Salis responded without taking his eyes from the scene.

"That *is* Ilyani architecture," Caidos said.  "They build with trees and plants, water and soil.  No buildings at all.  They sculpted that island and the banks on either side to form the waterfalls.  It took a generation, but the Ilyani are a patient people."

Caidos let the impact of his words and the scene before them help the companions begin to understand the people they were about to meet.  When they were ready to continue, Caidos led them down from the ridge and into the dense forest that covered the valley floor.

They came to a large, relatively clear area, and Caidos stopped, dismounted and looped Aquilo's reins around a nearby branch.  He indicated the others should do the same.  Caidos stood silently in the center of the clearing, as if he was listening. The others stood behind him, looking at the edges of the forest around them.

A subtle movement drew their attention to the area in front of Caidos. A section of thick vegetation seemed to move toward them. As it reached the brighter, but still low light, in the center of the clearing, the companions gasped. They saw eyes and a face and realized the vegetation was in reality a person approaching them.

The figure was tall and thin, over six feet in height, with long arms and legs and a green and brown covering that could have been clothing or skin, but appeared to be a cross between leaves and bark. The hair was short and twiggy, and framed a long and narrow face dominated by bright, green eyes.

"Caidos, One is pleased to meet again." The voice was light and musical, but gave no hint as to the gender of the speaker.

"Tilandrico, it is good to see you as well."

"One welcomes all of the companions." The person to whom Caidos had spoken raised an arm in greeting, then lowered it to the chest where a green stone rested. The travelers realized they were looking at the holder of the Ilyani fragment.

## Chapter 22

Caidos felt the knot in his stomach relax, knowing the Ilyani fragment holder was safe. He looked back at his traveling companions, and realized they were staring, most of them with their mouths hanging open and their eyes wide in disbelief. He began his introductions, expecting familiarity to dispel the surprise and feeling of unreality.

"Tilandrico-Lothrifora, Caretaker, may I introduce my companions?" The introductions were formal; Caidos always adhered to the customs of whatever country he was in.

"One would be honored," Tilandrico responded.

Caidos introduced each of the companions in turn, repeating the name Tilandrico-Lothrifora several times to help them learn it. The companions were formal in their greeting to the Ilyani, responding as Tilandrico had done. When Caidos introduced the Builder, Salis struggled with the name a time or two before asking, "Would you be offended if we called you, Til? It's a sign of friendship."

"One would not be offended. Should One call the Builder, Sal?"

Caught off-guard, Salis quickly suppressed a laugh, "One would be honored," using Tilandrico's words to Caidos. "May One say, that I think Ilyan is the most beautiful country I, I mean, One has ever seen. Your work here is inspiring."

"One thanks Sal for such remarks. The People are caretakers of this land, and strive to keep it sacred. If Sal, or any others, find it cumbersome to speak as the People do, One would not be offended, nor would any of the People, but One is pleased that Sal would make the effort."

"Perhaps as we ride to your city, Til," Salis said, "we could talk about the building you've done here. Or do you not call it building?"

"The People do not think of what is done for the Land as building. The People tend the Land that was given. One would be pleased to talk to Sal about the work of the People, but the People do not have cities, in the manner of the West, or even of Laria." Til spread arms out to encompass the glade in which they stood. "The People need no other shelter than that which the Land provides. This is the Meeting Place, where the People of this region gather."

"We'll stay here while we're in Ilyan," Caidos said, "Tilandrico, will others be joining us?"

"Perhaps later, Caidos. A fierce storm, earlier today, caused much damage to the Land, and the People are assessing and beginning repairs. The storm was the most recent in a hand-count of such storms since the full moon. One was made aware of the Companions' travel through Ilyan, and One left the work to meet the Companions here. One can see from the Companion's covering that the storm must have reached the Companions as well."

"Tilandrico, have you seen a Great Spirit in recent months? Something that has never been seen in the Land before?"

"One has not seen anything as Caidos has described, nor have any of the People."

"Colorful lights, speaking in many voices?" Caidos asked?

"No, nothing of this type."

Caidos shook his head. "I doubt the Shadow would have appeared to the Arkhanians three times, yet TA-KA is the only fragment holder we haven't talked to. And there are three appearances unaccounted for. That nagging feeling again; there is something I have overlooked. It's like a stone in my shoe, but no matter how many times I look for it, I can't find it."

The frustration was clear on Caidos' face. Til spoke softly, "One does not want to add to Caidos' problems, but there is another matter of great concern to One." Caidos nodded for Til to continue. "The People are very concerned that there have been no new sprouts for four cycles of the Moon. There has been a dramatic increase in both the number and intensity of storms. The ground shakes and the growth of the Land has needed more of the

People's aid than is normal. It is not the natural order."

"There has been an increase in storms and quakes in other lands as well, Tilandrico, but this news of the lack of sprouts is distressing." When Caidos saw the looks of confusion on the faces of the other companions, he explained. "The Ilyani give birth to new life more in the way plants do. An Ilyani will 'sprout', an offshoot, which is carried until it has grown enough to be planted in special ground that has been prepared. The Viriagalar will provide all nourishment needed, until the young one is fully-grown.

"I expected to hear of the problems with the weather but would not have thought it would transfer to the People in this way. The Ilyani have a power over plant life of every kind. This land is as lush and verdant as it is because the Ilyani have nurtured it, aided the growth. Would you like to explain it to them, Tilandrico?"

"One would be happy to do so," Til replied with a slight bow to Caidos. "One spoke earlier of the damage from the storm, and the repairs that may be required. If a branch has been broken by the strong winds, the People will repair it; help it to heal itself. Caidos has said that the People have a power over the plants, but One would say it is an understanding of what the plants need, a two-way connection between the People and the Land. The People can provide assistance to the Land, while the Land provides sustenance and life to the People.

"If a plant or tree has been damaged beyond the People's ability to repair, One will try." Til touched the green stone resting near the heart. "One has the fragment of the great crystal, Sefiron, and can sometimes succeed with its aid, when the People cannot do so alone. If the plant cannot be repaired, even with the aid of the fragment, then it will give its essence to the Viriagalar. The Land gives to the People, and the People give back."

"Well said, Tilandrico," Caidos said.

"One would be happy if Caidos would call One, Til, as Sal has suggested, for Caidos is friend to One."

"I'll try, Til, but I have called you Tilandrico for many years, and I'm used to that.

"That would please One as well. Does the lessening of new

sprouts and the changes in the weather forewarn Caidos of special events?"

"Yes, Til. All of the companions are with me, and we have come here to find you because we must rejoin the separate fragments of the crystal, to form a single crystal once again. We travel next to Arkhan, in the North. Will you join us?"

"He didn't ask me if I wanted to go," Salis whispered to Brandorin, "Did you get a choice?"

"I heard that, Salis," Caidos whispered back.

"One will travel with Caidos and the Companions. Is it necessary to leave at once? One would check on the repairs from the storm. If One's crystal is needed, One would like to provide its use before departing."

"We can rest for today, but I'd like to leave in the morning. If you would like to go now and check on the repairs, don't worry about us. I feel at home in this glade, and I can entertain the companions until you return."

"If the Companions would not be offended by One's departure, One will go and inform the People of the need for One to leave for a time." Til left the companions, melting into the surrounding forest after a few steps.

"What an amazing people," M'drani said after Til had left, "and the speech differences, no use of 'I' or 'we' or 'they'. Fascinating! How is it we've never heard of the Ilyani?"

"They are a very focused people," Caidos explained. They're dedicated to the land and plant life of Ilyan. They've never traveled outside their borders, and very few people, aside from Mages, have ever traveled here. You saw how dense the forests are; most people wouldn't be able to navigate within these surroundings. I had to have a guide meet me at the edge of the forest for many years before I felt comfortable traveling here on my own."

"How many Ilyani are there?" Brandorin asked.

"No one knows for sure. The People could probably tell you how many trees there are in Ilyan. If they couldn't give you an exact number, it's only because they aren't sure where the borders of their land lie. They aren't concerned with such things. I'd guess -

somewhere between five and six hundred thousand."

"Caidos, that can't be!" Brandorin protested. "Kartir is the most populous city in Zadania and there are only fifty thousand that live in the city itself, with another few thousand within a fifty-mile distance of its walls. All of Varsa would only be two hundred to two hundred and fifty thousand. We've traveled through Ilyan for eight days and have seen only one Ilyani."

"You've seen only one. I've seen more than I could count. At least three to five every hour since we crossed into Ilyan."

"You did? Why didn't you acknowledge them?"

"I did, many times. Sometimes they were busy with their work and didn't see us, but when they did, I nodded my head to them. It's what Ilyani do when they pass each other in the forest, if they don't know each other's names, as I didn't know theirs."

"That's what all the head-bobbing was about." Salis said. "I thought you were nodding off."

"They blend into their surroundings very easily. You saw how readily Tilandrico disappeared as he walked off.

"You called Til 'he'." Is he a man then? I couldn't tell," Matu said.

"No, Tilandrico is neither male nor female, but it's difficult for non-Ilyani to refer to someone without using a term such as 'he' or 'her'. Of course, now that Salis has provided us with the name Til, it might be easier. The People understand the way we speak in the west, and they wouldn't be offended if you said 'he', 'she', 'him' or 'her. I won't use 'it'. They are people, even though they may seem otherwise at first. Use whatever term is most comfortable for you."

"Have the Ilyani always been - that way, no male or female?" Lanata asked.

"As long as I'm aware of, though there are legends the People tell that would indicate at one time there were men and women."

"Can you tell us one, Caidos?" M'drani asked.

Caidos motioned for everyone to find a comfortable place to rest, as he sat on the ground with his back against a tree root. "One legend talks about the women of a village situated on a large and very deep lake. The women got water from the lake every day, which they carried back to the village in earthen vessels. One of the women, Lilordora, claimed there were great treasures at the bottom of the lake. The Ilyani of today have no interest in gold or money or other treasures, but the legend talks about a time when this was not so.

"Day after day, Lilordora would talk about the great treasure that was so close to them, yet they never tried to claim it. Finally, one of the other women, Sahtenyana, tired of hearing her story, asked, 'What would you have us do about this treasure?' She thought Lilordora would have to admit there was nothing that could be done, and she would stop complaining about not being able to reach it.

"But Lilordora had thought about the treasure a great deal, and had decided that if she could get some of the other women to go with her; she would dive into the lake and try to bring it up. She said she would only share the treasure with those that helped her dive for it. Most of the women agreed to go, thinking their husbands would be very surprised when they brought home the great wealth they found at the bottom of the lake. Sahtenyana was the only one that refused to go. She thought them foolish and greedy.

"They swam out to the deep water of the lake, and Lilordora and a few of the others began to dive. When they came up for air, the group that had not dived to begin with went down. They moved about the lake, diving in turns, looking for the great treasure. Then, when they were on the far side of the lake, the women waiting at the surface began to cry out. Those that were diving, including Lilordora, had not come up for air for a long time. They swam under the surface of the water to see what was happening, and discovered that the women were caught in the reeds and could not free themselves. They called to Sahtenyana on the shore to get help and then dove in after the other women.

"Sahtenyana knew that by the time she returned with help, the women would have run out of air. She had a knife with her and thought she could cut them loose from the reeds. She ran around the lake to the far side. When she got there she realized all of the women were now caught in the reeds. The only sign of where they had dived were their hands, reaching for the surface, breaking through to the air they so desperately needed. She dove into the water, and cut the women loose from the reeds, but she was too late. They had all drowned.

"Days later, Sahtenyana returned to the lake, feeling guilty for belittling Lilordora's dreams and feeling sorrowful at the loss of her friends. In her grief, she thought she saw their hands reaching up once again from below the surface of the lake. But when she looked closer she saw beautiful white flowers covering the area where the women had drowned. The flowers looked like the hands of the women, and since she had never seen such flowers before she thought she should name them. She decided to name them after Lilordora, and today we still call them by the name she gave them, Water Lilies."

"What a beautiful and sad story!" said M'drani, tears in her eyes.

"Caidos, will the Ilyani be offended if we light a fire tonight?" Salis asked.

"We've lit a fire every night since crossing into Ilyan. You have only to continue to heed my warning about using only dried out branches and logs."

"They won't want to add the broken branches to their special ground?"

"The Viriagalar? No, once a branch or plant has dried out, it's not used. The Ilyani are very diligent in watching the forests, ensuring that life is not wasted, but Ilyan is a large country and the forests are very dense. The dead branches you find to add to our fire will be returned to the land as well, just in another form. The Ilyani believe that no life is ever lost. The Viriagalar is proof of that. You may want to begin to look for firewood. There'll be less in this vicinity then in the other areas where we camped, and you found it sparse even then."

\* \* \*

The travelers had prepared and finished their evening meal before Til returned. Only Matu and Sadro had been aware of Til's approach, their hearing more acute than the rest.

"One has been to the site of the damage. The People have made great progress and will not require any further use of One's crystal. Have the companions been able to find all that is needed?"

"Yes, Tilandrico, we are content. Will you stay with us tonight?"

"Yes, Caidos, One is prepared to travel with the Companions."

"Was the damage from the storm severe?" Icara asked.

"It was not as bad as it might have been. Most is reparable, but a small kapok tree was uprooted. The People have righted it, and will provide special care over the next few weeks to ensure its survival. One used the crystal to advance the healing as much as possible. One would like to be able to monitor its progress, but One understands the necessity."

"Til, I have something to ask you," Salis said. "I have been given the task of planning the evening meals while we travel. Some of the others have certain preferences or dislikes in the area of food. I suppose you don't eat vegetables?"

"One does not eat."

"That's what I thought, but what about bread, flour, things made from plants like wheat?"

"One does not eat."

"All right. Then meat only? Is fowl all right?"

"One does not need to eat. The sun, soil, and water provide all of One's needs."

"You don't eat anything at all?"

"I think that's what he's been saying," Brandorin said.

"Til, you and I are going to get along just fine."

\* \* \*

The Ilyani had no need for horses and had no possessions, so as they traveled through the forests, heading northwesterly toward Arkhan, Til walked. In many places, while they were still in Ilyan, the lack of paths required the rest of the travelers to walk as well. In those areas where the undergrowth was less and the Companions were able to ride, Til had no trouble matching their pace, springing along beside one of the riders, talking easily though running.

On their third day since leaving the Meeting Place, they cleared the last of the dense forest. The dramatic change from the filtered light of the canopied forest to the bright sun of a clear, crisp day, caused the Companions to stop, waiting for their eyes to adjust to the disparity.

"I didn't think we were that close to the Pargona Mountains," Piritho said, as he gazed to the northeast, "and I wouldn't have expected them to be snow covered."

"Those aren't mountains, Piritho," Caidos told him, "they're clouds. But you are right, they do look like mountains, especially in this bright light after twelve days in filtered dimness."

Great storm clouds rested on the distant horizon. The tops of the clouds, catching the light of the noonday sun looked to be snow-topped peaks, while the dark lower portions, heavy with rain, looked like steep, forbidding slopes.

"We might as well stop here for a meal," Caidos told everyone, dismounting from Aquilo. "We have a fairly easy ride between here and Arkhan, which is just beyond Piritho's mountains. There's no distinct border, but the landscape differences signal the change in countries as well."

A few groups of trees scattered across the plain that led to the horizon, but the forest stopped where they stood. The gusts of air blowing in from the north were drier than the moist, heavier air under the canopy of trees, and the crispness it carried with it was a welcome change. The aromas carried on that wind hinted at lavender and mint and the more pungent scents of herbs and dry grasses, replacing the richer, mustier smells of the ferns and moss of the forest.

'Tilandrico, when we start again we will be riding at a faster pace," Caidos said. "You can ride along with one of us, rather than trying to run alongside."

"Kahdru has already carried Sadro and me," Piritho volunteered. "He's bigger than the other horses, but he's gentle and wouldn't let you fall."

Til looked at the horses with a look of apprehension. "One had not thought about falling off, Piritho. Does this happen often?"

"No, don't worry about that. Forget I mentioned it."

"Til, you can ride with me," Salis said. "It's easier with a saddle. I didn't even fall when he bolted off during the boar attack."

"Bolted off? One does not like the sound of that either."

"Perhaps it would be better if you gentlemen stopped trying to help," M'drani said. "Til, while we're resting here, why don't I show you what it's like riding a horse? You can ride behind me, and we'll walk, very slowly," she said, looking at Piritho and Salis. "Just around the area here. It's really a very nice experience. You feel at one with the horse."

"Yes, Til," Sadro added. "They have strong spirits, and there is nothing as free as a horse running across the plain."

"But we aren't going to run, Til," M'drani said, signaling to Sadro to allow her to handle this. "Just walk."

"One does not want to hinder the journey. One will try what M'drani suggests."

M'drani was about to walk N'jari to a nearby boulder, to allow Til an easier method of climbing up, but Til nimbly jumped and swung up behind her. She took Til's hands from behind her, and bringing them forward, wrapped them around her waist.

"Just hold onto me. It helps N'jari think of us as one rider," she added, not wanting to remind Til of the possibility of falling off. They walked around the other horses and out into the open area of the field. She thought it best to get out of hearing distance, considering the earlier remarks.

The companions watched as the walk increased to a slow trot and then a canter. By the time M'drani and Til returned to the group, they were at a full gallop. They stopped abruptly just short of the camp area. Til slid off the back of the white palfrey, a broad grin clearly evident.

"One has never felt such a feeling. It was quite exhilarating. Sadro was correct. One felt this freeness along with N'jari."

"Then you'll ride with us?" Caidos asked.

"One will enjoy doing so. Is the feeling much the same with every horse, or should One try others?"

"You can try other horses too, Til," Caidos said. "It'll help to spell the horses, so one of them doesn't have to carry two people all day."

\*     \*     \*

After the short break, they continued on their way, northeastward, Til riding with Piritho on Kahdru's back. A strong wind blew across the plain and the mountainous clouds that had hugged the horizon had sailed to other lands without releasing any of their moisture. The meadow gave way to dry grass and sagebrush, with only an occasional stunted tree, twisted and stark in the sharp light of the now cloudless sky. They stopped at the end of the day on the banks of a small river, which had cut its way into the hard-packed ground, forming a shallow ravine.

"Although we've probably been in Arkhan for many miles now, I always think of this river as the border. It's called the Hodara." Caidos was the only one of the party that had ever been through this land. "Tar-Kal, the capital of Arkhan is six days ride from here."

"Do we have to cross here, Caidos?" Brandorin asked. Although the ravine was not deep, the sides leading down to the river were steep.

"No, there's a better spot near here. I just have to decide if it's to the right or the left," Caidos said, scanning the area, looking for the landmarks he used as milestones. "I think we're on the wrong side of that small hill over there," he said pointing to the right. "Let me ride to the crest and see what's on the other side.

Watch for my signal. If I'm right, the ford should be just beyond."

He rode the mile to the low rise and once at the crest he looked eastward, then turned and signaled for the others to follow. When they caught up with him, the companions saw the landmark Caidos had been looking for. A twelve-foot high, unusually shaped sandstone boulder stuck up from the edge of the ravine. The passing river had eroded the base of the boulder before changing its course and cutting its way through the plateau floor. It stood, precariously top-heavy at the edge of the ravine, looking as if a strong wind would topple it in.

"It has always reminded me of a goblet," Caidos said, "as if it was a sign the river was here." Caidos looked out over the land with a frown on his face. "The area has changed. There is far more rubble at the base of these hills, and the river is running much higher than it ever has before. The more severe weather has marked this land as well."

"One senses a dramatic change in the land," Til said in a lilting voice. "Even though One is not familiar with this area, One senses an uncertainty, much as the People have seen in Ilyan. But this land is rich with many plants that One has never seen. One was sorry it was necessary to travel through this land so quickly. "

"There are many in this area as well, Til." Caidos said. "You can have a look while we're stopped. Hopefully the return trip will not be so hurried."

"There aren't enough trees around here to provide much firewood," Brandorin noted. "We may only find enough to cook our meal; that is if we can find anything to eat."

"There's plenty of animal life out here, you just have to look for it in different places," Caidos told them. "Matu, you and Sadro should have some success catching fish; there's an inlet to the east, around the bend. They go there to get out of the current.

"There are burrows in the hill we just came down. Around this time of the day, the residents, a surprisingly tasty prairie dog, start to return from their foraging. Lanata, your bow, and Brandorin's reflexes are probably the best methods for catching them. Take Zephyr with you, she makes an excellent herder. But be wary of their teeth, they're long and sharp.

"M'drani, if you want to come with me, there are some plants I'm sure you'll like. Though they look tough and fierce on the outside, the inside is succulent and flavorful. Whatever you find, catch enough for a couple of meals. There are fewer choices between here and Arkhan. We'll be using more of our staples in the next three days."

"Til and I can go hunting for firewood," Salis said.

As Icara moved to join the others, Caidos suggested, "Why don't you help Piritho to see to the horses."

"Don't be disappointed, Icara," Piritho said. A dejected look on her face made it seem she would have preferred to go with the others. "There's not much glory in it, but the horses appreciate it."

Despite the severity of the surrounding landscape, there was plenty for everyone. Til spent the time surveying the plants in the area, fascinated by the sagebrush, cacti, bristle-cone pines and wild grasses.

"One was not aware of so many plants that could flourish on so little water. The ground here must be very fertile. One looks forward to trying it."

"Try it how, Til?" Salis asked. "Are you going to take some back with you?"

"One uses the soil for nourishment, Sal. One will show Sal." Til walked a short distance away from the camp area, and stood still. As the companions watched, Til seemed to get shorter, and they realized the soil was now ankle deep. Til seemed to sink into the ground, stopping when the surface reached knee-level.

"One shares the resources of the land and is satisfied, in the same manner that the Companions find replenishment from the fish and meat being eaten."

"Does it taste different than at home in Ilyan?"

"One does not understand 'taste', Sal. If Sal wonders if the soil in this place is different than in Ilyan, if it will nourish One in a different manner, then One must wait before answering."

"That's an interesting way of taking nourishment," Icara said. "It'd be very handy when our form of food is scarce. There's always soil, and generally water. Have you ever tried our way?"

"One has discussed this with Caidos. The People were interested in his methods, but the taste cannot be felt, if that is a clear way of stating it. And One does not have the ability to process food in this way."

"Process food?" Icara asked.

"The Ilyani can't swallow. They have no stomachs. They have no need for one, since they don't eat," Caidos explained.

"Now that we've met the Ilyani, at least Til," Salis said, "I can understand why you didn't try to explain them ahead of time. It wouldn't have made sense without meeting Til first. Looking ahead, I know very little about Arkhan, and I wonder if what little I have heard is factual."

"What have you heard?" Caidos asked.

"That the Arkhanians are very large and very fierce. That a knife or sword won't cut them. Descriptions I've heard vary, but they all make them sound like monsters."

"They aren't monsters, but I don't imagine you believed that anyway. They *are* very large. TA-KA, the Defender, is at least seven feet tall, but he's also very muscular, very strong. They're fierce in battle, but are really a rather gentle people otherwise. I think it comes from the knowledge of their strength. They have stark, chiseled features, as if they were carved from rock. Their skin is thick and tough as hide; though it can be cut, it takes a great deal of force.

"The crystal fragment gives TA-KA the ability to change his appearance, his shape. He carries no weapons because he doesn't need them. He can best most foes with just his strength, but if he needs a better weapon, he can change his hands and arms into a knife or sword or ax."

"It'll be good to have him with us if Rhamak sends another attack," Brandorin said.

"But won't we be finished when we get to Arkhan?" M'drani asked. "That will be the last fragment."

"Once we have TA-KA's fragment we can complete the Kordunan replacement, which will give us eight, plus the crown piece," Caidos said, "but Rhamak may consider that the best time to try to gain control of the crystal."

"I thought the fragments could only be used by a member of the race to which it was given," Lanata said, "or did I misunderstand."

"No, you understood, but there are exceptions. The appearance of Sefiron's Shadow has given Brandorin, as the Protector, the ability to use the Umari fragment. The crown piece must be used by a mage, and though Rhamak was expelled from the Order over five hundred years ago, he has the skills to be able to wield it, and to complete the Rejoining.

"I have been worried about the fragment holders we hadn't reached, because if Rhamak were to capture any of us, he would have a strong leverage to gain control of the crown piece."

Til suddenly jumped out of the soil, with a look of surprise and confusion.

"Til, is something wrong?"

"This soil is different than the soil One is used to. It creates a burning from within. One cannot use it."

"Will the water and sun provide you with enough nourishment?" Caidos asked.

"These should be sufficient for a short time, eight to ten days. There seems to be an abundance of sun in this land, but One will need much water."

"Water is not as plentiful along our route," Caidos told him, "but there'll be an ample source once each day between here and Tar-Kal. Will that be enough?"

"One believes that will be sufficient. One has never been outside of Ilyan, and was not aware of the problems that might arise. If you will excuse, One will go to the river to store some extra water."

"If you don't mind some company," Lanata said, "I'll go with you."

"One would be pleased to have Lanata come along."

"I'll go too," Piritho said.

After they had left, Caidos said, "I'm glad everyone is getting along with Til. I know him well, but I wasn't sure if all of you would realize so quickly, how interesting Til and all of the Ilyani are."

"Larians have missed a great opportunity to get to know our neighbors," Matu said. "The Axana Mountains have created a separation between us and the west, but Ilyan is so close, and it's such a beautiful country. It's clear the Ilyani have a great reverence for the land, just as Larians do, if not more so. When we return, I will try to open up an interchange between our two countries, if I can figure out how to get it started."

"Til is well known among the Ilyani," Caidos told him. "Talk about your ideas, I'm sure he will be anxious to help."

\* \* \*

After everyone had eaten, and the extra food had been well cooked in order to bring it along for the next day, the weary travelers began to turn in for the night. Icara found M'drani alone and joined her.

"M'drani, were you going to go to sleep now, or do you think we could talk?"

"I'm not that sleepy yet. What did you want to talk about?"

"Nothing special, just talk. You and Lanata and I are the only girls, or women, on this trip, except maybe for Til, who isn't either."

"That's right. We women should stick together, shouldn't we?" M'drani said, sensing the younger girl was nervous, but not knowing why. "Have you ever taken one of these trips with Caidos before?"

"No. He kept promising to take me along, but it never seemed to happen. There was always something I was supposed to study back in Artara, which is mostly just a lot of old men, who are very set in their ways. They don't realize I already know how to do what they're trying to teach me."

"Aren't there any other female Mages?"

"Only three, including me, and the other two are very, very old."

"There must be other apprentice Mages that are closer to

your age."

Icara did not respond at first, and M'drani thought she had somehow said the wrong thing. She waited for Icara to answer, when she did her voice was quiet, and M'drani had to strain to hear.

"There are. Dozens of them, but they don't spend much time with me."

"Silly boys jealous of a girl being a better Mage than they are?"

"Yes, they are." Icara sounded delighted that M'drani understood. "I've known most of them for over ten years, but the only one I ever got to be friends with left over a year ago. Decided he didn't like being a Mage. So you see, that's why I hoped I could talk to you." Icara came to an abrupt halt.

M'drani suspected she didn't know how to broach the subject she wanted to discuss. M'drani wanted to help, but was not sure what Icara had in mind. "Is it something about your friend?

"Well, not exactly, but it's kind of the same thing. It's just that I have no idea how to talk to men."

"Do you mean just talk to them? Or are you talking about a specific man?"

"Yes, someone specific."

"To let him know you like him?"

"Yes. I know you must think that silly, because you're so beautiful, it's so easy for you. But where you look like a beautiful bird, I'm like a little mouse. Men don't even notice me."

M'drani looked at Icara, seeing not a little mouse but a sweet, quiet girl, with long, straight black hair, and inquisitive, bright green eyes, set off by high cheekbones and a perky nose. She was taller than M'drani, more statuesque, but she hid her figure in the long, loose robes of a Mage. M'drani had only known Icara for less than three weeks, but knew her to be thoughtful, bright, and cheerful.

"We can take care of that. Are we talking about one of the men on this trip?"

Icara nodded in response, but before she could say

anymore, Caidos walked over to join them. M'drani understood that the subject was closed.

"I'm rather tired," Icara said. "I think it's time to get some sleep." She left.

"How long have you known Icara, Caidos?" M'drani asked.

"Since she was a little girl. I knew her parents. She lived in Sibria in Varsa. She showed a great deal of talent at a very early age. Though they hated to see her go, they knew Artara was the best place for her to learn how to use those talents. I took her there soon after her eighteenth birthday."

"And she's been in Artara for over ten years?" M'drani said, surprised.

"No, I don't think it's been that long," Caidos said.

"She was just talking about knowing someone there for ten years, so it must be at least that."

"She would know better than I. Since I'm gone so much, I tend to lose track of the time. I'm glad she joined us on this trip. I've missed her."

"But, Caidos, that would mean she is twenty-eight at least," M'drani said. When Caidos seemed to take that at face value, M'drani added, "But she looks more like sixteen."

"That would be because she's a Mage. We age differently. I'm a hundred and eight, M'drani. Do you think I look that old?"

"No, you don't. I would say you only look sixty, if that."

"You're being kind, but kind words fatten the bones."

"But Icara looks like a girl, when in reality she is a woman. She's older than I am."

"I would have thought that was desirable. Looking young, not the other."

"No one minds looking young, but when a woman in her twenties looks that young, then people think of her, and therefore treat her, like a child. And that's not right."

"I'm beginning to think I walked into the middle of a private talk."

"It may have been for the best, Caidos. Now I understand the situation a little better, and I'll have time to decide what to do about it."

## Chapter 23

North of the Hodara River, they rode across the barren plateau heading toward Rin-Ka, which sat at the crossroads between Tar-Kal and Ti-Kee. There was no road over these lands; only Caidos traveled between Ilyan and Arkhan. A short, coarse scrub grass replaced the longer grasses of the plains, and the bitter winds carried a stinging bite as they picked up the loose sand and gravel that covered the plateau. A mournful cry was borne on those winds, as if someone was hurt or dying. Brandorin called for a stop.

"Those are the Soulful Winds," Caidos said. "It's the air moving through the caves and ravines in the hills, like blowing over the mouth of a jug or bottle. The Arkhanians say they are lost souls, people who were lost in the caves, or died in battle, or died too young; it depends on who you talk to. The more superstitious believe you can get caught in the song; the spirit can claim your body to use it to return, to finish its life."

"Caidos, since we've stopped anyway," Brandorin said quietly, "I've been wondering if the wind and the sun might be too much for Til. He's used to more shade."

"That's a good point," Caidos said.

"I don't know the Ilyani customs. Would Til be insulted if we offered him a cloak? Since they don't wear clothes."

"The Ilyani are not like that. They always seem to find the good in people. Til would see it as a sign of your concern. Why don't you suggest it?"

Brandorin pulled out his cloak and offered it to Til. "Too much sun can cause a burn too, Til, and the strong winds could drain you of moisture. Covering yourself with this cloak should protect you from both."

"Perhaps One should try that now," Til said. Attempting to put the cloak on, but not being used to clothing, Til had some difficulty.

Brandorin helped, wrapping it around the Ilyani's shoulders

and tying it around the neck. "You look very dashing, Til."

"One thanks Brandorin."

Til strolled around, turning so the cloak swung outward, seeing how it draped. "This journey is proving to have many new experiences for One."

                \*     \*     \*

They reached Rin-Ka, a sprawling encampment of tents that stretched out on either side of the road for a mile in either direction. The road from Ti-Kee bent at Rin-Ka, turning north. If not for the oasis at its center, the road would have angled towards Tar-Kal in a more direct route. Caravans transporting merchandise from the port to the capital, and returning with empty wagons and the occasional passenger, created a minor, but consistent need for limited commerce.

A few permanent tents served as shops, carrying essentials for travelers: water skins, blankets, knives, grain, and dried meats. A lone blacksmith made a good business, repairing broken wheels or harnesses. One enterprising merchant had raised a few tents to be used for temporary shelter for the smaller traveling parties, though most travelers preferred to stay with their wagons and merchandise to avoid the expense of shelter or stabling.

The companions got their first look at the residents of this country, and they felt small and insignificant amongst the huge Arkhanians. Even Brandorin, who was among the taller Varsians, only reached the shoulders of most of them. Arkhanians wore loose robes of light colors and material, which stood out in stark contrast to their rough and leathery skin. The members of different caravans were obviously well acquainted with one another, for the Companions witnessed several reunions of old friends.

Salis winced when he watched travelers greet each other with hearty handshakes and slaps on the back. "I hope that's not a standard method of greeting. If it is, I don't think I'd survive meeting more than one or two Arkhanians at best."

"These men know each other well. They travel the road

between the port of Ti-Kee and Tar-Kal continuously. Meetings here are always exuberant. They'll spend long hours in the taverns, catching up on news, and finding out where the best bargains are, as well as drinking a great deal."

"I wouldn't mind supplying these taverns with ale," Salis said. "I would imagine it would be very lucrative."

"Arkhanians drink kra-lon. It's made from a succulent plant that's found all over Arkhan. There are fields of them in this area, the only place I know of in all of Arkhan where you'll find farming being done. Each tavern makes its own brew."

"Are we going to have time to sample a little?" Brandorin asked hopefully.

"This air is very dry; a little something to drink would be nice." Piritho added.

"Very little would be all you could handle. It's an extremely strong drink."

"It's worth a try," Brandorin said.

"After we get settled in," Caidos told them. "I'll take you to a tavern where I know the owner, but only if you promise to take it slowly."

"Sure, Caidos," both Brandorin and Piritho promised, though Caidos heard a tone of confidence that reminded him of a young apprentice who always said he knew the incantations, but always managed to singe his eyebrows with every fire spell or topple whatever stack of objects he was trying to move.

They rode around the campsites of several caravans, finding an area on the north side Caidos had in mind. After they had established their campsite, Caidos took Til and a few others to the oasis. They needed to let their horses drink and fill their canteens, but Caidos wanted to make special arrangements for Til.

"Ra-Fa, it is good to see you, old friend," Caidos said to the large man that directed the flow of people and horses to the water supply. He was the largest Arkhanian the Companions had seen so far, at least seven and a half feet tall. He was as wide as Brandorin and Piritho standing side-by-side.

"Cai-Dos, it has been a long time since you've been through

here," Ra-Fa said in a deep, rich voice that could be felt as well as heard. The large Arkhanian embraced the Mage, and all of the companions cringed. He had the obvious strength to break an enemy's back, or even a friend, with an overly enthusiastic hug. "Looks like you brought some friends this time," he added when he noticed the others.

"Yes, this is the first trip to Arkhan for all of my friends."

"Then we will have to make them welcome, so they will want to return." He turned toward a group of Arkhanian travelers bringing their mounts to water. "You, back, wait for our visitors," he said, his voice getting deeper and more commanding. The Arkhanians he spoke to waited, though they didn't seem as anxious as Ra-Fa to ensure the travelers' satisfaction. Caidos directed the others to bring the horses forward, pulling Til aside to talk to Ra-Fa.

"My friend, Til, is from Ilyan, and has some special needs. I know this is not normal, but can we set up a place for Til to soak for a time? Perhaps an empty keg filled with water."

"This is unusual, Cai-Dos, but for you, anything. I will take care of this for you. Give me an hour, then come to my tent, I will have something ready."

"Thank you, Ra-Fa. I knew I could rely on you."

An hour later, Caidos brought Til to Ra-Fa's tent, where a keg of clear water had been prepared for Til's use. Caidos left Til in Ra-Fa's care, and returned to the camp.

"I better take you two, and anyone else who wants to go to that tavern now," Caidos said. "I know if I don't, you'll sneak off on your own. But I must emphasize the strength of kra-lon. Do not try to drink it quickly, or to drink more than one small mug. Do I have your promises to listen to my guidance in this?"

"Caidos, we *have* had some experience in taverns before," Brandorin said.

"Not like these. Do I have your promise?"

"Yes, Caidos," Brandorin and Piritho said, sounding like small children reluctantly agreeing to a parent's dictates.

"And I promise too," Lanata said.

"No, Lanata, I'm truly sorry, but you can't go to the tavern,"

Caidos told her. "Even Arkhanian women aren't allowed in a tavern. We must respect the customs of the people of this country."

Though she was obviously disappointed and a little annoyed, she conceded. "All right, I won't make a fuss, but you have to promise to bring me a taste."

"I'll bring some back for you, Lanata," Piritho promised.

"We'll go with you, Caidos," Salis said, referring to himself, Matu and Sadro. "It should prove entertaining to watch, and you may need help in getting them back here."

"I am going to regret this," Caidos said under his breath as he led the five men to a large tent a short distance away.

The interior was cool; dim light, filtering through the open-weave material of the tent walls, provided the only illumination. Patrons sat on carpets in groups of four to seven. Instead of the usual gaggle of many voices, the structure of Arkhanian speech, a language that consisted mostly of two syllable words; the overall sound blended together into a deep, rhythmic murmur with the cadence of a march.

Caidos led them through the sitting area to the back of the tent, where a dark Arkhanian stood next to a row of kegs and a stack of mugs. There was no bar or table as would be found in any tavern in the west. Lumber being in scarce supply in Arkhan, it was used for more important things, such as the large kegs holding the kra-lon.

"Cai-Dos, I never thought I'd see you in my establishment again. Not after the fight that broke out the last time you were here. Ready to give it another try?"

"Not me, Ja-Lar. I have brought some friends who insist on trying kra-lon."

A wide grin broke out across Ja-Lar's broad face, and the mischievous look in his eyes gave Brandorin second thoughts. "Wonderful. We have a fresh keg opened, a good brew." He raised his voice so all in the tent could hear, "We have some outlanders here, for their first taste of kra-lon. Everyone must have a full mug."

"They probably heard that back at the camp," Salis whispered to Brandorin, as he rubbed his ears.

There was a reverberant round of cheering as everyone filled their mugs from ewers readily at hand. Ja-Lar took out five large mugs and began to fill them.

"No, only two, Ja-Lar," Caidos said.

"But you have five friends here, Cai-Dos. Everyone must drink." Looking at Caidos, with a roguish glint in his eyes, he reached back for a sixth mug and added, "You must drink too, Cai-Dos."

"Only a taste, Ja-Lar, only a taste. Fill just two of the mugs, only a sample for the rest."

"What about Lanata, Caidos?" Piritho asked. "I promised I'd bring her back a taste."

"There'll be plenty for her to try," Caidos said. "You haven't seen his sample yet.

When Ja-Lar had served the kra-lon, he handed the companions each a mug, giving Brandorin and Piritho the full ones as Caidos indicated. He raised a filled mug for himself, and the other patrons did the same.

"Kra-lon cha-ta be-ra!" he declared. He drained his mug, as did all of the other Arkhanians. "Drink, drink," he told the companions.

"Easy," Caidos said in a final warning, as he took a small sip from his mug.

Each of the other men lifted the mug to their lips, and sampled a small taste of kra-lon. Salis spluttered and coughed as the liquid burned on the way down. Matu and Sadro were able to swallow theirs without too much difficulty.

Brandorin let out a long breath after taking a sizeable sip, then said in a hoarse whisper, "Oh, that's good." Piritho's reaction was very similar, and they both tried another taste, as the Arkhanian patrons raised their mugs in salute to them.

"It goes down easier the more you drink," Brandorin said.

"That's because it's numbed your throat. Remember your promises," Caidos told them.

"Cai-Dos, you have brought some hearty friends with you. We drink to them." Ja-Lar had refilled his mug, and soon drained it. Other Arkhanians returned to the kegs to fill their mugs or ewers, paying Ja-Lar as they did, and toasting Brandorin and Piritho as they returned to their seats. Caidos reached into his pocket to pay for the drinks he had ordered, but Ja-Lar stopped him.

"No, Cai-Dos," he said quietly, "I don't need your money. You're drinking so little, for all of you, and all of these toasts are more than making up for the little your friends will drink. But don't let anyone else know I have done this."

"I'll keep your secret, Ja-Lar, if you promise not to serve anymore kra-lon to my friends here. I need them to be able to walk out of here, and get back on their horses in the morning."

"A fair deal. It is done." His deep, booming laugh filled the tent.

Caidos looked at Brandorin and Piritho, checking the contents of their mugs, which were less than half full. Brandorin's usually clear blue eyes had a bleezed look. Piritho's might have been as well, but Caidos couldn't tell; Piritho seemed to be having difficulty keeping them open.

"Kar-lon," Brandorin said incorrectly, as he raised his mug, "very good." He took another swig, and swayed a little as he brought the mug down from his mouth. He steadied himself against a large keg that seemed to be the only thing preventing him from falling over. Piritho raised his mug as well, but his last sip of kra-lon stopped any comment he may have planned to make.

"Caidos, I think you're right," Brandorin said; though his words were a bit fuzzled. "I think my tongue is swollen," he added, as he tried to check for himself, though the effort seemed to make him dizzy. "Maybe we should go."

As they prepared to leave the tavern, it became obvious Brandorin and Piritho needed assistance to remain upright. Sadro supported Brandorin, while Matu did the same for Piritho.

"Don' forge' some for Lanada," Piritho barely managed to say.

"I've got it," Salis told him, as he raised his mug, which still had a fair amount of kra-lon. "We'll bring the mug back in a little while," he told Ja-Lar.

The patrons downed another round to the departing men, toasting them as they left. The companions could hear them cheering all the way back to their campsite.

When they returned, the ladies could see Brandorin and Piritho had not heeded Caidos' warning, even before they spoke and their words made it obvious.

"'lo, N'drami," Brandorin said. "We had a great time, sorry you could'n join us."

He exhaled in her direction and she stepped back saying, "I think I'm rather glad myself." Sadro eased him down next to M'drani, who helped to keep him from falling over. "How are you feeling, Brandorin?"

"Brrrrandorrrin," he repeated, exaggerating the trill in her voice, "I like the way you say my name." He looked at her dreamily.

"I'm glad," she said smiling. "Maybe you should have eaten before you went."

"You prob'y righ'. But I think I better wait 'til the ground stops movin'. Is that a quake I feel?"

"I'm afraid it's only moving for you, but I think you're right; you should wait," she said, suppressing a laugh.

"Here, Lanata," Salis said, "Piritho insisted we bring some for you. He would have brought it back himself, except I don't think he can feel his hands." Piritho was looking at his hands as if he had never seen them before.

She took the mug from Salis, looking at the two men, "It didn't seem to take you very long. It would usually take a full night of drinking to get someone that drunk."

"Not with kra-lon," Piritho muttered from his reclining position on the ground next to Brandorin.

"Maybe you shouldn't try it, Lanata," M'drani warned her.

"A little taste couldn't hurt," she said, as she drained the few swallows from the mug. "That's pretty good," she said, after licking her lips. After a moment she shook her head as if to clear it, and added, "Feel like I just ran a couple of miles. I like it."

"Is that all?" Matu asked her.

"It seems to have increased my appetite. What do you say we make supper?"

There was no loose firewood in Rin-Ka, so they ate from their stores. Brandorin was not yet ready to eat, and Piritho had fallen asleep.

As they prepared the meal, Lanata kept up a continual stream of a mostly one-sided conversation; the only affect the kra-lon seemed to have had on her was to make her talkative.

"I feel like I did on Tapping Day, after quite a few samples of the newly tapped kegs. I remember thinking I'd had too much because the ground was shaking, but when I saw that everyone else had noticed the tremors too, I realized it wasn't just me. I was in a little tavern just this side of the Ridamon Gorge. That was the day the bridge had collapsed. If I wasn't already planning on coming east, that would have decided me."

"Ah, Tappin' Day!" Brandorin murmured. "We missed that this year 'cause we're on the road by then," he told Piritho, who was in no position to hear anything.

As Brandorin slowly sank to one side, Ra-Fa arrived with Til, who seemed to be walking in an uneven manner, and was talking continuously about everything and nothing.

"What happened, Ra-Fa?" Caidos asked.

"I don't know, Cai-Dos. He was just sitting in the keg, and after a while he just started talking, 'One this' and 'One that'. He started to climb out of the keg, but seemed to be having some difficulty, so I helped him out and brought him back here."

"What kind of a keg was it?" Caidos asked.

"It was an empty kra-lon keg. But what difference could that make?"

"It would be too hard to explain, Ra-Fa. Thank you for bringing him back." Caidos looked at Til, who was talking to Piritho, who was sound asleep. "Three of them now."

"Three?" M'drani asked. "You mean Til is drunk? How could he get drunk? He doesn't drink."

"There was either a little kra-lon left in the keg or the water must have leeched it out of the wood, and then Til absorbed it with the moisture. We can sober those two up with some strong tea and food, and a good night's sleep."

"Which Piritho has already started on," Salis said.

"But I don't know what to do about Til."

"Maybe a run would help," Lanata suggested, "kind of burn it off, so to speak."

"It might, but he looks a little unsteady on his feet."

"I'll run with her," Sadro said, "we can each take an arm, and hold Til up between us."

"If you want to try it," Caidos said. "I can't think it would do any harm."

Lanata and Sadro each took one of Til's arms, and began to walk away, into an open area where they could run. Til was talking profusely the entire time.

"I should have known better," Caidos said, chastising himself. "I should have never let those two talk me into going to the tavern. I was just afraid they'd go on their own, and then I wouldn't have been able to control them. Kra-lon has a tendency to sneak up on you, faster and faster, until you just fall over."

"Do you know this from personal experience, Caidos?" M'drani asked.

"Yes, I have to admit I do. When I was much younger and traveled through Arkhan by myself for the first time, I failed to listen to Mandricon's warnings. I thought I would show the Arkhanians I was friendly, willing to learn their customs. I thought if I just sipped it very slowly, I'd be able to control it. The foolishness of youth." He looked at Brandorin and Piritho, not sure if he meant them or himself, but most likely both.

"No real harm done," she said, "they'll sleep it off, and will probably have a headache tomorrow. I would imagine they'll find the ride rather unpleasant, but you did warn them."

"It'll be more than just a bad headache. The after-effects of kra-lon overindulgence are rather severe. There *is* a cure, if I can find someone who knows the recipe, and if I can convince them to take it. It's rather unpleasant. But if I don't we'll either have to stay here another day, or we'll have to tie them to their horses."

"It's that bad?" Icara asked.

"I thought the cure was too disgusting, so I decided to take my chances with the kra-lon's after-effects. I was so very wrong. I've never felt so bad in my life. One day seemed to last a week. That decides it. I'll go talk to Ja-Lar."

By the time Caidos came back with the cure in two covered mugs, Sadro and Lanata had returned with Til, who had quieted down, though still seemed a little unsteady.

"Good, I'm glad the run helped Til, because this won't work since it must be drunk. Let's start with you, Brandorin, since you're awake ... somewhat."

"Start what?" Brandorin asked.

"Matu, Sadro, I'm going to need your help. Each of you, take an arm and hold him. He's not going to like this."

"No more kral-lin," Brandorin muttered.

"No kra-lon, this is something else. I promise you it will make you feel better."

"I don't feel bad," he said dreamily. "I don't feel anything."

"You may not now, but you will tomorrow. Let me have your sword, Brandorin." Caidos was worried the crystal would give Brandorin the strength to resist them.

"Lanata, you're strong. Stand behind him, and hold his head, and cover his nose. He won't swallow if he can smell this. I advise the rest of you to do the same or at least hold your breath. Ready everyone?"

As Lanata tilted Brandorin's head back, his mouth fell open, and Caidos took the opportunity to pour the cure in. He then closed Brandorin's mouth and held it. With Lanata covering his nose, Brandorin had no other option but to swallow, though he struggled against those holding him so hard he almost managed to overpower all three of them. All of the companions grimaced as they each caught a whiff of what Brandorin had been made to drink. It smelled of stagnant water and rotting vegetables, with cloyingly sweet overtones.

"That was horrible," he shouted, between gagging, coughing

and spluttering.  He struggled to get up, and Caidos signaled to the others to release him.  "What was that?  I've never tasted anything so bad."  He went for a water to wash the taste out.

"Stop him," Caidos told the others, who grabbed Brandorin, restraining him from drinking.  "No water for at least an hour.  I'll let you rinse out your mouth, if I can be sure you won't swallow."

"I promise," Brandorin said.

"You also promised to be careful in drinking the kra-lon to begin with, but I know how such promises are forgotten once you have started drinking that brew.  I'll accept your promise, as long as you understand, if you swallow any of the water, we'll have to give you another dose."

"Anything but that."  Caidos indicated Matu and Sadro could release him and allowed Brandorin to rinse the taste from his mouth, and was satisfied when he spit out the water.

"Now, will you tell me what that was for?" Brandorin asked as he sat back down, still feeling quite wobbly.

"That guaranteed you'll be able to move tomorrow.  If you had any idea what you would've felt like tomorrow without it, you'd be thanking me right now.

"I can't believe drinking that poison was the better choice."

"I think he sounds better already," M'drani noted.

"Just the shock of the cure," Brandorin said.

"Then you aren't feeling good enough to help us give Piritho his dose?"

"I wouldn't wish that on my worst enemy, let alone my best friend."

"It's good to hear you call him that again," Caidos said.

Brandorin looked confused for a few seconds, not realizing what he had said, but then it sank in, and he looked at Piritho sleeping nearby, and said, "It sure does."

Dosing Piritho with the cure was easier than with Brandorin since he gave them no resistance.  The potion was in his mouth and he had swallowed before he sat up and gaped at those standing, looking back at him.

"That kra-lon sure leaves a bad taste in the mouth."  Then

he rolled over and went back to sleep.

## Chapter 24

After creating his Maken, Rhamak had dismissed Chaubrel and returned to his chamber. He walked to the sideboard and poured a glass of wine; something Chaubrel would normally do, but he didn't want to be attended right now. He held the goblet for a few minutes, lost in thought, before taking a sip. He snarled at its bitterness, tossing it aside.

He'd been thinking of Gharvik. He didn't like thinking of his predecessor, found it disconcerting. He had dismissed Chaubrel so he could work through these thoughts alone.

*I suppose it was the transformations that made me think of him. He may have discovered the incantations, but he never employed them properly. What good does it do to change a dog into a cat? But to change a man into a dog, or into a creature that has never existed before, that takes an artist.*

*It takes a skill you never had, Gharvik. You showed me what I could do with my talent, I'll give you that, but you had no idea how far those incantations could take me.*

*You had no insight. You had a strong talent, but you wasted it. You wanted to control Febron. Why, I have no idea. Just because you were born there? Because no one else wanted it is more likely.*

*Why stop at Febron when you can have it all?*

*But you didn't know you could have it all because you never went to Artara. You avoided Artara because you didn't want to be subjugated to the Mirador. But I went. I put up with them to get what I wanted. And soon I will have it all.*

*I will have it, because of what I got from you, Gharvik. What I made you give me. Artara knew what you were doing. You thought hiding in Febron would keep them from seeing, but it didn't. Churlik took your fragment and gave it to someone else. You let them think you had died; everyone thought you had died.*

*But you got careless. Careless and vain. You were seen, and described. There were drawings. Hundreds of years apart, but they were there. I always laugh when I remember how angry I was when they gave me that stupid assignment. 'Go to Febron' they said, 'Study the demon trials.' I don't think they even had a reason, but I did it, and I found your trail. And then I found you.*

*I hated to have to stoop to blackmail, but you were so afraid of being exposed, and I had to know how you had lived so long. Over seven hundred years. I had already determined I was destined to be part of the Rejoining, but I needed your little trick to live long enough to make it happen.*

*And so you taught me. You taught me that, and transformation and mind probing. But you never saw how they could be used together. You fool!*

*But not as much of a fool as you might have been. You never told me taking another's life not only added their years to mine, but also their knowledge. If I had known that, I wouldn't have waited so long to take yours. I wouldn't have had to put up with your droning lessons; I could have just stolen your knowledge along with your lives. Yet there were incantations you held back: draining spells, power transfer, trigger spells. You had never even hinted such spells existed. You were afraid of my power, but you were so vain. You wanted to show someone what you had done. You should have been more afraid, and less vain.*

*Yes, it was the transformations that got me thinking about you. But I have moved beyond you now, and I will be moving further still. There have been setbacks, yes, but none of that will matter when I get to the final step. That is all that matters. Yes, Brandorin is getting in the way, but in the end I will win. I always do.*

*And why do I win, because I plan, and I weigh the possibilities, and I make the right choices. That's why Caidos will lose. He thinks with his emotions. He's too sentimental, cares too much for those fools out there. He would do better to take only those he needs, only the bearers of the crystal fragments, but what does he do? He allows others to go with them, and that's what will stop him in the end. Now, I have created a creature that will stop Brandorin, and with that big oaf out of the way, that sentimental, old fool won't stand a chance.*

* * *

By the next morning, neither Brandorin nor Piritho showed any ill effects from either the kra-lon or its antidote. Til was a little sluggish, and seemed to doze against Matu's back as they rode. North of Rin-Ka there was a well-worn road, but they had to compete with caravans for the use of it.

The country they passed through was rocky, but it nurtured both a plant and animal life as unique as its surroundings. The flat surface of the plateau was broken by buttes of layered sandstone of terra cotta, ochre and umber. Boulders of various and unusual shapes were strewn across the surface, jutting up from the flatness of the plateau.

Seeds born by the winds that sliced across the region found refuge in the crevices of rock-strewn hills. Trees had sprouted and grown at precarious angles and in unusual shapes, twisted and contorted by the same winds that planted them. Their roots had reached down beneath the rock to find a hold in the harsh terrain.

Cactus, agaves, and yucca scattered across the dry scrub grass to give the stark landscape a dash of color. Prairie dogs, mice and lizards skittered from sight whenever they rode by, only to return after they left, at least until the next caravan came through.

In some places the road passed through canyons cut into the rock by rivers that had long since dried up. The high cliffs provided a respite from the strong winds that raced across the plateau. Zephyr enjoyed flying through the narrow passages, soaring and swooping, hearing the echo of her calls. When they rode out into the open plateau again, she would return to her place in front of Caidos, where he would wrap his robe around her, protecting her from the sand and gravel that blew across their path.

A strong quake brought down a shower of rubble on them as they passed through a particularly narrow canyon. Caidos and Icara cast air shields over them to divert the rocks away and to the side as they stopped and waited for the tremors to subside.

Their first day's ride from Rin-Ka took them half the distance to Tar-Kal, where the road crossed the Din-Cha River. When they arrived, and began the nightly tasks of making camp, they found their cloaks caked with the gritty soil blown up by the winds. It had worked its way into every crevice, and into their eyes and mouths.

Everyone, except for Til, seemed to be suffering from a cranky surliness. "I think it's aching muscles as much as the weather and dirt," Brandorin told Caidos. "Maybe I should resume the nightly healings. The horses are paying the price too."

"Are you ready for that?" Caidos asked.

"As long as I can touch just the Umari stone," Brandorin said, though he felt Caidos was as aware of the deception as he was himself. His breathing had quickened when he said, "I might as well start now."

Brandorin hesitated before approaching his own horse; he could feel Caidos' eyes on his back. His last use of the Umari stone had resulted in extreme pain and had triggered the gut-wrenching fear. Sweat beaded his brow despite the cold night air that surrounded them, but once he got over the fear of beginning, the process seemed to revive him as well as Bristo, and he moved from one horse to the next with less and less hesitation.

While the companions ate, Til went to the river to recover the moisture lost during the day, but returned soon after. "One cannot use the water of this river. It produces the same burning as did the soil by the first river."

"Did you try the soil here, Til?" Lanata asked.

"One did, but it burns stronger than before."

"We will be in Tar-Kal tomorrow, Til," Caidos said. "It's a large city, and they have many sources of water. Will you be able to wait until then?"

"Yes, One will be fine. It has been only seven days since leaving the forests of Ilyan."

"Good. You can soak for as long as necessary. Once we're there, we'll have a week until the next New Moon, when we will reform the crystal. Perhaps we can find some rich soil for you as well. North of Tar-Kal the landscape is less harsh, and there are vast plains of tall grass."

* * *

The last day of their journey to Tar-Kal was uneventful, with the road and surrounding countryside looking the same as on the previous three days. The plateau stretched out flat and featureless, broken only by a few isolated buttes, rising from the surface of the plain like the last pieces on a giant chessboard.

Toward the end of the afternoon, a row of hills appeared on the horizon, forming a barrier before them.

"Does the road go through or around those hills?" Brandorin asked.

"Those aren't hills," Caidos told him, "that's Tar-Kal. Since there are no trees here, the Arkhanians build with stone. The winds across this plateau can get very fierce during the winter, and only stone can stand against them."

"Why would they build their capital in such a remote and barren land?" Salis asked.

"You'll get that answer when we get there."

"You do like your little surprises, don't you, Caidos?"

"You may know a carpenter by the sawdust and wood chips."

"Well, that may be true, but it's comforting to know it can never be later than midnight," Salis responded.

Til, who was riding with Brandorin, said, "One does not understand those comments."

"Don't worry, Til, none of us do either."

* * *

The capital city of Tar-Kal stood alone in the center of a vast plateau, an island in a calm sea. There were no walls to the city, for each building was itself as solid and formidable as a small mountain, which many mirrored in shape as well as substance. The base of each building was broad and thick in order to support the weight of the levels above, yet their facades were crafted with etchings and patterns that transformed the heaviness into works of art.

The streets of Tar-Kal were boulevards, with canals running down the centers and traffic flowing on either side. At the center of the great city, a palace of delicate beauty stood in contrast to the heavier buildings that preceded it. The base was constructed of hundreds of separate columns, chiseled and crafted to depict the trees and flowers that no longer grew in this land. The columns supported walls of marble depicting great warriors in battle etched into the stone and enhanced in gold leaf. The large volume of gold adornment on the walls caught the light of the late afternoon sun, and shone back at the companions, requiring them to shield their eyes.

"There's enough gold on those walls to pay for my cathedral, several times over," Salis said. He turned to Caidos, "That's why they built here; they found gold."

"Centuries ago. Gold *and* jewels."

"In the middle of a flat plateau?"

"There were rivers running across this plateau at one time, probably before the World Shapers arrived. The rivers dried up, but left the gold behind. The canals running through the city were once riverbeds. After mining the treasures they held, the architects decided to incorporate the resulting trenches into the city's design."

"But where did all the stone and marble come from?"

"There are quarries to the north of the city. The winters in Arkhan are very harsh, and they needed more permanent building materials than wood and thatch."

The companions rode to the entrance of the palace, where stewards took their horses to be stabled. Caidos debated sending Zephyr with the horses, but remembered that she had accompanied him to Tar-Kal once before; the Dalron had been particularly pleased with her. They climbed the stairs to the base of the columns, where an Arkhanian in formal attire stood to greet them.

"Cai-Dos, Doljon TA-KA has sent me to great you. He was aware of your arrival, but apologizes for being unable to meet you personally. He is meeting with the Cabinet."

"Thank you, Vor-Tra, we are honored the Doljon has sent a man of such status to greet us."

They followed Vor-Tra through the expansive corridors of the palace, to a large audience chamber. "The Doljon will be with you as soon as he is able. Please help yourself to some refreshment." He indicated a marble side table covered with a spread of food and beverages.

"I didn't introduce you to Vor-Tra, even though he is Chancellor, it would not be proper. When meeting with either the Doljon or the Dalron, introductions to them must be first."

The companions had time to eat an early supper, though Brandorin and Piritho seemed a bit wary of trying any of the beverages until they were assured there was no kra-lon. They were all relaxing when a trumpet blast signaled the arrival of the Doljon.

"Cai-Dos, welcome. I received word of your travels through Arkhan." A large Arkhanian, wearing fitted trousers and a loose tunic, belted at the waist with a band of gold, strode into the room. He had short dark hair, which framed a chiseled face with prominent brows and cheekbones, surrounding dark, penetrating eyes. A square chin underlined a full mouth and a flat nose. His voice was deep and rich, and carried across the chamber, greeting the companions long before his heavily muscled legs brought him there. His arms were equally as muscular and a gold band, holding an orange stone, encircled his right upper arm.

After greeting Caidos, he reviewed the companions, pausing the longest on Til and Brandorin. "You have brought some friends with you, Caidos, including an Ilyani and a warrior if I am not mistaken."

"You are not, TA-KA. May I introduce them?"

"Yes, do."

Caidos introduced the other holders of crystal fragments first, and when he added their titles along with their names and country of origin, TA-KA nodded in understanding. He waited until all of the visitors had been introduced before saying, "This is not a normal visit, Cai-Dos. Having all of the fragments in one place can only mean one thing."

"Yes, TA-KA, it is time for the Rejoining of Sefiron. Our arrival is a surprise to you," Caidos said. "Does that mean you have not been visited by the Shadow of Sefiron?"

"No, the Shadow has not come to us."

"This makes no sense," Caidos said, his confusion quickly changing to frustration. "The scrolls clearly stated that there would be six full cycles. There are three appearances unaccounted for."

Not wanting to concern the other companions, Caidos put aside his frustration, trying to make his voice more hopeful. "But we have all of the fragments now. TA-KA, could you have a Kordunan artifact brought from your museum?" The Arkhanian nodded to acknowledge Caidos' request and signaled his wishes to Vor-Tra standing against the wall. Caidos continued, "I can then finish the replacement fragment, and we need only wait for the next New Moon, which will be in six days."

"Then you will be our guests until then. I will tell the Dalron of your quest. I am sure she will wish an audience with you."

"We would be honored."

"But first you will be shown to rooms where you can rest and be comfortable." He clapped his hands twice, the snap of each percussion sounding sharp and clear as it echoed off the marble walls.

Servants led the travelers through the long marble-paneled hallways, to a wing reserved for non-Arkhanian guests. The rooms had open-air patios and enormous comfortable beds. For every four rooms there was a central bath. When the travelers had washed off the dirt from the road, and returned to their rooms, they found their dusty travel-worn garments had been removed, and a change of clothes had been provided. The men found tunics and trousers, with decorative belts, while the women were given soft, light dresses, fitted at the waist, with long flowing skirts.

The visitor's wing had an atrium in the center, where the companions met after they had bathed and changed. The men arrived first, but were soon joined by Lanata, who seemed embarrassed by the dress she wore. "Someone took my trousers, and left me this," she complained. Piritho stood, staring at her, his mouth hanging open. "Caidos, can you find out what they did with my clothes?"

"I'm sure I could, but you look lovely, Lanata, and I'm sure Piritho would agree."

"Yes, you are," Piritho finally managed to say.

"You like this?" she asked. "It feels funny when I walk." She demonstrated, and the light fabric of the dress swished and swirled, Piritho's eyes watching her every move.

"I like them," Icara said, walking in. M'drani had arrived with her, but waited in the doorway, watching the effect of the new clothes. Icara's hair was also different. It was pulled up and back, forming soft curls cascading down around her long neck.

"What do you think, Matu? These or my Mage robes?"

"Oh, these definitely."

"Salis, these?" The little man just nodded his head, enthusiastically. She asked each of the men in turn, and they all responded with a rousing affirmation.

"That's what I thought. Are you going to give them a chance, Lanata?"

"I don't have much choice right now. They took my other clothes," she said, though she didn't sound as sorry about the forced change as when she walked into the atrium.

The last of the companions to arrive in the atrium was Til.

"How was the water in your room, Til?" Caidos asked.

"One does not want to cause problems for the quest, Caidos."

"Did it burn as before?"

"Yes, but in a different manner. This water ... tasted differently, One thinks Sal would say. It would suffice for a short time, but there was no nourishment, and in absence of the nutrition from the soil, water is more important."

"We will be called to an audience with the Dalron shortly. Afterwards I will ask if there are other sources for water that might better suit."

A few minutes later, a steward, in the formal livery of the Arkhanian Home Guard, arrived to escort them to the Dalron's presence. He didn't say a word; he didn't have to. His uniform, bearing and a slight inclination of his upper torso and an outward swing of his muscular arm, spoke of his duty, as well as a respect for the Dalron's honored guests.

They retraced their path through the winding corridors, but instead of returning to the audience chamber, they were escorted to the throne room. The steward reached for an elegantly carved staff that rested in brass brackets. He struck the eight-foot long stave three times against the parquet marble floor, and as the third stroke still echoed in the stone-lined chamber, the massive entry doors swung slowly inward.

The throne room stretched before them; the entire Varsian cathedral would have fit twice over in the central aisle alone. Heavy granite columns that even a dozen Arkhanians couldn't have wrapped their arms around supported a marble-spined, barrel-vaulted ceiling. Salis tried to inspect the construction of the columns and capitals, his head swiveling up and back as they passed each massive column. Caidos caught his eye and gave him a reproving glare to stop his gawking.

The citizens of Tar-Kal flanked them on either side, each towering above the heads of the companions like the walls of a narrow canyon; their respectful murmuring was reminiscent of scree sliding down a mountain slope.

Well above the heads of even the mountainous Arkhanians were stained glass windows, with alternating scenes of epic battles and pastoral landscapes. The battles were depicted in intense colors that made the warriors portrayed appear capable of jumping from the window to continue their battle in the throne room. The fields and hills were presented in pastel, almost watercolor hues, which seemed as inviting as the battles were forbidding. The message was clear; the Arkhanians preferred a comfortable life, and were willing to fight to ensure it.

At the head of the room stood a dais of black marble, bearing three large, gem-encrusted thrones. TA-KA sat on the right throne, while the left-hand one was empty, but the woman seated in the center and largest throne drew their attention by her stature and majesty.

She wore a fitted gown with a long train, elegantly draped

on the floor before her feet, its material woven with threads of gold. She was as tall as but more slender than the male Arkhanians. A jeweled crown that rose from a gold scalloped circlet fanned out at the back of her head and framed her narrow face. The fan's alternating panels were covered in emeralds and sapphires. She wore no ring, but each slender finger was tipped with a gemstone instead of a fingernail. The companions could not tell if they had been added or were natural.

Following Caidos' lead, the visitors bowed or curtsied, and stood waiting to be addressed.

"Caidos, old friend, it is good to have you back with us." Her voice, while deep, resonated with a ringing sound, like metal striking rock. She gestured with the fingers of her right hand for him to approach. He subtly signaled for the others to wait, and walked the twenty feet to the bottom stair of the dais. "Are you healthy?"

"I am lucky in that regard, your majesty."

"The Doljon tells me of your quest. It is a long time in coming. Please, introduce your companions."

Caidos made the introductions, adding a formality befitting the occasion. The Dalron showed no surprise at the titles that accompanied each, but the Arkhanian subjects present were soon whispering together and craning to see those being introduced.

"Have you not brought your winged friend, Caidos?"

"I have, your majesty, but she is resting in my room. I can retrieve her if that is your desire."

"Do not trouble yourself, Caidos," she said, as she turned to Vor-Tra, standing to the side, and with a slight nod of her head, he left the room. She turned to a page, and waved her hand slightly. The man tapped his staff on the floor three times. As the sound traveled through the vaulted ceiling, it was carried even to the far reaches of the throne room. Without any word the Arkhanians turned and left the throne room, the ordered steps of their departure echoed throughout the chamber, like rocks tumbling down an embankment.

As the entryway doors closed with a distant thud that they

felt more than heard, the Dalron, TA-RA, heaved a relived sigh, "Enough of these formalities. I can't decide which gives me more of a headache, the strain to look so imposing, or this horrible crown." She reached up to remove it, but before she could do so, a servant came forward and took it off, setting it on the empty throne at her left. "Come, come forward," she said to the companions. "It is not often we have visitors from other countries, let alone so many."

Without any apparent signal from the Dalron, servants brought a cushioned chair for each of the companions. As they settled down into them, a strange buzzing was heard from the back of the throne room, and Zephyr came flying forward, preceding Vortra. She flew to the Dalron, sat comfortably on her lap, and closed her eyes as TA-RA began to stroke her. A contented purring from the firedrake vibrated through the quiet throne room.

"You have found no more of her kind?"

"No, TA-RA, but I am always on the lookout."

"Now that we are alone, we can talk about the quest. I never suspected it would come in my lifetime. To be frank, I never believed it would come at all."

"I had hoped the same, but Sefiron's Shadow has been seen twice that I know of. The voices said there are only two cycles left, and we are six days shy of the first of these two cycles."

"What can you do about the missing Kordunan fragment," the Dalron asked.

"There is a way to make another," Caidos assured her. "Then we will have all of the fragments. The presence of all of the fragments will draw the Shadow to us again."

"I no longer carry the Arkhanian fragment. As you know, I passed it on to TA-KA when he reached his majority six years ago. I would have been too old to accompany you on your quest, nor would I have the right, but may I be allowed to witness the Rejoining, since it will happen here, in my realm?"

"I was going to ask you if you would do so, TA-RA. It is one of the reasons I took this route to collect the holders and their fragments, so it would end here. You are the oldest living holder of a fragment, and you carried it longer than any that I know of."

"I take it you are excluding yourself, Caidos," she laughed.
"Of course. I am but the Watcher, not a true holder."
"It will be my last act as Dalron, to witness the ending of one era, and the beginning of the next. Once the crystal has been reformed, I will pass the crown to TA-KA, and he will become Dolron of Arkhan.

## Chapter 25

As they left the throne room, Caidos talked to Vor-Tra about alternate water sources for Til. Within the hour, the chamberlain had acquired five different vats of water from various places around Tar-Kal: a well, two springs and two rivers. The well that supplied water to the palace had been used for Til's initial bath and had proven to be a problem. While Til tested the waters, the companions, including TA-KA, waited in silence in the atrium.

Throughout the next forty minutes, sporadic sounds of impatience, exasperation and nervousness punctuated the otherwise silent room. When Til appeared in the doorway to the atrium, slumped shoulders and a disgruntled scowl made it evident that none of the water had helped. Vor-Tra was with him and if Til's expression had not told the story, Vor-Tra's would have.

"How bad is it, Til?" Caidos asked.

"One could not use these waters. Vor-Tra has explained it."

"The waters in and around Tar-Kal pass through leagues of limestone and sandstone," Vor-Tra told them. "I am guessing they contain a substance Til cannot tolerate."

"How long can you wait here, Til?"

"One cannot say, Caidos. One has never experienced this before. One feels a strong need for nourishment; stronger than it should be since the last soil time was only eight days ago. One believes the waters One has used over the last six days have placed this substance within."

"We can't wait here for the New Moon," Caidos said. "The Shadow will appear to us no matter where we are. We can't wait here for six days, then add the five and a half days back to Ilyani soil; it would be too dangerous for Til's health. The soil near the Hodara river wasn't good for you, Til. We'll have to return at least part way back to the forest."

"The Dalron will be disappointed," TA-KA said, "but she'll understand. I'll go explain it to her." Caidos accompanied the

Doljon when he left the atrium.

"Was any of the water here helpful to you at all, Til?" Vor-Tra asked.

"The first water was the best. It satisfied One for a time."

"Then I will see that you have an ample supply to take with you. We can provide you an extra horse to carry it." Vor-Tra left the companions in order to find a method of carrying a large amount of water that would also facilitate Til's use.

"One's needs require the Companions to ride again, when this place has such comfortable beds and such beautiful clothing for Icara, Lanata and M'drani."

"See, even Til noticed," Piritho told Lanata.

"We wouldn't be comfortable if you were sick, Til," Brandorin told him. "I'll be glad to go back to Ilyan."

"Maybe you can get a little more kra-lon on our way back through Rin-Ka," Salis suggested.

"You're a cruel man, Salis," Brandorin said.

"It wasn't that bad," Piritho added.

"You slept through most of it, including the cure."

"What cure?"

\* \* \*

When Caidos returned he carried a long staff marked with simple designs cut into the wood. He explained that it was a Rastor, the staff of power of the last Haldir (leader of the Korduna) and would serve as the necessary artifact he needed. He also told them the Dalron understood why they had to leave, and that she had invited the companions to join her in her private chambers for a late supper. They had eaten lightly on first arriving at the palace and though most of them could eat another meal, none of them were in the mood for a formal dinner with a reigning monarch.

Their expectations were nothing like the reality of the Dalron's idea of a late supper. They found an informal selection of meats, breads, potatoes and soups laid out on a sideboard, in a large room with a fireplace and enough big, comfortable chairs for everyone. The Dalron and TA-KA were talking quietly, sitting together on a sofa. It was obvious that mother and son were close and the companions felt they were interrupting.

"Come in, come in," TA-RA called, seeing them in the doorway. "No ceremony in this room. Of all the rooms in this palace, this is most like home to us. We welcome you."

She had changed out of the formal dress she had worn at their first meeting into one much like those Lanata, Icara and M'drani had been given, though fine threads of gold woven into the fabric carried a subtle reminder of her royalty. She wore no crown, but her fingertips still glistened with jewels. Serving as hostess, she secured each one of them a plate and encouraged them to take plenty of food. Directing them to the comfortable chairs, she instructed them to pull their feet up and "settle down in."

As they began to eat, and the light conversation signaled they had followed the Dalron's instructions to act as if they were in their own homes, TA-RA took Til aside and talked with him.

"Looks like Til's in trouble," said Salis.

"It's nothing of the kind," M'drani said. "I'm convinced she's apologizing for the water of Tar-Kal and making sure Til is not upset that his needs require us to leave."

"And that she will miss the reforming of the crystal."

"I'm sure she's not saying that to Til," M'drani continued. "If she's upset, she's keeping that to herself. She's a gracious lady."

"Yes, she is," said TA-KA, his voice booming down on their heads from where he stood behind them. He looked fondly at M'drani, and suspiciously at Salis.

"He was just teasing, TA-KA," Caidos said. "It's Salis' way, as much as I try to break him of the habit."

"He's right, TA-KA, I knew if I said that, M'drani would come to her defense. Just a friendly little baiting."

"Like tiger-chasing," TA-KA said, his hard-chiseled features taking on an incongruous whimsical slant.

"He doesn't really," Salis said in an aside to Caidos, who nodded confirming TA-KA's sport. "Yes, just like that," Salis told TA-KA.

* * *

Caidos and Icara sat at the center of the rotunda. Converting the prepared Zadanite to a substitute Kordunan fragment was tricky magic, and he didn't need any distractions.

Brandorin accompanied them reluctantly. At the end of the process Caidos would expect him to test the new fragment, which meant holding the Protector's crystal, something he'd been avoiding over the last two weeks. He barely noticed the murmured enchantments and the soft ebbing light pulsing from under Caidos' hands. His anxiety grew with the intensity of the light. The jumble of voices coming from the source of the illumination, seemed threatening, and his apprehension escalated.

Brandorin felt pressure in his temples and the air around him throbbed in time with his own rapid heartbeat. Bolts of light shot from the space in front of the two mages, now both mumbling over the globe of chaos they held in check. Beams streaked through the chamber, coming at him from every angle, and though he thought briefly of the pinecones Caidos had thrown at him in his first test of the Protector's crystal, the memories were quickly replaced by the illusion of swords and lances coming at him out of the dark. He fought the urge to cringe and collapse to the floor in an effort to make a smaller target.

He closed his eyes, squeezing the lids as tight as he could, blocking out the bombardment of light, but he couldn't stop the sounds, now so strong he could feel the pulsating beat. He clamped his sweating palms against his ears, and bent over, shaking with dread. His heart hammered so loud in his ears that it took him a moment before he realized the sounds had softened into a harmonious blend of voices like those that came from Sefiron's Shadow. Even the memory of those voices eased his tension.

He opened his eyes with trepidation; the room was now infused with a single light, a light without a source that contained every color he'd ever seen. An abrupt silence wrapped around him like velvet, and the blanket of light contracted to a warm red glow coming from Caidos' cupped hands.

The mage stood, holding both hands before him, and walked slowly toward Brandorin, the softly pulsing light guiding him in the now dark space between them, though Brandorin knew that it only seemed dark in comparison to the overwhelming light that had just vacated the chamber. In the short time it took Caidos to reach him, Brandorin's fear had re-escalated, and he couldn't take the gem. Afraid of what would happen, and afraid of dropping it with his sweat-slicked fingers.

For a brief moment he hoped it would fall. Fall and shatter so he wouldn't have to try and fail. Shamed for having thought of letting an easy way out for himself keep their mission from succeeding, he clutched the hilt of his sword, and calmly (at least outwardly) picked the crystal from Caidos' open hand. On seeing a flicker of surprise in Caidos' eyes, he briefly thought, *"Surprises me too."*

Expecting something like the spark of hot and cold he experienced on first taking the Protector's sword and awakening the Umari fragment, he scowled at the stone and glanced at Caidos who looked as puzzled as he felt.

"It should work," Caidos said then looked at Icara.

"We did everything the scroll said." The younger mage's confusion made her voice squeak.

Caidos considered the possibilities. "The artifact was authentic. The Zadanite? No, that was the right quality. 'At need', the scroll said. That may be it. We don't need it yet, not until the New Moon. That's it. It will work then."

Brandorin wasn't sure if it was his own concern of having to go through this all over again, but he felt that Caidos was not as confident as he acted. Icara seemed convinced, so he decided not to voice his doubt. He wasn't reassured by Caidos repeatedly muttering, "That's it. It will work." In any case, they'd know in six days.

\* \* \*

The companions spent a comfortable night in the soft down beds of the Dalron's palace, and woke to a splendid selection of eggs, breads, and cheeses laid out in the atrium. Their traveling clothes had been returned to them, cleaned and pressed, with the occasional tear repaired. Lanata and Icara had been given a set of traveling clothes, made from the same kind of material as the dresses, but stronger and warmer, cut in the same fashion as M'drani's trousers and tunic.

As they stood at the peak of the mountainous stairs leading to the palace entrance, the Dalron and her Chancellor were present to bid them farewell and wish them luck on their quest. Two enormous draft horses flanked their own mounts, making them seem like ponies being protected by their sire and dam. The first and larger of the two, a sorrel colored hunter with a white blaze, was TA-KA's mount. The second was laden with animal hides filled with water for Til. Vor-tra explained the hides came with a frame and were made in such a way that Til could step inside and soak.

Til rode with Sadro when the holders of all eight crystal fragments, along with their friends, left Tar-Kal. The spirits of all the companions were dampened by their worry for Til's health, and even Zephyr seemed to understand something was wrong. She remained with Caidos as they passed through the first canyon, instead of flying through and playing with the echoes. They stopped for only one short break, to spell the horses, then continued on to their first camp at the Din-Cha River, where they arrived an hour before sunset.

Til had tried the water at this river on their way north, and had found that it burned. They unloaded the water bags and set up the frame which allowed the bags to be used as a standup tub, but Til could only stand in the water for ten minutes before he felt the burning sensation.

"It seems to be getting worse, Caidos," Brandorin said, as they walked away from the others to discuss the situation. "The water worked for a longer time when we were in Tar-Kal. And Til seems to be weakening. Instead of looking at the plants in the area, as he did on the way north, he is sitting quietly."

"I noticed that too," Caidos said. "Perhaps when we get to Rin-Ka. The only trouble with the water there was the kra-lon in the keg."

"We should try for a very early start in the morning, and pick up the pace a bit, try to get to Rin-Ka as soon as possible. Do you think there's any point in bringing the water from Tar-Kal?"

"It didn't seem to help at all. What did you have in mind?"

"If we leave the water, but bring the bags and the frame, Til could ride that horse. If we aren't doubling up on one of the other horses, it will be easier to go faster for longer."

"But will Til be able to ride alone, especially such a large horse."

"Til doesn't have to control the horse," Brandorin said. "TA-KA can continue to lead it as he has been doing."

"It's not just the control. In Til's weakened state, he may fall off if there is no one there to hold him."

"Then let's transfer the supplies from our horses to the spare Arkhanian horse. That will give each of the horses a lighter load. I think the Arkhanian horse can take it."

Brandorin went to groom and heal the horses from their hard ride across the brutal Arkhanian terrain. Caidos was encouraged by Brandorin's actions, but healing the horses didn't require Brandorin to hold the sword directly. He was able to use the Umari crystal with the sword sheathed. Holding the sword directly still caused him intense anxiety and touching the Protector's stone resulted in the return of the bone-chilling fear.

By the next morning, Til had weakened considerably. Til's coloring was fading to a dull brown with eyes a listless, murky green. Brandorin looked at Til, holding his sword, and looked at the Umari crystal.

"Do you think this would help, Caidos?"

"No, I don't think so. The healing process requires you to take on the wound or illness of the other person, and heal it in yourself. Your workings are too different from Til's. I think it would be a futile attempt that could do more harm than good." Caidos had heard the doubt in Brandorin's voice and saw the release of tension in his shoulders when he had advised him not to try.

Piritho suggested Til ride on Kahdru with him, but that Til ride in front, where Piritho could hold him. He didn't have to say that his suggestion was made from a fear Til would not be able to hold on. When they stopped for a quick midday meal, Piritho eased Til off the horse, where the Ilyani lay on the ground, without moving. They rode the horses as hard as they could for the rest of the day, and arrived at Rin-Ka by late afternoon.

When they took Til to the oasis, even Ra-Fa noticed the change.

"Til, my friend, what has happened to you? It wasn't the kra-lon, was it, Cai-Dos?"

"I think it's the water in general, Ra-Fa. It's not what Til's used to in Ilyan.

"This is not good that a visitor should suffer so from the water of Arkhan. What can I do?"

"We think the water from your oasis was better for him. We have containers we would fill." He lifted up the animal hides given to them in Tar-Kal.

"Fill them, take all you need. I will help you to carry them wherever you would go."

They filled one of the hide bags, and helped Til to place feet and legs into the water. Within minutes a weak cry told the companions it wasn't working. Too weak to get out of the water, they lifted and carried Til to a bedroll.

In a voice barely above a whisper, "Caidos must promise One."

"Promise what, Til? Anything."

"If One withers completely, Caidos must take One's remains to the Viriagalar.

"I promise, Til, but it will not be necessary."

"Must give One's essence back to the People." Til could not speak further, but fell back, eyes staring forward.

"He isn't breathing, Caidos. We must do something," Icara said desperately.

"Ilyani don't breath as we do. One breath a minute is

normal. In this weakened state, it might only be one every three or four minutes. It's like hibernation, they go dormant."

Caidos saw everyone looking to him for an answer, a way to help Til.

"We'll get up very early, so we can leave at the first light of dawn." He held up his hands to stop their protests. "I appreciate you would all be willing to leave earlier, but there's no road between here and Ilyan, and we can't risk a horse breaking a leg because he can't see in the dark. If we ride faster, we should be able to reach the Hodara River by mid-afternoon tomorrow. Then at most it's a half day's ride back to the forests of Ilyan, but I think we will find suitable fertile soil before that."

"How will we know if it's suitable?" Sadro asked.

"By the plants. When we reach the tall, softer grasses, we should be fine."

"Do you think it would be better for one or two of us to take the fastest horses and go ahead with Til?" Brandorin asked.

"It may come to that once we cross the Hodara, but you can't ride a horse at full gallop for an entire day, even if we stop and let you heal them."

"We should keep a watch, sit with Til through the night," Lanata said. "I'll take the first watch."

"I would like to take the watch," TA-KA said. "It is because of the soil and water in my country that Til is in danger."

"It's no one's fault, TA-KA," Caidos told him. "It is just the nature of life."

"Lanata, you and TA-KA can take the first watch," Brandorin said. "We'll do two at a time in two hour shifts, and everyone should find a few hours out of the next ten when they can sleep."

Til barely moved all night, just a turn of the head to acknowledge a new watch. When dawn broke and the companions were ready to leave, the morning light showed that Til's coloring had worsened; the once bright green eyes were now a dull gray.

"It's not too late, we'll get Til back in time," Caidos declared; though he suspected he had done little to allay anyone's fears. He could hear the doubt in his own voice.

They rode fast, with little or no conversation, stopping every couple of hours to allow Brandorin a moment with each horse, to ease their rapid breathing and freshen them for the next leg of their journey.

Brandorin insisted on carrying Til with him the entire day, but he noticed there had been a dramatic change in weight; Til was much lighter than before. The Ilyani's skin looked like the accumulation of decades of decayed leaves dried out under the summer sun; Brandorin was afraid Til would crumble if held too tightly.

Caidos watched them both closely; worried Brandorin might still try to heal Til if everything else failed. He felt guilty when, for the first time, he was grateful for the fear spell that was sure to keep Brandorin from recklessly attempting to heal the ailing Ilyani.

They reached the Hodara River by late afternoon and after letting the horses drink, hurried across the plain for another hour before stopping.

"The grasses are longer here, Caidos," Brandorin said, pulling on Bristo's reins to stop him. "Do you think this will work?"

Caidos dismounted and looked at the plants and trees in the area. The trees were short and twisted, and when he reached down for a handful of soil, it was hard and caked. Walking over to Brandorin, who still held Til protectively, he looked in the Ilyani's eyes, "Til, can you hear me?" Til did not respond to Caidos' words. "I think trying too soon could be more harmful than waiting another hour. Come Brandorin, you and I will race across the plain."

Caidos returned to his horse and jumping on he shouted to the others, "Catch up to us as you can. You'll be able to see where we're going."

Aquilo and Bristo took off at a full gallop before any of the others could react, and they quickly covered ten miles across the plain.

"Here!" Caidos shouted, as he gently reined Aquilo down to a walk. He dismounted before she came to a full stop. A small stand of birch trees stood off to their left, and when Caidos bent to grab a handful of soil he came back up with a lump of dark, moist soil.

Brandorin slipped from Bristo's back, holding Til's still figure in his arms, "What do we do?" he asked.

"Dig." Caidos was already on his knees, digging into the soft, rich soil. "It doesn't have to be deep; we just need to get past the topsoil and plants."

Brandorin gingerly laid Til down next to Caidos, and joined him in deepening and lengthening the hole the mage had started.

"Don't throw the soil, pile it nearby. We'll need it again."

When they had uncovered a strip about two feet wide and four feet long, they moved Til onto the fresh soil, covering legs and lower torso with the dirt they had removed, so Til was in direct contact with the soil all around.

"I'll stay here," Caidos said. "Ride around and see if you can find a source for water."

"We didn't bring the hide bags," Brandorin said in frustration. "All I have is one canteen."

"Take the one from my saddle. The others should be along shortly. If you find water, give a shout."

By the time Caidos turned back to Til, it seemed as if the Ilyani was deeper into the soil. Caidos looked at Til's hands, and saw that the fingers had elongated and were burrowing into the soil. It was like watching the roots of a tree, seeing the growth of years in a matter of seconds. He jumped to his feet, shouting, "Yes. Yes."

Twenty minutes later the other companions rode up. Matu, the first to dismount, ran up to Caidos shouting, "Were we in time?"

"Yes, Til will be fine. Brandorin rode off that way to look for water. Circle around and see what you can find. We will need it for the horses as well as Til. We have ridden them hard for three days; we'll go no further. They deserve a rest."

They found a stream of clear water near a small stand of trees about a mile away. The white stark trunk of a dying birch tree dominated the setting. Its bare, twisting branches reached out like arms to the surrounding trees, just beyond their reach. The other trees leaned away, trying to increase the distance, as if they knew the birch was dying from some infectious disease.

They made camp there, expecting to move Til when it was possible. M'drani and Icara stayed with Til, while the others set up camp. By the time Caidos and Brandorin returned to check on them, Til was sitting up and talking quietly, legs still buried in the earth. Til's color was not back to normal, but the eyes were brighter and the skin did not look so wilted and dry.

"One thanks Caidos and Brandorin for the effort required to bring One to this place. Caidos learned much from the People, to know how to prepare a fertile bed."

"I pay attention," he said quietly, his voice choking with emotion. He placed his hand on Til's shoulder, squeezed it gently and smiled.

"We have an even better bed waiting for you at the camp," Brandorin told him. "There's a stream, and the soil there is so fertile, even I can smell the difference."

"One is beginning to think that Caidos and Brandorin, that all the Companions would make good Caretakers. One will go to this place the Companions ..." Til paused looking at each, then with an effort added, "all of *you* have prepared, if One could get a little assistance in standing up."

\*   \*   \*

They would have a full day of rest before the next New Moon; Sefiron's Shadow would appear to them at dawn of the following day. Though most of the day was spent at rest, the horses, run so hard for three days, garnered a great deal of attention. Brandorin healed their swollen tendons and overworked muscles, while the others washed and groomed them, combed their manes and tails, and cleaned their hooves. There was no need to hobble them; the Larian horses saw to it that none of them strayed. Brandorin smiled as they romped through the meadow like young colts and fillies; feeling relief from their aches and the strain of the desperate drive from Tar-Kal.

"We'll be missing the Harvest Celebration, Sadro," Matu said. Was that what was bringing you to Numina?"

Sadro looked at his fellow Larian for a moment in confusion, "The Harvest Celebration? That wouldn't be until next month."

"All of this travel has confused my calendar, too," Salis told him. "I don't even know what month this is. Are they still working on the cathedral, I wonder? That is if they found someone to continue my work. Work! I don't even know what I'll be doing after tomorrow. I don't have a job anymore."

"Come to Numina, Salis," Matu told him. "You wanted to learn our methods of building. We'll find a place and work for you."

"Maybe I'll do that."

"I would enjoy spending some time in Numina," Icara told them, "that is if I can convince Caidos I don't have to go back to Artara and study."

"What will you do after the crystal has been rejoined, Caidos?" Lanata asked.

"There'll be much to do. Learning what kind of world we'll have afterward will be the main task, but I think I'd like to go back to Artara for a while. Just to rest, and study, and talk."

"I can travel for you for a while, Caidos," Icara said.

"That just might work."

"You must all come back to Arkhan," TA-KA told them, "I will be made Dolron, and I would like you all to be at the coronation. Til, we'll bring vats of the proper water, and wagons of Ilyani soil, so that you may come too."

"One would enjoy that."

Sadro walked over to where Brandorin was cleaning his saddle and inspecting Bristo's bridle. "Where will you go after the quest is over, Brandorin?"

"It's been a long time since I was home. I must go back to Kartir."

"Will Piritho go there as well?"

"You'll have to ask him."

"It's just that I haven't fulfilled my Debt of Life to you. Because of his help, and Salis' as well, I owe them a Debt too, but not as great as the debt I owe you."

"So you're planning on following me around until you've saved my life? You don't have to."

"I must, Brandorin. It's the Larian way."

"It would be difficult for you in Varsa, Sadro," he said, looking at the cat-like features that now seemed so familiar to him, but would be foreign and disconcerting to the citizens of Kartir. "We're obviously strangers to Numina, but no one there stared at us, or made us feel unwelcome. I'm sorry to say Varsians are not as tolerant as Larians."

"Brandorin, you've just answered everyone's question," Caidos said. He suspected Brandorin had not heard the questions, so he explained, "Lanata asked what I would do, once the crystal was reformed, and my job as Watcher was fulfilled. Matu, you said you wanted to get to know your neighbors. Icara, you want an assignment that will take you away from the dreary lessons in Artara. I think it's well past time the citizens of Zadania get to know one another."

\* \* \*

The stream running through the glade flowed out of Ilyan. With its nutrient-rich water and the soil along its banks, Til's color and energy quickly returned. Despite the companion's insistence that further rest was needed, Til rose from the soil bed and walked to the dying birch tree. Til placed one hand on the trunk of the ailing tree; the other hand rested on the green crystal fragment. Til slowly moved around the tree, tracing its trunk and branches with one hand.

"Look," M'drani whispered. "Look at the branches."

The others followed her gaze. All, except Caidos, were amazed to see the dull grayness of the dying limbs begin to whiten. Thin, straggly dead offshoots thickened and grew, as small yellow-green buds of life appeared at the tips, quickly unfurling into fully-formed, vibrant green leaves. In a matter of minutes, the dying birch had been revived and stood with a full, spring-fresh cover of verdant foliage.

Instead of tiring Til so soon after recovering from the ill effects of the Arkhanian soil, the renewal process seemed to have worked both ways. Til's eyes were once again bright and brimming with life, and a smile broke across the face that had so recently been decimated.

"One could not sit idle when the crystal was needed," Til said.

"It seems to have helped you as well, Til," Caidos said. He had seen Til perform the job of Caretaker a number of times, and recognized the dumbfounded looks on the rest of the companions.

"One always feels renewed in the use of the crystal. One may have helped the birch, but the birch helped One as well. The Land gives to the People, and the People give back."

"Til, you've been nourished, now I think it's time for the rest of us. Salis, when do we eat?"

Salis had plenty of help preparing their evening meal. The day's rest and the anticipation of the next morning seemed to be giving everyone nervous energy. Hunting and preparing the meal as well as collecting wood for the fire were handled without any fuss.

"TA-KA," Salis asked, "I've seen you eat primarily meat, with some bread or potatoes, but when we were traveling through Arkhan, I didn't see enough wildlife to keep you big guys satisfied. What do you eat up there?"

"Chi-ma."

"What's that? And where were you hiding them?"

"Chi-ma travel in great herds, mostly north of Tar-Kal. There are great plains of tall grass where the Chi-ma graze. The Chi-ma are about as tall as your horses, but are broad and very meaty. They have thick pelts that provide leather for shoes, belts, harnesses, even the water bags that were made for Til."

"Kind of like cows."

"I have seen cows," TA-KA said with a scowl. "Chi-ma are much bigger, more fierce. They have jagged horns and sharp teeth, which we use for daggers and knives. It takes many men to hunt Chi-ma. They don't sit still waiting to be slaughtered. When the

Chi-ma run across the plain it feels as if the ground is moving. It can be felt for many miles."

"Wouldn't it make more sense to raise them, in pens, so you didn't have to chase them?"

"That would not be fun. Not for Arkhanians, not for the Chi-ma. It is a game we play. Sometimes the Chi-ma win, mostly the Arkhanians."

\*   \*   \*

At the end of the meal, Caidos talked about what would happen with the dawn.

"I think we should keep a watch tonight. Nothing is going to happen before the dawn, but I don't want to run the risk of missing the Shadow in the morning. And there's a distinct possibility Rhamak may arrive. We should be on our guard."

"What do we do tomorrow, Caidos?" M'drani asked.

"When Sefiron's Shadow appears, I will direct each of the holders, in turn, to take their fragments, and holding them aloft, we will place them together. We'll start with Brandorin, who'll take the two fragments he has, the Protector's and the Healer's and hold them together."

Brandorin looked at the stones in the hilt of his sword, worrying about how it would feel to hold the Varsian stone directly, without the sword. He felt the fear begin to rise in his throat, and he fought it back, refusing to give into a magically produced emotion. He felt some of the others looking at him, as if they knew he was afraid. To forget the fear, he asked, "How do we get the stones out of their settings?"

"They will be released by the voice of the crystal; just have your sword ready. I'll direct each of you to add your fragment. Once all of the other pieces are in place, including the substitute Kordunan fragment, I'll add the crown piece."

"And that's it?" Salis asked.

"That's it. Except for what Sefiron will have to say."

"We should stand watch, three at a time," Brandorin said.

"I'll take the first watch with Matu and Sadro, and the last with Caidos and TA-KA. Piritho, Lanata and Salis can take the middle watch. It's only nine hours until dawn, three watches will be enough."

\* \* \*

A half-hour before dawn, Brandorin paced the camp, nervous about the Rejoining. Caidos and TA-KA stood together looking out over the plain toward Arkhan, but he couldn't stand still. The fear gnawed at him even when he wasn't touching the Protector's stone. The thought of holding the stone directly, without the surrounding hilt of his sword, caused him to break out in a cold sweat.

He had wandered near the sleeping companions, and in the dim light of Day Spring, he could see M'drani sleeping peacefully under the newly restored birch tree. She hugged her blanket against the cold of the night, and he was reminded of a bird, nestled in sleep. Her soft violet eyes were now closed, long lashes brushing against the velvet blush of her cheek. Her lips, parted slightly, twitched as a fretful dream caused her eyelids to flutter. He wanted to touch her, to smooth away the crease that furrowed her brow, but was afraid to move, to startle her into wakefulness. Afraid she would take flight and leave him.

Brandorin turned, hearing a noise behind him.

"It will be dawn soon," Caidos whispered, "we should wake the others."

Brandorin turned back to M'drani, who was now sitting up. He smiled at her, and extended a hand to help her rise. Caidos moved amongst the other companions, waking them.

Although he had been sleeping soundly, Salis didn't complain about being awakened this time. The fragment holders sat together, in a circle, with the others sitting nearby. Caidos felt an almost kinetic energy in the air, carrying a hint at the beginning of all things, an anticipation of the potential of Sefiron Rejoined. The time dragged on as they sat in silence waiting.

Matu was the first to see a faint light glowing outside their circle, the first sign that the Shadow was with them. He stood, without speaking, but the others knew what he saw, and stood with him, facing the growing light that now pulsed and swirled a few feet away.

"Take your fragments from the sword, Brandorin," Caidos whispered.

Brandorin had been holding the sword, already drawn from its sheath, his hand resting on the Umari stone. He hesitated, knowing how it would feel when he touched the Protector's stone. He wondered if Rhamak had planted the fear spell, to make him hesitate, to delay or prevent the reforming of the crystal. That thought gave him the resolve he needed to move.

He put his hand over the crystals, feeling the fear surge like an icy hand clenching his insides. It rose quickly, and he felt his mouth go dry. He could not breathe properly. There wasn't enough air. He couldn't get the stones to release, his fingers kept slipping. He fought against the fear and tried to pry out the Protector's stone. His hands shook, but the stone would not release. He turned the hilt, tried for the Umari stone. The fear quickly subsided, allowing him to get a good grip on the indigo crystal. He realized the problem was not the fear.

"They won't release, Caidos."

"Neither of them?"

"No, neither one."

"Perhaps you were not meant to be first. Everyone try your fragments."

Each of them reached for the fragment they had carried with them for years, but not one of the stones could be removed from its setting.

The light of Sefiron's Shadow had grown in intensity and was starting to take on form and sound. The voices intensified, male and female combined in a song of joy. When the voices began to speak, all present, including those who did not carry a stone, could understand it.

"Caidos, the Watcher, you have done well. You have

gathered all but one of the fragments. The Lost Ones must not be forgotten. Take all our children and go through the Labyrinth. The last cycle begins."

The Companions watched as the light of the shadow separated and scattered across the plain, each beam of light accompanied by a note of the song. The last trace of voice and light faded as the first light of dawn broke the darkness of the night.

No one said anything for some time; the effect of the Shadow lingered long after the last light and sound had faded. But as the morning dawned, the feeling faded as well, and was replaced by the disappointment.

"It didn't work," whispered Lanata.

"Did we do something wrong?" TA-KA asked.

"Who are the Lost Ones? Sadro asked Matu.

"Where is the Labyrinth?" Icara asked.

"Wait everyone," M'drani said, "give Caidos a few minutes. He'll explain it."

Caidos had walked out into the plain, standing where Sefiron's Shadow had appeared. The lingering feeling of contentment he had experienced a month earlier was absent, replaced instead by a sense of loss and disappointment. He looked over his shoulders at the others, and could almost feel their questioning stares. He turned slowly, and walked back, his feet dragging in the grass.

"I'm sorry. I was wrong," he said, his voice sounded dejected and lost. "Our journey is not over."

"Do you know who the Lost Ones are?" Sadro asked.

"The Korduna."

"Do we need to find them?" Matu asked.

"The top of the hill is harder to find than the bottom."

"And the Labyrinth? Where is that?"

"Even the wisest cannot solve the labyrinth unless he has something to lean on."

Salis turned to Brandorin, an uncharacteristic look of defeat on his face, "He doesn't know."

## Chapter 26

Caidos stared at the dark orb of the new moon. Barely visible, he felt it mocking him. Like the solution to the current problem; it was there, but he couldn't see it. Why had Sefiron mentioned the Lost Ones? Would the fragment he made not work after all? If it wouldn't work, why provide instructions?

He turned to his companions, knowing their disappointment, but even in the low light of early morning as he scanned all of the anxious faces staring back at him, he saw no accusation in any of them. Like the trust of young children for a parent, they believed he would know what to do. Then he decided. Though he may not have the answers now, he would get them, and the people here, his friends, would help him.

"We must go to Artara," he told them, not wasting the time to admit to frustration, to tell them what they already knew. "There are scrolls I must consult, to know what our next step will be. There is one cycle left. We have another forty-five days."

"Where is Artara?" Lanata asked.

"In the southwest," Icara answered, "among the Eastern Islands."

"We'll need a ship," Brandorin said. "The dock in Laria is a long trip over land, and we can't be sure of finding a ship there."

"We can take a ship from Ti-Kee," TA-KA told them, "it is northeast of here. We've come a little out of our way, but it's more east than north."

"We'll have to bring the hide bags with water for Til," M'drani said. "Should we bring soil also, Til?"

"How long will the trip from Ti-Kee to Artara take?"

"Three to three and a half days," Caidos said, gaining comfort in having a course of action to follow.

"One will be satisfied by this water and the sun. One has learned that using the wrong soil is worse than waiting for the right soil."

"The soil in Artara should be like this soil, Til," Icara said, "some of the same plants grow there."

"Icara is correct in judging the soil by the types of plants that flourish in it."

"Once we are in Artara, and I have read the scrolls," Caidos said, "I'll know where we have to go next. Then we can decide if we need to take extra precautions for Til on the next leg of the journey."

"Can we travel to Ti-Kee through Ilyan?" Matu asked.

"For most of the way. Traveling across the plains will allow us to make the best time." Caidos stopped to picture the terrain and distance between their current position and the port city of Ti-Kee, in Arkhan. "It will be three hundred to three hundred and fifty miles. I would say we should be in Ti-Kee in a week and a half, at the outside. Time to Artara is less than four days, with favorable winds. Much depends on being able to find a ship that will take us."

"I will find us a ship," TA-KA said with the authority of his position, and though it seemed incongruous in such a large man, he added sheepishly, "There are certain advantages to being Doljon."

"Marvelous. Then let's get ready to depart." Caidos looked at the companions and saw hope, where a short time before he had seen dejection and concern. They seemed to have forgotten the Kordunan fragment, though he had not.

\* \* \*

The travelers were ready and on their way within an hour, a sense of purpose in their actions sustaining them. They rode across the plain, heading northeast, staying within Ilyan, where the soil and water were nutritious for Til. Although they had not been able to rejoin the crystal fragments, the companions were in good spirits. Their travels together had created a bond between them, and no one wanted to see that end.

M'drani riding with Icara said, "I think your new clothes are making a big difference in the way the men are looking at you."

"Do you think so? Even these?" she said, indicating the

lighter traveling clothes she now wore in place of the shapeless robes of a mage.

"Oh, definitely. In fact I heard Matu talking to Salis about the change."

"They were?" Icara turned in her saddle and looked back at Matu and Salis riding together behind them. She could not stop from smiling, so she waved back at them.

"That was subtle."

"I guess I shouldn't have done that."

"That's all right; it will give them something to think about."

\* \* \*

"What was that all about?" Matu asked, referring to the look and wave from Icara.

"I don't know. You can never be sure what women are doing," Salis said.

"Women? She's just a girl, though I do admit she looks quite different in the clothes she got in Arkhan."

"She's not really that young. Mages age slowly. Look at Caidos, you would never guess he's two hundred years old."

"Salis, stop that. I know how old Caidos is, and it's not two hundred. How old is Icara?"

"I don't know for sure. Women don't tell their ages, but I've known her for eight and a half years, and she'd been in Artara a couple of years by then. I'd say, upper twenties."

"Oh, I had no idea. Interesting."

\* \* \*

TA-KA rode with Til, behind Matu and Salis, the Doljon still feeling responsible for what had happened to Til in his country. The Ilyani's green and brown plant-like skin against the Doljon's stark features was reminiscent of the sporadic growth of plant against the stark stone walls of the Arkhanian canyons.

"You only saw a little bit of Arkhan, Til. We have some very beautiful country, filled with plants you've probably never seen before."

"One would be pleased to return to Arkhan and to study these plants. Caidos was correct; the People have stayed in Ilyan for too long. There is much to see beyond the Land the People tend."

"I've seen some of Varsa, but this is the first time I have been in Ilyan. Once I am Dolron, I will travel and meet the leaders of the other lands. Talk to them about an exchange, a sharing between countries."

\* \* \*

Lanata rode between Piritho and Sadro at the rear of the line. TA-KA's booming voice carried down the line of travelers.

"I think TA-KA is right. That's why I left Varsa and rode into Laria, to see other lands. I'd only been in Laria a week when I ran into you. Now in this short time I've seen Ilyan and Arkhan too. I didn't know how well my wish would be fulfilled."

"Mine either." Piritho said.

"Did you come along to see other lands too?" Sadro asked.

"Other lands? Oh, yes. Well, actually I'm hoping to find Rhamak."

"Why would you want to find him? From everything I've heard he'd be the last person I'd want to see."

"It's kind of like the Larian Debt of Life, but turned around. Instead of saving a life, Rhamak took one, and I'll take his in payment for that life."

"Not this again," Lanata said. "I was hoping you'd given up on the revenge business."

"I can't, Lanata. I made a vow."

"I agree Rhamak deserves to die, but don't do it for revenge. Do it so this quest can be fulfilled, or to stop him from taking other lives. Killing Rhamak won't bring Ilona back and as for the rest of your vow ... well, I don't want to hear about that ... that part is just a waste." Lanata spurred her horse and caught up with M'drani and

Icara.

*   *   *

Brandorin looked back as Lanata rode up, but knowing they weren't close enough to be heard, he asked, "What will we find in Artara, Caidos?"

"Didonno's scrolls. They should explain about the Labyrinth. I remember passages I didn't understand when I read them, but in the light of Sefiron's message; I'm convinced they refer to a Labyrinth. What I don't remember are any passages that say *where* it is. I've read those scrolls hundreds of times. I should know where we have to go, should've known it from the beginning."

"I'm sure the location is in there as well. But what about the Lost Ones? Will the fragment you made work?"

"I believe it will, if it is needed? The Shapers wouldn't condemn all of Zadania because one fragment was lost. But you see, I no longer believe it *is* lost."

"Then where is it?"

"I have no idea" Caidos said with a mischievous glint in his eye. "But I don't need to know, because if the fragment is truly lost, then the fragment we made will work. But if it is not lost, as I suspect, I am convinced Rhamak has it. In which case, he'll find us, probably at the Labyrinth. And once we have the Kordunan fragment, we know you'll be able to use it."

"All we have to do is get it away from him," Brandorin said with an air of false bravado, as the licking murmur of dread crept through his veins. He reached for his water skin; his mouth had gone as dry as the Arkhanian sands. He changed the subject. "How will *Rhamak* know where the Labyrinth is?"

"Remember he lived in Artara for a time. I'm sure he found a way to view the scrolls and learn their contents."

"Could he have modified the scrolls? Changed it so we wouldn't be able to find the Labyrinth?"

"It would be very difficult to have changed them without someone knowing, but even if he could, that wouldn't serve his purpose. He needs us to bring the rest of the fragments there. They must be held by a member of the race to which they were given."

"If that's true, Caidos, why has Rhamak made so many attempts to stop us?"

"His attempt to stop me is easily understandable. The crown piece is what controls the Rejoining. If he has that, he doesn't need the others. And being a mage, he could use it.

"That explains the raptor attack; it was directed specifically at me, and therefore the crown piece. The boar attack could be explained as well for the same reason; it's just that others were present at the same time."

"But then how do you explain the attack on Salis at the cathedral?"

"Rhamak must have known we were on the way there. The hawk M'drani sensed and flushed out of the trees was undoubtedly one of Rhamak's spies. Another lapithi. Remember what she said about the hawk flying through her spirit? A sense of helplessness, and an image of a man. It had to be Rhamak. He has probably been watching us every step of the way, through birds most likely, since they can bring the information back by the easiest and fastest way.

"I'd guess Rhamak was not in Medora, but had sent his spies and assassins with explicit instructions, but not the true purpose of the attack. We arrived in Medora the evening before the attack. As far as Rhamak knew, we were with Salis by that time."

"But none of that explains sending Piritho to attack me at the wedding. I didn't even have the crystals yet."

"No, you didn't," Caidos said, a little deflated. He thought for a moment, and began speaking again, thinking out loud. "Rhamak drew me away from the wedding to ensure his plan would succeed. I think we can accept that as fact. Since you hadn't been given the sword yet, I can only assume you were the target, rather than the fragments. Perhaps Rhamak wanted you out of the way before he began to put his plan into action."

"But how would Rhamak know this was the time to rejoin the crystal?"

"There are still three appearances unaccounted for. They could have appeared to Rhamak, which would be another argument for him having the Kordunan fragment. Maybe because he wasn't the true holder of the fragment it was kind of a warning to get it to the right person. But that's just speculation, and even if that's true, I don't understand why it would have appeared to him all three times."

"But why me, why not my father?"

"I think it's because Rhamak sees you as a threat to his success. He knows the kind of warrior your father is, would have heard stories, maybe even saw him in battle. But you're an unknown. I am beginning to suspect he's afraid of you."

"So he sent a spell that would make me afraid of everything," Brandorin muttered under his breath.

They rode in silence for a time, Caidos waiting for Brandorin to adjust to what he had just said, before he asked the question that had been on his mind for days.

"Do you accept my theory?" Caidos asked.

"It does fit, but that doesn't mean it might not be something else."

"Have you thought about the fact the boar attack was half-hearted at best? Three boars, against nine of us. The raptor attack was five against one. It was almost as if he wasn't trying as hard. No, I think the boar attack was sent so someone would get hurt, and you would use the Umari crystal to cure them, and that's when the real attack succeeded."

"You mean the fear that came from curing Sadro."

"Yes. Rhamak is afraid of your ability to defeat him, so he sends a spell to make you afraid to try. That's why I must ask you a question and why you must give me a complete and truthful answer. Is the fear gone?"

"No," Brandorin said reluctantly. "M'drani helped to control it in the beginning, and whatever she did has helped since. But it's still there."

"Is it always present, or only when you touch the Protector's crystal?"

"It's there most of the time, without touching the crystal. Even now, I have this feeling that something is there, stalking me, and I want to look over my shoulder, but I know there'll be nothing there. If I touch the Umari crystal that feeling goes away, but touching the other stone makes me feel like my blood has been replaced with black ice and I have only as much strength as a dried leaf. I wasn't lying when I told you it was getting better. I think I just had myself partially convinced that it was. The only time I didn't feel it was after drinking the kra-lon."

"You weren't feeling much of anything then. You haven't had to test it against an attack, in a situation where the fear could cause you to hesitate. Rhamak had to have sent the boars for the sole purpose of triggering the fear spell. He'll send another attack, I'm sure of it. And he expects you to be afraid."

"He expects me to die."

\* \* \*

Rhamak sat at one end of the expansive table in the dining hall, the breakfast before him untouched. "They'll have tried to reform the crystal this morning, but it didn't work. My how disappointed Caidos must be! They'll go to Ti-Kee and then to Artara, but by the time they arrive there, Brandorin will be dead."

"Yes, sire," Chaubrel said. "May I ask how you know they will go to Artara?"

"Because Caidos is confused. He doesn't know what to do, and he has nowhere else to turn. He'll look for answers in the scrolls. But he won't find them. Not all of them anyway. Just the ones I want him to find."

Chaubrel, feeling brave because Rhamak was in a good mood asked, "Which answers will he find?"

"He'll find out where the Labyrinth is. He'll learn what is expected of him when he gets there. But he won't learn where the last fragment is."

"No, sire."

"But Caidos won't expect that answer to be in the scrolls.

How could that old fool Didonno have written about that? He couldn't have known I would obtain it, but I wouldn't be surprised if Caidos suspects I have it.

"Will that cause a problem, sire?"

"No, it shouldn't. He'll expect me to be at the Labyrinth. He'll even be prepared for me to try to take the other fragments from him. He won't have time to prepare for what he'll find there.

"Unless he's clever. There is a way, but even that won't matter. Let him bring an army. Let him fight to stop me. It won't work, because he'll be fighting the wrong battle, in the wrong place, in the wrong way."

"What would be the right way, sire?"

"You're being rather daring this morning, Chaubrel." Rhamak paused, and Chaubrel wondered if he had gone too far. "But it doesn't matter. Your question is a good one. That's what Caidos won't know, until it's too late to do anything about it. He won't even know he's been fooled and that he's lost, and that I have won. I've known how this play would end for a long time, Chaubrel. Have known what would happen every step of the way." He looked away, staring out the window.

"Except for one thing. I hadn't expected the Korduna to die out just because I took the crystal. That didn't make sense. Over four thousand years holding the crystal; their survival instincts should've been inherent by then. Would you have expected that?"

"No, sire," Chaubrel said quietly, not daring to give an honest answer.

"I didn't want that to happen. It wasn't necessary for my plans. Why didn't they just leave, go somewhere more habitable? There was nothing keeping them up there in that wasted country. If they couldn't survive there without the crystal, they should've moved south. I had to have the fragment. You understand, don't you?"

"Yes, sire."

Rhamak sat quietly, nibbling at the food before him. A servant stepped forward, a paper in his hand. He looked briefly at Chaubrel, then stepped past him to hand the message to Rhamak directly.

"This message just came in for you, My Lord."

Rhamak looked at Chaubrel, and then at the man. He took the message, reading it he asked, "What's your name?"

"Kalga, sire," the man said, keeping his eyes averted.

"Kalga? Your name and your face seem familiar. Good news, Chaubrel," he said, referring to the message he held in his hand. "The Maken are in place."

Rhamak stood, lifting Kalga's face, forcing him to meet his gaze. Chaubrel began to speak, but a motion from Rhamak stopped him. "No, Chaubrel, not this time." Rhamak had not broken his gaze with Kalga. "I remember you now. Chaubrel saved you the last time, distracted me with news. From Laria, wasn't it, Chaubrel?"

"Yes, sire."

"What are you trying to do, Kalga?" The servant was frozen in place by Rhamak's gaze, his body trembling.

"Chaubrel, this man would like your job. Would you like to give up your position? Give this man a chance?"

"No, sire." He had saved him once before, managed to distract Rhamak, but the discussion of the Korduna and their fate had made this a bad day for Kalga to try again. Rhamak would not be swayed.

"I didn't think so. You have a nice job, don't you Chaubrel?"

"Yes, sire."

"You get special food, special clothes, jewels, a nice room. It appears Kalga would like some of that special attention. Would like to move up in the world. Is that it, Kalga?"

The man could not respond, but Chaubrel suspected he had changed his mind.

"I think we should grant his wish," Rhamak said, as Kalga began to rise from the floor, his feet now dangling a foot above it. "Do you like your higher station? No? Perhaps you would like a better view."

Rhamak walked toward the far side of the room, Kalga trailing along as if on a lead. By the time they reached the open window, Kalga's feet were high enough to clear the window ledge. When Rhamak stopped, Kalga continued to float out of the window, where he stopped, twelve feet away from the ledge, and outside.

"Is that high enough? I admit on the other side of the castle it would be higher, but this will probably suffice."

Rhamak turned from the window, severing his gaze and his control over Kalga, who fell, screaming, one hundred-twenty feet to the surface of the plateau.

## Chapter 27

Caidos was on edge the entire trip to Ti-Kee, and Brandorin's anxiety increased with each passing day. What started with the tense way he held himself in the saddle worsened until he jumped at any loud or sudden sound.

They traveled within Ilyan for as much of the trip as possible, allowing Til to use native soil and water to fully recover, but the lack of roads in Ilyan slowed their progress. Before heading north to hook up with the Rin-Ka-Ti-Kee road they used the Arkhanian hide bags, to bring fresh water and Ilyani soil with them.

Ti-Kee hosted a continual flow of caravans, most coming in empty and leaving full. Though not as busy a port as Setabri, Ti-Kee had more dock space; necessary to berth the larger ships designed to accommodate an Arkhanian crew. Ti-Kee was the only Arkhanian city regularly visited by Westerners, all of them ready to get their share of Arkhanian gold.

The travelers would have been lost children amid the flow of sizable Arkhanians, but TA-KA was in his element. They followed in his wake as he strode confidently through the bustling merchants and tough seafarers at the docks. He moved with a surety that wordlessly told others to make room. He found the harbormaster, who recognized him as the Doljon and moved them to the top of the list for bookings, allowing them to leave immediately.

The ship, the Sarnika, was manned by Westerners and heading out on a return trip to Setabri. Gorbik, her captain, was a Varsian who had spent most of his fifty-two years on board a ship.

"I sailed with you to Artara once before, Caidos, though you most likely don't remember me. It was well over twenty year ago, and I was but deckhand, mostly on the night watch. We had rough seas that trip, but you fared well. I be glad to have you on board the Sarnika. Will bring us luck no doubt."

"We could use some luck, Captain. Once we get to Artara, we need you to wait a day for us, before you take us to our next port."

"Where would that be then?"

"We won't know until we get to Artara. Is that a problem?"

"I don't question the ways of Mages, and you being the Head Man and all, it's no never mind to me. You're paying me well, and is an honor to have you aboard, and His Highness, the Doljon as well. Once the rest of your party are on board we can set sail."

They were out of the harbor and into the Umari Sea before they had settled their horses in the hold and stowed away their packs in the cabins below decks.

They had arrived in Ti-Kee about noon on the twelfth day after the appearance of Sefiron's Shadow, and they watched the sun set over Ilyan as they sailed south for Artara. They were the only passengers on board, and the ship carried no cargo, so they sailed high in the water. The winds were strong and the captain estimated that if they stayed that way, they would make landfall in Artara on their third day out.

Caidos was the only one that knew Til well enough to recognize that leaving the land was causing some concern. Enthusiasm for the ship and its sails and the view from on board soon overcame any doubts. Caidos had told Til that the sea water contained salt, which would be as harmful as the waters and soil of Arkhan. When on board, Til wore a cloak to prevent absorption of the salt sprays. Before retiring for the night, the water from one hide bag was used to rinse before soaking in the other.

The companions awoke the next morning to becalmed seas and a heavy fog, which had thrown a velvet curtain over the world, cutting off the light and deadening sound. The mist surrounded the ship, blocking off all sight of land and even the sea around them. Til felt at home in the dampness of the fog, and sat on deck talking to the sailors who had little to do while the fog held.

Screams from the bow of the ship brought everyone up from their cabins. The companions and sailors alike had weapons in hand by the time they reached the deck. Tall, muscular creatures with black, lifeless eyes were boarding the ship on all sides. Their mouths were filled with double rows of sharp dagger-like teeth, and their strong hands were armed with razor-sharp claws that ripped into the flesh of anyone that stepped within reach.

Seven of them stood in formation behind the largest, which scanned the people on deck as if looking for someone specific. Four others were still climbing on board. The companions stood, waiting for Brandorin to direct their defense, but he stood staring, and had not yet drawn his sword.

Lanata positioned herself on the bridge, the raised platform allowing her better aim on the creatures attacking. She shot three arrows; all finding a target, by the time any of the others reacted. Piritho, knowing why Brandorin had not drawn his sword, called out, directing the others to follow him.

The deck was strewn with the bodies of the sailors that had been on deck when the attack started; their spilled blood making the deck slippery. Piritho advanced on the leader, swiping his sword first at its midsection, then its arms and legs after he saw the cuts had no effect on the creature.

He fought a dual-sided battle, staving off two creatures at once. Their razor-sharp claws swept at him, requiring him to duck after each sweep of his sword blade. His foot, slipping on the slick, blood-soaked deck, brought him down to one knee just as one creature's arm swung with enough force to cast him overboard had it connected. He rolled out of reach before coming up. Matu and Sadro were having no more luck than he.

The creatures seemed out of their element on board the ship, their movements slow and unsteady. Their heavy muscular structure made their movements cumbersome and deliberate. They loped forward, shifting their weight from leg to leg as they advanced, sweeping at the companions with their long arms. The quick reflexes of men trained in battle prevented the dagger-tipped fingers from finding a target.

Salis directed his power at the creature in front of him, lifting it from the deck and making it an easy target for TA-KA, who had transformed his hands into large broadswords. The Arkhanian's first powerful swing would not even penetrate the tough gray hide of the creature, so he changed one to an ax and the other to a large sledgehammer. The ax had only minor effect, though TA-KA had struck with enough force to slice the creature in two. He switched to a needle-sharp rapier and stabbed into the area of the heart. The blade didn't go in very far, but it had hit its target. The creature went slack, hanging from nothing, until Salis released it and it crumbled to the deck.

Salis turned toward the next closest creature, but no sooner had he raised it from the deck, than another creature came up from behind him and backhanded him across the side of the head. Salis fell to the deck, unmoving, and the creature he had lifted sank back to the deck.

Caidos and Icara positioned themselves on opposite sides of the ship, casting fireballs at the creatures. The creatures swatted at them, sweeping them away like flies. The sea would have provided an unlimited source of energy to draw upon, but they soon learned the fog not only blocked their view, but shielded them against the boundless energy. They could only draw from the small area within the fog's curtain.

Zephyr darted about, diving at the creatures and shooting small flames at them. When one of her blasts hit a creature in the eye, it howled and raised its arms to protect them.

"The eyes, the eyes," Piritho shouted, "aim your fire at their eyes." Caidos and Icara changed the large fireballs they had been throwing, to arrow-shaped fire bolts, aimed at the creature's eyes. When Icara struck one directly in its eye, it let out a ghastly shriek and fell back. Losing its balance, it toppled over into the sea.

Lanata's arrows were finding targets, but not doing enough damage. On hearing Piritho's shout, she changed her tactics, and began to aim for the eyes. The first two were close, but the arrow hit the skin at an angle and skidded off without causing any ill-effect to the creature. She had only one arrow left. She took her time and waited for the right shot. When one of the creatures turned in profile to her, she let the arrow fly. It shot straight through the eye, killing it immediately.

Caidos was finding it difficult to draw enough energy to power his defenses. If he didn't find a magical solution quickly, he would not be able to do so at all. The fire bolts he and Icara had been trying were not working. He needed to dramatically change his tactics; try something Rhamak would not expect. With the last of the energy he could muster from the air within the fog shield, he enchanted everyone's sword, turning the blades into crystal-blue, razor-sharp scythes of ice.

The creatures had arrived in the dim light caused by the heavy fog, but they were now illuminated by the glowing blue ice of five swords and three daggers. As Piritho and the others swept their shimmering swords, the light of the blades cast trails of sapphire radiance that lingered in the air like birds of blue flame flying across the deck.

M'drani, who carried only a dagger stayed near Til, who had no weapons at all. The largest of the creatures approached them, and M'drani struck at it from one side. Her dagger was stopped completely, the brunt of the impact numbing her entire arm.

It swept out its powerful arms, knocking her down, as it barreled on through to Til. It picked Til up with both hands, its claws cutting deeply into back and sides. When Til raised an arm in defense, the creature caught it in its mouth and bit down hard, severing it above the wrist. It threw Til aside and continued on toward its target. Brandorin stood, frozen with fear, his hand on the hilt of his sword, still in its sheath.

\* \* \*

When Brandorin heard the screams of the dying crew, the rest of the companions rushed up on deck, but he felt the cries within him as the fear he tenuously held in abeyance broke free and seeped into every muscle. He fought its paralyzing grip and managed to reach the deck, but as soon as he saw the creatures, the fear enveloped him.

He was almost knocked over by the force of it as it swept over him in cold waves. He gasped for breath as if he were drowning in it. He watched, frozen, as Piritho took charge and began the attack, but he couldn't get his shaking legs to move. He saw the others charge forward, each engaging one or more of the creatures, and he felt alone and abandoned. They would fight for themselves; they had forgotten about him.

He knew he was the Protector; he should be fighting in defense of the others, but he saw only the gaping mouths of the merciless creatures bearing down on him. Saw the rows and rows of jagged teeth, could almost feel them biting into his flesh. He was on his own, and he knew he would not be able to raise his sword in defense. For the first time in his life, he felt certain he would die.

As the lead creature bore down on him, he wanted to flee, to lock himself in his cabin, but his legs would not respond. He was frozen, as fragile as an icicle; if he tried to move, he would shatter.

His heart pounded in his chest, his pulse throbbing in his fingertips as he gripped the hilt of his sword, touching the Umari stone. It wasn't powerful enough to dim the level of fear that pulsed through him now. An iron fist gripped his insides and twisted them until he thought he would be sick.

Then the creature struck out at M'drani, and picked up Til, cutting deep gashes in his back. After seeing what the creature had done to his friends, the heat of anger began to melt the ice that had formed in his veins. Brandorin withdrew his sword and swept it ineffectually at the creature, afraid to look at it.

The creature grabbed Brandorin just below his shoulders, pinning his arms to his sides. He dropped his sword as the creature squeezed him in a vise-like grip. It raised him above its head and let out a cry of triumph; a shrill, grating squeal that reverberated through Brandorin's head, so close to the creature's gaping mouth.

The other creatures, on hearing the victory call of their leader, paused in their attacks on the other companions, and turned to join the leader. They knocked aside anyone within the sweeping arc of their arms. They advanced on Brandorin, still held in the grasp of the leader, blood flowing down his arms and sides from the cuts made by the creature's claws.

The creature opened its mouth wide, and Brandorin could smell its foul breath, could see row after row of sharp teeth lining every inch of the wide maw. The image before him embodied the feeling of fear he had borne since healing Sadro. He could no longer see his companions or the ship. His sight, his hearing, all feeling was overwhelmed by the black void enveloping him, as the razor-edged teeth closed on his neck.

Then light again, and a horrible shriek filled his head. The sound of his own death.

* * *

Brandorin had fallen to the deck, suddenly released. Sadro had taken his ice-blue crystal sword and thrust it deep into the creature's side, aiming upward towards its heart. As the other creatures hesitated at the fall of their leader, Matu and Piritho stepped in, thrusting their ice-cold swords as Sadro had done. It took an incredible amount of force to break through the tough hide, but together they managed to kill another.

TA-KA had taken care of another two creatures, leaving four still intent on reaching Brandorin, who cowered on the deck behind Sadro, who stood over him, protecting him from their attacks.

Icara had managed to blind one with a couple of fire bolts, but could not draw enough energy to form another. The creature groped blindly across the deck. TA-KA charged it, smashing its legs out from under it. Once it was on the deck, Piritho jammed his sword down through its heart. TA-KA continued forward, felling the next creature from behind, and Piritho dispatched it in the same manner.

The first of the two remaining creatures stepped toward Brandorin, but Sadro stood his ground. He thrust his sword directly at the creature, but it swept out its arm, deflecting the blade. Sadro was thrown off balance by the blow. The creature's other arm swept out, slashing him across the stomach, but before it could strike again Matu and Piritho struck from either side. The creature froze, swords impaling it in the neck and side, before it fell to the deck.

Salis, recovering from the blow he sustained, saw the last creature moving in his direction. He used his power to lift it from the deck and hold it where it could not reach anyone. Its legs continued to move, as if it was walking. TA-KA approached the creature from behind, both arms now ending in massive hammers, and swung his arms together, catching its head between them.

The companions stood, searching the surface of the deck, waiting to see if any other creatures would attack. The thick fog that wrapped them in a shroud deadened the only sound, the moaning of the injured.

Matu ran to Sadro, while Piritho checked to see the extent of Brandorin's injuries. Brandorin backed away from him, but he was able to determine that the wounds on his arms and sides were not severe. Despite his feeble protests, Piritho was able to bandage the cuts with the shredded sleeves from his shirt. After finishing the makeshift dressing, he moved on to Sadro.

"Help me, over here, it's Til." M'drani's voice penetrated the stillness. Caidos and Lanata were the first to her side. Til sat, staring forward, a thick, dark green liquid seeping from the cuts on sides and back. M'drani gently held Til's left arm. The cloth of her tunic wrapped around the end, did not hide the fact that the arm stopped much sooner than it should have.

"We must do something. Could Brandorin help him?" The others, having seen Brandorin frozen with fear, looked on silently.

"No, his healing powers won't work on Til," Caidos told her, "but there is no need."

"No need? It's serious, but not beyond help."

"M'drani, you misunderstand. There is no need because the Ilyani heal differently than we do. Look." He pointed to the wounds on Til's side, which had stopped oozing liquid and were sealing themselves even as they watched. "Til is in a trance, concentrating on self-healing."

"What about his hand?"

"That too will grow back. That's the easiest way to say it. If you take the cloth off, you'll see the healing process has already begun."

M'drani carefully removed the cloth. The raw edges that had been there when she wrapped it had evened out, and a small stub of growth had formed at the end.

"The missing part of the arm will be formed by the end of the day. By tomorrow morning, the hand should be back. Til will be good as new before we reach Artara. Now, what about the rest of you? Is anyone hurt?"

"I think I'm going to have a black eye," Salis said, holding a cloth to his bleeding face.

"Let me see it, Salis," Icara told him. He removed the cloth, and she cringed when she saw the abrasion and swelling on his face. "We should go clean that out."

"Anyone else?"

"One of them back-handed me to the deck," M'drani said. "My shoulder hurts, but there's no cut."

"Caidos, over here," Piritho shouted. "You'll want to hear this."

Caidos hurried to where Piritho stood. Matu sat on the deck in front of him, holding his shirt against the wounds on Sadro's stomach. The shirt was already soaked with blood and the Larian's skin was deathly pale.

Caidos was trying to decide if there was a chance Brandorin could heal these wounds, when he was struck by what Sadro was saying.

"It was me, Caidos." The words were barely a whisper, but he was still trying to speak. Caidos bent down to put his ear to Sadro's lips, and with his dying breath, Sadro spoke his final five words.

Caidos stood unsteadily, his face a mask of incredulity. He stared at the dead man, trying to make sense of what he had heard.

"What did he say, Caidos?" Piritho asked. He asked twice more before Caidos finally heard him.

"He said, 'I was the third boar.'"

\* \* \*

Caidos was astounded.

"That simple statement answers so many questions, yet

creates so many more. It explains how the fear spell was triggered. I said I could understand it if Brandorin had healed one of the boars. How stupid of me! He did."

"What fear spell?" Salis asked.

Caidos had not noticed the other companions join them. Had not even realized he had stood there, thinking, for minutes after Sadro's death. Salis' question had brought him back, and he looked at all of them now as they stared back at him. All that is except for Til, who was sitting on the deck. And except for Brandorin.

"Brandorin, where's Brandorin?" Caidos cried.

"He was there when the last creature was killed," Piritho said. "I checked and dressed his wounds. He was too afraid to go anywhere. His sword is still here."

The companions spread out, searching the deck for Brandorin. He'd been attacked at the top of the hatchway and Caidos, picking up the sword, descended the ladder to look for him below decks. He found him, sitting on the floor in his cabin in the dark. Caidos walked in, closing the door behind him.

"Are you all right? Everyone is looking for you up on deck." When he didn't answer, Caidos put the sword aside, worried Brandorin might feel threatened. He started to light a lantern.

"Don't light that, please." Pain and sorrow permeated his voice so strongly Caidos barely recognized it as Brandorin's.

"Let me go tell the others I found you; then I'll be back." Caidos left the cabin, and returning to the ladder, he climbed back up enough to call to Piritho, who was standing nearby. "I found him, he's all right." When Piritho moved to follow Caidos back to the cabin, "No wait up here. Tell everyone else. He'll be fine."

"What should I tell them, Caidos? They're asking about his behavior. How he froze. Your comments about the fear spell."

"You and M'drani can explain it to them. I should have done that myself when it happened."

Caidos returned to the cabin. In the dim light he was not sure Brandorin was still there, but then he heard his ragged breathing. He walked over and sat in front of him, waiting for him to speak. Minutes passed before Brandorin's voice, hesitant and quiet, broke the silence. "Was anyone hurt?"

"Til suffered some serious wounds, but Ilyani are self-healing; Til will be back to normal by the end of the day tomorrow. Sadro was severely wounded. I'm sorry to say, he's dead."

A sharp exhalation of breath carried a single word rich with torment, "No!" Then silence.

"It wasn't your fault, Brandorin."

"Not my fault? I just stood there. With those creatures attacking everyone on board. Everyone was fighting them, even Zephyr and I couldn't move. Sadro saved my life and I did nothing. At least when Ilona died I *tried* to do something." His voice broke with emotion and they sat in silence in the dark.

Caidos finally spoke, "It was Rhamak's spell and you know it. The fear was Rhamak's doing. This self-pity is your own."

"What?"

"Sitting down here, in the dark, wrapping yourself in a cloak of shame and self-pity. It's very unbecoming."

"I saw how they looked at me when the attack started. I don't want to see that look again."

"Brandorin, those people are your friends. Don't you think they'll understand? Yes, they were surprised to see you freeze when action was needed. They've learned to trust your leadership. Learned to trust you. They knew nothing about the consequences you've suffered for healing Sadro. I didn't tell them about the fear. That's my mistake; I should have. Instead I told them you were just tired, exhausted from the ordeal of healing. Maybe I thought not voicing the problem would make it go away. It didn't. But M'drani and Piritho are telling them now."

"No. I don't want everyone to know."

"Do you think they won't support you in this?"

"I don't know. I don't know anything anymore. Everything I thought I knew about myself has just been shattered."

"Is that all you think of yourself? That you're a warrior?"

"That's what I was raised to be. A warrior, a leader. The Protector. But I didn't protect anyone up there. Til was hurt, Sadro died."

"You don't know yourself very well then, Brandorin. After knowing you for only a day, M'drani knew you better than you seem to know yourself. In fact, I would say that every one of your traveling companions knows you better than you seem to."

"M'drani? What did she say?"

"That you were brave ..."

"She got that wrong."

"That you were brave," Caidos repeated, with emphasis, "intelligent (that may be what she got wrong), forgiving, perhaps a little angry, and compassionate. She thought you would make a good healer, but then she said something that seems very appropriate now."

"What?" Brandorin asked, when Caidos did not continue.

"She said you must first learn to heal yourself." Caidos stood and walked to the door. "I'm going on deck now. You come up when you're ready to let your friends help you."

Caidos left and returned to the deck, where the other companions were waiting. M'drani and Piritho had told them what had happened to Brandorin as a result of healing Sadro. Caidos was not sure his talk with Brandorin had been the right way to handle the situation, but he could tell from the look of concern on their faces that he had been right to tell Brandorin his friends would understand and support him.

An hour passed and still Brandorin remained in the cabin. None of the companions had moved from their places.

"Maybe we should check on him?" Icara said.

"No, he'll be ..." Caidos stopped, noticing Brandorin standing by the hatchway, his hand on the pommel of his sword. Then the others turned and saw him too. M'drani stood, and walking over to Brandorin, took him by the hand and brought him to sit with his friends.

\*   \*   \*

The fog dissipated soon after the attack and the favorable

winds returned. Three crewmen had been killed in the attack, and a few others injured. The companions huddled together on the foredeck, trying to make sense of Sadro's revelation.

"From the way Sadro was talking when I first reached him," Matu said, trying to sooth M'drani's worries about not sensing the deception, "I think he was unaware of it himself up to that moment."

"We never saw Sadro's wounds. We assumed he had been gored by the boars, but they must have been our sword cuts," Piritho said.

"I placed a cloth on that wound," M'drani remembered. "It didn't look like a sword wound."

"Why did Sadro change back and the other boars didn't?" Salis asked. "And why was he dressed when the others were naked when they reverted back to men?"

"That's right!" Piritho said. "It was a few hours after their deaths before they were men again. I didn't change back even after the lust to kill had abated. Then when the Larians changed me back, they had to give me a robe to wear."

"All part of Rhamak's plan," Caidos said. "Whoever drove the wagon could have changed him back, even directed one of the other boars to gore him. If Rhamak can transform a man, he could have also transformed the clothes along with him. He probably purposely selected a Larian while the others were Varsians. So we would assume exactly what we did. That all three boars had been Varsians; that it was natural for a Larian to be in the area."

"Sadro was surprised when I said we'd be missing the Harvest celebration," Matu told them. "He thought it was a month away yet."

"Being a lapithi tends to make you lose track of time," Piritho said, "believe me."

"Why did Sadro save my life?" Brandorin asked quietly.

"I was wondering the same thing," Salis said. "Don't get me wrong, I'm glad he did. But didn't that kind of go against Rhamak's plan? Rhamak goes to all that trouble to transform men into boars, plants a fear spell for Brandorin to trigger. Then he's sure to die when he can't fight back during today's attack. It was actually pretty clever. Sorry, Brandorin."

"Once he reverted back to a man, Sadro was bound by his beliefs," Caidos said. "One of which was the Debt of Life. Rhamak didn't plan for that."

"His choice of a Larian for his plans backfired," Matu said, his voice carrying pride for his fellow countryman.

"That fog seemed rather convenient for the attack, Caidos," Piritho said. "Is your magic that powerful? To calm the sea, and change the weather?"

The mage nodded, "It can be. It's very difficult, and requires an expert, but it can be done. Our code forbids such interference. The ramifications of such tampering can have far-reaching consequences. But that fog was definitely magically produced. It not only covered the arrival of those creatures; it was also shielding Icara and me from using the energy of the sea.

"I asked the Captain, and he said the watch had seen another ship behind us. It sailed just this side of the horizon, at least until it grew dark. Rhamak was probably on that ship, following us. He has the power it would take to still the sea and create the fog. If those creatures were on board, then all they had to do was swim across and board the ship."

"Did anyone notice the way they attacked?" Caidos asked.

"They didn't seem to be interested in anyone except Brandorin," Piritho said. "They had ample opportunity to attack any of us, but they didn't fight us except in defense. They looked for Brandorin, and once finding him, headed straight for him."

"Sadro, Salis, and M'drani, even Til stood between the creatures and Brandorin. They saw you as obstacles in their path."

"So if Sadro hadn't tried to protect me, he wouldn't have died."

"Maybe not. But you would have," Caidos said. "It was his choice Brandorin, a Debt he felt obliged to honor."

"How would they know what Brandorin looked like?" M'drani asked.

"It may be the one who reached Brandorin first was the only

one that knew him by sight. Once he's reverted to human form I want you to look at him, Brandorin; see if you know him."

Brandorin shuddered slightly, as though the thought of looking at one of his attackers caused him fear. Only Caidos noticed the gesture.

\* \* \*

The sun was well past its zenith, and the companions still sat together on deck, recovering from the attack through their fellowship. They had talked about many things before the topic that Caidos had avoided finally came up.

"Caidos, Sefiron talked about the Lost Ones, who you said were the Korduna," Lanata said. "What were they like? They must have been a strong people to survive in The Void."

"Survive is the key word," Caidos told her, "Ironically, the title for the Kordunan fragment holder was the Survivor. Yet they did not. The power of their fragment helped them to survive in such a harsh land. They had no cities, but traveled in large groups, which they called Chatas. Each Chata had a region they would roam through, staying in one place for a season or two, then they would move on. There were ten Chatas, and periodically two or more would cross paths where the regions joined. They always saw this as reason for celebration. Those celebrations would last for a week or more. When you live in such harsh conditions all the time, you take advantage of any occasion that allows you to celebrate."

"How did the Sefiron's power help them?"

"It gave them the ability to put up with harsh conditions. They could survive on short rations, even allowing them to go days without either food or water. They were supposed to be able to smell water, even if it was deep in the ground. When the Chata selected a place to camp, they would plant seeds, and much like Til can do, they could nurture the seeds, so they grew in a short period of time. They lived in tents, and used camels to travel and carry the few possessions they cherished."

"What did they look like?"

"They died out before I was born, but there were drawings. They looked like most Westerners. They had narrow eyes, to protect them from the harsh sun. Their skin was tanned, seemed cracked and tough. I remember thinking they must have been very durable, and I wondered how they could have died out."

"What if we can't find their fragment?"

He thought for a while, trying to decide what to tell them, not wanting to discourage them.

"There's no reason to hold anything back, Caidos," Brandorin said. "I can attest to that. No secrets among friends."

"You're right. I won't make that mistake again. I doubt we'll find the Kordunan crystal, but that doesn't mean we won't succeed. When the Shadow appeared to direct the mages to stop Gharvik, they didn't have the Febronese fragment, yet their rejoining worked. The Spirit said we should not forget the Lost Ones. I believe that means their crystal is not lost."

"Isn't that a contradiction, Caidos?" Salis asked.

"No. And it's not one of my proverbs. The phrase 'the Lost Ones' refers to the Korduna. They died out because they no longer had the power of the crystal to aid them. They didn't have the crystal, but I am convinced the Kordunan crystal is not lost. Rhamak has it."

"Then we're going to have to overpower Rhamak to get it." Brandorin said, with more bravado then he felt.

"Rhamak will go where we must. To the Labyrinth."

"He won't be alone."

"No. I expect him to have an army of some sort, to try to overpower us, to take the crown piece. The Kordunan fragment gives him no special power. Having it merely prevented us from being able to rejoin the crystal without him. It forces us to go where he'll be waiting for us. To be forewarned is to be forearmed, but don't let that make us overconfident. Rhamak allowed an entire race of people to die so he could have their fragment. He'll do anything necessary to try to stop us."

"I think I liked it better when you kept secrets from us," Salis said.

Caidos could see his words had not only discouraged the companions; they had made them afraid, afraid of Rhamak and what he would do. Afraid that after everything they had done, after everything they had survived, that they might still fail.

"Wait a minute Caidos," Salis said, a thought suddenly coming to him. "Why is it such a terrible thing for Rhamak to take the crown piece? We have to hold our own fragments, I understand that. Reforming the crystal is necessary to calm the weather and the upheaval across the lands; even Rhamak wouldn't want to stop that. What does Rhamak gain by being the one that places the crown piece?"

"We can't rejoin Sefiron without it. To control the crown piece, is to control the power of the crystal. The Mirador is sworn to return that power to the fragment holders and to the people. But Rhamak would keep the power for himself. He would do anything; use anybody, to get the crown piece and the power it represents."

## Chapter 28

"Then I guess we better get ourselves an army too," Brandorin said. Everyone looked at him, wondering if the attack and his fear had made him irrational. "We have four weeks, give or take a day. We need to send out messages and get the armies moving."

"Just like that?" Salis said. "And where are they going to move to?"

"We won't know that until we read the scroll in Artara, but we have two days before we get there. We can use those days to plan, write some messages, and when we find out where we're going, we send those messages."

"How?"

"Zephyr could take them," Icara suggested, "she's smart enough to understand our instructions, and she can fly faster than a ship can sail, in a more direct route, and over land."

"Good for you." Brandorin gave her a pat on the back.

They discussed their plan, what the messages would be, and the best route for Zephyr to take in delivering them. Caidos could see that drawing on his training as a soldier was helping Brandorin to forget his fear, as well as the embarrassment over his inaction during the attack. He would not be caught so ill prepared again.

"The Ilyani have no army, no weapons, but Til may be able to provide some unexpected surprises for the enemy." Caidos looked at Til, who was still in a healing trance.

"What can he do?" Salis asked.

"Accelerate the growth of plants."

"I'm afraid I don't see the benefits of horticulture in battle."

"The advancing army may suddenly find a wall of hedges in front of them. And if those hedges have long thorns, they may find it a bit difficult to get through or climb over."

"That would be sneaky. I like that."

\* \* \*

The second morning on board, the Sarnika sailed through a channel between the mainland and the Eastern Islands scattered across the eastern horizon. Brandorin found M'drani standing at the port rail looking out at the islands. Looking for something to say, Brandorin said, "Til's awake. The hand has completely grown back."

"I saw. Til said it didn't hurt, at least not the way it would have for us."

They stood without talking for a time, Brandorin taking comfort in the nearness of her. "I wanted to apologize ... for yesterday."

"For what exactly?"

"For letting that creature get to you."

"For not protecting me?"

"Well, yes."

"Brandorin, there are eleven people on this trip, not counting the crew. We all look out for the rest."

"It's just that I promised your mother ..."

"Promised my mother what? Did she ask you to look out for me?"

"Yes, when we said good-bye."

"I should have expected that. I know she's worried. When we send the messages with Zephyr, I'll add an extra note for her."

"I wanted to talk to you about something else, too. Something Caidos told me you said. About me. About learning to heal myself."

"He told you that?"

"I guess he thought it would help, after ... what happened yesterday."

"If you can't even say the words, Brandorin, how do you think you're going to heal?"

"Is that all it takes?"

"It's a start."

He had talked to Caidos, but wasn't sure he would be able to tell M'drani. Caidos was more like the old family confessor, someone you could talk to because you knew he wouldn't tell your secrets, knew he would understand, no matter how terrible those secrets were. He would have told Ilona, but he had known Ilona....

He stopped; he had been thinking that he had known Ilona for so much longer than he had known M'drani, but that wasn't really true. Yes, he had met Ilona when he was nineteen, but then he hadn't seen her again until two months before the wedding. He had been on the road with M'drani for longer than that now. In many ways, their mutual fight against the fear had brought them closer than he had been with Ilona.

He was suddenly aware of M'drani's stare. He didn't want to tell her what he had been thinking about, so he just started talking.

"It's hard to admit to being scared when you were raised by the bravest man in Varsa. There's nothing my father would be afraid of." His words were a surprise; he hadn't realized he had felt that way.

"Did *he* tell you that?"

"No, he wouldn't boast."

"He never had to face the kinds of creatures you have, Bran. The raptors, those boars, and those things yesterday ..." She stopped suddenly aware of the way he was staring at her, surprise and a quirky little smile giving him an almost comical look. "What is it?"

"You called me 'Bran'."

"Oh, I'm sorry. An old habit, I guess. Everyone in my family does it. My mother calls me 'dran." She trilled the 'r' and stretched out the 'ah' sound. "All those syllables sound so formal."

"Don't apologize. It just threw me for a second. Piritho used to call me that when we were young."

"Did you call him 'Pir'?"

"Not too often," Brandorin said, laughing. "He hated that. It was usually Thiro. But I don't mind Bran."

"All right, but back to yesterday ... I'm not going to let you distract me so easily. Were you afraid when you faced the raptors?"

"No."

"The boars?"

"No."

"Did you even think of your own safety when you started to heal Sadro?"

"No, there wasn't time."

"And yesterday?"

"No, I wasn't afraid," he said sarcastically at first, but he stopped, took a deep breath, and resumed in a serious whisper, "I was terrified. I couldn't move I was so scared. I only moved when I saw that thing attack you, and then Til."

"You broke through the fear because of that?" she turned to him, placing her hand on his arm.

"Yes, but not enough to make a difference."

"But, Bran, don't you see what that means?"

"No. What?"

"That it's possible to fight it. The fear you felt was magically induced. Instilled in you by a spell, an incantation. It isn't real, so it's impossible to overcome. But you did. Maybe only a little, but you did it."

"That doesn't mean ..."

She interrupted him, "We must tell Caidos. He'll understand what I mean." She took his arm and pulled him from the rail. "You aren't as excited because the fear is still there; it's making you feel you can't win. But you can, you've proven that." They found Caidos, just climbing up from below decks.

"Ah, there you are, Brandorin." Caidos said. "The lapithi have completely reverted back to their human form. I want to find out if the leader was someone you knew."

"Wait, Caidos," M'drani said, "we have to tell you. Brandorin was able to control the fear for a time yesterday. During the attack, when the leader was bearing down on him, at the worst possible moment."

"You did? You didn't tell me that. That's amazing! Why didn't you say so?"

"I didn't think it was anything. I was still so scared."

"But you broke through and were able to take action,"

M'drani said. "At a time when the fear should have had its strongest hold on you."

"Do you know how you did it?" Caidos asked. "What were you thinking about?"

"About M'drani," he said quietly.

"Oh, that's it, is it?"

"I had just been attacked, along with Til," M'drani clarified. "He reacted to his friends being harmed."

"That's the key then. We'll have to work on that. Now let's have a look at the leader."

Brandorin shook his head, saying to himself, "I don't know why you're making such a fuss over a slightly lesser degree of fear."

They went to the hold where the bodies of the creatures had been taken after the attack. Gorbik had protested, saying they should be thrown overboard, but despite the fact a captain's word was law upon his ship, he had acceded to Caidos' wishes.

Pulling back the canvas that covered the body of the leader, Caidos asked, "Have you ever seen this man before? Take your time."

Brandorin took the lantern in order to focus the light clearly. He felt the fear rise in him again, not knowing if it was a false fear, or if he was afraid of seeing the face of another friend that had been tortured by Rhamak and sent to kill him. He fought to keep the lamp steady; to prevent his hand from shaking with the fear that rippled through him.

"Do you recognize him?" He heard Caidos' voice coming to him from the dark, and he realized he was standing over the man with his eyes tightly closed. He opened his eyes, and looked into the face of the dead man.

"No, I don't think so. No, he's not at all familiar." Relief swept over him, and he took a small bit of solace in knowing the fear that had gripped him as he stood over the dead man was not magically induced, just normal human fear.

"Rhamak must have had a drawing of you. Just look at the others to be sure, then we can give them a burial at sea. I think we'll cover them in their shrouds down here, so we don't have to try to explain to the captain where eleven dead men came from."

\* \* \*

The gull had watched the Maken attack the crew and passengers of the Sarnika from the top of the main mast. It had flown for a day and a half, under strict instructions from Rhamak to return as soon as possible. Rhamak had rushed to the solar to view its report, transforming the bird back to his human form as he sprinted into the room.

"Show me," Rhamak demanded.

Chaubrel waited just inside the solar. Rhamak watched in silence for a long time. His first word, shouted with uncharacteristic excitement, startled Chaubrel.

"Yes! Oh, marvelous! He can't move. He's terrified. The Maken have seen him. Yes, get them out of your way. It has him." Rhamak was ecstatic. He held his hands up over his head, as if he was lifting something. He practically squeaked with delight. Then he stopped and he did something Chaubrel could not recall him ever doing before. He shouted, his voice hoarse with rage. "What are you doing? You fool!"

It stopped, almost as soon as it had begun. The echo slowly faded, as Rhamak continued in silence. His hands were fisted at his sides, and his teeth clenched, the jaw muscles rippling with constrained anger. For the first time in many years, Chaubrel feared for his own life, but he dared not leave without Rhamak's permission.

"Chaubrel. Get out. Now." Rhamak's voice was quiet but the strain was evident. "Now." Chaubrel froze for only a second; then he ran.

## Chapter 29

Chaubrel had left the solar, going as far as he could get and still keep an eye on the doorway. Within seconds, the screams began. Each scream carried both the shriek of a bird and the sound of human agony. A flickering light from the solar doorway told Chaubrel the room was on fire. But Rhamak had not come out. The light built to an eye-squinting blaze, then was snuffed out.

Rhamak walked out, a blank look on his face, and he turned away from Chaubrel, heading for his private chambers. A black odious smoke followed him out of the room.

Chaubrel had knocked on Rhamak's door an hour later. Rhamak called through the door. "I will find you when I need you."

It was now almost thirty-six hours later and Rhamak had yet to come out. Chaubrel had never known Rhamak to be alone for so long. At first, the solitude was a unique pleasure, but now it made him edgy. He waited on a chair across from Rhamak's door. He was not worried about Rhamak's welfare; he just didn't know how to react to this uncharacteristic behavior.

The door swung inward, but there was no sign of Rhamak. His voice came from within the chamber, "Come in, Chaubrel." There was no hint of anger in that cool disembodied voice, but Chaubrel tried to swallow and found he could not. His knees shook as he stood and walked in.

"I'm sure you have deduced that the Maken attack was not successful." Rhamak sat in the shadows at the far corner of the large chamber.

"Yes, sire." Chaubrel was surprised his voice sounded so normal and so calm.

"Sit down."

Chaubrel moved to the chair that Rhamak indicated, his knees holding out just long enough for him to sit. Rhamak had never asked him to sit before.

"Why do these things keep happening? Brandorin should have been dead. Another second and he would have been. Why would he have saved him?" Rhamak was no longer angry, Chaubrel could tell that, but for the second time in thirty six hours he heard something new, something he had not heard in all the many years he had served at Kalarak. Rhamak sounded truly puzzled.

"I don't know, sire?" Chaubrel's caution-ridden words reflected his unease. "It's difficult to plan for every contingency."

"No, Chaubrel. Don't tell me what you think I want to hear. I really want to know what you think."

Chaubrel didn't know how to answer. Rhamak didn't want to know what he really thought; he was not prepared for that answer any more than Chaubrel was ready to give it.

"I don't know what happened, sire."

Rhamak showed uncharacteristic patience in describing the attack to Chaubrel. After a few questions, which Chaubrel asked more for a delay than for clarification, Rhamak wanted an answer.

"Did you instruct him to kill Brandorin, sire?"

"The Maken? Of course, they were told to kill him."

"Sadro. Did you tell him."

"No, Sadro was given no such orders."

"Then this is different than with Piritho." Chaubrel was moving cautiously; hoping Rhamak would draw his own conclusions.

"I don't understand that one either. I gave him express orders to kill Brandorin, and he refused. But I see your point. I didn't tell Sadro to kill him, and I never told him *not* to save him."

Chaubrel mentally sighed with relief.

"Sadro was killed. He wasn't in any real danger; yet he went out of his way to save Brandorin. He gave his life for someone he barely knew. Why would he do that?"

"Perhaps, because Brandorin saved his."

"You think so? Would you do that, Chaubrel? Give your life for someone you hardly knew?"

"It's hard to say, sire."

"How could I have anticipated *that*? I am disappointed, Chaubrel, I'll admit that to you. Brandorin has been lucky so far, but this gives me the chance to dispatch him myself."

"Are you hungry, sire?"

"Yes, I'm famished." Rhamak strode out of the room, but Chaubrel could not stand. His legs were weak with relief. He could hear Rhamak talking as he moved down the corridor, but he was temporarily distracted by a leather journal on Rhamak's bedside table. He heard Rhamak's receding steps, but he still shocked himself by walking not out the door to follow after, but toward the journal. Knowing he only had seconds, he flipped open the cover. He cursed under his breath; not only because of what he saw, but because he knew he wanted to read more.

\* \* \*

The ship was now within sight of their destination, and the companions prepared to disembark. Caidos felt a sense of exhilaration, of coming home after a long absence, and though only Icara had ever been to Artara before, the others seemed to feel it, too. They were ready long before the ship pulled into the natural harbor on the north side of the island.

The deep cobalt waters of the Umari Sea changed abruptly to clear turquoise as the ship sailed into the shallower waters of a cove that ended at the white, soft sands of the island of Artara. The narrow beaches encircled the dark, lush hills, which were topped by a large white building. To the mages that lived there, the building, not the island was Artara, and they considered it home.

There was no one at the docks to meet them; the normal supply ship would have been there only a week before, and was not expected again for at least three weeks.

"They are all little moles," Icara said. "They'll be burrowing their way through a scroll, or still debating over what to do about the scroll I brought to you."

A rickety old mage met them at the door, a look of surprise flitted across his face. He waved his hands around, while he stammered, "Mirador, you've returned."

Salis leaned toward Icara and whispered, "He looks like he just found an extra nut in his cookie."

"That's about as excited as he gets."

"Caidos, we have found a new scroll. I will go get it for you." Before Caidos could stop him, he had scurried off.

"I told you," Icara said. "They haven't even noticed I took it."

Once within its walls, the companions recognized the comfortable feeling of a place that housed the members of a close-knit community of scholars and teachers. The corridors were lined, not with tapestries or paintings, but with shelves and tables filled with scrolls and books and artifacts from every country in Zadania. The rooms were decorated with large tables for research, and comfortable chairs where groups of students could sit and talk. Caidos led the companions to the antechamber to his own rooms, rooms assigned to the Mirador.

"The apprentices will show you to your rooms, but come back here once you've settled in. There'll be a meal set out for you. Go ahead and eat when you return. I want to go to my study to review the scrolls. Icara, after you've eaten, please join me there."

Icara beamed with pride at being invited to review the scrolls with Caidos. "I'm not hungry, Caidos. I can go with you now."

"I appreciate that, but give me an hour at least, then join me."

An hour and one minute later, Icara knocked gently on the study door.

"Come in." Caidos said, then on seeing it was his apprentice, he asked, "Would you find Brandorin and bring him back with you? Ask him to bring his sword." Icara looked worriedly at Caidos. "Don't fret, there's no problem."

When Brandorin returned with Icara, Caidos motioned them to come in and asked Icara to close the door.

"There's much here we should review, and I've not yet found the passage which tells me where we must go, but I *have* found this." He passed a small scroll to Brandorin. "I found that wrapped within a larger one. It's sealed and it's clear the seal has not been broken."

On the face of the scroll were three words,

*For The Protector*

Brandorin took it and looked it over. "I don't see a seal."

"It's not a physical seal, but a magical one. I've read the scroll in which I found it from start to finish a hundred times and I never saw that before. Like the scroll Icara brought us, the seal must have prevented it from being found, until now. Until it was needed, or perhaps until the Protector's crystal was nearby."

"What do I do?"

"Open it and read it."

"But what about the seal."

"You're the Protector; it will open for you. I asked you to bring your sword because the presence of the Protector's fragment may be needed to release the seal; you may even need to touch the scroll to the crystal. What you find inside is for you only. You may share or withhold what you find inside, as you see fit."

He directed Brandorin to a chair on the far side of the room, a lamp already burning and waiting for him. "You can read it over there. Icara and I will be reviewing the rest."

For the next hour, the only sounds in Caidos' study were the shuffling of parchment, like leaves against wood, and the occasional frustrated expulsion of breath or the soft ah's of small discoveries. Chair legs scraping on the stone floor made Caidos and Icara look up; Brandorin walked toward them, his scroll in hand.

"I know where we have to go now," Brandorin told them.

"It was in there. Then I'm not getting addled," Caidos said, heaving a sigh of relief. "I didn't understand how I could have read these scrolls so often and not known where Sefiron must be rejoined." He looked anxiously at Brandorin.

"The heart of the Central Desert."

"Of course, where Sefiron was created. We can get there in time; it will be easier for each of the armies to meet us as well. We'll take the ship to the dock in Laria, and travel north to the southern end of the Desert." He stood, and started to look around, still talking to them. "It will be easier there. Here, I have a map."

Caidos walked to a table on the far side of the room and began riffling through some large parchments on a table by the wall, he returned with one. "See, here at the southern end, between the Chiron Ridge and the Jarbon Cliffs. There's a gradual decline to the floor of the desert. From there to the center is no more than - oh, about twenty-five miles. We can direct the armies to meet us there, and we can advance together to the Labyrinth."

Brandorin's silence made Caidos pause.

"What is it? What else was in that scroll?"

"There'll be traps, challenges in the Labyrinth. One for each of the fragment holders to solve."

"Yes, it covers that in another of the scrolls as well."

"With each problem there'll be a Key. Once the problem has been solved, the Key will be revealed. The one who resolved that problem must take the Key. It will open or reveal the next passage."

"We can do that. That's not what's worrying you though."

"It stated very clearly - wait - let me read it to you." He opened the scroll, scanning for the passage he wanted. "Here, *'For the powers of the Watcher shall have their limits within the Labyrinth, for each of the fragment holders must address the challenge alone, drawing upon such powers as Sefiron provideth him.'*"

"I understand that too," Caidos said, still not understanding Brandorin's concern. "The problems will be set so it requires the special powers of that fragment holder to resolve it. My powers wouldn't help."

"There's more. *'Only when the challenge has been solved will the Key be revealed, and will the passage beyond be opened.'* How will we get past the problem that's set for the Survivor? We won't be able to solve it, and even if we *can*, we won't know where to go next."

"That's covered in one of the other scrolls." He scanned through the scrolls; frustration growing, he tossed parchments aside, as one after another failed to reveal the passage he wanted.

"Yes, that's the one," he said when Icara handed it to him. *"'The way to Sefiron will be twisted and confusing, but those who hold the fragments must solve the challenges they will face on its path. The fragments will awaken the challenge by their presence.'* I think that means when we approach the challenge set for the Healer, for example, the presence of the Umari fragment will spring the trap, so to speak. If we don't have the Kordunan fragment, then that challenge won't be triggered and it won't have to be solved. If we obtain the original, or if the substitute fragment works, you'll be able to control it."

"That may be, but I hold two fragments, so I'll have to solve two of the problems. If we get the Survivor's fragment that will mean three challenges."

"Undoubtedly."

"It's the job of the Protector to lead the fragment holders through the Labyrinth, to determine which problem is meant for which holder."

Caidos began to understand the reason for Brandorin's concern, noticed his quickened breathing and nervous twitching of his fingers.

"What if I can't do it? If I'm too afraid to move, to face the problems I have to solve?"

"You'll do it, Brandorin. I know you will," Caidos told him, though inwardly he was concerned. Too much depended on Brandorin; and Rhamak's incantation was standing in the way.

"Let's call the others together," Caidos said. "We can tell them what we've learned. They can complete their messages, and Zephyr can be on her way."

Fifteen minutes later the companions were assembled together in the antechamber. Caidos filled them in on what they had learned from the Protector's scroll.

"The Central Desert. There's something about the Central Desert, something I can't quite remember." It was Piritho that had spoken. He looked distracted, trying to remember.

"Something about Rhamak?" Caidos asked.

"Yes, Rhamak. That's it. That's where his fortress is. Along the Chiron Ridge, at the western edge of the Central Desert. That's where they took me when they captured me outside Kartir."

"Does he have an army?" Brandorin asked.

"I don't know about an army, but I'd say there are at least a thousand men in that fortress. And he had a foundry; I could smell it. They've probably been making weapons for some time. That was over four months ago."

"Try to remember what you can, Thiro," Brandorin told him, "we'll go over it later. It may help us prepare the armies."

Caidos didn't think Brandorin realized he had used his old name for his friend, but Piritho had been very much aware of it. A silly grin now adorned Piritho's face.

"Is there any hint about the types of problems we'll face?" Salis asked.

"No, but I don't think they'll require great powers of deduction to resolve," Caidos told him. "They're there to ensure only the true fragment holders reach the center of the Labyrinth. The problem you'll face will be solved by the power of your fragment and the inherent abilities you possess as the holder of that fragment.

"I know you already understand the importance of our quest, but there are sections from the scrolls I think you should hear directly." He picked up the scroll he had brought with him from his study. "This portion covers Salis's question the other day, about the reasons we don't want Rhamak to control the crown piece.

"'He who completes the Rejoining of Sefiron by placing the crown piece, shall be of the Order of Mages, and must adhere to the precepts set down by the Order, for the power of Sefiron is the power for the world.

"'A Mage must have compassion in his heart for he shall control the power of Sefiron and give it to all the people of the world. Let no Mage of evil heart control the crown piece.

"'If a Mage who follows not the Code should complete the Rejoining he would become the power of the Crystal and even death itself shall be denied him.'"

He set the scroll down before continuing. "If Rhamak obtains the crown piece he will become immortal, and he'll have control of all the power he could ever hope to gain, and he'll make the rest of us serve him in a world of his making."

\* \* \*

Hours had passed since Caidos had gone to his bed chamber. The messages had been written, and Zephyr given her instructions, and he had watched her in the moonlight, as she flew west on her critical mission. She would go first to Numina, and then circle Zadania from B'Zuri, through Varsa, to Arkhan. They had decided to leave Febron to the Falconry to notify if they could design a plan that would motivate them without telling them about the crystal fragments, something the Febronese would do nothing to protect.

Having that taken care of should have set his mind at rest, at least for a while. All the companions were here, and they were all safe, but every time he started to doze off; he woke again, a niggling idea just at the edge of his consciousness begging for attention. An elusive thought, a feather on a light breeze, it scampered away every time he tried to pin it down.

He rose from his bed, stretching the aching muscles that had kept him from finding a comfortable position for sleeping; he walked to the windows that gave him a panoramic view of the harbor and the sea beyond it. The partly cloudy night that had seen Zephyr on her journey was gone, replaced by roiling clouds and sparks of lightning out on the horizon. The brief glimpses revealed by each strike showed high waves out on the open sea, cresting over the breakwater, churning the usually clam waters of the harbor.

A violent crash of thunder rattled the panes in the windows, and the clouds released a torrent of rain that hit the glass so hard Caidos jumped back. Worried that the panes would crack with the force of the onslaught, he was prepared to cast an air shield of protection.

By the time the next glimpse came, the sea had escalated its assault; the Sarnika rocking in the wake of wave after wave pouring over the breakwater. Thunder and lightning were now pounding and sparking so fast Caidos felt as if a battle were being waged against the island. The peals vibrated his bones and he retained images in his vision for seconds after the explosive flashes so that he became confused by what he was seeing.

One strike hit so close he could smell the lightning and saw a large banyan tree hit, splitting the trunk in a terrible wood-ripping roar. The afterimage gave him a chance to realize that men were running up the dock toward the ship, and when the next flare came, he saw that the Sarnika had torn loose from its hawsers and was free of the dock, bobbing in the churning waters of the harbor. But he couldn't be sure he had seen the mountainous wave that appeared to be bearing down on the ship. It crested even with the tips of the masts, and was breaking immediately behind the Sarnika.

He held his breath for the long seconds it took for the next flash to show the ship again; swamped by the wave, sinking rapidly.

## Chapter 30

They had used the few hours until dayspring in hopeful search for the eight crewmen who had been aboard the Sarnika as nightwatch. Three bodies had been found, washed ashore in the harbor; the other five we still missing.

Dawn broke, but little light penetrated the still heavy clouds drizzling on the calmer but still choppy waters of the harbor. Caidos directed a handful of mages, positioning them along the dock and shoreline to illuminate the water around the tips of the masts, the only part of the Sarnika visible above the surface. Captain Gorbik sent his best divers down to inspect the wreckage.

"She's listing at about a thirty-degree angle," Gorbik explained once his divers had reported, "the starboard side is up, but it's partially covered in a drift of sand. The masts are secure, and as far as they can tell there is no damage to the hull."

"Is there another ship on the island?" Brandorin asked

"No, I'm afraid there isn't." Caidos' hair was a visible sign of his frustration; it leapt from his head in every direction. The mage began to pace, scratching and ruffling his hair into a white halo around his head.

"And because we sent Zephyr with the dispatches already we have no way of sending a message for another ship to come. There are regular supply ships that come here from Setabri, but the next one is not due for three weeks. That would only give us a little over a week to get to the Labyrinth. It's not enough time."

"How well is the ship built, Captain?" Salis asked.

"She's the strongest in these waters," the Captain said proudly. "For all the good it will do us with her on the bottom."

"That may not be as hard to manage as you'd think," Salis said, giving Caidos an enigmatic look that made the mage look hopeful again.

"What are you thinking, Salis?"

"Remember, I can move things it would take dozens of men to lift."

"You can't try lifting that ship, Salis. It's too much."

He was no longer speaking out loud, but everyone could see his mind was still going, as he muttered, "It just might work."

\* \* \*

Zephyr arrived in Numina eighteen hours after leaving Artara. The first part of her flight had been at night, but Caidos had told her to follow the moon, which in its three-quarter phase provided enough light to see the water below, followed by the Larian shoreline.

The light of the moon gave the landscape below an eerie ghost-like quality; casting the greens of the plains in a silvery gray that made the grasses below, undulating with the wind, look like the waves on the sea she had just crossed.

When the moon set she flew down and rested until the sun began to rise. Matu had drawn a few easily recognizable landmarks that would steer her toward Numina. She saw the narrow ridge of rock that ran predominantly east and west, and pointed her in the direction of the Larian city. When she saw a thick wood, a solitary island in a silver sea, she turned to the left and headed toward a broad hill rising from the plain on the western horizon. Then, finally she saw the walled city, and she flew over it, heading toward the center and the large pavilion Matu had drawn.

She flew to the front of the council chambers. The Larians were able to understand her easily, and they brought her to Korlu, who was already in the Council Chambers with the rest of the Elders.

Matu's message told him the companions would be arriving in Numina in a few days, on their way to the Great Central Desert. He had not detailed the purpose of their trip, but Korlu already knew the nature of their journey. He also understood the importance of Matu's request for military support. After seeing Zephyr was fed and given a quiet place to rest before she started her flight to B'zuri, Korlu returned to the Council to inform them of Matu's request and to decide what must be done.

Zephyr left Numina the next day at first light; it would be too dangerous to attempt to cross the Axana Mountains in the dark. The winds over the mountains buffeted against her, sometimes sending her off course, sometimes dropping out from under her unexpectedly.

At one point the winds were so strong she could make no forward progress against them, so she landed on the leeward side of a low peak and rested for a time. When she sensed the winds had shifted and now came out of the east, she took flight again, gaining speed with the strong tailwinds.

She arrived at the steppes north of Setabri just as the sun was setting, and she flew into the dense branches of a tall spruce tree, too exhausted from her flight to look for food.

Hours later, much rested, her hunger wakened her. After ensuring there was no one in the area, she left her haven in the tree to hunt for her meal. Caidos had thought it safer for her to fly through much of Febron in the dark, and she crossed the more populous areas of that country by the time the skies lightened again.

\* \* \*

Caidos started by using focused streams of water to wash away the sand that had mounded over the starboard hull, causing the ship to list. When the ship failed to right itself, he continued to remove sand from under the starboard side, creating a shallow trough. Without the cushion of sand beneath, the ship slowly straightened, until it was only a few degrees off vertical.

"That will be enough for now," Salis said. "Captain, can we have your men dive again, to inspect the port side, now that it's accessible?"

While the hull looked intact, Salis wanted to be prepared. He had already talked to some of the mages who specialized in alchemy, and they were preparing patching materials that could be used to seal any cracks they might find later.

"I've tested samples of sealing compounds that will be

spread on any cracks we find to create a watertight seal," Salis told them. "If there are holes, we can make patches and seal them in place with the same substance. The mages have done some wonderful research. They have one mixture that spreads well, and adheres easily, even underwater, then after an hour it sets into an excellent seal. They are going to make enough to repair even a large number of cracks.

"Parts of the process require the mixture to sit for a time between steps, but they assure me they'll have enough by midday tomorrow. If all goes well, we could start removing the water by the end of the day tomorrow. That's your job, Caidos."

"Quite literally. I've decided that I'll do that part myself. I'll have some assistance from Nallidor, who also has the ability to do what's needed. We can't simply take the water out of the ship while its decks are still below the surface. It would just fill in again. Nallidor and I will use air cushions to push the water away from the area above the ship, and he'll hold the sea back while I get the water out.

"I'll create a fountain of water, which will come from the holds of the ship, and will empty out into the harbor, outside of Nallidor's shield. Then as the ship empties, it will grow lighter, and start to rise."

"Theoretically."

"You mean you aren't sure, Salis?" Brandorin asked.

"It's not like I've done this before. If it needs a little help, I can do some lifting."

"Just be careful," Caidos told him. "I've seen mages try to apply their powers to a task that was too much; it can have severe repercussions."

"I will. But we have to get that ship up so we can sail out of here the day after tomorrow."

"It'll work," M'drani told them.

"It's going to be an amazing sight to see," Icara added.

As the companions left, Salis added quietly, to just Caidos, "That's what I love, an audience that has no idea of how much can go wrong."

"Hopefully they'll never know the error of their ways."

\*   \*   \*

Chaubrel had been telling himself every day since glimpsing the journal in Rhamak's room that it was insanity to return for another look, let alone taking the time to read it in detail. Yet he was walking toward Rhamak's private chamber knowing Rhamak was not there.

He had convinced himself that Rhamak had wanted him to see the journal; that it had been left out for exactly that reason. In all the years Chaubrel had known Rhamak, he had never revealed anything about his past; at least not before the appearance of Sefiron's Shadow. There was something in that journal that Rhamak wanted Chaubrel to know.

As he entered the room, he half expected an alarm to sound; triggered by some spell Rhamak had set against intruders. But none of the servants would go anywhere near this room, and Rhamak trusted his chamberlain. Rhamak was on the other side of the fortress, and would be there for at least another hour. Despite the fact that Chaubrel was convinced Rhamak wanted him to read the journal, his heart was pounding and he couldn't slow his breathing no matter how hard he tried to take a deep, slow breath.

The journal was no longer on the bed stand, and though he told himself to walk out, his feet seemed to have other ideas, as they led him over to the shelves at the far side of the room. The binding on the journal had been distinctive, bound in rich cordovan leather with a ribbed spine. But Chaubrel had retrieved and replaced many volumes on these shelves, and he had never seen that particular tome.

No, that book had never been on the open shelves; it had to have come from a chest or compartment Chaubrel was unfamiliar with. He turned slowly as he scanned the room, seeing only those things he had seen a thousand times before. On his second circuit he stopped at the tapestry that hung at the head of the bed. It depicted a castle on a hill overlooking sheep-scattered fields. Not unusual for a tapestry, but Chaubrel stared at it with dropped jaw. There were no other tapestries anywhere in the fortress. Why had that never occurred to him before? Without realizing he had moved, Chaubrel was at the tapestry and was drawing it back to reveal the wall behind.

The journal rested on an ornate metal stand within a small alcove. On display, but hidden; a place of honor and shame.

Chaubrel withdrew the journal, taking it to the table to read. He looked again at the inside cover, at an illuminated list of names, a genealogy. Names that had riveted his attention at first glance, names he recognized from history, names of kings and queens. And at the bottom, the final name that had drawn him back to this volume, Rhamak's.

He scanned the pages that followed, seeing dates from a thousand years before. The only sound in the room, the distinctive crinkle of the thick vellum pages turned to reveal glimpses into each reign. The authors seldom acknowledged the ones that came before, but the change in handwriting stood witness to the transitions of one monarch to the next. He found comments written casually about momentous events he had learned as history, and a few rare passages written with obvious emotion about simple family matters.

Chaubrel froze while turning a page, not because of the writing before him, but because of the soft susurrus of a robe against stone that he had heard behind him. He rose slowly, controlling his breathing, then turned, keeping his eyes downcast, and said only, "Sire."

The silence that followed almost tricked him into believing he had been mistaken, until the toe of a leather shoe and the hem of a dark blue robe floated into his vision.

Rhamak finally spoke, without hint of emotion, "What have you learned?"

"Your lineage, sire," Chaubrel whispered with caution, stalling for time to decide how best to answer. "I have always known you must have been of noble birth; your intelligence, your bearing, your taste for fine food and wines. But, sire, your line, it was royal."

Rhamak's slow, controlled exhalation of breath told Chaubrel he had succeeded in diverting the worst of the vituperation. In a marble voice; cold, but laced with a dark vein of threat, "Read the last page."

Feeling like a condemned prisoner presented with his final meal Chaubrel turned to the last entry. The cramped script coupled with the pressure of Rhamak's tangible gaze on his back, made the words difficult to read. The emotion conveyed drew Chaubrel in as he found lines expressing worry, a father's worry about his son's future.

"Read it aloud."

Chaubrel began to sweat, knowing Rhamak would not enjoy hearing the unflattering remarks, even if they were expressed long since passed. His voice cracked as he began, and he stumbled over the first few words. "'Rhamak is following the wrong path. I have seen his eyes when he is directing the troops, or even simple instructions to a servant. He enjoys the power too much, and I fear what kind of leader he might be.'"

There was no more. Rhamak waited so long to speak again that Chaubrel hoped he had left. The heated reaction of the moment of discovery passed, Chaubrel felt safe enough to look up, though not directly at Rhamak.

"Do you see the irony?" the mage finally asked. "I could have had then, what I am so desperately trying to obtain now." Rhamak turned and left the room.

Chaubrel turned to close the journal, glancing at the date at the top of the page. It triggered a memory; something from history. A terrible fire in the Varsian Palace. The source of the fire had been a mystery but everyone in Zadania knew about the tragic end of the four thousand year old Dravonian dynasty. But it had not ended; the last of that line had just left the room.

Chaubrel knew the cause of that fire, and why it had been so difficult to extinguish, and he now knew why Rhamak hated Brandorin so strongly.

\*   \*   \*

It was late in the day by the time the alchemists were satisfied that their patching materials were ready if needed. Caidos and Nallidor had tested their incantations in another area of the harbor, in order to perfect the strengths required and the proper timing. By the time both the ship and the mages were ready the sun was low over the western horizon.

The companions waited on the dock, while the adjoining shoreline was crowded with the all of the mages of Artara and the crew of the Sarnika. Salis, Brandorin, the Captain and the two mages sat in a large rowboat out in the harbor, twenty feet from the tips of the masts. From this position, they could see the ship sitting at the bottom through the clear water of the cove.

Caidos and Nallidor began the first step of the process by casting an air incantation focusing on the water over the ship. It started as a small depression in the water, directly over the middle of the ship. Slowly the depression got deeper as the edges moved out farther and farther. At first it was a round hole in the water, but as the edges reached the ship's rails, it stopped expanding sideways and began to elongate, until slowly the hole took on the exact shape of the ship, and its depth reached the decks.

While Caidos and Nallidor concentrated on controlling the water and forcing it outward, Salis, Brandorin, and the Captain watched closely to see if there were any leaks in the walls of air that held the water back. They had thought at first they would only have to clear the area over the hatchways, to allow the water within the holds to be extracted, but Salis had pointed out that if the water remained over any part of the decks, its weight would hinder the ship's ascent.

Once the walls of the air cushion had been adjusted to match the exact outline of the Sarnika, the floor of the cushion was pulled back from the center. Though it looked no different, the cushions were now just walls around the outside. They couldn't allow the air cushion itself to hold the ship down. Caidos asked Nallidor, "Are you ready to hold the shield in place on your own?"

"Yes. Start slowly from the stern, and move forward, releasing it to me."

Caidos began to release his hold on the air shields as Nallidor had described. At one point, a hole opened in the shield and water began to seep back through, but Nallidor saw it and closed it before much water had poured back onto the ship. When Nallidor had full control of the shield, Caidos began to create the fountain to pull the water from the hold.

It started as a single, thin stream climbing from the center cargo hatchway. Caidos had pulled the water high enough to clear the surface of the water, then arched it over the wall of air and poured it back into the harbor. Once the initial fountain was in place, he increased the amount of water being poured up and out. As it reached its apex, the water fanned out forming an upside-down waterfall which caught the light of the setting sun, giving the scene the illusion of a river of gold pouring up out of the hold.

Salis listened for sounds of wood cracking or splintering. The ship had not been built to hold back the weight of the water now pushing against it. A minor crack caused by the storm could blossom into a major gap as the weight of the water pushed only from the outside of the ship.

He had discussed this concern with the Mages, and they had decided that as Caidos pulled the water out, Nallidor would force more air into the hold, to help push the water up, and to help support the walls against the weight of the water.

"She's starting to rise," Brandorin shouted. The others could now see the prow beginning to lift off the floor of the harbor.

"I'll keep her even," Salis said, using his abilities to help lift the stern, to keep it level with the prow. "Can you pull more water from the stern, Caidos?" he asked from between clenched teeth.

"I think so," Caidos said.

Salis felt some relief from the strain after a minute. "That's better. She's moving now."

The deck was now only ten feet below the level of the rest of the harbor. As it continued to rise, it started to list toward the starboard, and water began to pour back in when it tilted beyond the edges of the air shields.

"I got that, too," Salis shouted, as he pulled the ship back until the masts were straight again.

Once the decks were above the surface of the surrounding water, Nallidor slowly released the air shields. He started at the stern and prow, which were higher than the deck in the center.

"The air shields are gone, she's up," he announced.

"She's still sitting low in the water, the holds aren't empty yet," Gorbik said. The water continued to flow out of the holds, but everyone could see the water stream had lessened, and within a few minutes it had stopped completely. The Sarnika rested gently in the water, just as she had when they had docked two days before.

The companions, crew and mages watching from the shore began to cheer, and their excitement slowly grew, until everyone was jumping up and down and clapping each other on the back in congratulations.

Brandorin turned to Salis and the two mages. "You did it."

"Did you have any doubts?" Caidos asked.

"Not one."

"Well, I did," Salis said, breathing heavily from the strain of his efforts. "I was sure the hold was going to give in, or unseen cracks would split her wide open, or she'd tip over, or the water would come gushing in, despite the air shields, or ..."

"And all this time I thought you always knew exactly what you were doing," Caidos said.

"That's the sign of a true Master Builder. Presenting an air of confidence in times of total panic."

## Chapter 31

The bodies of four crew members had been found in the hold of the Sarnika. They were buried along with the three found on the shoreline. One man was never found though a marker was placed next to those of his comrades. All the members of the Artara community, the companions and the remaining crew gathered to commend their souls to the World Shapers.

Caidos selected ten mages to accompany them on their journey; choosing mages with the abilities that would help in their defense against Rhamak. They were limited by the number of horses they had brought with them to Artara, for there were no horses on the island, and each would have to carry two people from the dock in Laria until they reached Numina, where they would get more.

Captain Gorbik and his crew had spent the evening after the memorial service, checking the integrity of the hull. A few small cracks and leaks were patched with the alchemists' compound, the patches held in place by air shields until they could set. Only when they were satisfied the hull was sound did Gorbik approve their departure. They sailed with the first light of day, heading northwest until they were clear of the islands around Artara, then they turned west heading across to the Larian shore.

\* \* \*

At about the time the companions and mages were landing at the dock in Laria, Zephyr was leaving Tasago, a military post at the eastern end of Varsa. Brandorin had added that stop after learning where Labyrinth's location. They would have the shortest distance to travel, and could best bring the most supplies.

Zephyr's trip across Varsa, from Kartir, had been the shortest leg of her journey so far, but she had covered two thousand miles in five days, and was weary. With three more hours of daylight left, she departed for Tar-Kal in Arkhan, expecting to rest when the sun set. She could then finish her journey in the morning.

She was flying easily, riding the hot air rising from the arid plateau beneath her, when a large hawk, diving from above, swept into her, its talons open to slash at her as it passed. Before she had time to recover, another came at her from behind, stabbing at her with its sharp beak. She pulled in her wings and rolled, losing height rapidly.

She collided with a third hawk, flying beneath her. She went into a free fall, struggling to correct her uncontrolled plummet. Spreading her wings, and holding against the force of the fall, she pulled up just thirty feet from the ground.

Zephyr circled, trying to see her attackers, but before she could make a full sweep, two hawks attacked, one from either side. One cut her neck with its talons and the other grabbed at her tail. Too close to the ground to dive, she struggled to extract herself from their attacks.

Searching for a place to hide, she saw a large dark structure, lights shining dimly from the battlements. She flew in that direction, hoping to lose the hawks as she picked up speed. The hawk attains its fastest speeds when diving from a great height, but when flying straight and climbing, their speeds were slower than Zephyr's. If she had not covered so many miles in so few days, she could easily have outpaced them, but her shoulders ached and her flying was sluggish.

Two of the hawks raced up behind her, while two others, between her and the distant structure, were closing in and ahead of her path. She maintained her direction, waiting until the last possible moment, when she turned abruptly, climbing steeply. The four hawks suddenly found themselves flying into each other.

She had finally gained some distance from her attackers when a fifth hawk she had not seen before, grabbed her from above, digging its talons into her already aching shoulders. She went limp, forcing the hawk to carry her dead weight. The two of them dropped rapidly, but the hawk would not release, and she found herself caught in the middle of five fierce birds of prey.

They cut and slashed at her with beaks and talons, and she reached within herself, trying to find a reserve of strength. She inhaled deeply and released a blast of flame, far more than the tiny sparks and hisses she had ever been able to generate before.

One hawk ignited and plunged to its death. The other hawks, stunned by the flames, pulled back and Zephyr swung around. She shot a second blast, catching two flying close together. The fourth swerved out of her range.

The last hawk swung up from behind, planting its talons at the base of her wings and freezing them, it began to peck at her neck and head with its beak. They dropped rapidly, as before, but Zephyr could not turn her head to strike the hawk with her fire. The surface of the plateau rushed up at them from below, when the hawk suddenly released her to save itself.

Zephyr tried to fan out her wings as brakes, but the deep gouges at base of her wings sent a shooting pain through her shoulders. She couldn't hold against the force of the wind rushing up at her.

She turned her body, trying to stretch out parallel to the ground, with her head aiming slightly down. She stretched out her wings again, and held them despite the shooting pain. The drag of her wings against the wind slowed her descent and she swept out over the desert floor, adding a much-needed two hundred feet to her descent.

The wounds inflicted by the hawks were bleeding badly and she floated down toward the desert floor. She scanned the cliffs as she passed, looking for a crag or crevice in which to hide. The call of the hawks as they flew out beyond the Ridge told her they were still following, and she knew any hole large enough for her to crawl into would also afford access to the smaller hawks.

She decided to make her stand on the desert floor, knowing a hawk was more at home in the sky than on the ground. Her four legs gave her more maneuverability. She stood with her back to the steep cliff, limiting the hawks' access. They were cautious in their approach.

Zephyr knew she was weakening; she could not afford to wait while she lost more blood and became too weak to fight back. She moved to her left, looking over her shoulder in quick glances toward an outcropping that would afford her more protection. As she did, she tripped, and as she fell, the hawks dove in. But she was ready for them. Shooting a long tongue of flame, she caught the wings of the closest hawk, and it fell to the ground, where she easily sprayed it again.

The last hawk stayed outside the range of her flames, waiting for her to weaken. Zephyr rolled in the sand, staunching her wounds. She watched the hawk carefully, but it made no motion to move in. She had to take the initiative.

Her first attempt to take-off was unsuccessful. She sank back to the ground, now ten feet away from the protective cliff wall. The hawk began to circle. Zephyr collapsed, and the hawk moved in for the kill.

When the hawk swooped in; Zephyr rolled onto her back, shooting a blast straight into its chest. Its wings caught fire, and as it flapped them it only fueled the flames higher and within seconds the last hawk was dead.

Zephyr began to crawl toward the outcropping she had seen. When she reached it, she saw a crack at its base that opened into a cool dark crevice. With the last of her strength, she crawled in and collapsed.

\* \* \*

The companions and mages left Numina within two hours of their arrival, heading northwest toward the foothills of the Axana Mountains. The first day was slow as the mages adjusted to riding. Many of them had never ridden a horse, and those that had, had not done so for years.

The plain they traveled stretched out from their right to the mountains on their left. The flat plains gave way to gently rolling hills, which gradually increased in width and height as they met the steep lower slopes of the Axana Mountains, which sat on the western horizon, giants guarding against travel to the west.

The ground shook often with mild tremors, and they could see, even from a distance, the rockslides precipitated by the quakes. A sudden, violent storm on the third day left their clothes damp and chilled everyone to the bone, but when they stopped for the evening a few of the mages made the rounds, using air incantations to dry out everyone's cloaks. The mages paired up with the companions, forming air shields over their heads to protect them from the rain and much of the wind.

On their fifth day out from Numina a quake shook the ground with such force that all but the most experienced riders were thrown from their horses, and large gaping holes opened at their feet. While Matu and Piritho ran to stop the panicking horses, others checked the condition of each of the riders, feeling lucky that no one had suffered more than minor scratches or bruises.

One of the younger mages, J'faro, stood at the edge of the crevice that had just opened before him, marveling at his close call. The ground beneath him suddenly crumbled. As he slid into the fissure, he grasped at vines that gave way, rocks that rolled with him and ground that crumbled beneath his fingers. The sliding scree filled his mouth when he tried to call for help, his cries stopped in his throat. Just when he was sure nothing would stop his descent, he felt hands around his waist, though no one was there.

As he rose up out of the crevice, Salis stood at the top, his arms and hands stretched out in front of him, as if he was indeed holding the young mage. As the Builder swung his arms away from the gap, J'faro floated that way too and gently touched down on solid ground again. He coughed and choked on words of gratitude that Salis understood, even if he couldn't hear them.

## Chapter 32

Two weeks after leaving Numina, they reached the top of the Jarbon Cliffs, wet and bruised from the rough journey along the Axana Mountains. As they rode along the eastern and southern ends of the Central Desert, and the cold winds they'd been experiencing were replaced by hot, arid ones. The Chiron Ridge ran along the western edge of the desert, down to the southern edge, almost meeting the Jarbon Cliffs. Between the two, the ground sloped gradually, forming a mile wide slope down to the desert floor.

They turned east, knowing they would find the Larian troops, and hoping they would find the other armies as well. Zephyr had left almost three weeks before. Korlu had confirmed her arrival in Numina, but Caidos was worried that crossing the Axana Mountains may have proven too much for her.

By early afternoon they had found the outskirts of the Larian camp. Guards had been posted to watch for them, and were to guide them to the command post at the center of the mile-wide entrance to the desert.

Lata and Gaila, the two Elders that had transformed Piritho back to his human form, were in charge of the Larian forces. Caidos didn't have to ask if the other armies had arrived; he could see a thousand men encamped just west of them. Hundreds of tents spread out before them, a small uniform mountain range.

"What army is that?" he asked as he dismounted.

"The Kartirian cavalry and the N'varian Falconry," Lata told them. "They arrived together two days ago. The Protector himself led them here."

"My father is here?" Brandorin exclaimed.

"He said when he received your note, and knew you were alive, that Rhamak himself could not have prevented him from coming to your aid."

"What do you mean, when he knew I was alive?"

"He said he hadn't seen you for almost five months. I got

the impression something happened that made him question your safety."

"But I sent him word months ago, when Caidos and I started our journey. I told him about the quest."

"Apparently he never received the message."

"My mother. What have I put her through?" Brandorin leapt onto Bristo's back as he spoke, the horse sensing his agitation, was skittish. The horse pawed the ground, snorting, waiting for his master's signal to run.

"Where is he? I have to see him."

"Isn't that him riding up now?" Caidos said pointing to the northwest though Brandorin had bolted off before the mage had finished the sentence. A group of four horsemen approached from the west, a tall, handsome man in full dress uniform riding in front. His resemblance to Brandorin was unmistakable, though the dark auburn hair was graying at the temples and the years and the responsibility that went with them were etched across his face.

When Dilardin saw his son, he spurred his horse forward, closing the distance between them in seconds. Before either horse came to a complete stop, the riders had dismounted and embraced each other. No one heard the words they spoke at their reunion, but they were soon laughing together as they turned and walked back to the other companions.

"Caidos, it's good to see you," the Protector said as he approached the mage; his arms extended in friendship. They clasped hands, "Much has happened since last we spoke."

"Yes, Dilardin, it has. We've had a long road, but it has been comforting having Brandorin with us. I know the sword was passed on to him in an unusual manner, but he has become not only the Protector, but the Healer as well."

"Indeed?" Dilardin turned to his son. "I'm not surprised. If anyone could do it ..." He stopped as he noticed Piritho standing off to the side.

"Thiro, my lad, you're here too? How marvelous!" He walked over to Piritho, and embraced him as he had his own son. "We were worried about you." Dilardin's voice was hoarse and cracked with emotion.

"Yes, sir. I just want to say ... I mean ... I'm sorry ... I couldn't ..." Piritho began to stammer.

Brandorin interrupted, "Fell and hit his head. Wasn't himself for the longest time. He missed the wedding. He's sorry about that, but ..."

"I know he missed the wedding," Dilardin said, looking at Brandorin in a manner that only a father can. He knew he was not being told the whole truth.

"It's a long story," Brandorin said. "We'll tell you later."

\*   \*   \*

The other three men with Dilardin were Dagoru, the Commander of the Kartirian Cavalry; J'pahvro, Hawkren of the Falconry; and M'drani's brother-in-law, J'shurla.

J'shurla embraced M'drani. "I have a message from your mother. But I fear it will have to wait until our business here is completed."

"Nonsense. You're family, that comes first," Dilardin said, looking at his son, and then Piritho. "You go talk to your sister-in-law; we can take care of things here."

After the introductions were completed and they had moved into the Larian command tent, Dilardin said, "Clever idea using Zephyr as a messenger. A firedrake. Too bad there aren't more of them, they'd be very handy. Is she here?"

"No, she was to go on to Arkhan after delivering your message to Tasago," Caidos told him. "Do you know if she arrived there?"

"Yes, she did. The army should be here sometime tomorrow. Only eight hundred men, all the men that are stationed in Tasago. No other outpost would have been close enough for foot soldiers to reach here on time. And they're double-timing it all the way. If Zephyr hadn't gotten them advance notice, even that wouldn't have helped. We brought nine hundred men and horses. It saved us time not having to bring supplies for our stay here and the return trip. Another excellent idea."

"There's no sign of the Arkhanians," Caidos said, "so we don't know if she made it to Tar-Kal. I would've thought they'd be here by now."

Dilardin said, "I'm sure she made it, Caidos. She was tired, I could tell that, but she was determined to continue on with only a few hours rest.

"We saw a very large fortress sitting on the Chiron Ridge. It was north of our position, but I sent a detail out to investigate. They caught up with us a few days later. It was mostly deserted, but we believe it is Rhamak's stronghold."

"That's where they took me," Piritho said. "Huge place, looks like a monster's head?"

"Yes, that's what the scouts said," Dilardin said looking at Piritho, a confused look on his face. "Who took you there?"

"That's more of that long story, Father."

Dilardin looked at his son and Piritho, and decided the long story could wait. "Hawkren J'pahvro, why don't you give them a report of the Falconry?"

"Yes, sir. Within an hour of receiving your message, we dispatched riders to Medora, asking them to send as many men and arms as they could. We left B'zuri with six hundred riders. We rode to Tasago first, and met the Protector and his men there."

"I'll be very surprised if the Medorans agree to get involved," Dilardin said. "They won't bend a finger to protect the powers of the crystal."

"That's what I told them, Dilardin," Salis said. "They're only motivated by money and something they think is demonic. What did you decide on?"

"Well, actually a little of both," J'pahvro said. "The story is that a very, very large vein of gold was discovered in the southern Central Desert, and that an army of demons is trying to steal it. Anyone who helps to defend it will get a share of the gold."

Salis laughed, "We're probably going to be delivering the demons all right, but have you considered what you're going to tell them when they ask about the gold."

"I thought we'd just say the demons took it all."
"I don't think we should mention that until after the battle?"
"My thoughts exactly."

\*   \*   \*

The commanders had discussed strategy for the two days they were camped in the area. All agreed they could not afford to wait for the rest of the armies to arrive, but should head immediately toward the center of the desert.

Caidos, Brandorin and Dilardin rode out in the lead. The Companions and mages followed behind. J'pahvro rode with the Falconry on the left, and Dagoru, with the Kartirian cavalry, rode on the right. The Larians foot soldiers brought up the rear.

Brandorin could feel the fear rising within him. He struggled to control it; hide it from his father. He adjusted his sword to touch the Umari stone.

His father noticed the gesture and asked him, "I wasn't able to control the Umari stone. What can you do with it?"

Brandorin jumped when his father spoke, the fear making him edgy. He knew Dilardin had noticed, but covered as best he could by giving him a quick rundown of the situations where he'd used the Umari crystal.

"You healed a man gored by a boar? That had to have been pretty dramatic. How did it feel?"

Brandorin noticed Caidos over his father's shoulder, watching to see what he'd say. "You think that was dramatic? You should have seen the raptors." He heard himself running through various aspects of their journey. He felt he was rambling at top speed, but couldn't stop himself. It was taking all his effort to keep the fear from showing.

"You drank an entire mug of kra-lon and were still able to walk? I struggled through half a mug, and had to be carried out. The hangover was the worst."

"Then you must not have tried the hangover cure."

* * *

The floor of the desert was as flat as the still waters of a lake. The hard-packed, cracked surface looked like the scales of a great beast; the spiny cactus dotting the ground, the stiff bristles on its back. A dry wind blowing across their path carried loose sandy soil that stung their eyes and quickly coated the horse's flanks.

The wind stirred up the fine sand, thickening the air with dust, and preventing them from seeing more than thirty feet ahead. They had gone about twenty miles across the desert floor when the wind seemed to blow itself out. As the sand settled they saw staggered rows of eight-foot mounds standing end-to-end and stretching across their path. The mounds appeared to be formed from tilled soil.

"Those mounds look fresh. Why would anyone be working the ground in the middle of the desert?" Brandorin said.

"That looks like rich, fertile soil, not the type of soil you'd find here," Caidos pointed out. "Maybe we should get Til up here to check this out."

"Why worry about a few mounds of dirt," Salis said, "we can get around them."

"The point is," Dilardin said, "anything unexplained is reason to proceed cautiously." The conversational tones his voice had carried while talking to his son, had changed to the no-nonsense voice of a commander. "It's worth a few minutes to send men ahead to investigate." He looked to Dagoru, nodding his head once. Dagoru dispatched a squad of five men to scout ahead.

As they rode out, the others waited and watched. When the scouts reached the first row, the mound directly in front of them slowly unfolded. First a head, then shoulders and arms laboriously unwrapped from a creature that curled up from the mound. It rose to its knees and then stood, towering fifteen feet high. It let out an unnatural howl as it reached down with its massive arm and picked up one of the scouts, still sitting on his horse. Its skin was as dark and irregular as the soil it had appeared to be; its body thick and heavy, the face almost featureless. It had a large, gaping mouth and large dark eyes, but no discernible nose or ears.

The other mounds began to move and soon twenty giants stood in front of them. There was an army of at least a thousand men camped behind them.

Dagoru called to the scouts to withdraw and gave a command to his cavalry, "Form up and prepare to defend on my order."

J'pahvro shouted, "Falconry, alert."

Dilardin sat statue-still as he scanned the scene before him, assessing the situation. He saw not only the giants standing over them, and the army behind the towering creatures, but he was also aware of Brandorin's reaction to the scene. His son was openly fearful, struggling with himself to keep from turning his horse and fleeing. Bristo was atypically skittish, and Brandorin fought to maintain control of both his horse and himself. Dilardin felt uncharacteristically distracted by his son's reaction.

Both armies fanned out into position, establishing a row of defense between the companions and the enemy. The Larians formed up behind and around the companions. By the time they were prepared to move two of the five scouts had returned to the lines; the other three had been unhorsed and dismembered by the giants.

\* \* \*

The mages of Artara were used to following Caidos' lead, and they rode up to him now. The soldiers, seasoned in battle, showed no signs of fear as they faced the row of unnatural giants only a hundred yards in front of them, but the mages lack of military training left them in various states of agitation, from nervous to out and out panic. Caidos tried to calm them by drawing their attention away from the giants, redirecting it to what they'd been trained for.

"We're the only ones that can effectively fight those creatures, and we can do it from a distance. We can attack without being anywhere near them, but we must start first. The cavalry have no defense against those things. Follow my lead."

Caidos moved Aquilo forward, the mages following. He tried to create a gap in the Kartirian cavalry, but they would not part. "Dilardin," he called, "we must have clear access to those creatures to be able to fire."

"Agreed. Dagoru, leave room for the mages, but make sure they're protected."

"Yes, sir." Turning to the mages, he added, "Spread out along the line, at ten foot intervals. That will allow us to better protect you, as well as giving you a better line of sight on the creatures."

Caidos took a position in the middle of the front line, and the other mages spread out along the line that faced the giants, who merely stood watching their tactical movements.

"I think we surprised them, sir," J'pahvro said. "They're big, but they don't appear to be able to think for themselves."

"They haven't gotten their orders yet," Dilardin said. "This will be the best time to act. Caidos, begin."

Caidos released a series of fireballs, focusing on the giant directly ahead. The other mages, seeing him act, followed his example, alternately striking at the two creatures most directly in front of each of them. Though the barrage of fireballs was spectacular to see, the creatures sustained no injuries, just swatted at them and grunted at the annoyance.

After his experience with the other creatures Rhamak had sent, Caidos was disappointed, though not surprised to see that their efforts had no impact against the giant's tough and undoubtedly magically protected skin. He changed his tactics to the thin pointed arrows of flame that had worked so well on the Sarnika, aiming directly for the creature's eyes. The arrows caused only minor damage, which seemed to enrage the creatures more than hinder them.

Even though the mages' assault had caused no visual damage, the giants turned and began a slow, laborious walk away. Caidos spied a man on a gray speckled horse riding along the line of giants, issuing orders to withdraw. He could not see him clearly, but recognized the robes and the horse. He cast a spell, and whispered a name, which was amplified across the distance, though it still sounded like a whisper, it was clearly heard by the man behind the giants, "Vorago?"

On hearing his name the man turned his horse and faced Caidos, "Yes, Caidos, it's me. Surprised?"

"Why?"

"Why?" His mocking laugh amplified along with his voice. "Why would you need to ask? Because Rhamak is teaching me what you would not. I will live forever."

"But at what price?"

"Any price would have been worth it. I'll share the power of the united crystal."

"Rhamak will share nothing."

"You're on the wrong side, Caidos. But you have until tomorrow."

With those words, Vorago was gone, and the giants retreated along with the troops behind them.

"Should we go after them, sir?" Dagoru asked.

"No. They weren't ready for us," Dilardin said, "but we weren't ready for those giants. The sun will be setting soon, and it gets cold in the desert at night. Make camp and place watches all around the perimeter."

\* \* \*

The troops began the routine process of setting up camp; the seemingly random, chaotic actions flowed into an ordered structure as if by magic, though it was only the seasoned discipline of soldiers taking solace in knowing what was required of them.

Dilardin pulled Caidos aside, and said quietly, "Vorago was the one you were with the day of the wedding?"

Caidos' reluctant nod slowly changed direction as he shook his head in disbelief. "I thought Rhamak was the one who had led us both away, but it was Vorago. He led me to believe he was searching for Rhamak all this time. I've been a fool."

"Had he ever given you any reason to doubt him?"

"No, it's not that. There has been something nagging at me for weeks. Now it's so clear, but I should have seen it then. He advised me to avoid the Ridamon Gorge, saying the bridge had fallen in a recent quake; something that you, as the leader of Varsa, had no knowledge of. Later, Lanata told us she was there on Tapping Day when it collapsed. We were already on the road by then. The bridge couldn't have collapsed before the wedding. He delayed me so I would miss the wedding."

"And when we saw him in N'varia, he tried to get us to take the longer road." Brandorin said, "saying Mount C'zada was stirring. Probably trying to delay us."

Caidos continued, "A short time after we saw him in N'varia, M'drani sensed we were being followed. Vorago must have released the hawk she flushed out."

"Why would a hawk be a problem?" Dilardin asked.

"It wasn't really a hawk. Rhamak has learned how to transform men into birds, which he uses as spies. He can apparently change men into anything he wants, even creatures from his own distorted imagination. Like those giants, or the raptors that attacked me, any kind of beast he can conceive of."

"Then Rhamak sent the beast that attacked you at the wedding."

"Yes, sir. That was Thiro," Brandorin said with regret, watching from the corner of his eye for his father's reaction.

"Thiro? The beast that killed ... that poor lad. What Rhamak must have done to him to make him attack you like that. No wonder you wouldn't come home until you'd found him. But why would Vorago have risked you seeing him? Why wouldn't the hawk have just flown into the area on its own?" Dilardin asked.

"Because it would have been sensed long before it got to them," J'pahvro said.

"Exactly," Caidos told him. "He must have been hiding it with a spell to prevent it from being detected." Caidos snapped his fingers as he remembered something else. "Those dead trees in the woods, where we found Vorago's horse – he used their energies for his spell. But that wasn't the only thing I missed.

"We were attacked on the ship between Ti-Kee and Artara. The ship was suddenly becalmed in a fog that allowed the creatures to board the ship. Vorago is an expert in the weather; he would be the one mage I know, besides Rhamak, who is most able to do that."

"He can control the weather? So he may try attacking us with a lightning storm, or hailstorm, a tornado maybe," Dilardin speculated.

"I don't think we have to worry about that. It would be impossible to have the storm affect us and not them. They're too close. And once he started a tornado, even if he could, he'd have no control of it at all. It could turn on them as easily as bear down on us."

"Since he was obviously controlling those giants today, he could have just as easily been controlling the raptors that attacked me outside of Kartir, and the boars in Laria."

"The gray horse in the woods," Piritho said, "it *was* Vorago. I saw him."

"Why didn't you say something?" Brandorin said. "Well, not 'say', but I should have understood what you saw. I got the impression you hadn't seen anything."

"That's what Vorago wanted you to think, so he made me forget, and sent me on my way. Which brought me back in time to help you stop that last raptor."

"Another blunder," Caidos said. "Though I doubt Rhamak knows that Vorago helped you stopped those raptors, even inadvertently."

"Sounds like you've had a rough journey," Dilardin said. "Since you know Vorago, you may be able to anticipate what he might do, how he'll control those things."

"I obviously don't know Vorago as well as I thought I did. I'd never have thought him capable of this."

"Still, you know how he's controlled other creatures Rhamak has created. You know enough about him that you may be able to predict certain things about the way he might command. How were you able to defeat these other creatures?"

They described the attack on the ship, then the raptor attack ending with Piritho's role in distracting the final raptor so Brandorin could dispatch it.

"So Piritho was back to his natural form by then?"

"No, that didn't happen until we got to Laria," Brandorin said. "We understood each other, though. Caidos thinks it was the crystal."

"That and the fact the two of you are such good friends." Dilardin noticed Brandorin's sheepish look, but decided to wait until their story was finished to ask about it. "What about the boars?"

"They were also warded against my powers, but they weren't that difficult to kill." Caidos and Brandorin exchanged looks, and Dilardin thought he was getting closer to the explanation he'd been waiting for. Brandorin finished the story.

"The boars themselves weren't the main brunt of that attack. One of the boars reverted back to human form after being gored. We didn't know that at the time, so I used the power of the Umari crystal to heal him, but there was a hidden spell waiting for me." He stopped. Caidos started to explain the rest, but Brandorin interrupted him.

"No, Caidos, I have to do it. If I can't do this, how will I face the battle tomorrow?" Dilardin looked at his son in confusion. He had always thought Brandorin to be brave, almost reckless, even as a young boy he had never hesitated to do anything (a fact which often frustrated him as his father). Now he had seen fear and hesitation in his son, twice in a matter of minutes.

"There was a fear spell. I triggered it when I healed him."

"What kind of fear?"

"A cold, deep fear that grips me so strongly I can't even move. When I hold the sword, touch our crystal, it magnifies it, makes it unbearable. Even now I can feel it gnawing at me."

Dilardin reached for his son, placing his hand on his shoulder in sign of support. "When we were attacked on the ship, I was so terrified I froze. Sadro, the man I healed, saved my life, but died protecting me. When I saw my friends being attacked I was able to react a little, but not enough to do any good."

"Something like that happened to me once," Dilardin told his son. Brandorin looked at his father in shock.

"You, afraid, never."

"It's gratifying to think you see me that way, son. I hope this doesn't shatter your entire image of me, but I think the truth is more important right now. I was young, younger than you are now, but older than when you first went into battle. I wasn't prepared for the uncontrolled savagery that surrounded me. The enemy and our own troops were so intermixed I wasn't sure who was on which side. I was afraid of swinging at one of my own men, but I knew hesitation in trying to decide whether I should swing or not could cost me my life. I think it was that dilemma more than anything else that scared me. Swing too fast and I might kill a friend; not fast enough and I might be dead before I could. I stood there for what seemed like forever, not moving, watching the fight rage all around me."

"What did you do?" The timbre of Brandorin's voice, more than the question touched Dilardin deeply. He felt if he looked at his son now, he would see a boy of ten rather than the grown man that sat next to him. The question had held the sound of wonder and amazement that only a young boy, in awe of his father's every word, can project.

"I saw a friend being attacked a few feet away, and I moved to his defense before I'd had a chance to think about it. That's your enemy. Don't think about it, just feel it.

"Now, what're we going to do about those creatures tomorrow? Rhamak will have protected them from the use of your powers, Caidos. We saw proof of that already. Therefore we have to find another way to kill them. I'd also like to know what the nature of the enemy forces is."

"M'drani can help us with that," J'pahvro said.

"Yes, of course," Caidos said jumping up and pacing in front of them.

"She can Search," J'pahvro continued, "She can fly over the enemy camp and determine their numbers, their weapons, what machines they might have."

"That's it!" Caidos declared. Seeing their confused looks, he added, "Sorry, I've been working on our problem with the giants. Excuse me a moment. I'd like to get a couple of people started on a little idea I have. Be right back."

When Dilardin saw Dagoru and J'pahvro looking at Caidos as he hurried away, he explained, "He's a very wise man. I trust him to resolve this little problem for us. So we can move on to other things. J'pahvro, talk to M'drani and ask her to do this for us. Tell her what we need to know." Dilardin would issue orders to his commanders or troops, but he asked civilians to help when he needed them.

When Brandorin and his father were alone, Dilardin turned to him and asked, "Do you want to talk about this fear?"

"I know the fear isn't real, but it doesn't matter. Touching the Umari crystal helps, but touching the Protector's fragment makes it so intense I can't think of anything else. I don't know how I'm going to fight in the battle tomorrow."

"Then don't."

"But I have to. I'm the ...," Brandorin stopped.

"Yes, you're the Protector now," his father finished with both regret and pride. "I'm sorry the burdens of that role had to be passed on to you at a time like this, but all of this has happened for a reason. You were able to control the Umari crystal when neither your grandfather nor I could do it. You're the best of us. I saw that a long time ago. I'm sorry I never told you before. I should have."

"But I have to fight tomorrow. We have to get to the Labyrinth, and go through it. There'll be traps we have to solve. It's my place to lead them."

"Then do that."

"First you say don't do it, then you say I should."

"The solution is not as mysterious as it sounds. There're

many things I had to do as the Protector of Varsa, things I would never have thought I could do.  Things I might not have been able to do if I didn't realize I was the only one that could.  Things that were necessary for the survival of the people of Varsa.  I know you, Brandorin, when the time comes, you'll do what must be done, no matter the cost to yourself."  Dilardin hoped the cost would not be too high.

## Chapter 33

Brandorin left the command tent, his father's advice echoing in his head. He knew what he had to do, but the fear gnawed at his resolve. As he approached the campfire and saw his fellow companions, he turned away. The thoughts racing through his head gave him a nervous energy. He began to walk through the camp, passing small groups of soldiers sitting around their own fires.

He wasn't aware of the many conversations going on around him; his thoughts were turned within. Caidos and M'drani had told him his actions on the ship, albeit minor, had been a sign he could conquer the fear. They had been encouraged, almost elated that he had been able to take action in the face of overwhelming fear and panic. But he was not heartened by their beliefs. He could only remember his arms and legs feeling disconnected, unable to move them, his heart racing, his mouth dry.

"You're afraid because you think too much." The words came at him out of the dark. He stopped and looked to see who had spoken. When the voice came again, he realized the words hadn't been directed to him, but were spoken by a soldier, sitting near the fire with his comrades.

"You can't think when you're in the middle of all them swinging swords and lances. Just strike. You won't have time to be scared." The man speaking took his own advice, jumping up from the ground, drawing his sword, and slashing at an unseen foe.

"It's not that easy, Kitarhan. What if the enemy's behind you at the same time you're fighting the one in front of you?"

"That's why you have us, Sonok. We'll protect your back. Won't we, Mardeeso?"

"Sure, we'll watch your back," though Mardeeso didn't sound as sure as Kitarhan.

"This is your first battle too isn't, Mardeeso? You've spent too much time guarding the south gate back in Kartir. Wait'll you see. You'll love it, it's exciting."

Brandorin continued to walk through the camp, hearing

conversations very much like this one taking place at every fire. There always seemed to be someone who was scared, and someone else who was saying it was easy. But most of the men were quiet, lost in their own thoughts, undoubtedly remembering the sight of the giants they would have to face in the morning.

Brandorin had fought in at least a dozen battles against the Alithians. He was the Protector's son, but he had camped with the men he had trained with, yet he had never heard conversations like this on the night before his battles.

He realized his view of battle had been affected by the veterans he faced it with; would he have viewed those fights differently if he had not had their confidence to bolster his own. He walked the camp for over an hour, finding comfort in the common nature of the conversations, in being near the people that he was there to protect.

When he returned to the campfire where the companions had been sitting they were no longer there. He scanned the area, and saw TA-KA standing in a group close to the command tent, his head and shoulders towering over the rest. As he approached, he saw all of the others, as well as a number of the mages.

"Brandorin, thank goodness you're back," Lanata said. "It's M'drani. You have to do something." He could hear the panic in her voice, and he pushed through to the center of the group, bile rising in his throat. When he broke through to the center he saw M'drani, sitting on the ground, in the restful pose she assumed when Searching, but the look on her face was anything but peaceful. Her body, normally restive when Searching, was twitching and flinching, her face contorted in fear and pain.

"Caidos, what's happening?" he asked, when he saw the mage standing over her, worry written clearly on his face.

"I should've realized this could happen, but I was too concerned about what we were going to do about those giants."

"Caidos, what is it?" Brandorin had grabbed Caidos by the shoulders, his fear now focused on M'drani's safety.

"Where have you been?" Caidos asked him; suddenly realizing it was Brandorin who spoke to him.

"What difference does it make?" The fear surging inside him made him snap at the mage. "What's wrong with M'drani?"

"She was Searching the enemy camp, trying to find out how many men Rhamak has, if there were any other creatures; to tell Dilardin."

Brandorin wanted to shake him, make him get to the point. The indirect way Caidos was telling the story sent a spike of ice through his heart as he began to fear that the end was so bad Caidos was avoiding it.

"How long has she been gone?" he asked quietly.

"She started an hour ago. It should have taken maybe ten minutes, fifteen at most. Then she started that," Caidos said, motioning to her movements and facial expressions. "She can't come back."

"What do you mean?" Brandorin said, afraid he already knew the answer.

"Rhamak must have captured her spirit. Or maybe Vorago. But I doubt he has the ability."

"Did you know this could happen?" Brandorin shouted.

"No, I didn't, but I should have thought that it might. Tried to ward her against it." The guilt in Caidos' voice made Brandorin realize he had been accusing him, when he knew Rhamak was to blame.

"We have to get her back, now. We can't wait until morning. We can't wait until after the battle and hope she's still alive." Brandorin moved as if he was going to run off to the enemy camp, but Matu and Piritho reached for him, holding him back.

"What would you do? Her body is here. You can't go and carry her spirit back. If Rhamak has her spirit, she can only return if he releases her - or if he's dead."

*   *   *

M'drani could see Rhamak. He sat in a tall chair in the pavilion that served as his living quarters. A small cage surrounded her as she sat on the table in front of him. The cage was insubstantial, but it held her just as securely as if it had been real. Another man stood next to Rhamak, waiting, listening.

"I knew they'd use her to Search our camp. It was so predictable. I thought Caidos was smarter than that, though. I expected him to try to protect her, but it wasn't even a challenge." Rhamak stopped for a moment, considering. "Chaubrel, this might be a decoy."

"Do you mean that isn't M'drani?"

"No, this is M'drani. I can tell that much, but I'm wondering if Caidos is perhaps sneakier than I had thought. And I must remember Dilardin is here, and he's a worthy adversary. If he had powers like Caidos, that would be a rival worth fighting. Just to be safe, Chaubrel, tell Vorago to check the southern perimeter – no check all of them. Make sure they aren't getting ready to attack or try to launch a rescue mission for the little lady."

As Chaubrel left, Rhamak turned his attention back to M'drani in the cage. She wouldn't look at him, but she felt his gaze. The same cold decay she'd sensed when she helped Brandorin control the fear.

"You can't hold back from me for long, M'drani," he said, his voice falsely soothing. "I have too many ways to make you give in. You've only seen a few so far. But perhaps punishing *you* won't do it. What about your friends?"

A bolt of fear shot through M'drani, and she reminded herself that only the pavilion and Rhamak were real. The rest were just images.

"Caidos would be the obvious choice, but you talk frequently with the girl mage. What is her name, Chaubrel?"

Rhamak turned to look for his chamberlain.

"Not back yet? Chaubrel, you're getting slow."

"I'm sorry, sire," Chaubrel said as he scurried back into the pavilion. "You were saying?"

"The girl, what is her name? The mage."

"Icara, sire."

"That could get me the results I want. Let's see what happens."

M'drani saw the image of a round room with stone walls and a sleek black table. It felt as if she were there, though she knew she still had to be in the pavilion. Icara lay on that table, frozen in place.

"What would you think, M'drani, if I changed your little friend into one of my Talondrin. You didn't see the Talondrin, did you? But you saw the Maken. You got very close to one didn't you? And what did the brave Brandorin do? He just stood there and watched. Now you can watch. I find it fascinating, but I'm not sure you'll agree.

"Once she's transformed I'll direct her to kill you. What would you do then, M'drani? If you had a sword in your hand and a creature you knew to be a friend tried to kill you. Brandorin couldn't kill the beast he knew to be his best friend, even though it had killed his wife. Would you kill Icara to save yourself? Would you let me see what I want to see from your memory, to stop these images from racing through your mind?"

The image of Icara began to distort, the muscles in her arms and legs expanding, becoming grotesquely large. The bones forced to lengthen to fit the new shape. Icara writhed and twisted, screaming from the intense pain caused by the distortions to her muscles and bones. M'drani tried to reach her.

M'drani could feel the cold, dampness of the dungeon, could smell the stale sweat of those that had endured such torture before. She heard Icara's screams as they echoed against the hard stone walls, could feel the vibrations of those screams in her head. Could she stop Icara's suffering by letting Rhamak into her thoughts?

Icara's body had been transformed into one of the creatures that had attacked them on the ship. She turned to M'drani, pleaded to be released. Then her face contorted and expanded, until the features were no longer recognizable as Icara's. Her screams intensified.

The creature that had once been Icara rose from the table and walked to the wall, where Lanata, Piritho and Salis waited, their arms and legs chained to prevent their escape. The creature approached them, grabbing at them, tearing long gashes into their arms, chests and faces. The creature selected Lanata, and holding her so she couldn't move, it opened its mouth, filled with hundreds of razor-sharp teeth, and began to feed on her.

"Stop!" M'drani shouted; though no sound was heard in either Rhamak's pavilion or back in the camp. She struggled to reach the creature and pull it off of Lanata before it was too late.

M'drani realized she could not sense Icara's suffering, could not feel the others' fear. She knew her friends were safe and unharmed. She stopped her struggling and she banished the images before her.

"You're strong, M'drani," Rhamak said. "You should join me. Vorago did. He sees the true potential." His voice had softened, no longer threatening, but conciliatory. "What do you care about those others? They don't care about you? Caidos let me capture you when he could have prevented it so easily. They aren't coming to rescue you. They're more concerned about themselves. You won't miss any of them, would you?" Rhamak had lulled her into a restful state, and an image flashed across her mind, which he saw. It enraged him. "Brandorin. Why is it always Brandorin? You want him? Let's see if you still want him after I'm done with him."

M'drani could see Rhamak and Chaubrel and the interior of the pavilion. Rhamak turned his head to the doorway, nodding once. She saw two guards walk into the tent, supporting a prisoner between them. The man was in chains, and his head hung down so M'drani could not see his face. He hung limply, held up by the guards. They stood the prisoner in front of Rhamak, and walked away.

"He was trying to rescue you, M'drani. Foolish, considering the fact you aren't really here, but I don't think he's been thinking clearly lately. Have you, Brandorin?"

As the man struggled to remain standing, he lifted his head and M'drani's last hopes were shattered. It *was* Brandorin.

He had been badly beaten and his face was bruised and bloody, his lips swollen, his eyes barely open. He stood unsteadily, dazed, not knowing where he was, but when he saw Rhamak in front of him; he dropped to his knees, cowering in fear, pleading for his life.

Rhamak locked his gaze on Brandorin's and motioning with his hand, raised him up, until he was standing again, then lifted him higher, until his feet were no longer touching the ground, his body shaking violently.

"What do you think of your hero now, M'drani? What shall I do with him? You like that face? Do you find him handsome? I admit he's not looking his best right now, but it could be worse, much worse."

The muscles in Brandorin's face began to twitch, expanding and contracting. His cheekbones became more pronounced, the brow jutted out, and his mouth stretched into a wide grimace as he cried out in anguish.

M'drani tried to tell herself it was only an image of Brandorin; that he was not really there, not really feeling the pain that evoked those tortuous cries. The other images Rhamak had created had been set in other places, not the pavilion. Rhamak and his chamberlain were part of the images she was seeing now.

It was not what she was seeing that chilled her blood, however. She had been able to recognize the other images as illusions because she could not sense the feelings of those she saw before her. Now she could sense Brandorin's feelings, feel his pain and his fear. She was no longer sure this was just an illusion.

M'drani was forced to watch as Rhamak tortured Brandorin. He was convulsing from the pain and M'drani was now convinced of the reality of the scene in front of her. Brandorin had tried to save her and had been captured. Her mind reached out, trying to reach him, to find out what she should do. Would giving in to Rhamak now save Brandorin?

"I could stop this, M'drani, make it easier on him, but you have to decide for yourself. I can't let you confer with him." Her thoughts were blocked; she felt the iciness of Rhamak's magic stopping her.

\* \* \*

"There must be something we can do, Caidos," he said, desperation creeping into his voice. "Isn't there a spell you can cast? A way to bring her back?"

"I'm sorry, Brandorin. I've already tried everything I know to do. All of the mages here have tried."

Brandorin looked around, seeing the other mages for the first time. "Can you try together, all of you at once? Combine your powers?"

"We could, but there's nothing to apply them to. She's not here, and we have no way to reach her mind, wherever it might be."

"If you could reach through to her, could you bring her back?"

"Reach her how?"

"I don't know. I just know I have to try something. She pulled me back from ..." His mind raced through every possibility. He placed his hand on his sword, touching the Umari stone, the look of frustration and anguish on his face suddenly replaced by hope. "I could heal a wound, why not this? This is a wound of sorts."

"This is very different, Brandorin."

"How can you be sure? No one else has used the Umari stone for four thousand years. How do we know it won't work? It's worth a try. You said I would be able to control any of the fragments 'at need'. Maybe I can use M'drani's to follow her."

He sat down beside her. He touched the stone in the torque on her neck, resting his other hand on the Umari fragment. She had been flinching, pain and anguish showing on her face, but now she eased slightly. He sat for a time, his face mirroring hers, showing her suffering, but to a lesser degree.

"I can feel a little of what she's feeling, but it's faint, as if she's far away."

"Try using both your crystals ," Caidos said. Brandorin did not hesitate. He wrapped his hand fully around the hilt, the Umari crystal in the palm of his hand, the Protector's crystal under his fingers, his other hand on M'drani's fragment. The fear engulfed him, but he pushed it back, concentrating on reaching M'drani. His body trembled and he cried out, then he closed his eyes and he seemed to relax, his body taking on the same pose as M'drani's.

Long minutes passed without change. M'drani continued to tremble and shake, her face showing her suffering. Brandorin's head moved occasionally, as if he was tilting his head to hear better or looking at something in his mind.

M'drani's body began to shake more violently than it had so far, and Brandorin bent over, either in fear or in pain, the others could not tell which. He spoke one word, very quietly. Only Caidos was close enough to hear.

"Now."

Caidos put his hands on Brandorin's shoulders, and he could feel a trace of what he felt from M'drani. He turned to the other mages.

"Now, join me, reach for her."

The other mages quickly clasped hands and Caidos controlled the power they offered him.

\*   \*   \*

In the pavilion, M'drani sensed Brandorin reach out for her; he had gotten through Rhamak's block. She had braced herself for the shock of the pain Brandorin was suffering, but there was none. Instead, the tortured image before her relaxed. The grossly distorted face returned to normal and his body stopped shaking as it descended to the floor. He stood, looking at Rhamak, defiantly.

"What is this?" Rhamak said. "I didn't release him."

"I did, Rhamak," Brandorin's voice sounded within the chamber. Chaubrel obviously heard it too as he turned toward Brandorin. M'drani saw the look of loathing and triumph Brandorin gave Rhamak. Saw his lips move as Brandorin spoke again. "Now."

Brandorin reached for the cage, and once his hand was upon it, he said, "You can't have her." His image, as well as the images of Rhamak and the pavilion began to fade.

Rhamak screamed, "No!" as he reached out to grab M'drani, but she and Brandorin were both gone.

* * *

The mages could feel their energies being drawn into the effort of retrieving M'drani's spirit. Caidos was controlling those energies, feeding them to Brandorin, not knowing what he was doing with them. Brandorin's eyes opened and releasing his grip on the sword's hilt, he reached both hands out to M'drani, placing them on either side of her face. She opened her eyes, and stared back at Brandorin.

"Are you real?" She reached up and touched his face.

"Yes. You're back."

She looked around, seeing Caidos, the mages and all of the other companions.

"Thank you," she whispered, and collapsed, weeping quietly, as he wrapped her in the protection of his arms.

Cries of alarm came from the eastern end of the camp, and they were picked up and carried back from soldier to soldier until they reached the area around the command tent.

"They say we're being attacked on the right flank, something about demons and dragons," Lata shouted as he came running up. He ran toward the command tent, but by the time he reached it Dilardin and Dagoru had come out. Dagoru shouted orders to members of his cavalry as he ran for his own horse, and rode off to investigate.

Dilardin, seeing Brandorin holding M'drani, looked questioningly at Caidos, who nodded in confirmation. "He brought her back," Dilardin said, not asking.

"What should we do?" one of the mages asked.

"We wait for orders," Caidos told him.

They didn't have to wait for long. Within a few minutes, Dagoru came riding back, pulling his horse up to the command tent to report to Dilardin.

"False alarm, sir. The Arkhanians have arrived. And

apparently Zephyr is with them."

* * *

The eight hundred Arkhanians riding in on their large steeds had made the ground shake. That combined with the sight of such large men on huge war-horses coming at them from out of the dark had convinced the Larians they were under attack. The Arkhanian general, Pan-Ra rode up to the command post within a few minutes of Dagoru's announcement. Zephyr, who had been sitting on the saddle in front of Pan-Ra, flew off toward Caidos as soon as she saw him.

Pan-Ra dismounted, going immediately to TA-KA, paying tribute to the Doljon. The two Arkhanians and Caidos joined Dilardin, J'pahvro and Lata in the command tent.

"I beg your pardon sir," Pan-Ra said, addressing Dilardin as the ranking officer, "but I was instructed by the Dalron to report to Caidos immediately upon my arrival."

When Dilardin gave the general leave to continue, Pan-Ra told Caidos, "Zephyr was near exhaustion when she arrived in Tar-Kal. She was weak from the long journey and from loss of blood. She had deep cuts in her shoulders, on her back and at the base of her wings. The Dalron insisted on caring for her personally, and ordered me to carry her back to you." Zephyr, now greatly recovered, sat purring in Caidos' lap.

"You have performed a remarkable service for all of Zadania," Dilardin told the firedrake, not sure if she would understand, but knowing Caidos would appreciate the sentiment.

* * *

While the military leaders talked, Brandorin stayed with M'drani, now wrapped in a blanket against the cold of the desert night. She recovered rather quickly, but he continued to keep one arm around her, holding her close, while she told him what had happened. Often during her narrative, she would tremble from the memories, so he would wrap both arms around her and pull her closer to him until the trembling stopped.

"I was directly over the center of their camp. There are thousands of them. There was a large structure near the center, and I flew down to get a closer look. I wanted to see if there were any catapults or battering rams. Commander Dagoru asked me to look for such things.

"Suddenly I felt as if I was being dragged down. The ground rushed up at me, I was headed straight for the structure. Then I was through the roof of the building and I was in a cage, sitting in front of Rhamak." She shivered, and Brandorin held her to his chest, talking to her softly.

"I had never seen Rhamak before, but I knew it was him. He tried to get into my mind, read my thoughts. I wouldn't let him."

"Good for you."

"But that's when he started doing things, trying to make me let him in. I don't know how he did it, my body was here, but he caused such pain. I told myself it wasn't real, but it hurt so badly." She stopped, and leaning back, she looked at him, "Oh, Bran, I'm so sorry."

"For what?" He looked at her puzzled. He reached out and stroked her hair away from her face.

"I told you your fear wasn't real, so you should be able to control it. He made the images seem so real. If your fear is anything like the pain I felt ..."

"Don't worry about that," he said, putting his fingers to her lips. "It's over now."

She leaned on him again, and continued her story, "When I wouldn't give in, he would try another way, but I wouldn't let him in. I kept thinking, if he could do that without controlling my mind, what could he do if I let him?"

"You don't have to go through this again," he told her.

"That's all for now," she said. She stopped, relaxing into Brandorin's arms, feeling the comfort they provided. Dilardin came out of the command tent, and walked over to them.

"How are you feeling, M'drani? Dilardin asked.

"Better," she said.

Dilardin looked at Brandorin, a questioning look in his eyes. Brandorin nodded.

"I wouldn't bother you if it wasn't important, but if there is anything you could tell us about what you saw; it could save a great many lives tomorrow."

"Of course," she said, getting up to follow him back into the command tent. Brandorin went with her, afraid to let her out of his sight again. She told them what she saw, but they continued to ask her questions for an hour, until they had a clear understanding of everything she had seen in the enemy camp. They drew a layout of the enemy's position and the way the camp had been established. M'drani reviewed it and said it was a fair representation of what she had seen.

"We appreciate what you did, M'drani and I'm sorry you had to go through that," Dilardin told her. "If I had known that could happen I wouldn't have asked it of you."

"If it will save lives tomorrow, then it was worth it. There is no permanent damage. The more time that passes, the less it seems to linger."

"Brandorin, after you've seen M'drani back to her tent, come back here?"

They left the command tent and went back to the camp area where Icara, Lanata, Piritho, and Til were waiting.

"Where are the rest?" Brandorin asked. After what happened to M'drani, he wanted to know where everyone was.

"Matu went to the Larian camp," Icara told him. "Salis went off with Caidos earlier and hasn't come back. I think TA-KA is with the Arkhanian commander."

Brandorin turned to M'drani, "You can't go anywhere near the fight tomorrow. It would be too dangerous for you to get too close to Rhamak again."

"I don't think there's anything he could do unless I would Search again."

"We don't know that. Caidos didn't know he could grab your spirit like that. There's no point taking the risk." He felt her sense of duty might help, so he added, "You have to be able to carry your fragment through the Labyrinth."

Before he left, Brandorin pulled Piritho aside. "Watch her closely, Thiro, without letting her know you're doing it. Come get me if there's any sign of a problem."

After Brandorin had left, Lanata pulled Piritho aside, "That's a good sign don't you think?"

"What?"

"That he would ask you to watch M'drani."

"You mean after what I did to his last girlfriend."

"Stop that!" she said angrily. "You're always doing that to yourself. It wasn't your fault. What I was trying to point out was that Brandorin must be starting to believe that too."

## Chapter 34

Rhamak launched his offensive at dawn; ten of the giants lined up on the frontline, with an army of five thousand men behind them. The remaining giants were split, five on each side, flanking Rhamak's army. The Arkhanian cavalry had taken the frontline for the Companion armies, with nine hundred Kartirian Cavalry and six hundred N'varian Falconry directly behind. The one thousand Larian foot soldiers brought up the rear. Twenty-five hundred would face five thousand.

"Give Caidos the signal to begin the assault on the giants in the frontline," Dilardin said. Dagoru gave the order to the trumpeters, and a blast of their horns began the battle.

Salis had worked with the mages to devise a method of dealing with the giants and their magically empowered defenses. J'rafo, a young mage Caidos brought because of his expertise with fire, had developed a substance on Artara that he called Dry Fire, a powder that was harmless unless it came in contact with water. The alchemists had found most of the ingredients needed to make the Dry Fire, and what they could not find they were able to transmute from other substances readily available.

Salis stood near the frontline; waiting to test the first of two methods he had devised to implement the Dry Fire. A large sack tied with a string, slip-knotted around the top, sat on the ground in front of him. He looked at the two mages standing next to him and signaled for them to begin.

They pulled water from the air around them, forming large spheres floating in front of their faces. When each globe of water was the size of a man, Salis said, "That should be enough. Let's try that big ugly one straight in front of us," he said pointing at the giant he meant.

The mages hurled the water spheres at the creature, one aiming high, the other low. As the water hurled across the distance between the two frontlines, Salis levitated the sack in front of him, sailing it across the field to the now soaking giant. Just as the sack reached the giant, he used his power to release the string that held the bag closed, and he tilted the sack toward the creature. The Dry Fire poured over the giant, igniting as it came in contact with the creature's wet skin. Within seconds the giant became a fifteen-foot column of flame.

"That worked well. Let's go for another one, just make sure not to put that first one out when you throw the water on the second one."

As the mages began to form more water spheres, Salis moved more sacks of the Dry Fire from a stack behind them. He had insisted he be the only one to move the substance, since he didn't have to touch the sacks to do so. He was afraid with the heat of the desert and the nervousness associated with their first battle, the mages' sweaty palms could ignite any small amount of the Dry Fire that might be clinging to the sacks.

The first giant had collapsed to its knees but was still burning, a strangled cry coming from within the flames. Vorago could be seen, riding the line behind the rest of the giants. He directed them to begin their advance across the open plain, just as the mages and Salis launched the water and Dry Fire at the next giant.

Salis had known they wouldn't just stand there waiting, so he had provided the mages on the left flank a method of dealing with them.

The Larians carried spears, long heavy poles with large sharp tips. The mages had collected forty of these spears, and coated the tips with Dry Fire. The alchemists had created several batches that were slightly sticky, so a thick coat could be brushed onto the tips. The mages began to send the spears at the giants in front of them, using air incantations to provide them with enough force to penetrate the tough hide and to help direct them to their target. The first spear struck one in the stomach. When it became coated with blood, it ignited and began to burn the creature from the inside. After their first target had been impaled by three spears, the mages began to hurl the remaining spears at all of the giants within range.

Caidos knew Vorago would be controlling the giants, so he had assigned three of the mages to control him. They cast spells to interfere with his directions to the giants. Instead of bearing down on the Arkhanian cavalry in front of them, the giants began to falter. When they were no longer being directed, they had no destination. The middle ground between the armies was soon crowded with randomly ambling giants, many of them burning.

One after the other, the giants were doused with first water then the Dry Fire, and Rhamak's frontline became a vast moving inferno. The giants tried to beat the flames out, but only succeeded in spreading them, and the moisture on their hands merely fueled the fire.

Others were burning from within, the shafts of the spears sticking out of their hide in various places. Though there was no outward sign of flames, they were smoking and beating themselves trying to stop the burning. One of the giants, covered in flame, had been walking in circles when it finally chose a direction and began to walk over Rhamak's troops. The soldiers started to run in panic, trying to avoid it.

The purpose of the five giants guarding the flanks then became evident. As the men began to flee toward the side in an effort to avoid being trampled, the giants on the side prevented them from leaving, by trampling them and kicking them back into line.

"I don't think Rhamak trusts his own men," Dilardin said. "I like that quality in an enemy commander."

As the giants in the frontlines were dispatched, Vorago moved more up from the sides. Rhamak inspired his men to attack by projecting images of huge, fierce beasts behind them, driving them forward.

As Rhamak's troops moved out onto the plain, they could be seen clearly for the first time. Most were ragged, conscripted soldiers, but every squad of fifty men had a grotesque, troll-like captain. The captains were large and muscular, their faces contorted to make the men fear them. They wielded whips to flail at the men, driving them like cattle. Between the images of demons at the rear lines and the troll captains among the men, Rhamak had gotten his army of five thousand men moving toward the Companion armies.

The large Arkhanian horses sprinted across the distance to the dead, burning giants. Arkhanian's carried two weapons into battle, a large broadsword and a double-sided battle-ax. They used the sword while still on their horses, but once on the ground, they used the ax, sweeping it in a wide arc, cutting on both the outward and the return swing.

Salis and the mages had decimated the giants' ranks. Only two remained. Without the giants guarding the flanks, the enemy army had started to spread out to the sides. Dilardin signaled the Kartirian Cavalry and the Falconry to move up the flanks, closing in on the enemy from three sides.

One of the remaining giants gained the focus it had previously lacked, and it turned in the direction of the Companions, who waited at the rear of the line. The giant strode quickly across the plain, covering twelve feet with each step. Arkhanians tried to stop it, but the giant, over twice the height of the average Arkhanian, easily swept them aside. It broke through the Larians, ignoring them completely. Zephyr took flight, flying above the giant, but diving down into its face, flashing fire into its eyes, trying to draw it back.

Til searched the area for the few plants to be found on the desert floor. The cactus and brush grass scattered in the area suddenly began to grow at an alarming rate. Cactus plants that had been separated by ten to twelve feet, now reached each other, and began to grow in height. The two-inch spines that had covered the cactus, elongated to foot-long spikes. The scrub grass grew into vines, twining around the cactus hedge, making it stronger. By the time the giant reached the hedge, it was twelve feet high and four feet thick, and stretched out in front of and around the companions.

The giant was temporarily stopped, but it would soon break through, or decide to go around. Lanata reached into her quiver for arrows tipped with Dry Fire, and taking careful aim, she shot the first directly into the mouth of the attacking giant. It howled in pain, and stopped its assault against the hedge, as smoke began to issue from its gaping mouth. Lanata quickly fitted another arrow to her bow, and shot again, this one driving straight into the creature's left eye.

Salis and one of the mages had arrived, but Salis didn't want to risk getting Dry Fire on the Companions behind the hedge. The mage created a smaller sphere of water, only three feet across and doused the giant's legs. Salis followed immediately with a small sack of Dry Fire, and the flames starting at the legs, quickly raced up the creature's body, until it was a wall of flame. The Companions moved back as the giant toppled onto Til's hedge, setting it aflame. The giant burned in its own bonfire.

Caidos caught up with Salis to see what could be done about the last giant.

"We're all out of spears," Salis told him, "and I don't want to try to soak that thing while it's in the middle of our troops. We can't control it well enough."

"Let me talk to Dilardin, see if he can get our men away from that thing. Be ready and watch. When there's a safe margin, take action."

As Caidos rode off toward Dilardin, Salis directed the mages to form the water sphere. The dry air in the desert was getting even drier as the mages withdrew the little moisture it possessed to form the spheres.

Soon a trumpet call was sounded, and the Larian troops in the middle ground began to move to the flanks. There were still men in the area of the remaining giant, but Salis could see they were not Larians or Arkhanians, and the cavalries had been directed to the flanks, having not yet reached the middle ground. The giant had turned and was heading toward the companions.

The formation of the water sphere was progressing painstakingly slowly, but Salis controlled his impatience until he felt the sphere was large enough to coat the remaining giant. When it was, the mage hurled it, and Salis followed with the Dry Fire. They flew across the short distance to the giant, the water and Dry Fire reaching the creature together and bursting into flame as they hit.

Salis had finished his part in the battle, so he was escorted back to the rear, where the other companions waited with a protective guard of Larian soldiers. It soon became obvious Rhamak's forces were not seasoned fighters, and the battle shifted in favor of the companion armies.

The Arkhanians swept through the frontlines, killing every enemy within their reach; only the troll captains offered them any resistance. The Arkhanians fought fiercely, barreling into their opponents and sweeping their battle-axes in arcs of devastation, only to follow each sweep with a chopping swing of the broadsword.

The Larians, moving in from the front, fought with spears, swords and knives in hand-to-hand combat with Rhamak's soldiers. They threaded their way through the battle, weaving a tangled fabric of struggle and death.

The cavalry, flanking the enemy on either side, forced them centerfield, where they faced the fierceness of the Arkhanians or the deadly grace of the Larians.

The companion armies were outnumbered, more than two to one, but their experience and belief in their cause gave them the advantage. The battle came down to individuals fighting in a sea of men and swords, axes and spears.

Although the Companion armies were more experienced soldiers, the difference in numbers was taking a toll. Rhamak's armies fought desperately, trying to avoid being eaten by the demons they thought waited for them at the rear of their line. As the day wore on, and the heat of the desert climbed, the soldiers grew fatigued, and the weariness began to cost them. Rhamak's army was gaining ground.

A loud horn blast was heard from far behind the Companions, and as they turned to look, they saw another army approaching. Thinking it was Rhamak's second assault, they turned preparing to defend themselves on two fronts. Then they realized the Kartirian foot soldiers had arrived.

A second horn sounded, and Dilardin said, "The Medorans

are with them." He waited and a third set of notes blared over the cries of battle. "They have three hundred, plus our eight hundred, that's eleven hundred more foot soldiers. With the numbers we have eliminated, that makes things a bit more even."

The Kartirian and Medoran foot soldiers were fresh to the battle, though they had been on the road for over two weeks. The fight continued, but the numbers of Rhamak's army began to dwindle rapidly.

By late afternoon Rhamak's forces were down to less than a thousand, and the Companion armies had suffered only minimal casualties. The less experienced soldiers could see they were outmatched and now severely outnumbered. They began to turn and run from the fighters bearing down on them.

Rhamak, seeing his army so easily defeated, issued a challenge. His voice, magically enhanced, carried over the field, and was heard by every soldier on both sides.

"Caidos. Brandorin. I will fight you myself, if you will face me."

The fighting continued, but Caidos and Brandorin met with Dilardin. The other field commanders and the companions stood nearby.

"His army is still fighting," Dilardin said, "but he must know they're beaten. He was counting on those giants to cause more damage. Still, I have to wonder why he would do this?"

"He believes his power to be greater than mine," Caidos said. "He assumes he can best me, and that Brandorin will be afraid."

"Is he right?" Dilardin asked.

"If it was just me against Rhamak, I think I would lose," Caidos admitted. "It would be a long and difficult battle, but I think, ultimately, he would defeat me. But I won't be fighting with just my own power."

"The crystal will enhance your powers," Dilardin said.

"Rhamak expects that, but what he probably hasn't thought of is that I will also be able to draw on the power of the other crystals. Yours certainly Brandorin, because they'll be so close, but with all of the others so near, I'll be able to draw on the collective power of all of the fragments."

"Will it be enough for you to overpower him?" Dilardin asked.

"Yes, I believe it will. Or at the very least, I can control him long enough for Brandorin to deal with him."

Brandorin had not spoken, had said nothing about the challenge.

"I'll be there too," Piritho said.

"You weren't included in the challenge," Dilardin said.

"But I will go."

Brandorin looked at his friend, and knowing he had come all this way for just this chance said, "Yes, he must. Rhamak won't be surprised to see him. We'll go together."

"Will you have a surprise for Rhamak as well, Brandorin," Dilardin asked.

"He expects me to be afraid, but last night I overcame the fear when I needed to save M'drani. I will do so again today."

"Since Rhamak will expect you to be afraid, letting him believe you still are will be to your advantage. If he thinks you're too afraid to strike at him, he may let his guard down, expect the blow to come from Piritho."

"If I don't draw my sword until I'm ready to strike, then if I strike quickly, it will be over before the fear builds." He tried to sound confident, but suspected his father and Caidos recognized the growing signs of his fear.

"If we continue the fight, and win, then you'll still have to face Rhamak," Dilardin said. "So we should save the lives of these men, and accept the challenge."

Caidos cast a spell to give Rhamak an answer. "We accept, Rhamak. Brandorin and I will be joined by another. Piritho will come as well."

"How fitting. In one hour then."

"Caidos?" Brandorin asked, pulling the mage aside. "Will the incantation Rhamak cast to instill this fear in me be released when he's dead?"

"That is normally the case, but Rhamak has already demonstrated a skill with spells that I would not have thought possible." Caidos placed his hand on Brandorin's arm in reassurance before adding, "I can't be sure."

* * *

When the hour had passed, Caidos, Brandorin and Piritho rode out to meet Rhamak, the other companions riding out behind them. An expectant hush had descended on the battle field, as soldiers from both sides watched the three men ride out to the muffled sound of their horses' hooves on the hard packed desert floor. Through the wavering heat they saw Rhamak walking casually toward them. They dismounted and walked out to meet him.

"Here we are, all together at last," Rhamak said as they approached. Brandorin and Rhamak stopped at the same time, staring at each other across the few yards that separated them. "We could've saved ourselves a great deal of trouble and come here directly."

Brandorin's jaw was clenched with the will to control his trembling limbs and his racing heart. A cold trickle of sweat snaked its way down his sides, but outwardly, he hoped, he maintained a calmness he didn't feel as he stared at Rhamak.

Caidos began to draw on the power of the crystal, to be prepared for Rhamak's first move. Without taking his eyes from Brandorin, Rhamak said, "Caidos, starting already? Are we not going to exchange pleasantries first? I haven't actually met Brandorin before, but I guess we don't need introductions."

"Actually we met last night, Rhamak," Brandorin said, struggling to make his voice sound confident, but he could see from the look on Rhamak's face that the renegade mage recognized the signs of growing fear.

"You're always spoiling my fun, Brandorin."

"I'm glad to hear it," Brandorin responded, catching a hint of anger in Rhamak's voice.

"And Piritho," Rhamak said, finally taking his eyes off Brandorin, "you look very different from the last time I saw you."

"I am here to be sure you pay for that."

"I've always wondered why you didn't carry out my orders," Rhamak said. "Do you know you're the only one that has ever done that?"

"I notice you're carrying a sword, Rhamak," Caidos said.

"Yes, I thought I would fight fire with fire, to use one of your cliché phrases, Caidos. I'll use magic with you, but it's only fair for me to kill these two with their weapon of choice."

Rhamak cast his arm in Caidos' direction, almost knocking him over with a bolt of energy, but Caidos had been prepared, and had deflected it at the last second.

"I thought we'd get started," Rhamak said casually, as he sprinted forward to cover the distance between them. He swung his sword at Brandorin, who ducked it, rather than draw his sword and fight back.

"Still a little wary of that sword, Brandorin?" Rhamak taunted him as he parlayed a sword thrust from Piritho. He shot another blast at Caidos, who returned the fire. Rhamak deflected it with his sword, as he continued to swing at both Brandorin and Piritho.

Rhamak moved fluidly as he fought against Piritho, tried to get Brandorin to join in, and volleyed fire and air blasts with Caidos. Piritho tried to stay between Rhamak and Brandorin, giving his friend the time he needed to prepare. Caidos cast incantations guardedly, not wanting them to ricochet and strike either Piritho or Brandorin. Flashes of fire and crackling heat ricocheted off Caidos' and Rhamak's hands, as metallic clashing of swords rang through the rippling heat of the desert.

"I just want your fragment, Caidos," Rhamak said as he came close to slicing Brandorin's arm. "I'll settle for that."

"Is the Kordunan crystal not enough for you?" Caidos responded, sending a quick succession of fire blasts at Rhamak's head.

"So, you know I have it?" He touched his hand to his

forehead in salute; a white stone rested in the circlet he wore. "I needed it to be sure you wouldn't start without me."

Piritho thrust in at Rhamak's side, slicing the sleeve of his shirt. "That was too close," Rhamak said angrily as he waved his free hand, and Piritho went flying back ten feet, landing hard.

"I thought you were going to fight us without magic," Brandorin said, avoiding another blow from Rhamak's sword. He drew his sword for the first time, and bringing it down, grazed Rhamak's shoulder.

"I said I would *kill* you with the sword. You must play closer attention."

Caidos countered with a major assault against Rhamak, alternating balls of fire and blasts of air, trying to throw him off balance. Piritho took advantage of the moment, coming at Rhamak from the right, while Brandorin moved in from the left.

But Rhamak deflected all blows with ease, and stepped up his attacks on all three of them.

"Are you going to let these other two fight your battle for you, Brandorin?" Rhamak said taunting him. "The way you did on the ship."

Brandorin did not respond. He knew the verbal taunts were attempts to distract him. He tried to ignore them; he had to concentrate. The black ice of fear clutched at his heart, and gripped his muscles. It was like moving through one of Caidos' air shields.

"These other two are in the way, don't you think, Brandorin? This is supposed to be between you and me." He struck out simultaneously at both Caidos and Piritho, each one of them thrown back in opposite directions. When they tried to return they couldn't; a shield now enclosed Rhamak and Brandorin.

Brandorin glanced back at Piritho and Caidos, who were trying to break through the shield. He'd have to face Rhamak alone. His breathing sounded like ripping paper, and he felt just as ragged-edged. The fear clawed at his insides to the point he thought he would be sick.

"You've been trying to kill me for a long time now," Brandorin said, stalling as he struggled to regain even minimal control. "But it never seems to work, does it?" His voice sounded hollow, and he knew Rhamak heard the tremor that now raced through his entire body.

"You've been lucky so far, I'll admit, but you're on your own now. No friends to help you."

They fought, Brandorin feebly defending himself against Rhamak's sword thrusts; unable to initiate any direct action of his own.

"Brandorin, I must say, you surprise me. These feelings between you and M'drani. So soon after what happened to your bride."

Brandorin stumbled, his concentration temporarily broken. Rhamak moved in and Brandorin felt a sharp pain shoot up his left arm. It was a decisive cut. The heat of the pain helped Brandorin to focus, and his memory of Ilona's tortured body intensified his resolve. He began to attack, his training helping his arms to move without thought, as he fought harder and faster.

"That touched a sore spot, didn't it?" Rhamak countered. "But I understand your attraction to M'drani. She's quite lovely. I'll be sure to get to know her better once I've united the crystal. You won't mind."

Brandorin tried to ignore the taunts, expecting Rhamak to counter with an incantation at any time.

"Last night I showed M'drani what it will be like. You cowering before me, begging me for your life. She will watch when it happens for real." Rhamak cut off his comments when Brandorin's sword caught his hand.

"I'm done playing with you now, Brandorin." Rhamak sneered as he sent a blast of air at Brandorin, trying to knock him off balance. Rhamak was the one surprised, however.

The air blast rebounded back onto Rhamak, who fell backward to the ground. Caidos had cast an incantation protecting Brandorin from the use of magic. Brandorin pushed back the fear, refusing to let it control him, as M'drani had helped him do right after the boar attack. He moved in, his instincts taking over.

Brandorin lunged forward to where Rhamak lay on the

ground in front of him. Rhamak cast his left arm out and a visible blast of energy shot through the shield. Piritho was jerked off his feet and dragged back, in time to take Brandorin's sword thrust in the stomach.

Brandorin withdrew the sword, momentarily stunned by what he had done. Piritho grasped the wound as he fell to his knees, trying to staunch the flow of blood, which coursed out and over his hands. He collapsed.

Brandorin stood there for a moment, seeing Piritho's blood on his own sword. He remembered Ilona's blood on the day of his wedding, and he remembered the look of pain and fear on M'drani's face the night before. It took only a fraction of a second, but the fear was now totally forgotten. He faced Rhamak, who now stood before him, looking back at him in mock innocence.

Brandorin's reaction was not what Rhamak had expected; he could see it on his face. Rhamak had expected the death of his friend to increase the fear, or at least replace it with a mindless, impetuous rage. Instead, the heat of his anger coursed through Brandorin's blood and banished the fear, as the tempo of his sword thrusts pulsed in time with his own heartbeats. Brandorin moved with measured precision, his reflexes heightened, each move as calculated as if he had had hours to prepare.

He anticipated each move Rhamak made, countering it before it was half executed. His sword blurred as he slashed it through the air in front of him, each contact with Rhamak's sword still ringing when the next blow had already been struck.

He drove forward, pushing the mage back. Rhamak's sword seemed to slow even as Brandorin's moved faster, and Brandorin could see fear in his opponent's face for the first time. Rhamak's backward movement stopped suddenly as he backed up into the shield wall he had erected to keep Caidos and Piritho out. That fraction of a second of distraction was all Brandorin needed. He thrust his sword into Rhamak, just as his sword had struck Piritho. He withdrew it, and struck again, through the heart.

The shield wall dissolved and Rhamak fell to the ground, his cold, tawny eyes staring lifelessly into a clear blue sky.

## Chapter 35

Brandorin stood over Rhamak's body, waiting for him to get up again, not ready to believe he was truly dead. There was no sound, other than the hollow sound of his own ragged breathing, echoing in his head. A call from Caidos and he suddenly remembered Piritho, as if it had been hours since he had stabbed him through with his sword.

After Rhamak had pulled him back through the shield, it had closed again, so Caidos had not been able to reach him. When the shield collapsed with Rhamak's death, Caidos had gone to him, trying to staunch the flow of blood. He held the cloth of his robe over the wound, pressing to hold back the blood, but Brandorin could see it too was soaked through.

Piritho's face was chalky white and blood trickled out from between his lips. His eyes, half-open, stared dull and motionless, and Brandorin thought he was too late. Then, in the stillness of the desert, he could hear short gasps of breath. Piritho eyes focused on Brandorin's, as he tried to speak.

Brandorin bent over his friend, and answered the question Piritho was not able to voice. "He's dead."

Piritho's words carried no further than Brandorin, "Then I can go too."

"No." Brandorin said emphatically. "I won't let you."

Brandorin reached for his sword. He grabbed the hilt touching both stones and his last hope shattered. A chain of despair tightened around his neck; it would anchor him to this fear for the rest of his life.

"Brandorin, you can't do this." Caidos reached out to stop him. "He's too far gone. His wound is far worse than the ones you healed for Sadro. It could kill you. You must be here to reform Sefiron."

"My father can do that. He's the Protector too."

"There'll be a challenge meant for the Healer. We aren't sure Dilardin can control the Umari stone, even if he can take back the role of the Protector. It's never been tried. And he didn't read Didonno's scroll. It has to be you."

"I did this to him; it was my sword. I felt it go ..." His voice cracked with anguish. "I can't just sit here and let him die when I have the power to heal him."

"No, don't," Piritho said, his voice less than a whisper, his face contorted by the pain. "Let me go."

Dilardin and the rest of the companions rode up. Lanata leaped from her horse and running to Piritho's side gently picked him up and held him.

"What are you waiting for?" she cried. "You have to heal him. Haven't you punished him enough?"

Brandorin cringed from the accusation in her voice, knowing she was right. Yet fear's anchor held him back. He remembered the pain he had suffered when healing Sadro. Caidos was right; Sadro's wounds had been less severe than Piritho's. The memory of the intensity of that pain and utter feeling of loneliness surged up, and he knew he faced the possibility of that again.

"Is it the fear, Brandorin?" Caidos asked him. "Is it gone?"

"No, it didn't die with Rhamak. I'm fighting that as well as you."

"Remember how weary you were after healing Sadro. We have to go through the Labyrinth. You must be at your best."

"That was Rhamak's spell."

"There could be another. Rhamak transformed Piritho too. He could have planted something then, or just now, during the fight."

"We have time for me to recover. We have another day."

"There's no time to wait, Brandorin," Lanata urged him. "Help him, please."

Brandorin felt physically ill from the fear and the tempest of emotions assailing him: the fear of facing Rhamak, elation at the mage's death and the hope the spell had been broken, utter disappointment that it had not, guilt over being the instrument of Piritho's injury, and now the dilemma of taking action or endangering their quest.

Brandorin reached for the sword, holding it despite the aching loneliness and the fear. He moved Caidos' hands aside, replacing them with his own. The effect was instantaneous.

A surge of power shot through him and into Piritho, as a bright blue light burst from the hilt of his sword like a lightning bolt. The pain Piritho was feeling surged back into him, and he doubled over, fighting to keep his hands on the sword and on Piritho's wound. He threw his head back and cried out from the sudden intense pain that pierced his belly.

The companions watched as blood gushed from Brandorin's abdomen and seeped from his mouth. Dilardin, overwhelmed by his son's ordeal, moved to help him, but Caidos stopped him.

"He has started. He must finish."

Piritho sat up. He lifted his shirt, and after Lanata wiped the blood from the wound area, everyone could see there was no sign of a cut.

Brandorin was still clutching the sword, but he held it now to his stomach, his body bent over it, shuddering with the pain. He collapsed, releasing the sword. His breathing was shallow, almost nonexistent; his skin was deathly pale.

No one moved. No one dared to breathe, until finally Brandorin opened his eyes, breathing deeply, the look on his face triumphant. He sat up and looked at Piritho, his expression changing from confusion, to wonder, to awe and gratitude.

"You loved her too," Brandorin whispered to Piritho.

"How could you know?" Piritho looked back at him in confusion.

"I didn't before, but I do now."

"*She* didn't even know I loved her. She was destined for you."

"Who are they talking about?" Lanata asked quietly.

"Ilona," Dilardin said. "I didn't know, Thiro."

"But Rhamak did," Brandorin said; then to Piritho, "He learned that from you. That's what he used to make you attack me. Your jealousy for what I had. But you didn't."

"I couldn't."

"But why Ilona? You loved her too."

"That's what I've been asking myself ever since the Larians changed me back."

"You two have known each other since you were boys," Dilardin said. "You're like brothers. You may have loved Ilona, Thiro, but it was not as deep a bond as the two of you shared."

Caidos added, "When you couldn't kill Brandorin, the rage and need to kill that Rhamak had instilled in you was still there. You had to strike elsewhere."

"At the time I sensed some emotion connected with Ilona," Piritho said. "But I didn't understand what it was."

"The primitive beast couldn't understand an emotion like that," Matu said.

"Why do I understand all of these things now?" Brandorin asked.

"It was part of the healing. You picked all of this up when you healed him," Caidos said.

"This didn't happen with Sadro."

"In a way it did," Caidos said. "Sadro carried the fear. M'drani sensed a deep fear in him. Piritho's feelings for Ilona and the guilt of what he had done were part of the pain he carried. You healed that too."

Brandorin showed no signs of the exhaustion and fear that had followed Sadro's healing. "You seem to be recovering better than after healing Sadro."

"I'm not exhausted like I was then. I'm barely tired." He stood up easily, picking up the sword as he did. He held it by the hilt, looking at it with wonder, he clasped his hand around the hilt. "It's gone," he whispered.

"The fear?" Caidos asked, hesitation in his voice, hoping, but worried he was wrong.

"All of it. The fear, the terrible feeling of being alone. It's gone." He raised the sword, his hand firmly clasped around its hilt, and let out a joyous yell. He then turned to Piritho, clasping his arm he said, "Thank you, Thiro."

Brandorin walked over to Rhamak's body, standing over it,

he looked down and said, "We could have answered Rhamak's question."

"What question?" Dilardin asked.

"He didn't understand why Piritho didn't follow his orders and kill me. Rhamak understood jealousy, but he didn't understand loyalty, the bond of a lifelong friendship."

"He used the one, but wasn't prepared for the power of the other."

Caidos bent over Rhamak, staring at the white stone in the circlet on his head. It was a pure, but cloudy white that seemed to glow in the bright light of the desert sun, "I would have thought it would be colored, probably red, but no matter. We'll be needing this."

"No you won't," a voice said. They looked up, startled to see a stranger standing nearby. He wore colorful damask robes, had olive-toned skin and tilted eyes, with a recent scar above one. He seemed to have appeared out of nowhere.

"My name is Chaubrel," he said. "I think you've been looking for me."

The companions looked at him in confusion. Caidos said, "We haven't been looking for anyone."

"Well, maybe not, but you did want to know where this was." He held out one arm, and with the other hand he removed the cuff bracelet he wore, and held it up so they could see the red stone set in its center.

Caidos let out a great sigh of relief and said, "You're Kordunan."

"Yes," Chaubrel said with a dip of his head.

"But you said they died out two hundred and fifty years ago," Salis said.

"Except for me," Chaubrel said. "I am the Survivor."

\* \* \*

Dilardin pulled Caidos aside, asking, "Are you sure he's dead? Could it be a spell?"

"I've tested for every incantation I know of. There isn't even a hint at a lingering spell. If he was simulating death, there would be an echo of the magic, but there's nothing. He's dead."

Dilardin had Rhamak's body removed from the battlefield, and returned to camp, as the process of cleaning up after the battle began.

The companions rode back, Chaubrel riding with Caidos, who seemed unwilling to let him or his crystal fragment out of his sight. By the time they had returned, the sun was low over the western horizon. Caidos told them, "The trials in the Labyrinth will require our utmost attention; we can't afford to be tired when we face the challenges set for us. We'll start first thing in the morning."

The heat of the day was escaping rapidly, and the companions sat by a large fire, relishing each other's company. Lanata sat very close to Piritho; she had not been more than a foot from him since rushing to his side after the fight with Rhamak. Caidos had introduced Chaubrel to the other companions, and they all listened intently, as he told them what had happened over two hundred and fifty years before.

"Rhamak sent men to capture me and all of my Chata and with it, the crystal fragment. He had learned how to take a person's life, extending his own. When he does this, he gains not only the years that person had left, but all of the knowledge they had gained during their lifetime. He thought if he absorbed the lives of Kordunan he would be able to control the power of our crystal."

"But it didn't work that way," Caidos said.

"No, it didn't. He killed many of my people with his experiments, but never me. I was the only direct descendant of the original Kordunan who received the crystal from the Shapers."

"This was two hundred and fifty years ago?" Brandorin asked.

"More than that. He kept us in cages for years, hoping to find the right method of stealing our lives so he could control the crystal. Members of the other Chatas didn't know we were missing for a long time. He had captured others, outside our Chata, so he could continue his experiments. After a time, Rhamak found it harder and harder to find more subjects for his experimentation. I only learned this many years later, after all the rest of my people had died."

Chaubrel's strong contempt for Rhamak was evident in every word he spoke, but most specifically his name. He said it as if he had eaten some disgusting thing he wanted to spit out.

"I remember you," Piritho said. "You were very close to him."

"You're being very gracious with your choice of words," Chaubrel said. "You heard the way I spoke to him then, and notice it is not how I speak of him now. He killed my people, yet I served him, degraded myself before him."

"I'm sorry, I didn't mean to offend," Piritho stammered.

"No, don't apologize. It's true. I gave him what he wanted, because he gave me what I needed. I had long known a special destiny awaited me. But like Rhamak, I was born too soon. He extended his life because he felt it was his destiny to control the power of the crystal. But he confused lust for fate. He wanted the power so badly he convinced himself he was meant to live long enough to obtain that power." A look of ultimate gratification crossed Chaubrel's face. "But we see who is alive now, and who is not."

"He couldn't control your crystal, so he had to keep you alive to do it for him." Caidos said.

Chaubrel nodded slowly. "After he realized all of my people had died without the power of the crystal to help them survive, he took very good care of me. He made it clear that if he had my promise to stay with him, he would let me out of the cell, let me live near him." Chaubrel spit and cursed, "Chaos take him!"

"He said this as if it was a great privilege, that I should be grateful for his charity. But I knew I must live, so I could be here with you today. So I promised him, and I served him. He rewarded me, and I have hated every minute of it for all of those two hundred and fifty years.

"There were certain moments though - that helped - gave

me courage. I offer you thanks now for many of those moments."

He could see the companions didn't know what he meant.

"When the Mages of Artara found the Umari crystal, Rhamak was quite perturbed. I couldn't show my pleasure, but it was very entertaining to watch his frustration and anger. And Brandorin, you caused him a great deal of both, and gave me hope. Though it was better to keep my distance when he learned of your successes." He touched the scar over his eye.

"He did that?"

"After he killed the messenger which showed him how you saved Caidos from the Talondrin."

"The Talondrin? You mean the raptors?"

Chaubrel nodded. "Rhamak gave all of his creations their own special names."

"What did he call me?" Piritho asked.

Chaubrel thought for a moment, "He just called you 'that one'. Curious, I never thought of that before. Maybe he knew he really didn't have you under his control. He was very, very upset when you failed to kill Brandorin." He looked at Piritho and Brandorin. "I see you're friends again. I'm glad."

"Chaubrel, maybe you can answer a question for me," Caidos said. "When the creatures attacked us on the ship in the Umari Sea ... What did he call them?"

"The Maken."

"When the Maken attacked the ship, the leader was looking for Brandorin; that was very obvious. After they had reverted back to human form, Brandorin didn't recognize the man. How did he know what Brandorin looked like?"

"Rhamak showed him."

"Where?" Brandorin asked. "Was he following me?"

"No. Not like that. Rhamak could read another man's thoughts; all he had to do was look into their eyes. No one could resist. Except for you, M'drani. I'm very glad he wasn't able to control you. And that you were able to save her, Brandorin. He hadn't expected that." He laughed softly. "Oh, the simple pleasures."

"The Maken?"

"Oh yes, the Maken. Rhamak could control a man's thoughts. When he wanted them to do something, he would project his thoughts into their minds, so they would see clearly what he wanted. No misunderstandings, because they saw it all exactly as he envisioned it. Rhamak projected an image of you, Brandorin, into the Makens' minds, so they would recognize you."

"How is it that Vorago came to work for Rhamak?" Caidos asked, still upset at the betrayal, and that the betrayer had managed to escape.

"Rhamak knew Vorago was monitoring his movements, but he didn't want you to know of Kalarak. His fortress on the Chiron Ridge. He set a trap. He allowed Vorago to see him transform a man from his bird form, and read his thoughts. He believed Vorago would be curious about the skill. Later he used that curiosity to entice him into joining him. This all happened long before Vorago stopped providing reports to you."

"I wouldn't have thought Vorago could be turned so easily," Caidos said.

"I've made it sound simpler than it was," Chaubrel said. "I don't believe Vorago planned on following Rhamak in the beginning. I think he believed he could get the knowledge he sought and then leave. Or perhaps he thought he could do what Rhamak had done to his predecessor."

"Who was that?" Caidos said, surprised. "I never heard of another before Rhamak."

"Gharvik, of Febron."

"The fragment holder?" Salis asked. When Chaubrel nodded in ascent, he continued, "But he died hundreds of years before Rhamak would have been born, even with his long life."

"Gharvik let everyone believe he had died. But he had discovered many dark spells before the Mage Churlik took the fragment from him. It was he that had discovered the Life Stealing spells. Rhamak learned of him while in Febron and he tracked him down; threatened to expose him to the Mages if he didn't teach Rhamak his arts.

"Gharvik was smart enough not to teach Rhamak how to steal lives too soon, for as soon as Rhamak had learned what he wanted, he stole Gharvik's life. Then he learned that doing so passes on all knowledge as well as the years."

"Did Rhamak teach you these spells?" Caidos asked.

"No, he was very protective of his knowledge, and I didn't want to learn them anyway, even if I had the skill to apply them. Too much power becomes too strong a temptation. Vorago learned that, too late. He was already in Rhamak's power by that time."

"I agree with you, Chaubrel," Caidos said. "I am wary of the power of the crystal, and what will happen when I position the crown piece."

"If you approach the task with that wariness, Caidos, then I don't think you have anything to worry about. If Rhamak had obtained your crown piece, then we all would have worries beyond imagining. I'll never tell you all of the things I witnessed, and his power was not a fraction of what he would have gained if he were to complete the Rejoining. But I have known for some time Brandorin would prevent that from happening."

"Me? What do you mean?"

"Rhamak was so intent on your death in part because he knew you were destined to stop him."

"Why did he believe that?"

"The voices of Sefiron's Shadow told him."

"Then it did appear to Rhamak," Caidos said.

"Three times, the first time almost nine months ago. Then again at the next two New Moons."

"Why would it appear to Rhamak three times?"

"Because he called it," Chaubrel said.

"He did what?" Caidos and Brandorin spoke at once, but the other companions were quickly voicing their disbelief as well.

"He called it forth," Chaubrel continued. "I take it you didn't know this could be done. He seemed to feel that by calling it, he would have control over it, but the Shadow's words cleared up that delusion.

"They referred to you by name, Brandorin. That surprised

him."

"I'm surprised too," Brandorin said, "I hadn't taken the sword yet nine months ago ..."

"You're right," Caidos interrupted, "Dilardin was the Protector then."

"The voices said it was Brandorin's destiny to awaken the powers of the Healer," Chaubrel said. "They said that calling forth the Shadow would grant special powers to the Protector. That made him very angry. Chaubrel mockingly repeated Rhamak's comments, '*I* call the Shadow and the Protector gets the special power? I'll see about that.'"

"That's when Rhamak tried to steal the sword," Brandorin said. "I bet he thought that if he had it, it would give him those special powers."

"Only recently I learned of another reason for Rhamak's resentment of you." Chaubrel paused for effect, knowing there would be a strong reaction to his next revelation.

"Did you know that Rhamak was Varsian?" Pausing to see everyone shake their heads, he continued, "Then you will be surprised to learn he was Dravonian." The surprise and incredulity on the faces of all the Westerners put a small knowing smile on the Kordunan's face.

"I too was shocked to learn this, but what was even more surprising was that it seemed Rhamak wanted me to know. As you can well understand, the fact that you now hold the role that had once been his for the taking, and that you were destined to hold such power in the Rejoining, enraged him. He was intent on your downfall.

"He thought Piritho would accomplish that for him. When that failed, he planned that trap for you with the boar attack. He wouldn't say what the second attack was, 'the attack within the attack' he called it," Chaubrel mimicked Rhamak's haughty manner. "But when he received the reports, and learned you were afraid, he was joyous. He was sure the attack by the Maken would succeed, because you would be too afraid to defend yourself."

"But he didn't understand about the Debt of Life," Matu

said.

"No, Rhamak did not understand such gratitude or loyalty. I was sorry to hear of Sadro's death. I had wanted to help him when he was at Kalarak. He suffered more than most. Rhamak left him alone in the dark dungeons for a very long time. Tortured him with images I thought would drive him mad. All of that pain, so the fear he passed to you would be intensified. So you would feel his loneliness and sense of abandonment as well."

"Was there no one who knew he was missing?" Piritho had spoken softly.

"No. Rhamak questioned him about that. He wanted someone who would not be missed. I didn't understand that."

"When I was in Kalarak I knew Brandorin would be looking for me. I was actually worried about that. I didn't want you to come after me, because I knew what Rhamak would do if he caught you. That made it easier somehow, knowing it was better for me to be there."

"That's why healing your wound, also removed the fear spell." Caidos nodded his head slowly, thinking for a moment before continuing. "Rhamak fostered Sadro's fear and loneliness so that they would transfer to Brandorin with the healing. But Piritho, you didn't feel that way. You didn't feel abandoned. You carried a hope, even a certainty that whatever you had to endure at Rhamak's hand was at least saving Brandorin. That transferred to Brandorin with the healing, canceling the fear spell."

"Rhamak couldn't understand your strength, Brandorin. That you would be able to overcome such fear, and to act in spite of it; he was outraged."

"I'm glad to hear I was able to cause Rhamak such anguish," Brandorin said, "but I don't think it was enough. He died too easily."

"You call that easy?" Salis said.

"He didn't suffer, as he had caused so many others to suffer."

"Do you feel you didn't exact enough revenge?" Caidos asked him.

Before he could answer, Chaubrel said, "Be wary of revenge; it's a self-consuming emotion. I planned for many years how I would seek revenge against Rhamak, until it was all I could think about. Then I realized I was letting him rob me of even more of my life. He had already taken far more than he had the right to. I would not let him have any more. I released my lust for revenge, and focused on the future. On this moment, and on tomorrow."

\* \* \*

The companions sat together around the campfire. Tomorrow they would face the challenges of the Labyrinth. Rhamak had taunted him about the difficulty of the challenges, but Brandorin had no doubts about facing them now.

Brandorin looked at Salis, wrapped in a cloak, a blanket pulled over his head. "Salis, maybe you should move closer to the fire if you're that cold."

"Don't mention my name. Besides I'm not cold, I'm hiding."

"Hiding? From who?"

"Kortis. He's in charge of the Medoran army. He was on the Council, and he knows me by sight."

"You're not in Medora anymore. Besides, the Medorans didn't arrive until after you were finished with the Dry Fire."

"No, I'm not worried about that. But he would know about my skipping town after the attack at the Cathedral. I saw him earlier, and he looked at me, but didn't recognize me right off. If he puts two and two together, he may come around with a detail of men to take me back to Medora for trial."

"Well, we can't have that. I don't think you need to worry, though. He's busy trying to find out where all the gold went. And I don't think he's buying J'pahvro's story about the demons taking it."

"It would be just my luck if he tried to blame that on me too."

\* \* \*

"The Companions should be protected," Dilardin said. "Though Rhamak is dead, we don't know where Vorago is. I'm concerned he could still cause trouble."

"The Companions must go alone," Caidos told him. "That's very clearly stated in Didonno's scrolls."

"Then it should only be the Companions. Leave the others behind."

"They don't carry a fragment, but they are each one of the Companions. Lanata saved M'drani's life during the boar attack, killed more than one of the Maken, and saved all of the companions from one of the giant's in today's battle. Piritho has been key to our defenses since the beginning, and I would trust Icara with my life. Icara, as my apprentice, should see this. If you feel we need support, then let it be these three."

"I don't feel comfortable about this, Caidos. I know the importance of what you must do. I won't let it fail because I could have done something to prevent it and did not."

"I understand your concern, Dilardin, but I know that once we're in the Labyrinth, we won't be in any danger. If you feel you must do something, find Vorago. He's my only concern now."

"Could he stop you?"

"He could cause trouble. Delay us. And we must rejoin Sefiron no later than dawn the day after tomorrow, when the last cycle passes."

"May I take the mages that helped in the battle?"

"Excellent idea! Vorago is stronger than any one of them, but together they'll be able to control him."

"I urge you again, let me send support with you, at least until you reach the Labyrinth. They won't go in with you. They can remain outside, to prevent anyone else from entering."

"It is not allowed, Dilardin. We must make this last leg of the journey by ourselves."

## Chapter 36

Dawn broke across the desert floor. The cold night lingered as the eastern sky began to lighten from gray dullness to golden haze. Caidos stood at the edge of the camp and looked out over the flat surface of the plain to the desert's center, where his journey of both miles and years would finally end.

He found himself thinking of Mandricon, knowing his predecessor would have relished this moment. Mandricon had been Mirador for over two hundred years, and had spent much of that time studying the lore of Sefiron. He had learned everything he could of those who had carried the crystal's fragments and the powers they possessed. He had speculated and planned for the possibility of the Rejoining, dreaming of what could be accomplished with the power a united crystal would generate.

Caidos had never had such dreams. He had more than enough power on his own. Possessing that power had cost him dearly, had cost him the lives of his parents and a normal family life. He didn't regret his life as Mirador, however. He was close to the families of all of the fragment holders: felt like a grandfather to Brandorin and M'drani, like an uncle to Matu, Til and TA-KA, thought of Salis as a brother. Though he had lost his own family, he had gained a much larger one.

"Getting nostalgic, Caidos?" Salis asked him quietly. Though he hadn't heard Salis walk up behind him, Caidos was not surprised by his presence or his question.

"A little, I guess," Caidos answered, knowing Salis understood his reservations about what would happen this day. "I can't help but wonder what will happen after the crystal is rejoined."

"I've been wondering myself," Salis told him. "I've gotten so used to moving things around; it will seem strange to have to do it without the crystal. Makes me glad I've come up with all those machines."

"I wasn't thinking about the loss of power as much as the

other changes."

"You mean not having to travel all the time? Have you decided where you'll live?"

"Artara, I suppose."

"But the life of a scholar doesn't appeal to you, does it?"

"It would be nice to have some time to relax, to do things I haven't had time for, things I've thought about for years. Things that..."

"'Things?' Doesn't sound like something you're really enthusiastic about. You'd be bored after a few days. If you don't want to stop traveling, you don't have to. You may not have to check up on us fragment holders, but you can go visit your friends."

Caidos looked at Salis, and realized he had been getting foolishly maudlin. He had been so worried about how much he would miss his old life; he had never considered not giving it up at all.

"You want to travel with me for awhile, Salis? You don't have to go back to Febron."

"I was thinking of a new project. A little idea I had."

"Shouldn't we get started, Caidos?" Brandorin asked as he walked up behind them.

"Yes, we should. Are the others ready?" Caidos turned as he asked his question, and saw the other companions already on their horses. Dilardin was with them. He had reluctantly agreed to allow the Companions to complete their journey unescorted. He planned to see them off, before continuing the efforts of directing the cleanup of the previous day's battle.

"I'll station a lookout, to watch from here. If there is any problem, send up a signal, and we'll come to your aid."

"Once we're in the Labyrinth, we'll be fine, Dilardin. The only problems we'll encounter there are the challenges which are meant to verify our right to be there, not to endanger us."

They started out, riding closely together, their excitement for what lay ahead growing with the heat of the desert as the sun rose over the Jarbon Cliffs in the east. They had expected to encounter a mound or hill, something that would hold the

Labyrinth, but instead they saw only the miles of flat featureless desert laid out before them.

"Could we have passed it, or gone the wrong way?" Salis asked. "There isn't anything out here."

"Maybe it will only appear at dawn on the morning of the New Moon," Brandorin suggested.

"No, it's here," Caidos told them. "It's the job of the Watcher to find it."

They rode slowly, Caidos in the lead, each of the fragment holders behind him, riding together. Icara, Piritho, and Lanata rode at the rear. Slowly a mist appeared in front of Caidos. He stopped, as it thickened and began to swirl.

"What's a mist doing in the middle of a desert?" Salis asked. "There's not enough moisture out here for that."

"You always expect things to follow the rules," Brandorin told him. "I think you better be ready to accept a few things on faith."

The mist now enveloped them, as it magnified the golden glow of the early morning, wrapping them in a cocoon of light. A dark core began to form directly in front of them, and Caidos rode slowly toward it. The golden haze was slowly replaced by dull grayness, almost tangible enough to touch. The only sound, the horses' hooves on the hard-packed sand, deadened as if the mist around them was absorbing all sound. After thirty feet, they came upon the opening to a cave, in a hill that had not been there a few moments before.

"Is this one of the things you had in mind?" Salis asked, staring.

"I would think so," Brandorin said, sounding a little skeptical himself.

Caidos dismounted, and signaled for the others to do the same. He walked to the entrance of the cave, but little could be seen inside. Brandorin reached out, and putting his hand on Caidos' arm, he said, "Maybe I should go first."

"There are no enemies in there, Brandorin. I must go first. I need to open the door."

Caidos stepped forward into the entrance of the cave, and instantly disappeared as the blackness within wrapped around him like a blanket. Brandorin stepped forward, and took a defensive stance, his sword withdrawn, watching the entrance of the cave intently. As he watched, the blackness in the cave's entrance began to eddy like the liquid in a dark pool. Slowly, gray patches appeared within the black, until it finally dissipated and Caidos could be seen clearly, standing at the opening of a long sloping tunnel.

"All right. The door's open. It's up to you now, Brandorin."

"Not yet. The Code of the Challenge applies to you too, Caidos." Brandorin clarified, when he saw Caidos didn't understand. "The Protector's scroll. Remember it talked about the Keys? Each challenge will reveal a Key. There should be one for you too."

Caidos searched the entrance and found a small golden key embedded in the wall, but he could not extract it.

"Touch the crown piece while you remove the key," Brandorin told him. Caidos held the crystal in his amulet with his left hand as he reached for the key with his right. He lifted it easily from the surrounding stone.

"Hold onto that," Brandorin told Caidos, "We'll need those Keys later. I brought some torches, so we can see where we're going in there. Thiro, can you get them?"

"It won't be necessary," Caidos told them. When he saw the look of skepticism on Brandorin's face, he said, "Bring them if you want, but it's foolish to carry torches under the light of the sun."

Piritho had retrieved the torches and they lit them, passing them out to everyone. Brandorin called to M'drani, "I think it will be your role to help lead us through, to Search ahead when the way is unclear."

The passage was wide enough for two people to walk together, so Brandorin and M'drani led, while Piritho and Lanata brought up the rear.

The path twisted, turning left, then right, sometimes sharply, at other times in a gradual curve. They had walked about three hundred feet when the path took a sharp turn. As they rounded the turn, the path split, one way following the turn, and the other straightening out again.

"Here's our first choice," Brandorin said, looking at M'drani.

"I can't tell just by looking at them. Do you want me to Search ahead?"

"No, I don't think that's necessary. I think we should go this way," he said, pointing to the straight path. "I thought I would need your help, but somehow I know."

They went in the direction Brandorin had indicated. The path continued to turn; the further they walked, the more frequently it twisted. They soon lost all sense of direction, but whenever there was a choice, Brandorin selected one easily.

They had been walking through the Labyrinth for ten minutes, when Salis asked, "Getting in seems to be going just fine, but has anybody given any thought to how we're going to find our way out?"

"As a matter of fact, I have," M'drani told him. "You can't see it, but I have been leaving a thread to follow back out." Salis waved his torch around behind him, trying to see M'drani's thread. "It's more of a mental thread, Salis. I can see it. You'll be able to get out," she gave him a sly look, "as long as you bring me with you."

"I don't think this is anything to joke about, M'drani."

Brandorin looked at Salis. "*You* don't want to make jokes. I can't believe it."

"Salis," M'drani asked, "are you afraid of close spaces?"

"I wouldn't say afraid, exactly. I just prefer a clear exit."

"It will be fine, Sal," Til said. "One will not let Sal get lost."

"Lost? I wasn't worried about getting lost. Let's just drop the subject."

After the next couple of turns, M'drani stopped, putting her hand on Brandorin's arm. "There's something close. I can feel fear and pain, more than just one person." She closed her eyes, concentrating, "four, five, more than that. I can't tell how many."

They proceeded cautiously, but as they rounded the next turn, the passage opened into a wide chamber, the ceiling too high for the light of their torches to reach. A white haze filled the center of the chamber. It began to move as they entered, and as it moved a wind followed it, as if its churning created the wind, rather than the other way around.

The wind increased until it was difficult to stand, and the companions held on to one another to keep from being blown over. The wind blew out all of the torches, but the chamber did not darken; the light of the morning sun surrounded them even though they were inside.

The haze began to coalesce; forming shapes independent of the swirling wind, as keening cries of anguish filled the chamber.

"It's dreadful, they're suffering so." M'drani told them. "They're confused, don't understand where they are or why they're here."

"This is the first challenge," Brandorin said. "It's mine. It's for the Healer."

He dropped the now useless torch, and withdrawing his sword, he placed both hands on the hilt and walked forward into the swirling cold of the bone-chilling mist. It engulfed him, clinging to him so closely his shape could still be discerned within it. A new voice joined the wailing; Brandorin cried out along with those from the mist.

"He's taking on their pain," M'drani told them. "He's relieving their anguish."

A sapphire light glowed softly from the center of the haze, building in intensity as it brightened into a small blue sun, hanging in the center of the room. A silent explosion of light temporarily blinded the companions.

When their eyes readjusted to the light in the chamber, the mist was gone, and Brandorin was on his knees, his body bent over the sword. He knelt there until his rapid breathing slowed to normal; then he started to rise. When they saw he was having difficulty, M'drani and Piritho ran to help him.

"That was different," Brandorin said when he regained his strength. "There were dozens of them. They all came at me at once. I could feel them, understood who they had been, saw the events in their lives, heard their cries, felt their pain. It was everywhere. They've been here so long. Since the Devastation that followed Trevarre's betrayal."

"They were all the people that died when the World Shapers freed Zadan?" Piritho asked.

"No, I don't think this was everyone. I think there'll be more."

"We better keep going," Caidos said, when everyone stood still, wondering about the implications of Brandorin's statement. "As I said before, we won't need the torches."

"Wait, before we leave here, I have to find the Key. Brandorin said, circling the chamber. He reached to the rock at the side of a tunnel on the far side of the chamber, the middle tunnel of three. He withdrew the small gold key, which fit easily into the palm of his hand. "We go this way," he said pointing down the tunnel that had held the key.

Brandorin continued to direct them through the Labyrinth, never hesitating at any turn, the tunnels providing them with the light they needed to see their way. When they reached a large chamber, with eight tunnels leading out of it, Brandorin stopped.

"M'drani, I think this one is yours. I have no idea which way to go from here."

"I can't say either, but let me take a look." She sat on the floor in the middle of the chamber, assuming the pose she used when Searching. Her eyes closed and she breathed deeply, relaxing. The dove spirit rose from her, and headed for the tunnels, flying down each for a time, then returning to select another. In one case the dove flew into one tunnel; then a minute later came out a different one. After checking each passageway, the dove returned to M'drani's body, and hovering over her, settled down, merging back into her.

She rose, and walking to one to the right, she said, "It's this one."

"Couldn't we just have walked a little way into each tunnel to determine that?" Salis asked.

"If you had, you would have fallen into a very large, very

deep hole in that one," she pointed to her left. "Most of them have no light, and I have a feeling lighting a torch would not have helped. The darkness within seemed thick and cloying. I had to sense my way through."

"The challenge doesn't have to be difficult for the one it's meant for," Brandorin said. "The Key won't be revealed until the challenge has been met. Is there a Key in the entrance to that tunnel, M'drani?"

M'drani rested her left hand on the stone in the torque on her neck, and easily removed the Key with her right.

Soon after following the tunnel M'drani had selected, an orange light could be seen flickering ahead of them. As they turned a corner, they saw a large fire burning in their path. There were no turns or alternate tunnels between them and the fire. They would have to go through.

Caidos stepped forward. "This must be for me, I can put that out easily. There's plenty of moisture in here ... wait a minute. I can't draw energy from either the stone around us or the air."

Brandorin approached him, and quietly said, "Sorry, Caidos. This one's for Til."

"Til? What could Til do to put out a fire?"

"Til, can you take care of this for us?"

"One is meant to extinguish this fire?"

"Yes, I'm afraid so," Brandorin told him.

Til walked toward the blaze, searching the floor and wall of the tunnel. "One understands what to do now." Til raised an arm over the floor of the tunnel, and a small bit of moss which covered the floor and wall there began to expand. It started to cover the floor, growing over the flames. With the left arm, Til started the moss on the other side of the tunnel moving. It continued to grow, until it began to smother the flames from the left, and within a minute the blaze was extinguished.

"Is that what you had in mind?"

"That was perfect, Til. Now if you can find the Key under all that moss, we can move on."

Til found the key in the wall just past the spot where the

flames had burned. Til extracted the key while touching the Caretaker's green fragment.

"What were those flames burning?" Salis asked. "There was no wood, no vegetation, just stone."

"I told you you'd have trouble accepting some of these challenges," Brandorin told him.

"Fine, I won't say anything until it's my turn."

"That would be now," Brandorin said, standing at the end of the next tunnel, he had held his arm out to block M'drani from moving forward. A large chasm opened out before them. A bridge had at one time spanned the chasm; the jagged edge the only sign that anything had ever been there. The other side, a sheer rock face, was twenty feet away.

Salis approached the gap cautiously. Then looking at Brandorin and M'drani, he said, "She gets to fly around through a few tunnels. Til waves his hands and puts out a fire. I have to build a bridge?"

"Are you saying you can't do it, Salis?" Caidos asked him.

"I didn't say that. I'm just saying, it doesn't seem fair."

"I could have let you walk into that mist, and get hugged by all those ghosts," Brandorin suggested.

"You've got a point. Just give me a minute." He walked to the end of the stone path that spanned the chasm. He carefully looked over the edge and saw a fifty-foot drop to jagged rocks below.

"TA-KA, can you come here a second. Hold my legs. I trust you not to drop me." When TA-KA had a good grip on Salis' ankles, he swung out over the jagged end of the path. He studied the edge and the underside of the portion that extended out over the chasm.

"You can pull me up now. Thanks."

He looked at the walls of the tunnel on the near side of the gap, then began to inspect the far side. He walked along the edge of the chasm on a two-foot wide ledge, to get a better look at the wall on the far side. Finally he returned.

"I think I have it. I just need a little help from you, Caidos."

"I can't help you, Salis. Didn't you see what happened when

I tried to put out the fire? There are no energies in here for me to draw what I need for the incantation."

"I'm not asking you to solve the problem, I just need you to shoot a blast of something over at that large slab of rock on the other side of the chasm. I'll take it from there."

"Blast it how?"

"It's already split from the wall of rock behind it. I could see a gap when I walked over to the side to check. If you can hit it at the bottom, that should loosen it enough to allow it to fall away from the rest of the wall. Once it's loose, I'll use my powers to guide it down into place. It'll make a nice bridge. We can't just let it fall because it's too heavy, and it would break this base," he said as he stamped the rock TA-KA had helped him inspect. "But the base is solid enough to hold the weight if it's set in place rather than dropped."

"I'll try," Caidos said. Strain showed on his face as he tried to pull energy to power the incantation. "Nothing."

"That's the only way I can see us getting across this gap," Salis said.

"Caidos, can you use energy from people?" Piritho asked.

"It can be done, but it's not an acceptable method. Rhamak would do it, but that's no way to reach the Crystal Chamber."

"What would be the effect if you'd use me?"

"I can't ask you to do that."

"You don't have to ask. I'm volunteering."

"It would depend on how strong a blast is needed, but it would weaken you, probably knock you unconscious. For a few minutes to an hour maybe. I can't say for sure, I've never done it."

"You can't meet the challenge without this, Salis?" When Salis shook his head slowly, Piritho said, "Then I don't see we have any choice. I don't carry a fragment, so I don't have to go on from here. If it knocks me out, just pick me up when you leave."

"Doesn't look like we have any other options, Caidos," Brandorin said.

Caidos reluctantly agreed, "I'll use the minimal amount to accomplish Salis' request."

"All right. Let me sit down first. Wouldn't want to pass out and fall into the chasm." Piritho sat down, and Lanata joined him, ready to support him if he fell back.

"I'll stay with you," Lanata decided. "I don't have to go any further either. You can use my energies, too, if you need to, Caidos."

"All right, Salis, what do you need?"

"Hit it right at the base there, where that darker spot is. Just enough to loosen it, not break it. Wait until I'm ready. Let me stand over there, so I can see where I'm guiding it." Salis moved to the right of the gap, where he could watch the slab being lowered in place. "Anytime you're ready."

Caidos shot a short, highly concentrated bolt of energy at the spot Salis had indicated. The slab of rock remained in place. Piritho had passed out and fallen against Lanata, who said, "He's fine. I can feel his heart beating."

"Should I try it again?" Caidos asked

"Wait for it," Salis said, not taking his eyes from the slab. From the grimace on Salis' face, it was evident he was attempting to move the rock.

After a few seconds, the slab began to move slowly away from the wall. It moved a little faster as the gap from the wall increased, until it had reached the point at which it would start to fall over the chasm. Then it stopped.

"I have it now," Salis said between clenched teeth, his voice strained. The slab began to move again, now lowering slowly over the chasm, the strain of the great weight showing clearly on his face. It settled into place on the near side of the gap, about a foot to spare. A tunnel opened on the far wall where the slab of rock had been. Salis exhaled and flexed his arms, as if he had just lifted the rock physically.

"Who needs all those ropes and pulleys?"

Everyone began to cheer; congratulating Salis on what they had thought was an impossible challenge. Caidos and Brandorin bent to check on Piritho. He was out, but his breathing and heart were strong. Caidos whispered, "We didn't make a mistake bringing them with us, did we?"

As they went to cross the newly formed bridge, Brandorin looked down, and turning to Salis, he said, "I believe this is yours." He pointed to the top of the rock, which had been up against the wall only a few minutes before. A golden Key was imbedded in its surface. Salis removed the Key, while touching the stone in his belt. The rock slab he had lowered into place seemed to melt, as it merged with the stone floor below it, and the bridge became whole again.

"Nice trick," Salis said. "If I could do that, I wouldn't need mortar."

They crossed Salis' bridge in single file, and passed through the tunnel opened by the removal of the large slab of rock.

"Take care of him," Brandorin told Lanata as he turned to cross the bridge, leaving her and Piritho behind.

As they proceeded down a long, narrow tunnel, a large feline creature jumped out of a side tunnel, barring their path. It stood towering over them, snarling and roaring, its mouth wide, with long threatening fangs. Its paws were massive, and it swiped at them with long, sharp claws.

Brandorin drew his sword, and stepped in front of M'drani, but the creature showed no signs of attacking. It merely seemed intent on preventing them from passing. TA-KA moved to the front of the line, and stood beside Brandorin, his right hand changed into a broadsword.

"We aren't meant to kill this creature," Brandorin said. "We can't gain the crystal by taking a life, no matter what the form."

Matu stepped forward. "I would imagine I am meant to pacify this beast."

"That was my feeling, too." Brandorin stepped aside to let Matu pass.

Matu approached the beast cautiously, while it continued to growl and snarl at him. He listened carefully, trying to hear its voice, reaching out to it with his mind, trying to calm it. Slowly the beast calmed enough for him to walk up to it. Matu reached out his hand, and the beast flinched back, wary of his approach. He waited.

Finally, the beast submitted, lowering to a reclining position, Matu stroked its sides. He noticed a gold Key hanging on a chain around the creature's neck. He reached for it, and seeing that the beast allowed it, he took the Key. As he did, the beast slowly faded until it was gone.

With the beast gone, the companions were able to continue along the passage. They had gone only a short way, when Brandorin stopped.

"This isn't the right way," he said.

"But there have been no turns." Caidos said.

"Still, this is wrong."

He turned, and walking back to the place where they encountered the beast, he found a hollow cut into the rock, the place from which the beast had sprung. There was a small opening in the back wall of the hollow.

"This is the path."

"We can't fit through there," Salis said, as he looked at the opening Brandorin had found.

"At least not yet. TA-KA, it's your turn."

TA-KA came forward. He had to bend over to get close enough to the opening to inspect it.

"Let me see what's on the other side," he said. As he reached toward the opening, his arm and shoulder stretched forward, drawing out until they were thin enough to pass through the narrow gap. The rest of his body began to change shape as well, until there were no longer any recognizable limbs, just a long, thin shape squeezing through the narrow gap.

"There is a passageway on this side," they heard him say through the crack.

"I'm trying to keep an open mind here, Brandorin," Salis said, "but I don't see how the rest of us are going to get through there. Caidos can't blast through for us, there's only Icara left to leave behind."

"Do you see the Key, TA-KA" Brandorin asked, ignoring Salis' comment.

A moment of silence followed, then, "Yes, it is here."

"Remove it." Brandorin told him.

The gap in the wall expanded, until there was an opening large enough for the companions to walk through.

"All right," Salis said, "I promise to stop questioning your leadership."

The path moved more directly now, no turns or alternate tunnel choices. The companions accelerated from the slow, wary walk they'd adopted thus far, to a rapid pace, fueled by the excitement of being so close to their goal. The tunnel led into a large chamber with no other tunnels leading out of it.

"This is a dead end," Caidos said, as the remaining companions entered the chamber behind him.

"There were no other turns," Brandorin told him. "This is where we're supposed to be." As he surveyed the chamber, the entrance into the chamber began to close, sealing them in. But instead of being alarmed, Brandorin merely felt mild surprise, as if someone had told him it was raining on a day he had expected sunshine.

"I'm tired," Salis said through a yawn. "Do you think we can rest?" He didn't wait for Brandorin's response, but sat down against the wall, as his eyelids began to droop.

"I think we could all use a rest," M'drani said. As she lowered herself to the ground, gravity seemed to take over, and she plopped down.

One by one the companions sat, slouched or dropped, too tired to continue. Brandorin felt the same pull of weariness and kept shaking his head, as he fought the sudden exhaustion.

"This isn't natural," he said. "There's something wrong." He collapsed, falling to the chamber floor, unconscious before he came to rest.

\* \* \*

Dilardin had directed Dagoru to take command in the aftermath of the battle. Something had triggered his defensive instincts, told him to be wary, but he couldn't decide what it was. He felt at a disadvantage; yesterday had been the first battle he commanded without possessing the Protector's crystal. Was this how it would have been without it; doubting himself, missing things?

As a precaution, he had Dagoru send a platoon of men, along with six of the mages, to the center of the desert, to guard the entrance to the Labyrinth. Caidos had said they must make the journey alone, and they had done that. But there was no reason he couldn't send men to wait outside the Labyrinth for their return. One of the men had returned to report; they had found the Companion's horses, standing at the edge of a thick mist. Dilardin ordered the platoon to wait with the horses after circling the mist and ensuring themselves the site was secure.

That had been four hours earlier. He had found no solace in placing the guard. One by one, he ran through each of the conversations he had been involved in since arriving at the desert.

He smiled when he remembered his reunion with Brandorin. He was overjoyed when he had received the note Zephyr had delivered, but hadn't felt truly satisfied until he'd seen his son for himself. There was nothing in that meeting to cause concern.

A meeting with Caidos had followed that reunion. He had been happy to see Thiro safe. Thiro had been dancing around saying something, and Brandorin had stopped him. But that had been cleared up later, when he learned of Thiro's role in Ilona's death. That wasn't the cause of his distress.

He and J'pahvro had given Caidos a report of their trip to the desert, their numbers, the pending arrival of the rest of the troops. They had found the fortress; later learning from Chaubrel it was called Kalarak. It was Rhamak's stronghold. Had they been wrong to pass it by without a thorough search? There may be something there, but that wasn't the problem gnawing at him.

He had talked with Brandorin, hearing about his adventures. He was proud of his son: becoming the Healer, his defeat of the raptors, and the boars. But he had triggered Rhamak's spell, taken on the fear. That had concerned him, but the fear was now gone.

The request he had made for M'drani to Search the enemy camp had not gone well, but once again Brandorin had shown his true nature. He had overcome the fear and brought her back. The fear again, there was something about that fear. Why should it bother him, now that it was gone? The spell had been broken when Brandorin healed Thiro.

The battle had followed and Rhamak's challenge. That was not characteristic of the man, and Dilardin succeeded in battles because he learned to understand his enemies. But Brandorin had killed Rhamak. Vorago had escaped; he could still be in the area. That concerned him, but it was not the problem that plagued him now.

His apprehension increased; Dilardin knew there was something wrong. He kept coming back to the fear Rhamak had instilled in his son. But the spell had been broken. Yet still, there was something about that spell.

He decided to view Rhamak's body; perhaps looking at his fallen enemy would clarify his concern. He pulled aside the flap of his tent; saw a number of men standing in the area. He turned toward the tent where Rhamak's body had been taken, and two things hit him.

It *was* the spell. Not the spell itself; it was how it had been triggered. He turned back to the men. They were standing there, immobile, suspended in awkward positions, stopped during normal movement. Heading back to his tent for his sword, he caught movement out of the corner of his eye. He turned toward it.

He had time to speak only a single word. "Vorago."

He never made it back to his tent.

## Chapter 37

Chaubrel stood alone in the center of the chamber, looking at the other companions. One by one they had all succumbed. They lay there now, not moving, barely breathing. Once again Chaubrel had been the last to survive.

He knew this was the challenge set for him. He must find the Key and remove it in order to save the lives of the people who had welcomed him into their midst, accepted him as one of their own.

Based on the preceding challenges, he knew the release of the Key would also trigger the opening of another tunnel, one that would lead them out of this chamber. He began his search at the far side of the room, directly opposite the entrance tunnel.

He scanned the walls to either side, slowly circling the chamber, back toward the entrance. He passed the area where the entrance had been, without finding the Key, continuing until he was back where he'd started. It wasn't there.

He searched the floor of the chamber, moving each Companion to look beneath them. As he moved them, he worried about their limp and lifeless forms. Time was running out, and still he couldn't find it. He had not survived all those years, tormented by Rhamak, only to reach this point and fail. He remembered his life in Korduna and over two hundred and fifty years under Rhamak's tyranny. He had survived because of the crystal.

He reached for his cuff bracelet, removing it so he could touch the stone with both hands. He closed his eyes, as he often had done back in Korduna, when a sandstorm prevented him from being able to see where he was going, or when he needed to find the water beneath the sand. It had been two hundred and fifty years since he had called on the powers of his crystal fragment; would he be able to do it? He felt a tug, something directing him to a specific spot on the wall. He had looked there, but the Key could not be seen, it had to be felt.

He reached to the wall, rubbing one hand across the surface

while he held the stone in the other. He felt a lump in the wall, one that he somehow knew was not natural. He began breathing again, though he hadn't realized he'd ever stopped. He brushed at it with his fingers, and the surface fell away, revealing the key beneath. As he withdrew it, the wall surrounding the key dissolved, opening onto another tunnel. The doorway they had used to reach the chamber reopened and a cool breeze blew through the two tunnels. The fresh air revived the Companions, who began to stir. They recovered with no ill effects, and after thanking Chaubrel, resumed their journey through the passageway he had uncovered.

"We have all the Keys now," Salis said, "should we start putting the pieces together?"

"No, there's one more Key," Brandorin said. "The first Key was for the Healer. I'll have to solve a second challenge, as the Protector."

The pathway took them straight for a long time, no turns or side tunnels. The tunnel began to shrink, until they were forced to crouch down and walk in single file.

"I feel something ahead," M'drani whispered to Brandorin, who was walking directly in front of her, "and it scares me."

"Me too," he said. "Everyone hold back. Let me go on ahead."

Brandorin crouched to move into the tunnel, and he smiled, remembering the low ceiling at the inn in Medora. As he reached the end of the tunnel, able to stand upright again, he stepped out into a great chamber. A shadow passed over him, and he pivoted around, his sword drawn and his head tilted up to look at something high above him.

A huge creature stood at the far end of the chamber, facing Brandorin. Its back was to the entrance, so it didn't see the rest of the companions move into the chamber. They stood against the far wall; their mouths open and eyes wide, as they took in the sight of the creature towering over Brandorin.

It was taller than the giants they'd faced on the battlefield. Its powerful, muscular legs were jointed like an animal's and ended in cloven hooves. The muscles pulsed under the strain of its movements, completely visible, for the creature had no skin, no fur, nor scales, just raw evident power.

Muscles rippled across its torso and the bulk of its arms and legs. The long arms ended in hands so large they could crush Brandorin's head without effort, or slash him easily with the four-inch long curved talons at the end of the bony fingers. Its head was broad with a jutting bull-like snout filled with jagged teeth and curved tusks, matched by horns that jutted out over empty eye sockets. Its back supported two expansive wings that stretched across the width of the chamber. A long whip-like tail tipped with spikes slashed out at Brandorin.

This creature was more ominous than any Rhamak had created. An evil emanated from those vacant eyes, staring back with an intense hatred of all those that walked in the freedom of the world. But what caught Brandorin's attention was a golden Key hanging from a chain around its neck.

If Brandorin faced this creature with the fear of Rhamak's spell still plaguing him; he would have stood frozen until the creature had moved forward to crush him. But now he confronted it without hesitation, knowing what he must do. He poised for attack, moving warily, sizing up his opponent.

Darting forward, he closed the gap between himself and the creature. He rushed at the legs, the only part of the creature within his reach. The creature bent down to swipe at Brandorin, forcing him to pull back. The razor-sharp talons sliced across his back.

Pivoting around and swinging his sword at the arm as it swept by, he slashed across the back of its hand. The creature reared back, roaring in pain. The sound of its cry filled the chamber, echoing back like the voice of a dozen creatures.

The creature, now enraged, moved out from the wall. It advanced toward Brandorin, who stepped easily to one side, avoiding its grasp. As he pivoted away, he struck another blow to the wrist of the other hand. The creature's size made its moves cumbersome, but Brandorin flowed naturally, as if his steps were part of a dance well rehearsed.

It moved cautiously, keeping its back to the wall, Brandorin always in front of it. It bent over, sweeping at him with long muscular arms. Brandorin thrust his sword into the creature's arm, and anchored it there; using the sword to vault over as it continued its sweep past him.

Blood was now dripping from the many cuts Brandorin had inflicted. It oozed, black and foul, over the stone floor, making it slippery, filling the chamber with the smell of decay. Brandorin avoided the pools of blood, pulling back toward the middle of the chamber, drawing the creature out with him.

Whenever it reached down for him, he avoided its grasp. He continued to taunt it, trying to get it to reach further. When it did, he ducked in under its arm, rolling to the ground to keep it from grabbing him. He slashed at its legs as he came up. Brandorin imbedded his sword in the creature's leg, twisting it as it went in. As the creature bent over from the pain in its calf, Brandorin grabbed for the Key, but it hung still inches out of reach.

He swung his sword through the loop of the chain, cutting it, and caught the Key in his left hand. Straightening up abruptly, the creature bellowed, which resounded through the chamber, and as the echoes of that cry faded, so too did the creature. Brandorin was left standing in the middle of the chamber alone, holding the golden Key.

"I knew I didn't need to kill it," Brandorin told them. "This creature was the soul of Trevarre. Part of his punishment was to be imprisoned here, waiting for the Rejoining."

They stood in the middle of the great chamber, the only sound, Brandorin's rapid breathing.

"I'm not questioning your leadership, Brandorin," Salis said. "That was amazing. I'm sorry I complained about the challenge I had to solve. But what do we do now? There's no exit from this chamber, other than the one we came in from."

"We take the keys we've all collected. Hold them in one hand, and touch your crystal fragment with the other."

As everyone complied, they heard a grinding of stone from the wall behind them. The wall on the far side of the chamber began to move. From the opening a golden light emanated and the sound of voices raised in song filled the chamber. The Companions recognized the joy they had experienced with the appearance of Sefiron at the dawn of the new moon. What they had seen and felt before was merely a shadow of what awaited them within the adjoining chamber.

They all moved toward the song, Brandorin no longer leading. They knew what the next chamber held, and no one wanted to wait a moment longer. As they entered the Crystal Chamber, they were overwhelmed by the presence of the Shapers; their song and light enveloped them, as they stepped out into the pure clear sunlight after a lifetime in shadow.

The song and the light and the swirling images within were faint, as if they were being seen and heard from a great distance. Though the chamber was no more than fifty feet across, looking into the images within its center was like looking across the great expanse of the heavens. The light emanated from the center of the chamber, yet seemed to fill both the room and the companions.

"We should begin," Caidos whispered.

Brandorin drew his sword, and reaching for the crystals within its hilt, a brief flash of blue light flared. He easily removed first the Protector's crystal and then the Umari stone. The open setting that had held the Protector's stone for five thousand years closed, leaving the pattern on the hilt as complete as if it had never been there. He put his sword back in its sheath, and looked at Caidos, who gave him a nod to begin.

He took the Keys retrieved in the Labyrinth, and placed each in the palm of one of his hands. He then held the crystal fragments between his thumb and forefinger, one in each hand, ensuring the Key from the Healer's challenge was in the hand with the Umari stone, and the same for the Protector's Key and fragment.

He raised the crystals to eye level and reaching into the light of swirling images in the center of the room, he brought the fragments together.

A blue light glowed from within the Protector's crystal, while a single note from the faint song grew stronger, rising above the others, clear and strong. At the same time an indigo light shone from the Umari stone and a second voice was added. Brandorin could feel the stones taken from him, and he withdrew his hands. The separate fragments now joined as if they had always been one. They remained floating in the air before him, held by the images swirling about them. He looked at the palms of his hands, then on the floor in front of him; the Keys were gone.

M'drani stepped forward. She reached up to the torque on her neck, a flash of violet light, and she held her crystal fragment in her hand. The gold of the torque closed around the hole left behind. She followed Brandorin's lead, holding both the golden Key and the crystal fragment, as she reached up to the piece of crystal already waiting within the images of light. The light and song of the N'varian crystal were added to the other two.

One by one the companions stepped forward, removing fragments from settings that had held them for thousands of years. With each fragment placed against the others, the song became stronger and more complex, and the light that surrounded the images within the chamber grew richer.

Chaubrel removed the ruby stone from his cuff bracelet, and holding both it and the Key, approached the joined fragments of the other Companions. Tears filled his eyes. He had waited for this day far longer than any of the others present, and the pain and loneliness he had suffered at Rhamak's hands were forgotten as he felt the joy of the united crystal.

The crystal was complete, except for the crown piece. Caidos stepped forward. Reaching for the amulet around his neck, he removed the crystal, as a beautiful opalescent light began to glow from within its center. Holding the Key and crystal in one hand, he reached into the swirling images, to place the crown piece on top of the crystal floating there.

Before he could settle it into position, he felt the arms of someone grabbing him, pulling him to the ground. He turned to find Lanata's face next to his. Lanata's eyes were staring, as if she did not even see Caidos. They cleared and focused on him. A look of confusion replaced the blank stare, as Brandorin pulled her up and held her.

"What are you doing?" Brandorin asked angrily.

Lanata looked back at him, not understanding what had just happened. "I don't know. How did I get here? I was with Piritho, near the bridge and the next thing I was here."

"You attacked him," Icara said incredulously. "You came in, ran across the room and attacked him."

The Companions suddenly became aware of a change in the sound of the Crystal's song, as different notes scattered throughout the room, the light following it. Caidos stood at the side of the chamber, looking down, desperation etched across his face. The others moved forward, and following his gaze, saw the crystal crown piece, in shards on the ground.

* * *

The Companions stood looking at the shattered remnants of the crown piece. Caidos had talked about the ability to reform the crystal if one of the fragments was missing, but they could not do so without the crown piece.

"We've failed," M'drani said. "It's my fault. I'm so sorry." She began to cry softly, and Brandorin releasing Lanata to Matu, went to M'drani.

Holding her, he said, "This wasn't your fault. It was Lanata."

"But I told Caidos she was no danger to us. I sensed no evil intention. If I hadn't said that, Caidos wouldn't have let her come with, and the Rejoining would be complete."

"M'drani," Caidos said, "don't blame yourself. It was my decision." He walked to Lanata, where Matu still held her. "Let her go. She can do no damage worse than what she's already done."

Matu seemed reluctant to release her, but Brandorin nodded to him. Matu let go of Lanata, who collapsed to the floor. Brandorin grabbed the hilt of his sword, and he could see Matu had done the same. TA-KA had positioned himself in front of the doorway leading out of the chamber.

Caidos knelt down in front of Lanata. "Why?"

Lanata couldn't look at Caidos or any of the other

companions, and when she answered her voice was so soft it was difficult to hear. "I don't know. I don't even remember doing it, but there are images coming back to me now. Memories I didn't have a few moments ago."

"Memories of what?" Caidos' voice was gentle, not accusatory.

"Of a round room, with a black stone table in the middle. I don't know where it was."

"I think I do," M'drani said. "Were there chains on the walls? Chains to hold prisoners?" She shivered as she recalled the images Rhamak had made her view.

"Yes," Lanata said, remembering more of the room. "I was being held there, I was chained to the wall. There was a man on the table. He wasn't chained, but he couldn't move. Another man stood over him, his back was to me." Lanata stared straight ahead, as if she was seeing the images again, replaying them, trying to understand what had happened.

"It was Rhamak. He transformed the man on the table." Her voice dropped, "Oh, no. I remember now. I watched him transform all of them." She stopped, dropping her head into her hands in despair.

"The boars," Brandorin said. "You were there when Rhamak created the boars."

"But you weren't one of them," Matu said.

"No, but I had my turn on that black table. I can't talk about the things he made me look at."

"Did you really follow those wagon tracks or were you in the wagon, Lanata?" Brandorin asked.

"I did ride my horse across the Central Desert, but it wasn't under the Harvest Moon. I was in Kalarak then. I crossed later, with Vorago, as he drove the wagon carrying the boars. I remember doing it now, but it was like I was in a trance."

"Why didn't you recognize her, Chaubrel?" Brandorin asked. "You said you were always present when Rhamak created his creatures."

"I was ill soon after he began the boar transformations and

had to leave the room. I recognized the feeling; Rhamak had pulled energies from me. I was very surprised at the time; there were others present for that purpose. He didn't want me to see you, Lanata.

"He probably didn't trust me. He didn't like it that I held the crystal, and he couldn't control it. He never told me what the second attack was that day, the attack within the attack. It was the triggering of the spell and the Companions accepting you."

"What were your instructions?" Brandorin asked.

"I was told to watch the boar attack. To help you fight them, so I would gain your confidence and you would bring me with you. I didn't remember that at the time. I thought I was doing it because I *wanted* to help. Once I left Vorago at the wagon, I didn't remember ever being in Kalarak or seeing the wagon. I noticed the tracks without remembering I had helped make them. He blocked my memory so I wouldn't remember any of this, so M'drani wouldn't sense any danger. I can only assume I'm remembering it now because I've done what Rhamak wanted me to do."

"Yes, you played your role well, Lanata." A different voice drew everyone's attention to the doorway from the other chamber.

Rhamak stood there, gloating. Piritho stood behind him, his sword drawn and a blank look on his face.

## Chapter 38

Rhamak strode into the chamber, oblivious to the shock on the faces of those assembled there.

"Alive! You're still alive? I ..." Caidos' words were stopped by a nonchalant wave of Rhamak's hand.

"Caidos, there's no reason for you to speak. I already know what you'll say."

Brandorin drew his sword, and lunged for Rhamak, but Piritho stepped forward, his sword aimed at Brandorin's heart. Piritho stood between Brandorin and Rhamak, protecting the renegade mage. Although his friend had obviously taken Rhamak's side, Brandorin could not bring himself to strike him.

When Brandorin tried to move again, he couldn't; he was held by a shield, as were each the others in a separate invisible prison.

"Thiro, you can't let him do this," Brandorin shouted.

"Piritho works for me, didn't you know that? The Larians may have changed him back, but I never released him."

"You shouldn't have been so quick to forgive me, Bran." Piritho said; his voice filled with disdain and disparagement.

Brandorin stared back at him, the shock on his face quickly changing to outrage. "Don't call me that," he said, anger rising in his voice. "You don't have the right to be so familiar with me. Not if you've chosen to follow him."

"Bran? Was that what he used to call you when you were growing up? How endearing!"

Brandorin's face was red; the veins on his forehead distended with the effort of struggling against the invisible bonds that constrained him. Piritho stood stoically staring back at him.

"I'm not sure if you'd attack me or Piritho if you were to get free, but I have no time to speculate right now.

He spoke distractedly, his attention on the Crystal's swirling images. "Yes, Caidos, I am still alive. Your trite penchant for inane, outdated proverbs would have you telling us that 'A cat has nine lives', but that would do me an injustice, more than one. Firstly you shouldn't compare me to a cat. Although it's a predator of sorts, they're primitive and nowhere near as menacing."

He had reached the edge of the halo of light and the source of the song that still filled the chamber, though the intensity of the sounds had diminished with Rhamak's arrival. He put his hand out, just short of touching the pulsing lights, letting it linger as if he could feel the power it held.

"But more importantly, a mere *nine lives*?" he continued sarcastically. "A gross underestimate. I have hundreds! You can't kill me! I am immortal. I allowed you to think you had defeated me so you would lead me through the labyrinth."

He stopped, as if suddenly remembering something, and turned away from the Crystal, giving Caidos a judgmental look. "It was uncharacteristic of you to use human energies for your incantation. And then to leave Piritho and Lanata behind. Discarding them after they had served your purpose. But I needed them to be here. So I sent Lanata on her way, then revived Piritho to serve as my guard."

He turned to Brandorin, enjoying his moment of triumph. "You must be asking yourself, 'How did he do it? I know I killed him.' Let me satisfy your curiosity. It was the shield. It not only kept Caidos and Piritho out; it provided the illusion of my death, and transferred my spirit into this." He touched the white stone at his brow. "You fought me; that part was real. I wouldn't have missed that, but you killed a mirage.

"But enough of this reminiscing. I have something I must take care of now."

His hand reached up to the circlet on his brow. He touched the white stone and with a quick flash of light, it came away in his hand. He stepped away from the center of the chamber, and holding the stone aloft, spoke words in the Ancient tongue, slowly and methodically, words that had been long rehearsed.

The errant light and isolated song, circling the chamber since Caidos' fragment had shattered, increased in intensity as Rhamak continued to recite the incantation. The speed of their flow about the chamber increased as the path they circled grew tighter and tighter, centering on the stone Rhamak held aloft. Rhamak's spell came to an abrupt end as the light and song merged into the stone and the opalescent light that had once shone from the crown piece now shone from the stone in Rhamak's hand.

"I was destined to be here, at this time, in this place. You can't begin to understand the power Sefiron will generate. Nor have the slightest idea what to do with it, even if you could. You'd share it with the rest of the world. But a power like this can't be shared.

"I've prepared for this day for five hundred and thirty-eight years. I discovered the knowledge to let me live long enough to see this day. But I didn't waste that time merely waiting. I have prepared, have planned. I will be the one to control the power the crystal holds. I will remake the world."

Rhamak had created his own fragment, and with an obscure and unknown spell had captured the essence that had resided in Caidos' crystal for thousands of years.

"Didn't know I could do that, did you, Caidos. Did you think Didonno had only written those few scrolls you possessed? That the knowledge of such power could be contained in so few words?

"He was the first Mirador after the Dedication. At that time the instructions of the Shapers were fresh in their minds. He knew it would not always be so, felt he needed to record what he knew, to ensure it would be remembered. But many disagreed with him, felt it should be passed from Mirador to Mirador, by word of mouth alone. They feared it could fall into the wrong hands once it had been put to parchment. Ironic, isn't it? They fell into mine.

"The scrolls also explained how to call the Shadow forth. In 'a time of need' they said. The one who called it, would control it. That proved to be a little problem. It kept appearing to me in Kalarak. If that continued, I would have to travel to where you were, so you'd know to gather the flock. I wanted you to know, Caidos, so I wouldn't have to do all the work."

"But you made a mistake, Rhamak." Brandorin said, mocking him. "It didn't go to Caidos, did it? It came to me."

"Rhamak didn't do that, Brandorin," Caidos said. "You took your father's sword and became the Protector and the Healer. The shadow was drawn to you ..." Caidos' words were cut off, a look of excruciating pain contorted his face. Brandorin, too, struggled against a pain like none he had ever felt before, not even when healing Sadro or Piritho."

"Enough from you two. I'll do the talking."

The pain stopped as quickly as it had started. He strolled among his captive audience, relishing the moment, enjoying their futile struggles to free themselves, to try to stop him, the looks of failure so plainly written on their faces. Except for Brandorin.

He stopped; looking at the man the Shadow had predicted would be his downfall. He glared in triumph at his prisoner. Brandorin stared back into those tawny malevolent eyes, not admitting defeat.

"Your attitude is a might inappropriate for a man who has been beaten." They stared at each other, and Brandorin was rewarded by an unguarded look of surprise from Rhamak when he didn't cower and look away.

"I have other matters to contend with for now." Rhamak turned his attention to Caidos instead. "There was a mountain of knowledge in those scrolls. I have all of them, except those in Artara," he said, returning to stand before the pulsing lights of united crystal fragments. "If I took them all, they'd have been missed. I left those because they contained the information you needed; information I wanted you to have.

"Yes, I did need you to get through the Labyrinth for me," he admitted reluctantly. "I'd tried, but I couldn't solve the problems set for others. You needed those scrolls to understand about solving the challenges in the labyrinth. You explained that to them, didn't you Brandorin? Don't bother to answer, I know it was you.

"But the rest of the scrolls. Those were the real treasures! I have them all at Kalarak. You see, Didonno *had* heeded his detractors. He'd hidden most of the scrolls, but had left hints in the ones given to each Mirador. But Churlik had waited too long to expel me." He spoke the words derisively, making his disdain for the head of Artara clear.

"No one before me had understood it. Of course, if anyone after me could have, it was too late," he laughed. "I removed them from their hiding place. Had taken them from Artara long before they sent me away, or should I say, *thought* they sent me away. I let them discover my experiments so they'd cast me out." He waved his hands around, mocking the mages of that time.

"Once they'd labeled me a renegade, no one would take my research seriously. No one would be allowed to study the kinds of incantations I alone now master."

"The Shapers, you see, had wanted to give the stupid people that now populate this world every conceivable opportunity to survive. As if the power of the crystals wasn't enough! If life became too rough, too dangerous, the Shadow could be called. The storms and quakes, that was unexpected. Probably because I called it without any real need.

"Once the Shadow appeared, the powers of the fragments would be stronger, and joining them would provide even more power. They even anticipated the loss of a crystal. You found the instructions for duplicating a regular crystal; I didn't know it was there. But if one of the Miradors was careless enough to break the crown piece, the power it held, the essence of the Shapers, would remain in the area of the shattered fragment, waiting to be refocused into another crystal.

"But not just any crystal, mind you. It had to be a special crystal, and not just some enchanted piece of Zadanite." He enjoyed flaunting his knowledge and cunning before them, paused to increase the drama in his tale. "The instructions for creating an alternate crown piece were to be found in yet another scroll. That clever Didonno, he wouldn't put everything in one place. He scattered it about throughout the scrolls, made it seem as if the writings were random, idle thoughts of an aging mind. But I've had centuries to piece it all together.

"I will admit; I had a few failures. I tried repeatedly to capture the essence of the Kordunan stone. I suspected that if all of the people were dead I might have been able to gain control. But it was only a suspicion, and I didn't want to take that risk, when I had other options." He walked over to Chaubrel, standing frozen at the far side.

Chaubrel had dropped all pretense of respect or fear, and he looked at Rhamak now with a loathing that momentarily stopped the mage's tirade. "You kept me alive all these years, Rhamak, so I could be here today, to put the Kordunan crystal into place. But I used you too, don't you realize that? This long life you have given me has been a burden, but those born to great destinies must bear their share of hardships. And you have been mine." He stopped suddenly, intense agony etched across his face. He would have doubled over in pain if Rhamak's shield had allowed it.

"You know I never wanted your race to die out. I only wanted control of your fragment." He shouted in anger, losing his composure for the first time since walking into the chamber. "I gave you everything. I told you what I had never told anyone before. I looked at you as ..." He stopped. His teeth clenched, his breathing rapid as he slowly regained control. He released Chaubrel from the pain. The smug look on Chaubrel's face had been replaced by relief and the sweat on his brow. Rhamak continued, his voice measured and controlled.

"Yes, I need you for a little while longer, but once I complete the crystal, I'll no longer need any of you. But I will allow you to live, to see what I do with the power I will command."

He continued to sermonize about his power, his destiny, as he returned to the joined crystal fragments suspended in the swirling lights. He was so intent on the crystal that he didn't see Piritho move close to him, his sword poised. Piritho pulled the sword back, and putting all his weight into the swing, brought the blade around, aimed at Rhamak's neck.

The blade stopped an inch from contact, Piritho frozen in place like the others. "Piritho, you disappoint me once again. How you keep managing to defy my orders, I don't understand, but we'll have a great deal of time to find out. You *will* yield to me, and the first thing you'll do is complete your first assignment. You will kill Brandorin, in a manner that will make him suffer for all the trouble he has given me.  Then *you* will pay."

Movement from the corner of his eye caught Brandorin's attention.  He turned to see Icara carrying a stiletto as she lunged for Rhamak.  Without pausing in his litany of punishments, without turning to look at her, Rhamak swept his arm in her direction, as if he was swatting an annoying fly.  Her forward movement abruptly reversed and she was thrown against the far wall, where she lay crumpled, unmoving.

Her head lay at an unnatural angle from her body.  Those of the companions that could turn their heads to see, quickly looked away, not wanting their suspicions confirmed.  Brandorin looked to M'drani, knowing she could feel if Icara's spirit had left her body.  M'drani looked back at him, shaking her head as she cried silently for the loss of her friend.

"She might as well have tried to stop the sun on its westward course," Rhamak said.  "But I'm letting these distractions deter me from my destiny.  Look, it waits for me."

He gestured toward the united pieces of the crystal, still hanging suspended in the air in the center of the chamber, now one solid piece, but incomplete.  They waited for the crown piece to be placed on top.  The song of the crystal still hung in the air, quieter now than before, though the song had changed, taking on a softer melodic tone.

The companions struggled in their invisible prisons, trying to escape, to reach Icara in the hope she was not beyond their help, or to reach Rhamak, to revenge Icara and to stop him from completing the crystal.  Except for Brandorin.  He stood, silently watching Rhamak as he approached the crystal.

"Brandorin, we must stop him, we can't let him control the crystal," Piritho shouted as he struggled in place.  "What's wrong with you?  Have you given up?  Are you just going to let him do it?"

"*Let* me do it?" Rhamak responded derisively.  "I would think you of all present, would know you cannot stop me.  You see that, don't you, Brandorin?  You're smarter than I would have thought.  You know it's futile to fight against me.  And even now you're wondering if it's too late to join me.

"I won't share the power of Sefiron. Vorago made that mistake, believing I would let him control some of the power. He was a fool that proved useful. But maybe there'll be a place for you in my new world, Brandorin. But you must be prepared to pay for all the trouble you've caused me along the way."

Rhamak stood in the center of the chamber, the joined fragments hanging in front of him. Their light cast an eerie glow on his face, his stark features cadaverous. M'drani, her eyes cast down, was lost in her grief. Salis looked about the chamber for something he could use as a weapon, something he could hurl at Rhamak. Til and Matu watched the body of Icara, hoping for some movement. TA-KA continued to struggle, hoping that sheer force could break the bonds. Rhamak looked at them all, in disgust.

"This is the most important moment in the history of the world, and although you're here to witness it, you're not watching." He reached out his hand, and pulled it toward him, and all of their faces turned, as if pulled by invisible strings. They were unable to turn away, forced to watch. They were unable to prevent Rhamak as he reached up and placed his stone at the top of the incomplete crystal floating in the air before him.

Another voice was added, one more powerful than any of the others, but it was discordant with the song. The volume of the song increased and the light from within the crystal, now whole, now a pure white light, grew in intensity. It moved in a wider circle from within the crystal, until it enveloped Rhamak as he stood there still holding the final piece in place. The light grew so strong the companions thought they would not be able to look at it. They couldn't turn away, either because Rhamak still held them, or because the power of the Shapers did, but the intensity of the light did not cause them pain, nor did it blind them.

It continued to expand. As it reached each of them, they were released from the bonds Rhamak had used to hold them, but they remained in place, now held by the joy of a united Sefiron.

The light and the song grew to an intensity beyond human abilities to see and hear. The joy of the united Crystal infused them, as it exploded into separate fragments of color and individual chords of sound. It flew through the chamber in every direction, rebounding off the walls, joining together in new combinations, only to scatter, to return again and again, in ever increasing diversity and harmony.

The dance of visual song slowly decreased in its variety and intensity, as each of the individual melodies passed through one of the companions, then returned to the crystal from which it emanated.

The eventual silence seemed as powerful as an explosion. The aftermath of the experience so numbed the companions, they were unable to speak or move, even though they were no longer held in place by the bonds Rhamak had placed on them.

M'drani was the first to notice, "Rhamak is gone."

They looked at the united crystal, still hovering in the air where it had been reformed, much larger now than the total of the individual pieces. Rhamak no longer stood by the crystal, nor was he anywhere else in the chamber.

They all started talking at once.

"He must have gone back down the passage. He's waiting there for us to leave," said Lanata.

"Why would he leave the crystal? He has 'waited centuries' for this moment," Salis said, mocking Rhamak's tyrannical voice.

"He has gone to try his new power."

"At least he's not trying it on us."

"I'm sure he'll get to that."

"Maybe we could lose him in the labyrinth."

"Maybe he's fixed it so we won't be able to leave this chamber."

Only Brandorin was silent. He had walked up to the crystal, gazing into its center. "He's here," he whispered, almost to himself, rather than to the others, but in the closeness of the chamber his voice was heard over all of theirs.

They stopped their speculating and questioning, and looked at Brandorin, to see where he was looking, to see where he had found Rhamak. For a moment, no one spoke, as each of them searched the chamber once more, then they all started speaking again, asking.

"Where?"

"I don't see him."

"What do you mean?"

Then one by one they stopped their questioning and realized Brandorin was looking into the crystal, not near it or beyond it.

The image within the crystal had changed. It was different than the image they had of the Shapers when they first arrived in the chamber. Then it had been an ephemeral reflection of multiple spirits, both within the crystal and outside of it at the same time. Now it had a dark heart, which formed no tangible shape, but pulsed and changed form, totally contained within the very center of the crystal. A faint wail of pain and defeat could be heard coming from its center.

"Rhamak didn't understand the nature of Sefiron," Brandorin explained. "He only yearned for the power it possessed, thinking he could control it. Do you remember what Didonno's scrolls said? *'If a Mage who follows not the Code should complete the Rejoining he would become the power of Sefiron and even death itself shall be denied him.'* Rhamak thought he would control the power of the crystal. Rhamak's power and the many lives he absorbed will provide a power for the world, through the crystal, but he won't control that power.

"And he isn't dead," Brandorin added. *"The release of death 'will be denied him.'* There was also a little something Rhamak didn't know about," Brandorin said, a glint of mischief in his eye. "He never saw the scroll you gave me to read, Caidos."

"The one marked 'For The Protector'! That was only revealed after the Shadow had appeared. What did it tell you?"

"You thought *'The Code'* the scroll talked about was The Code of the Mages of Artara, but as I read The Protector's scroll and Didonno talked about the Keys, he often used the word Code for Key. The Keys served two purposes. The first was to ensure only the true holders of the fragments would face and complete the challenges; each Key released would open or direct us to the next passage.

"It wasn't necessary to hold the Keys while rejoining the fragments, but when the fear spell didn't end with Rhamak's death, I wondered if he *was* really dead. So I decided to set a little trap for him." Brandorin smiled mischievously before adding, "to thank him for the trap he set for me, with Sadro.

"Once I used the Keys to join the first two fragments, all of the others had to be rejoined the same way. Did you notice the Keys disappeared when the fragments were locked into place? It prevented Rhamak from being able to take control. When Rhamak put his new crown piece in place, he wasn't holding your Key, Caidos. If we hadn't held the Keys, the crystal would have been open for anyone to put the crown piece in place. Even one of us. Rhamak didn't use the Key. He didn't follow *'The Code'*."

"It would have saved me a great deal of concern if you had told me that," Caidos said.

"I couldn't. Apparently Didonno was trickier than Rhamak had realized; he'd set a magical trap that was triggered when Rhamak took those scrolls away from Artara. Rhamak knew about the Protector's scroll, knew it told of the Labyrinth's location and the challenges, but he didn't know about the Keys. The removal of the scrolls changed the keys' function. I couldn't reveal that, or it wouldn't have worked. And your key is still lying on the floor with the shards of your crown piece. I couldn't say anything or Rhamak could have used it.

"But I wasn't the only one keeping something back. I was worried for a while there, Thiro."

"I thought I had a chance to catch him off guard if I pretended he had control over me."

"Wait a minute," Caidos said. "Are you saying Rhamak wasn't controlling you? And Brandorin knew that?"

"He did control me at first, when we were still in the Labyrinth. He showed up at the bridge. I woke up, Lanata was gone, and Rhamak was there. Talk about being surprised. I was still a bit groggy, so he had no trouble controlling me. I couldn't think of anything on my own; I simply wanted to do his bidding. As soon as we stepped into this chamber, I revived; the Crystal's presence, I assume. I realized he had all of you in a bind, so I played along waiting for a chance to catch him off guard. I could see how upset you were, Brandorin, so I used our old signal."

"Signal?"

"It was when he called me Bran. The only time Thiro ever called me that was when he was hatching a scheme and wanted me to play along. I never knew what he was going for at first, but I always caught on in time."

"I knew what Rhamak was planning," Piritho said. "Something I remembered from my time at Kalarak. I only remembered when he mind-linked with me. I knew the crystal he wore would capture the lost powers of your shattered crown piece, Caidos. I couldn't let anyone stop him until after he'd gotten that far."

In the joyous aftermath of the completion of their quest, everyone had temporarily forgotten the price they had paid to get here. Caidos was the first to remember Icara. Although he'd never had any children of his own, Caidos had often felt a fatherly pride in the accomplishments of his young apprentice. He walked away from the companions, toward the far wall, where her body lay after Rhamak had thrown her.

As he approached her body, he noticed she was no longer lying in the position in which she had landed; her head no longer bent at the awkward angle that had so clearly indicated a broken neck. Instead she looked peaceful, on her back, her arms resting across her chest, as if she had already been laid out for her burial. Caidos stopped in mid-stride and felt his heart skip a beat when he noticed the faint but steady rise and fall of her arms and chest.

He closed the gap between them in two long strides, dropping to his knees just as she opened her eyes and looked at him. A slight, sweet smile on her face reflected an inner peace in stark conflict with her last conscious action.

"He's gone," she said, not asking a question, but telling Caidos what she should not have known. "He won't get out, not ever."

"How can you know that? We only just discovered that ourselves," Caidos said.

"I was dead, Caidos," she said, sitting up on her own, though Caidos tried to help, feeling she should have been broken and bruised. "But it wasn't like anything I ever imagined. I think I was *in* the crystal, with the Shapers." She spoke the final words in a quiet, awed voice.

"I could see all of you watching Rhamak. And he was so close, right in front of me, but I wasn't scared. I could hear their song, and yet I felt I *was* their song, or at least a part of it. I was infused by it, soared with it, felt uplifted by it." She paused, unable to find the right words to properly describe her experience. Salis and M'drani had joined Caidos in time to hear Icara's words, and M'drani added, "I felt you leave, I thought ..." but she was unable to finish.

Caidos, feeling a need to anchor his emotions on something concrete, asked, "How did you escape from Rhamak's incantation?"

"He was concentrating so much on holding all of us, especially you and Brandorin. Then he was distracted by Piritho's attempted attack. He never saw me as a threat. I had tried a counter-spell, but when that didn't work, I sort of shuffled the shield and was able to get loose."

"You 'shuffled'...? I didn't know that was possible. Rhamak underestimated you, but maybe I have as well," Caidos added proudly.

"I knew if I tried to release anyone else, he'd notice. I had to act quickly. One second I was running at him, and the next I was in the crystal. I never felt a thing. Well, no pain, I mean. What I felt when I was in there ..." she stopped, looking at the crystal. "I don't think we've invented the words to properly describe what I felt. But I understood, too."

"Understood what?" Salis asked when she didn't continue, sitting close to her.

"Everything! I knew Piritho was faking. I knew what Rhamak was going to do and I knew what would happen to him when he did. But that was only part of it. I understood what he knew. I understood everything you know, Caidos, everything." She stopped, shaking her head and looking at everyone.

"I could understand your thoughts, knew your fears. I wanted to call to you, tell you it was going to be all right, but I couldn't speak. Brandorin, *you* understood. You knew what would happen to Rhamak."

"I didn't know exactly what would happen, that he would be caught within the crystal, but I knew he wouldn't be able to control the power it held. If I had known what you were going to try, and I could have stopped you, I would have."

"I'm glad you couldn't. I don't seem to be able to remember all the things I understood while in there, and what little I do remember seems to be fading, but I remember how wonderful it felt, still feels. I wouldn't have missed that for anything."

"I'm glad you had such a wonderful time," Caidos said "but I could have done without thinking you were ..." he stopped, choked up with emotion, and pulling her toward him, hugged her tightly for a long time.

When he finally released her, he wiped his eyes. "I had always hoped to pass the position of Mirador onto you one day. Even though the primary task of assuring the reuniting of the crystal has been completed, there are many other roles for the Mirador to assume." He walked away from the others with his arm still around Icara's shoulder.

\* \* \*

"Thiro," Brandorin said, "you weren't here when Lanata ..."
"I know what she did."
"How could you? It happened before you entered the room."
"I know because Rhamak gave me those same instructions." Brandorin's mouth dropped open. "If you could see the look on your face! It's not all that surprising if you think about it. Rhamak wasn't taking any chances. He needed someone to break the crown piece if he couldn't obtain it himself. Once it was broken, the

powers would be released and he could capture them in the crystal he'd prepared."

Piritho walked over to where Lanata was sitting against the wall. He talked with her quietly, then they both returned to the others. She started to apologize for what she had done, but Brandorin stopped her.

"It wasn't your fault. It even helped us. If Caidos *had* placed his crown piece, we would've still had to deal with Rhamak. Now that's been taken care of for us."

"I guess we'll face new challenges when we return to our homes. Without the powers we've gained from our fragments, we'll all have to do things the Febronese way, without magic," Salis said.

"I don't think it'll be that bad," Caidos said, pointing to Salis' belt. "Your fragment is back where it started. And so is yours, M'drani," he added pointing to the torque around her neck. He lifted the amulet from around his neck and stroked the crystal, once again where it had been for thousands of years.

Brandorin pulled his sword from its scabbard, and stroked the familiar blue crystal imbedded there. "They're all back," he said. The rest of the companions checked, and each of them found their fragment back in its previous home. Brandorin turned his sword over, to look at the second fragment his family had carried for seven generations, but there was no stone there. "I guess that's only fair. My family was entrusted with the fragment to bring it here and see it was united with the others. We had no rights to it."

"I don't think it will go unused though," Caidos added. "Piritho, may I see your sword?"

Piritho withdrew his sword from its scabbard, but even without looking at its hilt, he knew there had been a change. As he pressed his palm on the hilt he felt a stone embedded there. He felt tingling run from his hand, up his arm, and ripple all through him. When he turned it to show Caidos, it reflected the light of a stone that had never been there before. It held the indigo crystal of the Umari.

"Why would *I* have this fragment?" Piritho asked.

"I can think of several reasons," Caidos answered. "You sacrificed a great deal to help reunite the crystal. The Umari fragment has always given its bearer the power of healing, and it seems fitting you carry it, and wield that power."

"Because I've caused so much pain to others?"

"I wouldn't put it that way, Piritho. You've been in a unique position that will help you empathize with those in pain. That alone will give you a sort of power, even if it weren't for the added help of the crystal. That has always been the way of the crystal fragments; the power, or the potential for the power, must already reside within the holder. That ability is then empowered by the crystal, making it stronger."

"But I've vowed to take my own life, as retribution for what I've done. Rhamak, although not dead," Piritho said, as he glanced toward the united crystal, "is beyond my reach, and I would say he's being punished for his evil actions and ambitions." He looked at Lanata with regret, and then at Brandorin and the sorrow on his face turned to resolve. "So, I must now fulfill my vow."

"I release you from that vow," Brandorin said as he approached Piritho, taking his hand in friendship. "You can't blame the arrow when it hits the target, you blame the archer who launched that arrow. Rhamak used you as a weapon to try to destroy me. You were a well chosen weapon," then when seeing the stricken look on his friend's face, he added "from his point of view. When the weapon didn't find the target, the weapon itself caused its own level of pain. I blamed you for what happened to Ilona, but I was wrong to do so."

He looked at his friend with pride. "It's quite an amazing arrow that can defy the intent of the archer. As you said, Rhamak is being punished for what he has done. Don't punish the rest of us, by leaving us again."

Piritho, overwhelmed by his friend's statement and demonstration of forgiveness, could not speak. Instead he embraced Brandorin in gratitude. When he stood back, there were tears in his eyes. As Piritho stepped back, Lanata was quick to take his place, and while embracing Brandorin, she whispered "Thank you" in his ear.

    Piritho, not understanding the reason for Lanata's action was temporarily disappointed by what he thought was a sign of affection on her part. That was quickly replaced by joy, however, when she turned to him, enveloping him in an embrace that removed all doubts from his mind as to her feelings for him. "I would have never let you do it, you know?" she whispered in his ear. "How would I ever find someone else who understands me the way you do?"

## Chapter 39

The Companions followed M'drani's mental thread on their way out of the Labyrinth. When they reached the outside again, the mist churned as the tempest winds returned, buffeting them into one another. Brandorin held onto M'drani, fearing the bluster would carry her away.

"We must get clear of the cave's entrance," Caidos told them. Away from the tunnel the winds subsided, though they still cycloned around the hill that crowned the Labyrinth. As the mist continued to swirl in the wind, it grew smaller and smaller, until both it and the hill were gone. They gazed out across a flat desert, the sun sitting low over the Chiron Ridge in the west. Their trip through the Labyrinth had taken the entire day.

The pounding of horses' hooves heralded the arrival of Dilardin, Dagoru and J'pahvro, followed by a contingent of Kartirian Cavalry and Falconry. Their own horses were waiting nearby with a platoon of soldiers.

"Are you all right?" Dilardin called to them as he rode up and dismounted.

"Yes, we're fine, Father," Brandorin told him. "Sefiron has been reformed. We won't have to worry about Rhamak again."

"But we do, that's why we're here. He isn't dead. Vorago came back and cast a spell on all of my men, and myself, immobilizing us. He revived Rhamak. But when Rhamak emerged from the tent, he no longer needed Vorago. Rhamak froze him along with the rest of us. I had to stand there and watch Rhamak ride off in this direction, knowing he was coming after you. I also realized something else..." he stopped, looking in Lanata's direction.

"It's over, Father. It's a long story and we've had a long day."

"No, you don't. It's always a 'long story' with you. If I'd made you finish your story about the boar attack, I would've realized then what I finally realized too late."

"What was that?"

"Rhamak was too precise in his planning to leave anything to chance. Sadro could've too easily died before you had a chance to heal him, or you might not have even seen him at all. Rhamak must have had a back-up plan."

"He did. Two actually."

"All right, so you know that now, but it would've been better to know that before you went to the Labyrinth."

"Maybe, but I think it turned out pretty well."

Dilardin looked at him, seeing a different attitude in his son. His journey over the last few months and what happened in the Labyrinth had changed him. Dilardin wanted very much to hear the full account.

"Let's compromise," Brandorin said. "I'll tell you everything on the ride back to camp. I'm suddenly dead tired and very hungry. Where's Bristo?"

When Brandorin turned to look for his horse, Dilardin saw the gashes across his back. His fatherly instincts taking over, he decided to see to his son's well-being before asking for details.

"Piritho, would you like to see what you could do as the Healer?" Caidos asked him.

"I didn't even think about that," Brandorin said. Piritho withdrew his sword, but looked confused as to how to proceed. "Just hold the hilt, and place your hand over the wounds on my back," he told Piritho. "It doesn't hurt that much, so it shouldn't be too great a shock."

Piritho did as Brandorin had directed him. The characteristic blue light glowed from under Piritho's hand, and within a minute Piritho jerked back as Brandorin's wounds were transferred to his back. Brandorin felt the gouges on his back dissolve away, and he turned to look at his friend who stood, cringing slightly and stretching his back muscles. He quickly relaxed, however, as the crystal helped him to heal.

"That was a very odd feeling," Piritho said. "The power just coursed through my whole body."

"Good job," Brandorin said, slapping his friend on the back.

Piritho recoiled from the blow, saying, "They aren't totally gone yet."

"Sorry. It did take longer the first time I did it and it might take a little longer for you, without the Protector's stone."

Brandorin made sure Piritho got to his horse, and on their way back to camp he gave his father the details about the Rejoining of Sefiron.

\* \* \*

By the time Dilardin was satisfied that he'd heard the full story of their adventures in the Labyrinth, it was long past sundown. A gap in the heavy cloud cover opened onto a river of stars, floating along like the flotsam of an ice-choked river.

"The armies will begin their marches back to their own countries tomorrow. Will each of you be returning with them?

"I will be returning to Tar-Kal," TA-KA told them, "and Til will ride with us as far as Ilyan."

"One wishes to show the People the joy of riding a horse," Til said.

"I'll be returning to Numina with my people," Matu told them.

"I'd like to go along with you, Matu," Salis said. "Kortis is still looking for me, and I think it would be better if I'm heading in the opposite direction. I can start to study Larian architecture. I have a little project in mind."

"The Medorans were not very happy when they were told the demons took all the gold," Dilardin told them. "But they were very helpful in cleaning up. I think they hoped they might find some gold left behind. What will you do now, Caidos?"

The mage had sat quietly with Zephyr, content to let Brandorin tell the story of the Labyrinth, happy for once to just sit in the background.

"Piritho and Lanata are going to Kalarak to make sure the prisoners are released and taken care of. I think I'll start by going with them. I want to find the rest of Didonno's scrolls, and there may be other things Rhamak has collected that will be worth looking into."

"I can draw you a layout of the rooms," Chaubrel said. "Show you where you'll be likely to find Rhamak's treasures. But I can't go back there with you."

"I understand. I doubt I would either. After that I think I'll take whatever I find back to Artara and spend a long time reading, and doing all of the other things I haven't been able to do."

"A holiday?"

"Something like that. Icara can come with, and I'll begin to pass the role of Mirador onto her," he said, with a great deal of pride in his talented apprentice.

Icara gave M'drani a questioning look; when she nodded encouragingly, Icara said, "If it'd be all right with you, Caidos, I think I'll go to Numina for awhile."

"Why? What's there?"

"Can we talk about this later?"

"Not you too? I think you've been listening to Brandorin too much."

"Brandorin, will you be coming back to Kartir with us," Dilardin asked his son. "Your mother is very anxious to see you."

"Not immediately, though I promise to come back after I make one stop on the way."

"Where will you go?" Dilardin asked, though he suspected he knew already.

"To B'zuri." He stopped, looking at M'drani, who smiled back at him. "M'drani and I plan to be married, and she'd like to tell her family, before coming to Kartir with me to meet the rest of mine."

The rest of the companions were enthusiastic in their congratulations. Brandorin looked at his father, wondering if he should have told him privately first. Dilardin smiled broadly.

"What about you, Chaubrel?" Dilardin said. "If not Kalarak, then where?"

"It will be hard to return to Korduna after all these years, knowing my people are no longer there. Everyone has extended an invitation to join them in their country, and I'm warmed by the offers of hospitality. I've decided to first travel with TA-KA on his journey. He has promised to find companions to join me on a trip to my homeland. After that? I don't know yet."

"If you'd like to come to Kartir, I'll find a job for you. Let you see what it's like to work for someone voluntarily."

"You're most gracious."

\* \* \*

The next morning the companions breakfasted together, their last meal before separating to go in different directions. The first parting divided their group in two, one heading west, the other east.

"How long will you be in Numina, Salis?" Caidos asked him. "I could stop in Numina and pick you up on my way from Kalarak to Artara. The idea of traveling alone is not as appealing as it used to be."

"I'll be there for at least that long, but if I'm not, they'll know where you can find me, though I don't think I'll have time to go traveling for a while. I hope to have a little project of mine started by then."

"You mentioned that before we started out for the Labyrinth. What is this project?"

"I'd rather not say until I have the basic details worked out. It may not even be possible."

"Sounds like you have something challenging in mind."

"Challenging and rewarding."

"Salis, have you developed an altruistic streak?"

\* \* \*

There were tearful farewells and promises of reunions in the months to come, as the two groups of companions parted. Brandorin and M'drani rode with Piritho and Lanata as the armies pulled out and headed west. Caidos, with Zephyr, rode along with Dilardin.

"Did anyone find out what Salis' 'little project' was?" Brandorin asked.

"No, he's being very secretive," Piritho told him.

"I think it has something to do with what the Shadow said to him," M'drani said, "when we saw it in Febron."

"I don't know what they said," Brandorin said, "but Salis was talking about a Testament."

"He said something later about it not being the Cathedral," M'drani added, "because that wouldn't last for countless generations."

"We'll have to make a side trip to Numina when we go to Arkhan for TA-KA's coronation."

When the armies reached Kalarak, a few skirmishes broke out between the patrols and a small, armed force left behind by Rhamak. He had apparently placed the guard to keep the servants and slaves within, as much as a protection against entry. Once Dilardin and Caidos had convinced the guards Rhamak was dead and would not be returning, they willingly surrendered.

Piritho and Lanata made their way to the dungeons. As they descended the stairs marked on Chaubrel's map, they instinctively reached for each other's hand. They found themselves in a round room, a glossy, black stone table at the center. Despite the cold dampness of the room, Piritho felt a flush of heat rise within him, and he heard again the horrible cries of anguish that had poured from his mouth when Rhamak had transformed him into the beast. Pain shot through his hand, just as it had when Rhamak had reformed his fingers and had forced sharp claws through their tips.

When he realized only one hand was hurting, he also realized the pain was not the same. Lanata was squeezing his hand, and he knew she too was reliving her time in this room. He faced her, turning her away from the scene before them, and engulfed her in his arms. After a time, her soft sobbing ceased and she wrapped him in her arms, and he poured out his own anguish.

Still holding her with one arm, he reached to his side, placing his hand on the hilt of his sword. A blue nimbus of light surrounded them both as the healing power of the Umari crystal absorbed their suffering and released their pain.

They held each other for a long time after the blue light faded, then without a word they turned and walked the long corridor that led to the cells. Weak from hunger and neglect, the men within cowered in their cages, thinking their time on the black table had come. Even the light of a single torch burned their eyes like the light of the desert sun.

Lanata spoke to them softly. She told them Rhamak was dead and they were to be set free. Many didn't believe her, thinking it was another of Rhamak's tortures; others just sat and cried, unable to form words of gratitude. Piritho used the Umari stone to heal as many as he could. Food, water and freedom took care of the rest.

\* \* \*

The door to Rhamak's study would not open; it was locked by a series of complex spells. Caidos sent everyone else away before working his way through the layers of incantations protecting the door. The spells triggered traps if released improperly. When a loud explosion accompanied the release of one lock, Dilardin himself rushed up the stairs that led to the private chamber.

"I'm fine," Caidos assured him. "Before I attempt to release each lock, I protect myself against any possible repercussions."

"I insist on being here when you've cleared the locks, before you enter the room."

"Dilardin, there are no enemies hiding inside, but I'll call you before I go in."

Almost two hours later, Caidos had released the last of the locks, and with Dilardin by his side, they opened the door and entered Rhamak's private sanctum. The room was expansive, stretching beyond the limits of their torch's reach. There were no windows, so Caidos cast an incantation to light the interior. What the light revealed took their breath away.

Tall shelves lined both sides of the room, from floor to

ceiling, filled to overflowing with books and scrolls, chests and vials. Tables scattered across the main body of the room were covered with maps, charts and drawings. Some of the drawings appeared to be architectural plans for the fortress they were in, renditions of possible designs that Rhamak had rejected, and floor plans that Caidos put aside for later review, in case they showed rooms that might otherwise be hidden. One table, in the center of the room, was bare; an ornate, high-backed chair sat like a throne before it.

"This is where he would've studied the scrolls and first learned the secrets of Sefiron." Caidos spoke softly, almost reverently, but Dilardin knew the respect he showed was for the Crystal and the scrolls, not the man who had stolen them.

"Who is that?" Dilardin asked. Caidos looked up, and on seeing the direction of Dilardin's gaze, followed it. A large oil painting mounted on the far wall showed a dark image of a man with hypnotic eyes.

"Gharvik."

"The man Chaubrel told us about. It's not like Rhamak to pay tribute in this way," Dilardin said.

"He wasn't paying tribute to Gharvik, he was gloating." Dilardin looked to Caidos for an explanation. Caidos pointed to the case below the portrait. It was filled with rolled parchments. "Didonno's missing scrolls."

The third Mirador had written five times as many scrolls as Caidos had thought. In addition to Didonno's scrolls, Caidos found many Rhamak had written: journals of his experiments, and his quest for power. There were also books on obscure knowledge, some that had been lost centuries ago; vials of powders and solutions that would need to be analyzed, devices of unknown purpose.

Rhamak had not exaggerated about not wasting the years he waited for Sefiron's Rejoining. He had amassed the single largest collection of magical knowledge Caidos had ever seen, probably in the world. Caidos had thought he would be able to relax, to take a long deserved rest. He could spend the rest of his life studying these writings, learning the treasures they held.

Caidos, Piritho and Lanata remained at Kalarak when the armies continued their journey west. Dilardin had insisted on leaving a protectionary force with them, despite Caidos' insistence it was not necessary.

"Vorago is still out there somewhere," Dilardin warned him.

"I suspect he's been here already," Caidos told him, "there are signs someone was rummaging through Rhamak's treasures. He never made it into Rhamak's study, however. If he had been able to break through the locks, which I doubt, he would have never bothered to recast the incantations. If he returns, I can handle him."

"Still, I'll feel better if there is a guard here."

Caidos was staying in Kalarak to organize and pack up the contents of Rhamak's study. He had sent Zephyr to catch up with the ten mages that had served with the Companion armies. He would need help in getting these treasures back to Artara.

Piritho and Lanata worked day and night helping the residents of Kalarak. The kitchen and household servants Rhamak left behind volunteered to help. They had had a more comfortable existence than those working in the mines and foundry. Chaubrel had told Piritho about the chests of gold and jewels stored in his chambers, suggesting the treasure be divided amongst the victims of Kalarak, a start on their new life.

\* \* \*

A third parting took place at Tasago. The Kartirian Cavalry would continue west, while Brandorin and M'drani traveled southwest with the Falconry.

"If you aren't in Kartir within the month, Brandorin, I'll send a platoon out to bring you back," Dilardin told his son. "I'll be in enough trouble with your mother for not bringing you back directly."

"You can tell her the wait will be worth it," Brandorin said. "She'll get to meet her future daughter-in-law when we return."

"That may get me off the hook. This gives your mother time

to get the estate ready to receive her."

"I wouldn't want her to make a fuss, sir," M'drani said.

"She enjoys such things. She loved every minute she spent planning ..." Dilardin suddenly stopped, uncharacteristically at a loss for words.

"Planning Brandorin's and Ilona's wedding," M'drani finished for him. "Don't worry, sir. I know about Ilona, and I understand."

"I'm beginning to realize having the Searcher in the family will be a very good thing. Why don't you and I have a little talk." Dilardin put his arm around M'drani's shoulder and walked away, letting Brandorin know with a simple look, that he should stay back. As they walked away, Brandorin heard his father saying, "To start with, you can drop the 'sir', family doesn't need to be so formal."

As they headed south with the Falconry, Brandorin asked M'drani, "What did my father talk to you about?"

"Mostly you."

"Me? What did he say about me?"

"He told me all sorts of things," M'drani said mysteriously. "It was very revealing." She laughed lightly when she saw the worried look on his face. "He's very proud of you. Did you know that?"

"You mean what I did for the Rejoining?"

"Not just that. I think he's more proud of who you are. Everything you'd done that led up to that."

"What are you talking about? I always thought I didn't really measure up to what he expected the son of the Protector of Varsa to be."

"He knows you thought that. I think that's why he talked to me. So I could tell you."

"I don't get it."

"He knows he was very tough on you, set very high standards for you to meet. He knew what he was preparing you for, you didn't."

"He was preparing me to take over as the Protector of Varsa."

"No, he wasn't. He knew you had no interest in politics. I think he knew you would be the Protector of the Crystal. Hoped you would also be the Healer. That's what he was training you for. I told him he had done a very good job."

M'drani reached her arm across and took his hand. Brandorin didn't speak for many miles.

\* \* \*

As the rest of the companions headed east, Salis noticed a light green stalk on Til's side that had not been there before. He stopped to ask about it.

"One is aware of this, Sal. It is a sprout."

Salis remembered their conversation in Ilyan, and realized what this meant. "One is pregnant!" Salis declared.

Til looked at Salis with surprise. "One is happy for Sal," Til said enthusiastically. "One thought that this worked differently for non-Ilyani."

"No, no, not me," Salis stammered. "I meant you. Til is pregnant?"

"Yes. The power of the crystal has returned life to its normal ways."

\* \* \*

When the Larian army headed south, Icara rode with Matu for a while. Salis was riding behind them, and saw them talking together. Icara pulled her horse to the side, and waited for Salis to catch up, while Matu continued on ahead.

"Matu said you talked to him about your special project, but he wouldn't tell me what it was."

"I asked him not to say. I want to make sure this is going to work before I tell everyone."

"He said he would be working on it with you."

"Yes, I'll need to get both the Larians and the Ilyani involved."

"I would help too, Salis."

Salis nodded, thinking he understood Icara's reasons, "So you can be near Matu." Icara looked at him surprised. "Didn't think I'd guess? It was a little obvious you like him."

"M'drani was right," Icara said.

"Oh, she thought I'd figure it out?"

"No, she said men can be very stupid about such things."

"What? What do you mean?"

"It's not Matu I like. It's you."

"Me? But you're always hanging around him."

"Only when you're with him."

"You mean ... I'm the one ... Oh, no, what's Caidos going to say about this?"

"He thinks it's a wonderful idea."

"You talked to him already?"

"I had to tell him why I wanted to go to Numina."

"I don't know what to say."

"Does that mean you don't like me?"

"Like you? I think you're wonderful. I just never thought I had a chance."

"Good, then that's settled."

\* \* \*

Autumn had passed into winter and the winds blowing in from the Lorapan Sea were cold and full of moisture. Though the volatile weather caused by Sefiron's waning powers had ended; winter in N'varia was no time to be on the road. Brandorin and M'drani had gotten caught in a sleet storm on the way to B'zuri. The road had turned into a river of mud, and they had been soaked through and frozen to the bone by the time they reached M'drani's home.

Brandorin remembered the deep comfortable bed he had slept in on his first visit, and was so anxious to sink his frozen limbs into its warm embrace that he didn't mind the lack of meat with his dinner.

They stayed for only a few days. Brandorin used the excuse of his father's deadline and the poor conditions of the roads in the wet, early winter weather. But he admitted to M'drani that the real reason was a deep, unexplained longing to see his home. He'd been away for almost six months, having left under the worst of circumstances, and he wanted to be back before the Winter Festivals, a time of celebration and thanksgiving.

M'dori hated to see her daughter leave again so soon, but understood Brandorin's need to go home, even without him voicing it. She wrapped them in thick wool cloaks and warm boots before seeing them off at the docks.

Caidos and Brandorin had taken twelve days to travel from the site of the raptor attack to B'zuri, but early autumn and dry roads were long gone. Brandorin and M'drani had rain, sleet and cold winds biting at them all the way to Kartir. If the roads weren't bogged by gripping mud, they were frozen into rough, irregular ruts that made for treacherous footing and slow progress. The autumn colors had been plucked from the trees, leaving a few stalwart specimens that clung to their branches, flapping in the blustery weather with hummingbird-winged speed. Shorter days put an early end to their travels each day, as they searched each afternoon for a sheltered spot to make camp out of the wind.

Three weeks after leaving B'zuri, almost five weeks after parting with his father in Tasago, they rode up to the southern gate of Kartir. The winds blowing in from the Lorapan Sea snapped the pennons on the parapets so strongly, Brandorin commented, "Sounds like they're applauding our return."

An hour later they arrived at the Protector's estate. Brandorin stopped his horse at the gate. M'drani didn't need to ask him why. He had last seen his home on the day of his wedding. He had rushed out to hunt down the beast that had killed his bride, only to learn the beast was his best friend. Now, here he was, seven months later, returning from a journey that took him around Zadania and back, his new bride-to-be at his side.

"Do you think she'd understand?" he asked, though he knew M'drani couldn't hear him over the wind. It would be easy to blame

Rhamak for Ilona's death, but he would always believe she had died because he had failed her. He looked at the woman at his side, and he silently vowed never to do so again.

## EPILOGUE

Brandorin and M'drani met Piritho and Lanata in Tasago, and traveled together to the southern end of the Central Desert, where they met Salis, Icara, and Caidos. It had been almost a year since the Rejoining and Salis was finally ready to show them the project that had kept him too busy to attend their weddings.

"The rest are already there," Salis told him, "so let's go." They turned their horses north, and started to ride out across the dry plain of the Great Central Desert.

"Have you seen this yet, Caidos?" Brandorin asked.

"No, between going to Tar-Kal for TA-KA's coronation, and trips to Kartir for the weddings, I was mostly in Artara, going over the scrolls I found in Kalarak."

"Do you have any idea what he's built out there?"

"No, and I've tried to find out. Icara knows but she's not talking either."

"Why would he build in the middle of the desert?" Piritho asked.

"It must be a memorial," M'drani suggested, "to the men who died in the battle. Even those on the other side. They were being forced to fight by Rhamak."

"You aren't far off the mark," Salis said, turning around to talk to her, but he would say nothing further.

They began to talk about other things, and before long it felt as if they were back on their journey over a year before. The miles ticked away and they didn't even notice the heat of the desert.

They had covered twenty miles when Brandorin, looking ahead, said, "Salis, I think you've taken a wrong turn. We must be heading back into Laria, or into Ilyan."

"Why do you say that?" he asked, though Brandorin could tell by the sound of his voice he already knew the answer."

"Because those are trees in front of us."

"No, that's what he's building," Caidos decided. "You liked the way they built in Numina, so you created a building that looks like trees."

Salis didn't respond, neither confirming nor denying Caidos' guess. Excited for them to see what he had done, Salis picked up the pace. When they had covered another five miles, Brandorin suddenly stopped. The others reined in and looked at him.

"Those aren't buildings, Salis."

"No, they aren't."

"You haven't been building, you've been growing. You've created an oasis."

"I'm not doing it by myself. Til has brought the Ilyani into it. They're the ones who got the plants started again. We have a long way to go. When it's ready, Matu and the Larians will bring the animals back in."

"It's not just an oasis," Icara said, too proud of what Salis had done to remain quiet any longer. "He's rebuilding. He can't really recreate what was here before the devastation, but he's bringing it back to life."

"Salis, what a wonderful thing to do," M'drani said.

"When I saw what the Larians and the Ilyani had done, I felt like I was just a kid building sandcastles. This will last."

"For countless generations," M'drani said. "It's what the voices from the Shadow told you." She turned to Icara, "Now I know why you love him."

They quickly covered the distance to the trees and found the rest of the companions waiting for them in the middle of a beautiful garden. Plants of every kind filled the area. Not just palm trees providing limited shade, but desert willows, covered with orchid-like blooms, towering fig and umbrella trees, their fanlike leaves providing shade for the flowers, shrubs and grass that carpeted the oasis floor. Plants that would normally not be blooming this late in autumn were heavy with colorful and fragrant blossoms.

After they greeted each other, an Ilyani, much smaller than Til walked into the garden, and stood looking shyly at the five companions that had just arrived.

"May One introduce One's offspring, Salbrandrani Pirlanaidos," Til said. "It is a custom among the People to select a name that does honor to those important in One's life."

"We are honored, Til."

After a great deal of talk and celebration of reunited friends, Salis showed everyone what the Ilyani had done. The garden was centered on the spot they had entered the Labyrinth. It spread out for two miles in every direction. He told them of his plans to do the same for the rest of the desert. Chaubrel had joined them, and with Icara's help was finding natural water springs, and areas were being dug out to create lakes and ponds.

Salis had named the area Sefiron's Garden and after it was formally dedicated; Salis and Icara were married in front of all of their friends.

**THE END**

## Acknowledgements

Special thanks to all who read the early drafts of this book, and helped with the challenges of figuring out how to write that first novel. Your input was invaluable.

Dolores Cilia

Jay Schnurr

Mike Schnurr

Roxanne Kaufmann Elliot

Ralph Smith

Sarah Scarborough

And a few anonymous on-line critiquers: Charles, Robert, Snig, Alice, and Dave

Thanks!

Made in the USA
Charleston, SC
28 September 2014